COLLECTION Vol:5

Enid Blyton

THE MYSTERIES

COLLECTION Vol:5

3 books in 1

EGMONT

EGMONT

We bring stories to life

The Mystery of the Missing Man First published in Great Britain in 1956
The Mystery of the Strange Messages First published in Great Britain in 1957
The Mystery of Banshee Towers First published in Great Britain in 1961

This edition published 2013 by Egmont UK Limited
The Yellow Building, 1 Nicholas Road, London W11 4AN

ENID BLYTON ® Copyright © 2013 Hodder & Stoughton Ltd

ISBN 978 1 4052 6792 2
1 3 5 7 9 10 8 6 4 2

www.egmont.co.uk

A CIP catalogue record for this title is available from the British Library

Printed and bound by CPI Group (UK) Ltd, Croydon, CR0 4YY

55565/1

Stay safe online. Any website addresses listed in this book are correct at the time of going to
print. However, Egmont is not responsible for content hosted by third parties. Please be aware
that online content can be subject to change and websites can contain content that is
unsuitable for children. We advise that all children are supervised when using the internet.

EGMONT

Our story began over a century ago, when seventeen-year-old
Egmont Harald Petersen found a coin in the street. He was on
his way to buy a flyswatter, a small hand-operated printing
machine that he then set up in his tiny apartment.

The coin brought him such good luck that today Egmont has
offices in over 30 countries around the world. And that lucky
coin is still kept at the company's head offices in Denmark.

CONTENTS

1. OFF TO MEET OLD FATTY

'I do wish old Fatty would hurry up and come back from wherever he's staying,' said Bets. 'We've had almost a week of the holidays without him already – such a waste!'

'He's coming back today,' said Pip, passing a postcard across the breakfast table to his young sister. 'Here's a card from him. Three cheers!'

Bets read the card out loud. ' "Back tomorrow by bus from Warling. Meet me at bus stop if you can. What about a nice juicy mystery? I feel just about ready for one, Fatty." '

'A nice juicy *what*?' said her mother, puzzled.

'*Mystery*,' said Bets, her eyes shining. 'You know how something always seems to happen when Fatty's about, Mummy – there was the mystery of the pantomime cat – and the mystery of the vanished prince – and . . .'

Her father groaned. 'Look, Bets – I'm tired of

1

all these adventures and strange happenings that seem to pop up whenever your friend Frederick is about. Just try and steer clear of any trouble these holidays. I was hoping that Frederick was staying away for a nice long time.'

'I wish you wouldn't call him Frederick, Daddy,' said Bets. 'It does sound so silly.'

'I should have thought that Frederick was a much better name for a boy in his teens, than the absurd name of Fatty,' said her father. 'I wonder Frederick allows people to call him by that old nickname now.'

'But the name suits him,' said Pip. 'Anyway I don't think *my* nickname is very suitable for me now that I'm a bit older. Why can't I be called by my proper name of Philip, instead of Pip?'

'Simply because you're a bit of a pipsqueak still and probably always will be,' said his father, disappearing behind his newspaper. Bets gave a sudden laugh, and then a groan as Pip kicked her under the table.

'Pip!' said his mother, warningly. Bets changed the subject hurriedly. She didn't want

Pip to get into any trouble the very day that Fatty came home.

'Mummy, where's the bus timetable?' she said. 'I'd like to find out what time old Fatty's bus arrives.'

'Well, seeing that there are only two in the morning, and the bus from Warling takes two hours to get here, I should think he'll be on the *first* bus,' said Pip. 'Otherwise he'd be really late!'

'It should be about a quarter to ten,' said his mother. 'That means you'll have plenty of time to clear up the fearful mess in your playroom first. I could hardly get into it yesterday.'

Pip groaned. 'WHY do we always have to tidy the playroom when we plan to go out?' he demanded. 'I really do think it's . . .'

'Enough said,' said his father, from behind his newspaper, and Pip became silent at once. He looked across at Bets, and she grinned at him happily. Fatty was coming back! Fatty, with his wide grin, his twinkling eyes, his mad jokes – and his extraordinary habit of suddenly finding himself in the middle of peculiar mysteries! Oh the times they had had with Fatty – the excitement – the adventures! Why was it that some people *always* found themselves in the middle of something thrilling?

If Fatty was cast away on a lonely desert island, something extraordinary would immediately happen, thought Bets. A mermaid would pop up and let him swim away on her back. Or a submarine might arrive and . . .

'Bets, what are you dreaming about?' said her mother. 'You've carefully buttered your bread on *both* sides!'

Pip and Bets tore upstairs as soon as breakfast was finished, only one thought on their minds – Fatty was coming back!

'Let's hurry up and tidy the playroom,' said Pip. 'I want to go round to Larry's and see if he and Daisy know that Fatty's coming back today.'

He began to throw everything into the big toy cupboard, higgledy-piggledy, bang, crash, wallop!

'Mummy won't like that,' began Bets, but Pip only laughed at her. 'All right – *you* do it properly, old slow-coach. Good-bye – I'm off to Larry's. See you later!'

But Bets couldn't bear to be left behind, so

she shoved in the last few things, flew to get her coat and raced down the stairs after Pip, falling over the cat sitting on the bottom stair.

'Sorry, Puss!' she panted, and raced down to the front gate. 'Pip! WAIT for me!'

Soon they were at Larry's house. The front door was open, and they could hear Daisy calling to her brother. 'Aren't you ready to meet Fatty? You'll be late!'

In a few moments, all four children were on their way to the bus stop. 'What do you bet that old Fatty will play one of his tricks on us, and come in some kind of disguise?' said Pip.

'Well, I hope he does,' said Larry. 'We'd soon see through it!'

'Look, we're *just* in time,' said Bets. 'Here comes the bus. Let's run!'

The bus, a double-decker, came to a stop, and the four children ran to the exit at the back. People were crowding off, and the conductor was shouting loudly, 'Hurry off, please, and mind the step!'

Larry suddenly nudged Pip. 'Look, that's Fatty – he's disguised himself, just as we guessed he would. He's carrying a dog basket too, and I bet old Buster is in there. Stand back – don't let him see us!'

The fellow who was carrying the dog basket was stout, and wore a bulky overcoat, a yellow scarf round his neck and chin, and a cap with a large peak pulled down over his nose. He coughed hollowly as he stepped down from the bus, and held a large green cotton handkerchief to his mouth.

Bets giggled. 'That's Fatty all right!' she said in a low voice to Pip. 'Let's not say a word, but just follow him solemnly home!'

They set off, keeping just behind him. The fellow went off at quite a pace, limping slightly with his left foot.

'Yes, that's Fatty!' said Larry. 'Sort of thing he *would* do, in disguise – put on a limp or something! He can't fool *us* though!'

They followed the limping youth down the street, round a corner and up the hill. Then Larry shouted to him.

'Hey, Fatty! Stop! We know it's you!'

The youth swung round and glared at them.

'Don't you dare call after *me*!' he shouted. 'Cheeky young brats!'

'Go on, Fatty – we can't *help* knowing it's you!' said Pip. 'And we know you've got old Buster-dog in that basket, too. Let him out!'

'Buster? Who's Buster?' said the fellow. 'Are you mad? There's a *cat* in here, not a dog! Have a look!'

He slipped the catch of the basket, and opened the lid. Out sprang a most enormous ginger cat, spitting and hissing!

The four children stared in the greatest astonishment. A CAT – not Buster! So this fellow *wasn't* Fatty after all. Gosh, what an awful mistake!

'Er – we're very sorry. It's all a mistake,' stuttered poor Larry, his face scarlet. 'We do beg your pardon.'

'Now you just listen to me,' said the fellow, angrily. 'See that policeman over there? Well, I'm going to complain about you, see? Following me about! Whispering behind my back. Calling me names! Come here, Pussykins – that's right, you hiss at these kids!'

To the children's horror, the fellow went

across the road to a corner – and who should be standing there but Mr Goon, the village policeman. Mr GOON! He was no friend of theirs! What in the world could they do?

'Better get away quickly, before Mr Goon comes after us!' said Pip. 'Gosh, what a mistake we made!'

He turned to run, and bumped hard into someone standing just behind him, grinning, a little Scottie dog in his arms.

'FATTY! It's you! Fatty, we thought you were that fellow over there, with the dog basket!' cried Pip, overjoyed to see his friend again. 'We followed him, and now he's gone to complain about us to Mr Goon!'

'And *I* followed *you*!' said Fatty. 'I was on the top deck of the bus, and I saw you, though you didn't see me! I carried Buster because I was afraid he'd go careering after you, and give the game away. Give your friends a lick, Buster!'

He held up the little Scottie, and Buster most ecstatically licked all his four friends, whining in joy. Then Fatty put him down on the pavement, and alas, Buster suddenly spotted Goon the

was staring angrily at the policeman across the road.

child gave a yelp of delight and raced across the road at top speed. Ah, here his old enemy! What about dancing round his ankles and pretending to nip him? Buster felt just like a little exercise after his long ride on the bus!

Mr Goon glared at the excited Buster in disgust. 'Ha – you little pest of a dog! So you're back with your master, are you? Get away, now! Clear orf!'

'Buster's only telling you how pleased he is to see you,' said Fatty, as the burly policeman tried to skip away from Buster's attentions. 'My word, Mr Goon, you ought to learn dancing! You're really nippy with your feet – almost as nippy as Buster is. Heel, Buster! The dancing lesson is over!'

Goon went purple in the face. That boy! That toad of a boy! What wonderful peace and quiet there had been in the village for at least a week, with that boy away! Now he was back, and something would turn up to make things uncomfortable, Goon was sure. That boy was

always in the middle of p
some sort!
.......................openings of

Fatty joined the others who, fe
the fellow with the at had compla re that
them to Mr Goon, were keeping well awa bout
the angry policeman.

'I must say, that I think you were all a bit
silly following a chap-with-a-cat instead of a
boy-with-a-dog!' said Fatty.

'All right – don't rub it in,' said Larry. 'I'll buy
us all ice creams to make up for our mistake.'

'Sorry – but I think I *must* get home first,' said
Fatty. 'Mummy will be looking out for me. But
let's have a meeting this afternoon – a meeting
of the famous Find-Outers and Dog! Come to my
workroom about half past two. Come on, Buster,
old thing! To heel! and DO remember to be polite
and shake paws with my dad and mum as SOON
as you see them!'

Larry and Daisy went off together and so did
Pip and Bets. Bets' mother was amused to see
the little girl's happy face. 'I can see that you met
Frederick all right!' she said.

'We're having a meeting at Fatty's this

THE MYSTERY OF
BANSHEE TOWERS

afternoon,' said Bets, her face glowing. 'It's the first meeting the Find-Outers have had for ages!'

'Find-Outers?' said her mother. 'Let me see now, that's . . .'

'Oh, *Mummy*! You *know* we're the Five Find-Outers – and Dog!' said Pip. 'Don't you remember all the mysteries we've solved? I daresay we'll find out another and solve it *these* hols!'

'*If* one turns up!' said Bets.

Don't worry, Bets. Things always happen when Fatty is around. I don't expect you will have to wait *very* long before a nice 'juicy' mystery looms up for every one of you!

2. DOWN IN FATTY'S WORKROOM

Bets felt excited when at last the time came to go to the first meeting of the holidays. Her mother had not allowed her to race off immediately after dinner, but had sent both her and Pip up to their playroom.

'I don't know if you think that what you did this morning to tidy up the room was anything *like* enough,' she said. 'Throwing things higgledy-piggledy into corners and cupboards isn't *my* idea of clearing up. Please do the job properly before you go!'

'Oh *blow*!' said Pip, exasperated. 'Now we shall be late. Come on, Bets, you do your share.'

It was soon done, and they raced off down the garden path, happy to be on their way to Fatty's house. They joined up with Larry and Daisy, and were soon in Fatty's workroom at the bottom of his garden, well away from everyone, and *almost* out of range of any shout from the house!

'Grown-ups want an awful lot of things done if you're within shouting distance, you know,' Fatty said. 'But if they have to go and *fetch* you, they're sure to decide it's too much bother – so they do the things themselves!'

The shed was certainly well tucked away, and very, very comfortable. An oil-stove gave quite enough warmth, and on the floor was an old tiger-skin rug. 'Oh, Fatty,' said Bets. 'I do think this is a most exciting shed. It's lovely to be back again, after so long at school.'

'Nice to have you here, little Bets,' said Fatty, in the 'special' voice he sometimes kept for the little girl.

'Got anything to eat, Fatty?' asked Larry. 'I had quite a good dinner, but somehow I always feel hungry when we meet down here.'

'There are some chocolate biscuits in the cupboard,' said Fatty, who invariably seemed to be provided with a vast variety of good food, wherever he was. 'By the way, please look firmly the other way if Buster tries to beg any food from you. He is on a diet – slimming, you know. He over-ate himself while he was away. Too many cats about!'

'But surely he hasn't begun to eat *cats*!' said Daisy, shocked.

'No, idiot! But with plenty of cat-dishes around always ready to be licked clean, he did far too well,' said Fatty. 'Buster, stand up. Show your tubby figure – oh what a middle you've landed yourself with – disgraceful!'

Buster certainly had a tummy. His tail drooped when Fatty scolded him, and he went sadly into a corner and curled himself up, eyeing the chocolate biscuits sadly. Bets felt very sorry for him. 'I'll just let him *lick* my chocolatey fingers, Fatty,' she said. 'That's all, I promise. I just can't bear to see him looking so left-out. Here you are, Buster – lick my fingers.'

Buster was pleased. He licked Bets' fingers and then sat down as close to her as he possibly could. He loved kind-hearted little Bets. She put her arm round him again.

'Fatty, is this meeting about anything special?' she said. 'I'd be just as pleased if there wasn't any mystery to solve at the moment. I mean – I do hols. My father made a list of interesting spots we could go to see. He said we shouldn't just mess about doing nothing, he said . . .'

'He *said* that – but what he really meant was that he didn't want you under his feet all the time,' said Larry. 'My father's like that too – I mean, he's an absolute sport, and I'm really proud of him – and he is of me – but I do notice that after about ten days of the hols he always gets this idea of us going off for the day – not just one day, but every day. And *mine* made out a list too – here it is. I'll read it out.'

He took a neatly-written list from the pocket of his trousers and read from it. 'Old water-caves at Chillerbing. Museum of age-old fossils at Tybolds. Norman Tower at Yellow-Moss . . .'

'Gosh, those are down on *my* list too!' said Pip, scrabbling in his pocket for it. 'Yes – all those are down – and two or three more. Roman remains at Jackling Museum. Sea pictures at Banshee Towers, at the top of Banshee Hill. Old musical instruments at . . .'

'I don't want to see *any* of them!' said Bets, suddenly looking very woebegone. 'I wouldn't so much mind the sea pictures – I like sea pictures – but I *don't* like those ugly fossily things, or those . . .'

'All right, Bets, you won't spend lovely spring days in museums or Norman towers or caves,' said Fatty, putting his arm round her. 'But we might go and see Banshee Towers. You know why it's called that, don't you?'

Nobody knew. 'Well,' said Fatty, 'a banshee means "a woman of the fairies" – and it shrieks and wails when any misfortune or unhappiness comes to the family in whose house it lives.'

'How very unpleasant,' said Daisy, at once. 'I'm very glad *my* family doesn't own a banshee. I should be scared stiff. Does Banshee Towers own a banshee, then?'

'I suppose it did once, when the family lived in it,' said Fatty. 'But now that it's a museum – or a picture gallery or something – I expect the banshee has retired!'

'I don't want to go to see Banshee Towers if the banshee still lives there,' said Bets, decidedly. 'So you'll have to find out, Fatty.'

'I honestly wouldn't worry,' said Fatty. 'It

would be a pity to let an old-time "woman of the fairies" frighten you from seeing wonderful sea pictures. And I believe they really *are* wonderful!'

'Well, we'll make a few expeditions to show our parents that we really are not the lie-abeds they think we are,' said Larry. 'It should be rather fun, actually. We could picnic in these places – and I could use one of them for my holiday essay. It would be something to write about – especially the banshee howling. I hope it wails like anything when we're there!'

'I won't go if it does,' said Bets at once. 'Hello, who's that at the door? Golly, that loud knock made me jump!'

'Who's there?' demanded Fatty.

'It's me – Ern,' said a well-known voice outside. 'I've been sent to stay with my Uncle Theo – Mr Goon, you know – because one of my sisters has measles and I haven't had it – at least, Mum can't *remember* me having it. Can I come in?'

'Of course! Come along in, Ern, we're all here,' said Fatty, and opened the door. Ern stood there, grinning in delight to see his friends again.

Buster at once made a great fuss of him.

'Coo, it's nice to see you all again,' said Ern, sitting down on the floor and hugging the little Scottie. 'I didn't want to come and stay with my uncle – I don't like him and he doesn't like me – but I don't mind putting up with him if you'll let me be with *you* now and again. Any mysteries going?'

'Not so far, Ern,' said Fatty. 'Help yourself to the chocolate biscuits, but DON'T give Buster any. He's slimming.'

'Luvaduck, is he really?' said Ern. 'I must say he feels a bit solid-like.'

'It's good to see you, Ern,' said Fatty. 'We are planning to go on some interesting rambles – and you can come with us, if you like – if your uncle will let you.'

'Coo, I'd like that!' said Ern. 'Well, Uncle says I've got to turn to, and look nippy, and not get under his feet, and use my loaf . . .'

'Your *loaf*?' said Bets, in surprise. 'Do you have a loaf of bread of your own then?'

'You don't know much, do you?' grinned Ern, so delighted to be with his old friends again that his eyes shone like stars. 'Using your "loaf" means using your brains, see?'

'Ah yes,' said Fatty, gravely. 'Well, if we all intend to go sight-seeing and learning about banshees and old musical instruments, and Roman remains, we must ALL use our – er – loaves. Are we allowed any butter with them, Ern?'

But dear old Ern didn't see the joke, though the others roared in delight. Ern didn't mind. It was sheer happiness to him to be with Fatty, Bets, and the rest. They could pull his leg, correct him, laugh at him – they were his friends and he was theirs. Let them do whatever they liked, as long as he could be with them!

3. BINGO - AND BUSTER!

It was fun to have Ern again. He enjoyed the company of the five friends so much, and entered into everything with the greatest delight. He sat listening intently as they went on discussing their plans for the next two or three weeks.

'I suppose I couldn't come with you sometimes?' he said, at last. 'I daresay Uncle would let me off now and again. So long as I do the jobs he sets me, of course.'

'Yes. If he's kind enough to have you to stay, you must certainly help him in any way you can,' said Fatty. 'His garden, for instance. I passed it the other day – shocking! Full of weeds!'

'That's what my uncle said,' agreed Ern, mournfully. 'Trouble is – I dunno weeds from flowers. Oh, and there's another thing – he's letting me have my dog with me while I'm here. What do you think of *that*?'

'*Dog*? I didn't even know you had one, Ern,' said Pip, surprised.

'Well, he's a bit new, like,' said Ern. 'I've had him for three weeks. I'm trying to train him good and proper – like you've trained old Buster there, Fatty.'

'Good!' said Fatty. 'Very good. An untrained dog is a nuisance – nobody likes him. Where is this dog of yours – and what's he called? What kind is he?'

'I don't rightly know what kind he is,' said Ern. 'He's a bit of a mixture really; he's not very big, but he's got a mighty long tail with a mighty big wag in it – and nice ears that prick up like Buster's here – and rather short legs. Pity about his legs, really, he looks funny when he runs, you see, and all the other dogs laugh at him.'

'They don't!' said Bets disbelievingly.

'Well, they stand and stare at him, and sort of wink at one another when he comes scuttering by,' said Ern. 'His name is Bingo – good name, isn't it? It suits him too – you wait till you've seen him. I like him an awful lot – it's the first time I've had a dog of my own. He's potty about me you know – thinks I'm the world's wonder!'

'Just like old Buster then,' said Bets. 'He thinks Fatty's the world's wonder, don't you, Buster?'

'Woof!' said Buster, agreeing heartily. He went to Fatty and licked his chin, and then put his head on Fatty's knee, looking up at him adoringly.

'Loving old thing,' said Fatty, and patted him. 'Well, Ern, I'm awfully glad you've a dog of your own. Good for the dog – and good for you, too. You'll like having someone who looks up to you and thinks that everything you do is right! But look after him well, won't you?'

'Where is this Bingo?' asked Larry.

'I've locked him in the woodshed at Uncle's,' said Ern. 'You see – well, I didn't know if you'd like me to bring him along. Buster mightn't like him.'

'Rubbish!' said Fatty, getting up. 'Any dog is a friend of Buster's if he belongs to one of us. Let's go and visit this dog of yours, and take him for a walk.'

'You're a real sport, Fatty,' said Ern, his

face glowing. 'Come on, then.'

They all went out of the shed and made their way to Peterswood Village, Buster dancing round in joy, sniffing along the hedges, barking at a sparrow, wagging his tail without a stop.

'Is your uncle in a good temper today?' enquired Larry.

'So-so,' said Ern, with a grin. 'He smiled when I cleaned his big boots for him – and he frowned when I upset the milk. He doesn't know I've come to see you.'

'Why didn't you tell him?' asked Bets. 'You're not *scared* of him, are you?'

'Oh, I'm proper scared of Uncle all right,' said Ern. 'Bit too free with his temper, he is. I don't think he'll be too pleased if I go about with you too much, so I won't tell him anything.'

They came to Goon's little house, which stood not far from the police station. As soon as they opened the gate, a terrific volley of blood-curdling howls greeted them, and something hurled itself against the woodshed door.

'That's him – that's Bingo,' said Ern, with pride. 'I hope Uncle's out. He wouldn't like that noise at all. Hey, Bingo! I've brought friends to see you.'

Buster the Scottie was astonished and rather alarmed to hear the extraordinary noise from the shed. He put his head on one side and pricked up his ears to sharp points. He gave a little growl.

'It's all right, Buster,' said Ern. 'That's my dog in there. Hey, Bingo, come along out!' And he slipped the catch of the door and opened it.

Out shot something at sixty miles an hour, gave one horrified look at the crowd of children, and disappeared at top speed through the gate.

'That's him!' said Ern, proudly, as Bingo shot down the road. 'What do you think of him, Fatty?'

'Well, I really only caught sight of his tail,' said Fatty. 'But that certainly looked fine. Look out, here comes old Mr Goon, your uncle, Ern. He looks pretty bad-tempered too.'

Mr Goon had opened his front door, and was standing there in his uniform, helmet and all, glaring in his best manner.

'ERN! What's the matter with that dog of

yours, barking like that? Has he gone mad or something? Where is he?'

'I don't know, Uncle,' said Ern, truthfully. 'He shot off at top speed. I only hope he hasn't gone back to my home. He might catch measles, and come out in nasty spots.'

'You and your measles!' snorted Mr Goon. 'I said you could have that dog if he behaved himself – and if I could borrow him at nights when I go down into the rough part of the town; but I tell you this straight, Ern, if he's going to act silly, and bark at nothing, and rush off like a mad thing, I won't have him. And you might tell him to keep away from my feet. He's tripped me up twice already.'

'Oh, I'm very sorry about that, Uncle,' said Ern. 'Er – I just brought my friends to see him.'

'Well, you can take them away again,' said Goon, ungraciously. 'They may be your friends, but they're not *mine* – especially Frederick Algernon Trotteville – pah!'

'Who's he talking about?' said Ern, in wonder, as Goon went indoors and slammed the door.

'Me, I'm afraid,' said Fatty. 'Those are my real

27

names, you know, Ern. I try to forget them, though I can't say I like my nickname either. Now, what about your dog, Bingo, Ern? Where do you suppose he's gone?'

'I don't know,' said Ern, suddenly looking desperate. 'I can't think why he went off like that. I suppose my uncle went and shouted at him in the shed or something. Let's go and look for him.'

But before they had gone more than a few steps, Mr Goon was at his door again, shouting for Ern.

'Ern! You come back! What about those jobs I gave you to do? You come back, I tell you.'

'Better go, Ern,' said Fatty. 'Cheer up. We'll have a look for old Bingo. He won't have come to any harm.'

Ern went slowly back through the gate, looking angry and troubled. His thoughts were full of Bingo, his beloved dog. He might get run over! He might get lost! He might even be stolen. He's so friendly and good-natured, he would go with anyone, thought poor Ern, and began to run as he heard a stentorian shout from inside the house.

'ERN! You come on IN! I've got to go to the police station, and I want you to peel the potatoes for supper and get things tidy. ERN!'

Poor Ern disappeared into the house. He longed to slam the door, just as Goon had done, but he didn't dare.

The others walked slowly through the village, talking about Ern, and keeping a look out for Bingo. There was no sign of him. Fatty thought he must have gone to find his way back to Ern's own home. They decided to go to the bun shop and have tea there. Buster was pleased. He knew that this usually meant a few tit-bits for him!

Just as they reached the bun shop, they heard a little whine – a very small and pathetic one. It seemed to come from the hedge nearby. Buster went at once to investigate. He slipped through the hedge and then gave a sharp bark.

'Buster, what is it? Come back!' called Fatty. Buster appeared again – with something trotting behind him – Bingo!

'BINGO!' said everyone, in astonishment, and Bingo wagged his long tail, went flat on his tummy, and began to crawl anxiously towards them, in a most humble manner.

'Poor Bingo!' said Bets, in her gentle voice, and at once Bingo shot over to her, pressed himself against her, and gave a funny little high whine. He wagged his long tail so hard that it slapped against Bets' legs, but she didn't mind. She patted him and stroked him, and he went nearly mad with joy. Buster stood nearby and watched gravely.

'Well, you're a bit of a comic, Bingo, I must say,' said Fatty, looking at him from all angles. 'What a tail! Pity you didn't have legs to match, old boy! But my word, you've real doggy eyes!'

Yes, Bingo had good, bright, faithful eyes, and a tongue always ready to lick any friend. The children decided that Ern was lucky. 'What do *you* think of him, Buster?' said Fatty, seeing Buster standing and watching everything, his eyes bright, his tail wagging just a very little.

'Woof,' said Buster, and went straight over to Bingo. He stood nose to nose with him, each sniffing at the other. Then Buster danced round Bingo, and Bingo gave a joyful bark, and away they went together, tearing down the road like mad things!

'Buster approves,' said Larry. '*I* rather approve of him too. A comical dog, but a real little sport. Well, if we're going to have tea at the bun shop, what about it? And please don't eat more than six buns, Fatty – you want to be able to squeeze out of the door again!'

In they all went, made for their favourite table, and sat down. Fatty, as usual, had plenty of money, and that meant a good tuck-in for everyone. In the middle of the meal, the door was pushed open with a heave, and in trotted the two dogs, panting, their mouths open as if they were both laughing!

'Buster, go and shut the door after you,' said Fatty sternly. 'Have you forgotten your manners? Bingo, please notice that doors must be pushed shut, not left open, when you come in and out of rooms.'

'Wuff,' said Bingo, head on one side, listening carefully. He trotted over to the door and helped Buster to shut it, using both paws and nose.

'He's "one of us" already!' said Larry. 'I'm

beginning to like you, Bingo, old thing. Now, *sit*! Buster, teach him how to sit. Gosh, look at that, Fatty – both sitting down side by side, as good as gold! We're going to have some fun with old Bingo!'

4. MR GOON LOSES HIS TEMPER

Ern had been very busy indeed while the others had gone to the village. Mr Goon was in one of his worst tempers. He always was when he had met Fatty, whom he disliked very much.

'That boy!' he said to Ern. 'I don't trust him an inch. Never did. It's a pity he's not as stupid as he looks. Too clever by half, he is!'

'He *doesn't* look stupid, Uncle,' said Ern, emptying some potatoes into a bowl of water to peel. 'How could he when he's got such marvellous brains! You should hear him talk – luvaduck, he knows pretty well everything!'

'I'll luvaduck *you* if you don't get on with those potatoes, Ern,' said Mr Goon. 'That boy's a menace – yes, that's the word for him – a menace!'

'What's a menace, Uncle?' asked Ern. 'Anything to do with manners? Sounds a bit the same.'

'I don't know if you're being rude, or just plain stupid, Ern,' said Mr Goon, majestically. 'But this I do know – you'll get a clip on the ear soon.'

'And one of these days my dog will bite you if you clip me!' cried Ern, almost at the end of his tether. 'Now, Uncle – don't you come any nearer. I'll throw this bowl of potatoes over you, if you do!'

Ern looked so fierce that Goon retreated hurriedly. 'Now, now,' he said, 'don't take things so seriously, Ern. Can't you see a joke?'

'Depends who makes it,' said Ern, feeling suddenly victorious. Then his spirits fell again as he remembered his dog. Where *was* old Bingo? Had he run away for ever? He sniffed a little as he went on peeling the potatoes, and when he remembered how Bingo ran to meet him and licked him lovingly each time he came home from school, a tear fell plop into the potato bowl.

I'm an idiot – that's what Fatty would call me, thought Ern. But I dunno – there's something about a dog that gets you – especially if it's your own.

Mr Goon went off to the police station, his boots well polished by Ern, and his helmet and uniform well brushed. Ern was glad to see him go. As soon as his uncle was out of sight, he thought he would whistle for Bingo – just to see if by *any* chance he would come.

So he whistled. Ern had a most piercing whistle, shrill, long and alarming. It made everyone within hearing jump in surprise and annoyance. Ern stood at the front gate and whistled for at least five minutes. No Bingo arrived – but a good many windows and doors were opened, and people began looking out to see if anything was the matter. They thought that it must be Goon blowing his police-whistle for help!

A small boy arrived, panting, at the front gate. 'Any help wanted?' he asked. 'We heard the police-whistle being blown.'

'That was only me whistling for my dog,' said Ern, astonished. Then, seeing people looking out of windows and doors, he shot inside Goon's house in a hurry. They'll tell Uncle I was using his police-whistle, he thought desperately.

Luvaduck, what a day! Wish I was at home, measles and all!

About half past five, Mr Goon returned home to see if Ern had put on the kettle and had made him some toast, as he had commanded. Fortunately for Ern, he had everything ready. Ern was down in the dumps: no Fatty had come back, no Buster, no Bets – and certainly no Bingo. Ern didn't want any tea at all, a most unusual thing.

'This toast is burnt,' said Mr Goon, grumpily.

'It's not,' said Ern. 'It's just right. That's how my Ma likes it, anyway.'

'And you've put too much tea in the pot,' said Mr Goon, peering in, holding the lid in his hand. It was hot and he had to drop it very suddenly. It fell to the floor and broke. He glared at Ern as if *he* had dropped it!

Ern gave a sudden giggle, and his uncle went red in the face. 'Pick them pieces up,' he commanded, 'and take that grin off your face, Ern.'

'I can't. It's stuck there,' said Ern, suddenly feeling cheeky.

'ERN!' said Mr Goon, in a terrifying voice, and stood up. Ern promptly stood up too, and ran to the door. He opened it and Goon came after him. Ern went down the hall to the front door and opened that, and then shot down the front path with his uncle on his heels – at exactly the same moment as Fatty and the rest, with Buster and Bingo, came in at the gate.

Somehow or other, Mr Goon became mixed up with the two excited dogs as they raced towards the front door – and down he went with a thud. Bingo leapt up at the astonished Ern, and tried his hardest to lick him in as many places as he could, barking madly all the time. Buster, finding his old enemy, Mr Goon, on the ground and at his mercy, sailed in gleefully to the attack! It really was a sight to be seen!

'BINGO! You've come back!' shouted Ern in joy, and lifted up the delighted dog, who at once plastered his face with loving licks.

'CLEAR ORF, ALL OF YOU!' roared poor Mr Goon, trying to push Buster away. 'I'll tell your parents about this! WILL you order this dog away, Frederick Trotteville? One of these days I'll clap you in a cell, yes, and the dog too. Get away, you brute! Lemme get up! Ern, help me up.'

It was Fatty who pulled the heavy policeman to his feet and dusted him down, murmuring apologies in a polite voice that simply infuriated Mr Goon!

'Bad luck! Did you trip over your feet? Hey, you'll scare the girls, if you roar like that. Buster, behave yourself. BUSTER! Are you deaf? Stop dancing round poor Mr Goon. Here, let me help you up – up we come – that's it – upsadaisy. You all right now, Mr Goon?'

Mr Goon glared. He saw that quite a crowd had gathered round his front gate – and some of them were daring to laugh! Laughing at the law! What were things coming to? Most majestically, Mr Goon went to the gate and scowled at everyone there. 'What's all this? Clear orf, now! You're creating a nuisance, you are. Move on, there. MOVE ON!'

Only a few people moved away. Fatty felt sorry for poor Mr Goon. 'Perhaps if you told them to move OFF instead of move ON, they'd understand better,' he suggested. 'Let me help you, Mr Goon.' And Fatty waved an imperious hand and shouted in a suddenly enormous voice, 'MOVE OFF, WILL YOU! MOVE OFF!'

And, rather astonished, the lookers-on moved off at once. Fatty was rather astonished too – he hadn't thought it would be so easy! Mr Goon was more than astonished. He was exceedingly angry.

'Think you're in the police force now, do you?' he said, fiercely. 'Well, what about *you* moving off – *or* on – I don't care which. Funny how trouble always comes when you're about, isn't it, Frederick Trotteville? Now I'm going back to finish my tea in peace and quiet. Clear orf, all of you! I'm sick of the sight of you. You get indoors, Ern – and take that dog to the woodshed. Tripping me up like that. You can consider him arrested and put into a cell, see? And there he'll stay out in the woodshed, night and day!'

'Oh *no*, Uncle – that would be cruel!' said Ern, upset. 'Fatty, tell him. He might listen to you.

You can't lock up a dog, night and day.'

'All right then, you go home!' stormed Mr Goon. 'I do a kindness and take you in – and that silly dog too – and this is what happens. Go on home! Catch the measles!'

Ern didn't know what to do – but Fatty did. He whispered something in Ern's ear, and Ern's face broke into a delighted smile. He took hold of Fatty's hand and shook it hard. 'You're a friend, Fatty – yes, that's what you are, a friend,' said Ern, warmly. 'I'll go and get my things straightaway. Would you mind Bingo for me, till I come out? Uncle's in such a temper, he might scare him. WHAT a pity he tripped over Bingo!'

Bets and Daisy had been very scared by all the upset, but the boys had rather enjoyed it. Fatty couldn't help feeling a little sorry for Mr Goon. The policeman did not shine when things went wrong; but Fatty felt sure he would be sorry and feel guilty when he had had time to ponder over things. That was the worst of a hot temper – it led you into doing silly, rash things you were sorry for afterwards

– and then it was probably too late.

Ern had disappeared into his uncle's house. He was there about three minutes and then came out again, carrying a canvas bag. Bingo trotted joyfully over to him. Ern was beaming all over his round face.

'Where are you going, Ern?' asked Bets, in surprise. 'Home? But you can't go there, with measles about!'

They all went out of the gate together, leaving Mr Goon staring after them. He was just beginning to wish that he hadn't lost his temper.

'Ern, come back! You come and apologise and I'll let you stay!' he shouted.

'Sorry, Uncle,' shouted back Ern. 'I can't stay where I'm not wanted – or where my dog will be locked up night and day. Sorry, Uncle!'

'Where's Ern going?' asked Pip.

'He's going to stay in my workroom till his family are clear of the measles,' said Fatty. '*And* Bingo as well. Nice dog, Bingo. Be good for Buster to have company too. The workroom is nice and warm, and I can put a camp-bed there. But nobody is to know, see? You are all to keep your mouths shut. Ern is our friend, and we've got to stand by him.'

'Oh *good*, Fatty! You always think of some fine way out of things when they go wrong,' said Bets, squeezing Fatty's arm. 'Ern, are you pleased?'

'Pleased? I feel like a tail with two dogs,' said Ern, looking down at Buster and Bingo trotting amicably together. 'No, I mean a dog with two tails. Coo, luvaduck – wasn't poor old Uncle in a temper, all because he fell over Bingo! To think I'm going to stay in your workroom, Fatty. You're a friend, you are – and I can't say more than that, can I?'

'No, that's about the best thing anyone can say about anyone else,' said Fatty, with one of his grins. He gave Ern a little punch in the back. 'I bet I'll say that about *you* someday, Ern!'

Ern glowed. He looked round gratefully at the little bunch of friends walking with him. Yes, that was about the best thing that could happen to anyone – to have friends, whether they were two-legged or four-legged.

And to BE a friend to someone is just as good,

thought Ern. Well, maybe it's even better. I'll have to ask Fatty about it sometime. He's sure to know!

5. FATTY IS A REAL FRIEND!

The little company went in at the back gate of Fatty's garden, and trooped down to the shed – Fatty's cosy little workroom. The two dogs trotted along amicably together, Bingo occasionally giving Buster a friendly lick. Bingo's tail never stopped wagging or waving.

'You'll wear it out if you're not careful, Bingo,' said Ern, as they went in close file down the path, Bingo's tail slapping against the nearest legs. Bets laughed. She didn't feel scared any longer – just pleased and excited. She was glad that Ern had got away from unkind Mr Goon. It would be nice to have him at their meetings.

The workroom felt warm when they opened the door, and was full of a golden light from the sinking sun.

'Well, here we are once more,' said Fatty. 'Get out the toffees, Bets – they're in that cupboard.

I'll just go up to the house and see if I can find a camp-bed – or a spare mattress, if not.'

He disappeared, and Bets went to find the toffees. Trust Fatty to have something to chew or suck or drink! Good old Fatty to think of rescuing poor Ern!

Fatty was in the middle of hunting about for a camp-bed when his mother appeared. She was astonished to see him in the spare room. 'What in the world do you want, Fatty?' she said.

'Er – well, I just wondered if there was a camp-bed to spare,' said Fatty.

'A *camp*-bed? Whatever for?' said his mother. 'Fatty, I will NOT allow you to sleep out in the garden yet! You'd catch your death of cold!'

'Mummy dear, I'm not *thinking* of such a thing!' said Fatty. 'I like my own warm bed much too much to want to shiver outside, with beetles and frogs and ants all over me. I just wondered if we *had* a camp-bed to spare, that's all.'

'Fatty, why are you so mysterious about it?' asked his mother. 'Look at me! Why this sudden idea of a camp-bed?'

'Mummy, you are always so *curious*,' said

Fatty, taking her hand. 'Can't you trust me? I don't want to sleep on it. I don't want to sell it. I don't even want to take it off the premises. I just want to *borrow* it. I'm afraid if I told you *why* I want it, someone might ask you questions, and then you'd answer – and someone else might suffer. Please trust me, Mummy, and believe that, like the Boy Scouts, I am about to do a good deed!'

'I never in my life knew anyone who could wheedle things out of me like you, Frederick,' said his mother, beginning to laugh. 'All right, I won't ask you any questions. I'll trust you – as I always do, dear! There's a spare camp-bed in the cupboard under the stairs.'

'Bless you, Mummy, you're a pet,' said Fatty, and gave her a smacking kiss on the cheek. He went to the cupboard and found the camp-bed. In no time at all, he had carried it down the garden, unseen, and Larry was helping him to take it through the door of the shed.

'Did you have any bother getting it?' asked Larry. 'I always have to go into long, long explanations when *I* want to borrow anything like a camp-bed.'

'No. Fortunately my mother trusts me as much as I trust *her*,' said Fatty, putting up the camp-bed with Ern. 'Nothing like trust in a family! I can recommend it thoroughly.'

Ern stared at Fatty. What odd things Fatty sometimes said – but they were worth remembering, Ern thought. 'Nothing like trust in a family.' That meant trusting one another. There was quite a lot in that idea. Ern decided to think about it when he was in bed. He felt excited when he saw the camp-bed neatly made up in a corner of the workroom.

'Luvaduck!' he said. 'It's a miracle, this! Me sleeping here, all on my own, safe as houses, and my uncle not knowing a thing about it. I don't know how to thank you enough, Fatty, that I don't.'

'Well, don't try,' said Fatty. 'Bets, did you find the toffees – ah, yes, I see a lump in your cheek, and one in Pip's.'

'Fatty, can we do anything to help Ern?' asked Bets. 'I mean, bring food, or something like that. Cook will always give us bits and pieces.'

'Well, I vote we all bring what we can, without arousing any *suspicions*,' said Fatty. 'Ern had better send a postcard to his mother, saying "Getting on fine, quite happy", or something like that – in case Mr Goon tells her that he's sent Ern off. But I don't somehow think he will! He'll imagine that Ern has rushed back home, with awful tales about him!'

'I'm going to enjoy myself,' said Ern, bouncing up and down on the camp-bed. 'Wish *I* could do something for somebody – you, Bets, for instance. I'd do anything, really I would!'

'I've no doubt your chance will come someday,' said Fatty. 'Now, what about a game? Or shall we first of all decide what expeditions we are going to make this week?'

'It sounds as if we were explorers or something,' said Pip. 'How nice to be able to say "What about exploring the Sahara?" Or "I think we should row down the Nile and count the number of crocodiles there"!'

The others chuckled. 'Well, let's take a vote on where we should go first,' said Fatty, taking two sheets of paper from a shelf. 'Here are the lists made out by Pip's father and Larry's – together with a few notes of my own. I think we'll take a vote as to which two places we would prefer to visit. We can always go and see the others afterwards, if we want to.'

He read out the list of places. 'Well, there you are. Now just choose two of those, each of you, and scribble them down, fold your papers in half and give them to me. I'll open them and see which places the majority of us want to visit.'

Soon they were all busy. Bets asked how to spell 'Banshee' so everyone at once knew *one* of her choices! The notes were handed in to Fatty and he opened them.

'Well, the two places that the majority of you want to see are the old water-caves at Chillerbing – and Banshee Towers, on Banshee Hill. Bets, I'm surprised *you* put down Banshee Towers. I thought you'd be scared of any places connected with banshees wailing in the night!'

'Fatty, I only chose Banshee Towers because you said there were magnificent sea pictures there,' said Bets. 'I won't go if there are *still* banshees, though – unkind fairies wailing and foretelling horrible things! I'd hate that.'

'Dear Bets, banshees only belong to fairytales,' said Fatty, seeing that Bets looked rather scared. 'We shan't see or hear a single banshee – but we *shall* see a magnificent set of sea pictures. I believe some of them reach from floor to ceiling. We shall feel quite seasick if we gaze at them too long.'

'I shall take some seasick medicine with me, then,' said Bets, solemnly.

Everyone roared with laughter. 'I'm only teasing you, Bets,' said Fatty. 'Hey – look at those two dogs!'

They all turned to look – and there were Buster and Bingo, *both* squeezed into Buster's basket, fast asleep, so entangled that, as Larry said, 'T'other couldn't be told from which!' Pip glanced at Fatty and Ern. Both had such pleased, admiring looks on their faces that Pip laughed.

'Look at Fatty and Ern,' he said. 'Did you ever see such dippy looks on any faces except dog-lovers?'

'Yes, I did – on yours on your birthday when Granny gave you two white rabbits!' said Bets at once. 'You looked at them just like Auntie Sue looks when she goes to see if her twins are asleep! *Quite* dippy!'

That made Pip go red, and everyone laughed. 'You're getting quite smart, young Bets,' said Fatty. 'Well, to come back to Banshee Towers. I see that four out of five have voted for that, so we'll go there. And three out of five have voted for the water-caves. So those are our first two expeditions.'

'*I* voted for Banshee Towers too,' said Ern, to Bets. 'I'm mad on sea pictures. You see, I want to go into the Navy when I'm old enough, so I *had* to vote for the sea picture place. And don't you worry about banshees, Bets. The moment I see one, I'll whistle like this, see, and I'll make them so scared they'll fly out of the window and never come back!' And Ern suddenly put two fingers into his mouth, screwed up his face, and gave a very sudden, very long and extremely piercing whistle. It made everyone jump violently, and the two dogs in the basket leapt straight up into the air as if they had been shot.

Buster barked and Bingo howled, and both

dogs tore round and round the room after imaginary enemies. Ern was quite overcome at the commotion he had caused.

Fatty glared at him. 'ERN! Do you want to bring all the policemen in the neighbourhood here? That whistling of yours is EXACTLY like a police-whistle. You'll have my father and mother down here if you don't look out.'

'Luvaduck!' muttered Ern, trying to catch Bingo as he tore past him for the third time, really scared.

Fatty heard a shout from somewhere outside, and groaned. 'Somebody *is* coming!' he said. 'Switch off the light, Bets, quick – the switch is just behind you. Shut up barking, Buster, you idiot. Now, no noise, anyone. We'll sit here in the dark and hope nobody comes to find out what on earth we are doing here. SHHHHHHH!'

Not a sound was to be heard in the darkened room except some rather heavy breathing from a scared Ern. Suppose he was found here by his uncle or somebody and sent home? Ern wished and wished that he hadn't shown Bets how he proposed to frighten a banshee.

After five minutes had gone by, Fatty judged it safe to put on the lights again. As he did so, there came a call from his house, away up the garden. He groaned.

'That's my supper. Where *has* the evening gone to? I'll have to go. You and Pip ought to go too, Bets.'

'Gosh, and so had we!' said Larry, pulling Daisy to her feet. 'Good thing our father and mother are out tonight, and there's only Cookie to see to us. Goodnight, everyone. Sleep well, Ern. So long, Bingo-dog. Be good!'

'Wuff,' said Bingo, pleased to hear his name. He accompanied everyone to the door, his tail wagging nineteen to the dozen. The two dogs gave each other a quick lick, and Buster trotted up the garden with Fatty.

Ern was left alone in the shed. He was astonished to hear Bingo growling softly twenty minutes later, and horrified to hear soft footsteps coming to the door. His heart sank. Was it his uncle, coming to fetch him? But how could he *possibly* know where he, Ern, was? The door opened and a torch shone in, lighting up the darkness in which Ern sat. Ern trembled and shook, feeling most alarmed.

'Ern! It's me, Fatty. I've come to bring you some supper – and to tell you there's a torch in the table drawer, if you want to see to eat or to read. I won't be able to come down again to the shed tonight, so goodnight, and sleep well. I'll bring you some breakfast in the morning.'

'Coo, thanks, you're a wonder, Fatty,' said the grateful Ern, and took the tray that Fatty handed in.

'There's a bone for old Bingo, from Buster,' said Fatty, giving him a paper bag. 'So long, Ern. See you tomorrow!'

'So long,' said Ern, gratefully, and sat down to eat a nice piece of fried fish, mashed potatoes and greens. He gave the bone to Bingo, who was thrilled. He made such a noise gnawing it that Ern felt sure it could be heard for miles around!

'Bingo, old dog, are you enjoying this?' said Ern, when at last he had undressed and slipped under the rug that Fatty had left for the camp-bed. 'Come on under the rug with me

– we'll keep each other warm. That's right. Snuggle down. Goodnight!'

Goodnight, Ern and Bingo. You're quite safe, though somebody has peeped in at the window, and knows you are there! Don't worry, it was only the black cat next door – and she fled as soon as she saw Bingo! Sleep tight!

6. OFF TO BANSHEE HILL

Ern had a happy, but very restless night. Bingo kept imagining that he heard rats running round outside the shed, trying to get in, and leapt on and off the camp-bed every few minutes, rushing to sniff round the corners of the shed, his long tail waving in excitement.

'Bingo! I'd much rather have rats nibbling my toes than you jumping off and on my tummy all night long,' said Ern at last. 'For goodness sake, come and lie down.'

Tired out at last, Bingo cuddled under the rug and fell asleep. Ern put an arm round him and went to sleep too, dead to the world until morning.

He awoke to hear a stealthy knocking on the door and flew out of bed to open it. Fatty was there – good old Fatty – his pockets bulging. Buster was with him, and immediately went to rub noses with Bingo.

'Hello, Ern,' said Fatty, pushing his way in quickly to prevent the excited Bingo from rushing out. 'Got to be a bit careful, the gardener's here this morning, and he'd better not see you in the shed. He might tell Mr Goon!'

'I'll be very careful then,' said Ern, as Fatty pulled a hastily-wrapped packet from one pocket, and some apples from another.

'Here you are, Ern,' he said. 'Best I could do for the moment. I didn't dare to take too much from the larder, but there were plenty of eggs, so that was something. How's old Bingo? Was he good last night?'

'Well, he seemed to be hunting round for rats for *hours*,' said Ern, unwrapping the packet Fatty gave him. 'Coo, hard-boiled egg sandwiches – smashing! And two buttered rolls – with honey inside! You're a brick, Fatty, straight you are.'

'You'll find some little bottles of lemonade in that cupboard,' said Fatty. 'And an opener too. I daren't bring you a pot of tea. Mummy would start asking questions!'

Ern sat happily munching his egg sandwiches,

a glass of lemonade beside him, with Bingo sitting expectantly at his feet. Buster went sniffing at the bottom of a second cupboard, and Fatty laughed.

'He knows a packet of his biscuits is kept there, and he wants to give old Bingo some,' said Fatty, getting up. 'Am I right, Buster, old thing?'

'Woof!' said Buster, dancing round excitedly, his tail wagging. Bingo joined him, having heard the word 'biscuits'! Soon he and Buster were amiably sharing a packet, crunching up the biscuits in delight.

Buster was overjoyed to have Bingo to play with. He suddenly went completely mad and began to rush round and round the room at top speed, barking wildly. Bingo joined him, and the two boys hurriedly leapt out of the way.

'Shut up, Buster,' said Fatty. 'Don't do your racehorse gallop in here. Gosh, there goes the lemonade! BUSTER! Have you gone completely mad?'

'BINGO! Oh my goodness, he's got hold of the rug now,' said Ern. 'He'll tear it to pieces – look at them having a tug-of-war. Fatty, you'll have to take Buster away. They'll wreck everything!'

A cautious knock came at the door and the two dogs left their play and rushed to it, barking madly.

'COME IN!' yelled Fatty. 'MIND THE DOGS!'

It was little Bets, come to bring Ern a packet of food. Ern gave her a hug and opened the packet. Bets had made him some potted-meat sandwiches, and brought him two currant buns as well. 'And next time I come, I'll try and bring a pot of jam,' she said. 'Oh, look at Bingo – he's sitting up and begging! Did you teach him that, Ern?'

'No,' said Ern, in surprise. 'Perhaps Buster did. Good, Bingo, good! You can stop begging now. Those sandwiches are for *me*.'

'I brought Bingo a ball,' said Bets, feeling in her coat pocket. 'Here, Bingo – catch!'

The ball-game became very boisterous, as Buster also joined in, and soon chairs went flying, and rugs slithered about. In the middle of it, Fatty's mother looked in at the door.

'Whatever is going on?' she said. 'I knocked, Fatty, but there was such a noise I suppose you didn't hear. Why, *Ern* – you here already? You're very early. How is your uncle, Mr Goon?'

Ern was rather takenaback. 'Er – well, he has a bit of a cough,' he said.

'Dear, dear, I hope he didn't cough all night, poor man,' said Mrs Trotteville.

'I don't know. I didn't hear him coughing at all,' said Ern, truthfully.

'You and Bets are here very early today,' said Fatty's mother. 'Is there a meeting – or are you going out together, or something?'

'Yes, Mummy, yes, we're all going off on an expedition,' said Fatty, hastily. 'We shall be starting pretty soon. Er – any chance of sandwiches for Ern and me?'

'I'll tell Cook,' said Mrs Trotteville, and disappeared up the garden path, much to everyone's relief. Fatty frowned at Buster.

'It was your silly barking, and Bingo's, that made Mummy come and see what was going on,' he said. 'Sit! And you too, Bingo – SIT!'

Buster promptly sat, looking up at Fatty with pricked ears. Bingo took one look at him and did the same.

'And now, not another bark out of you, see?' said Fatty to Buster, and Ern pointed his finger at Bingo, and said exactly the same. Bets giggled.

'They look like two naughty little boys – and do look, Bingo is putting his tongue out at you, Ern!'

Sure enough, Bingo's tongue was lolling out of his open mouth, as he sat panting on the rug. His bright eyes were fixed lovingly on Ern.

'Couple of idiots,' said Ern, very proud of his dog. 'Now just keep sitting till we say you can get up.'

'Look,' said Fatty. 'I rather think we'd better set off on this first expedition of ours this morning, as I've said we were going. Bets, go and round up Pip and Larry and Daisy, will you? Tell them to be here in half an hour, with bicycles, sandwiches and drinks.'

'Right, Fatty,' said Bets, happily, and off she went. An expedition all together – to Banshee Towers! It really would be fun.

In just over half an hour, everyone was ready. Pip came with Bets, Larry with Daisy, all on their bicycles. Now, how could they get Ern's bicycle too? – it was in the shed at Mr Goon's!

'Uncle will be at the police station by now,' said Ern. 'I could nip by and get it.'

'All right, but for goodness sake don't get caught,' said Fatty. Ern shot off, and ran all the way to Mr Goon's house. He went to the woodshed, opened it, and was thankful to see his bicycle still there. Good thing Uncle didn't think of it, or he'd have locked it up! he thought, and rode off at top speed, keeping a wary eye out for Goon. Fortunately, he was safely at the police station, very busy indeed.

Soon they were all cycling away down the country lanes, very happy to be going on a picnic to Banshee Hill. The spring sun shone down, the birds sang in the hedges, and the sky was as blue as in summer.

'I can feel some portry coming into my head,' said Ern to Bets, who was riding beside him.

'Poetry!' said Bets. 'Oh, Ern, you're so clever at making up poetry. Do tell it to me! How does it go?'

Ern loved making up what he called his

'portry'. He went on cycling, his head full of the things he saw around him – primroses in the ditches, cowslips in the fields, new green leaves on the hawthorn, cows grazing, pigeons cooing . . .

'Well, it hasn't quite come yet,' he said. 'But I know what I'm going to call it – "*Coo*".'

'Oh, is it a song the *doves* are going to sing – all about the spring?' said Bets. 'Say it to me, Ern.'

Ern sailed along on his bicycle, loudly chanting the 'portry' that had suddenly come into his head.

> *Coo, look at them primroses down in*
> *the ditch,*
> *Smiling all over their faces.*
> *Coo, listen to all the birds up in the hedge,*
> *And larks in the big open spaces.*
> *Coo, look at the cows and the cowslips too,*
> *And . . . and . . .*

'And what?' said Bets. 'Do go on, Ern. It's wonderful.'

'Can't seem to think of the end of it,' said Ern,

frowning. 'That's the worst of me when I think of portry, Bets – it comes and goes – and now it's gone. P'raps Fatty can think of the ending.'

'We'll ask him when we have our lunch,' said Bets. 'Look, isn't that Banshee Hill up there?'

'Coo – what a hill!' said Ern, sounding as if he were beginning his 'Coo' song again. 'I bet we'll have to walk half the way up it. I'll push your bike for you, Bets.'

Yes, it was Banshee Hill – a very high one, running up steeply, with a winding road twisting to the summit. As they came near to it, the sun suddenly went in and a great black cloud blew up behind it.

'I suppose that's Banshee Towers right at the very top,' said Bets. 'Strange-looking place – it stands there as if it's glowering down at us. I don't like it very much – especially with that black cloud behind it.'

'You're right,' said Ern, as they began to cycle slowly up the winding road that led to the top. 'Very banshee-ish, I should say. Looks as if it wants to grumble and growl and wail!

Hurry up, young Bets – I believe it's going to pour with rain. Here, let me wheel your bike for you, it's too steep to ride just here!'

Fatty had just turned round to see if the girls were managing all right, and was pleased to see Ern wheeling Bets' bicycle for her. Ern might be rough and ready sometimes, but he had very nice ways, thought Fatty. He called to Daisy.

'Want any help, Daisy?'

'No, I'm all right,' said Daisy, panting. 'I just hope we'll get to the top before it pours! Hey – that looks a pretty grim place up on the hill, doesn't it?'

'Yes, more like an old fortress than anything!' shouted back Fatty. 'Look at the two dogs – we've left them far behind! Never mind, they'll catch us up sometime.'

They arrived at the gloomy old place at last, and stacked their bicycles in a convenient shed. Then they made their way to the entrance.

'This way to the wailing banshee!' said Larry, grinning at Daisy and Bets. 'Make ready to run for your lives!'

'Idiot!' said Fatty, seeing Bets' alarmed face.

'I'll make *you* run for your life if you say any more, Larry! Come on, we have to pay to go in, so cough up!'

7. INSIDE BANSHEE TOWERS

'How much to go in, please?' asked Fatty.

The dour-looking man behind the turnstiles told them.

'Whew – that's rather a lot for us children to pay,' said Pip. 'Don't we get in for half-price?'

'You do not,' said the man, looking at them severely over the top of his spectacles.

'Do you charge for dogs?' asked Fatty.

'No. They are NOT allowed in here,' said the man. 'Anyway, you haven't any dogs with you.'

'We seem to have lost them,' said Fatty. 'Er – do you charge for cats? I can see one sitting in your office.'

'And what about horses?' said Larry, joining in. 'Any objection to horses or a sheep or two?'

'No horses and no sheep,' said the man, 'And no silly children either, so be careful if *you* want to go in, see?'

'He's smarter than he looks,' said Fatty to the others when they were safely inside. 'Let's buy a catalogue, shall we? I say – what a place!'

'And what a VIEW!' said Daisy, going to one of the great windows that looked down over the countryside. 'Glorious! You can see everything for miles around!'

'Fatty! Come and look at this picture!' called Bets. 'It's so real you can almost hear the swish of the waves!'

They all went across the stone floor, their feet clattering, to a wall where a great picture was displayed – a stormy sea, the waves rising high, the spray flying.

'I feel as if my face is getting wet with spray when I look at that,' said Bets, in awe. 'Isn't it magnificent? Do buy a catalogue, Fatty. I want to see what it says about this picture.'

Fatty went back to the man at the turnstiles, took a catalogue and put down a coin. The man didn't even look up. Surly fellow! thought Fatty and went back to the others, leafing through the catalogue to find a description of the picture that Bets liked.

'It's called "Fury of the Storm",' he said. 'It says the artist is one of the most famous of sea-artists – and would you believe it, that picture was painted more than a hundred years ago! And yet it looks as fresh and clear as if it had been finished yesterday.'

Someone clattered over the stone floor, set down a stool, and put up an easel in front of a picture on the opposite wall. He proceeded to set up a large canvas on the easel. The children went over, in curiosity.

'Hello, kids,' said the man, a shock-haired fellow in a loose black painting overall. 'Come to worship at the shrine of sea art? Mind you don't bump into the banshee. It wails one day a week, you know, so you *may* hear it.'

'I don't want to,' said Bets, at once. 'Anyway, there isn't a banshee. It's just imaginary.'

There was further clattering, and three more artists came in, carrying easels. They set themselves down in front of various pictures. Fatty stared in surprise.

'Are you *copying* the pictures?' he asked the man beside him, who was now sitting on a stool, mixing colours on a palette.

'Yes. We all belong to a School of Art,' said the man. 'Those who are good enough are sent here to copy these pictures for practice – we can sell them all right afterwards, you know.'

Bets looked at the picture on the man's easel. It didn't seem very good to her. 'You haven't painted that wave the right colour,' she said, pointing.

'Well, alter it for me,' said the man, offering her an enormously long paintbrush.

'Oh, I couldn't,' said Bets.

'See that fellow over there?' said the man, pointing with his brush. 'Well, he's the best of the lot. He doesn't belong to our art school, though. You go and see *his* work – better than the original artist's, I sometimes think!'

They went over to look at the picture the other man was copying. He sat in front of a lovely seascape, that shone on the wall opposite the man. It was a picture of a blue sea swirling round the bottom of a high cliff, tumbling over the rocks. On his big canvas he was reproducing a marvellous copy. He scowled at the children.

'*Allez vous en!*' he growled.

'That's French for "Go away",' Bets whispered to the surprised Ern. 'We'd better go.'

But Ern wouldn't move. He stood staring at the picture on the wall, his face full of wonder and awe. To think anyone could paint the sea like that – why, it was *real* – you could almost hear the wind and the roar of the waves – you could feel the spray and . . .

'Wake up, Ern,' said Larry. 'You'll shout for a lifeboat if you look at that picture any more!'

'It's smashing,' said Ern. 'Ab-sol-utely smashing. Wish *I* could paint. Gosh, if I'd painted that picture there, I'd never do anything but sit and look at it all day long!'

The French artist who was copying the picture suddenly lost his temper as Ern breathed heavily down the back of his neck. He leapt up and hissed at Ern with a long string of what sounded like complete gibberish.

'Come on, we've upset the fellow,' said Fatty, seeing the alarm on Bets' face. 'Sorry. Ern, come with me. ERN!'

But Ern was still staring at the picture on the

wall. Fatty and Larry took him firmly by the arms and led him to the opposite side of the great hall, where other pictures were.

Ern and Bets could have stayed there all day, staring at the pictures. There seemed to be some magic about the seascapes that appealed to each of them in a way that the others did not feel. Soon they left Bets and Ern to themselves and wandered into the other rooms. Here there was old armour on the walls, and old weapons in cases. The four examined them with much interest, and Fatty longed to take down a great old pike from the wall, and caper about with it.

'I don't see why we shouldn't have our picnic in *here*, do you?' said Larry, looking out of one of the great windows. 'That enormous black cloud is now pouring down sheets of rain. We can't picnic out of doors. We needn't make any mess at all, and we'll take all our litter home with us.'

'I bet that bad-tempered fellow out at the turnstile won't let us stay,' said Fatty.

'What's it to do with *him*?' said Larry. 'We've paid, haven't we? Anyway, I'm really hungry. Gosh, was that thunder?'

It was! The children felt all the more determined to stay in Banshee Towers for shelter, and have their lunch there. Ern was longing to – not because of the lunch, but because of the pictures. He simply could not take his eyes off them!

The six sat down in a corner of one of the great rooms, behind a kind of large settee. Now if that turnstile man looked in, he wouldn't see them and turn them out!

'Wonder where the dogs are?' said Fatty, suddenly. 'They ought to have been here long ago.'

'Gone rabbiting halfway up the hill, I expect,' said Ern. 'Or else that turnstile man wouldn't let them in! They'll be all right. They'll either turn up – or go home!'

'Some of those artists are leaving,' said Larry. 'I can hear them packing up and shouting good-bye. Hello, who are these? Peep through the arms of the settee, Fatty – visitors, do you think?'

Yes, they certainly looked like sightseers. There were three women and a man, and they ambled aimlessly round, looking at the pictures and the old armour.

'Not worth the money to come in and see all this junk – and I never did like sea pictures,' said one woman. 'All those picture waves that never break, but just rear up and keep still! Gives me the willies!'

To the children's dismay, the visitors sat down on the settee behind which they were hiding, and began to rustle paper, unpacking their lunch. 'All them silly tales too, about banshees wailing!' said the man. 'We've wasted our money. It would be *worth* it to hear a banshee wail – but there, I never did believe in things like that.'

It was at this moment that Fatty suddenly felt impelled to be a banshee. The idea came to him in a flash, and he couldn't stop himself. He opened his mouth and let out a marvellous wail, eerie, long-drawn, high-pitched and really terrifying!

'E e e e - o o o o o - o h h h h h h - e e e e - o h - oooOOOOOOO!'

The man and the three women leapt up from

the settee as if they had rockets under them. One of the women screamed, and then they all four fled at top speed to the door and out into the great hall to the entrance where the turnstiles stood.

Not only the visitors jumped almost out of their skin. Larry, Daisy, Pip, Bets and Ern jumped too, and clutched in fright at one another, when the eerie wail echoed round them. Larry realised almost at once that it was Fatty, and he gave him a very hard punch.

'Idiot! What did you do that for? I almost died of fright! Look at poor Bets – she's trembling!'

Fatty, overcome with laughter and shame at one and the same time, couldn't say a word. Gradually the others joined him in laughter, and the six of them rolled about, trying not to laugh too loudly.

'Oh, their faces!' groaned Fatty. 'Oh, what made me do it? I'm awfully sorry but it just sort of came over me. Oh, how they skedaddled! And *your* faces too! Oh, I *must* laugh again, and I've such a stitch in my side!'

'I bet any artists left skedaddled too!' said Pip,

wiping his eyes. 'You're a horror, Fatty. The things you think of! Honestly, if it had been a real banshee wailing, it couldn't have done it better. I do think . . .'

But what he thought the others never knew, because a most extraordinary noise gradually began to echo all around – high-pitched, wailing, unhappy! It went on and on, and Bets and Daisy clutched at the boys in real terror.

'Fatty, that's *not* you this time, is it, Fatty?' said Daisy, in a shaking voice. 'Oh, what is it? I don't like it, I don't, I don't. Tell it to stop.'

But the wailing went on and on, mournful and miserable, and soon the children huddled together in fear, amazed and frightened.

At last it stopped, and they all heaved a sigh of relief. 'Let's get out of here,' said Larry. 'It's all right, Bets. It was probably just a silly echo wailing round the hill. Cheer up! Fatty, bring the lunch – we'll have it somewhere else. DO come on!'

8. A STRANGE DISCOVERY!

Fatty collected the lunch and they all crept out from behind the large old settee. They walked with rather shaky legs across the room to the great hall where the artists had sat, copying the pictures. Now only one was left – the Frenchman who had been copying the picture that Ern had liked so much.

He was rolling up a canvas very carefully, whistling below his breath. He jumped when he saw the children coming in, and looked annoyed.

'So, you have no fear of the banshee?' he said. 'You are brave, brave, brave! See, all the others have gone. *Ils avaient peur* – they were so, so afraid. But I – I am not afraid of the banshees – nor of – how do you call it – goosts?'

'Ghosts,' said Fatty. 'Do you *really* mean to say you weren't scared?'

'No, but today there was something

– something – how do you say it – peculiar? First there was *one* banshee wailing – and then, there was a *second*. I suppose, *mes enfants*, you know nothing of the *first* banshee?'

Fatty felt himself going red, but he wasn't going to admit anything to this laughing man. He didn't like him very much.

'Are you going?' asked Fatty, seeing the man tying the canvas he had been rolling up.

'Just to the village to my car – and then back again to paint, paint, paint!' said the man, and dug Fatty in the chest with his roll of canvas. 'And you – you stay here to wail, wail, wail? Ah, what a naughty boy!'

And taking no notice of Fatty's angry face, he strolled across the hall and vaulted over the turnstiles as easily as an acrobat.

'I suppose he thinks he's very clever,' growled Fatty, not at all enjoying being laughed at by the artist. 'Listen, it's still pouring with rain. We *can't* picnic on the hills, we'll have to have it here, banshee or no banshee. Don't look so scared, Bets – a wailing can't hurt us.'

'The turnstile fellow has gone,' said Larry,

looking across to where the man had sat when he took their money. 'Gone to have *his* lunch, I suppose. Well, we should be pretty safe in this hall. Come on, let's eat something. We'll feel better then!'

So they went over to where a great wooden seat stood, beside an old oak table. Fatty unpacked the lunch, and soon they were all sitting down, eating it, surprised to find that they were so hungry after their fright.

'Ern, tell Fatty your poem,' said Bets, suddenly, seeing a piece of paper sticking out of Ern's pocket, and feeling certain that Ern had managed to find time to write down his 'pome'.

'Poem?' said Fatty, surprised. 'Have you been going in for poetry again, Ern?'

'Er – well, Fatty, it's only a silly sort of pome – I mean poem,' said Ern, blushing. 'I've called it "Coo".'

'Ah, it's about doves or pigeons then, is it?' said Fatty. 'Cooing.'

'Well, not *exactly* that sort of coo,' said Ern, anxiously. 'It's really the sort of "coo" you say when you're surprised, like. I've got it written down here. I must say I feel like writing a pome about the sea too, now, after seeing all those sea pictures.'

'You're a wonder, Ern,' said Fatty, and meant it. 'Come along, where's this poem?'

'I couldn't *finish* it, Fatty,' said Ern, looking at it. 'That's the worst of me. It all comes in a rush, like, and then fades out and I can't think of a good ending.'

'Well, read it, Ern,' said Fatty. So Ern, blushing again, read out his 'pome', at top speed.

> *Coo, look at them primroses down in*
> *the ditch,*
> *Smiling all over their faces.*
> *Coo, listen to all the birds up in the hedge,*
> *And larks in the big open spaces.*
> *Coo, look at the cows and the cowslips too,*
> *And . . .*

Ern stopped and looked pleadingly at Fatty. 'I can't think of the end, Fatty. I just can't.'

'Oh *yes*, Ern – there's only one *possible* ending,' said Fatty, and carried on at once.

Coo, look at the cows and the cowslips too,
And the lions so dandy and yellow,
And the cups full of butter for me and
for you,
And hark where the bulrushes bellow!
Coo, look at the runner beans, how fast
they go,
And . . .

By this time, the others were laughing so much that Fatty had to stop for breath and laugh too. Ern stared at him in admiration. 'How do you do it, Fatty?' he asked, solemnly. 'Takes me ages to think of even one line, and you just go rattling on and on – coo, I'd never have thought of that line, "Look at the runner beans, how fast they go!" That's very funny, Fatty.'

'Dear old Ern, your lines are poetry, and mine are not,' said Fatty, clapping him on the back. 'Yours are just a bit too "cooey" that's all. "Coo" isn't a good word for poetry, unless it's said by a dove!'

'You're a wonder, you are,' said Ern, remembering another of Fatty's lines. 'Lions so dandy and yellow – you meant the yellow dandelions there, didn't you? – honest, Fatty, you're a genius.'

'Let's change the subject,' said Fatty, feeling rather a fraud. He could reel off verse without stopping, ridiculous, amusing and clever, and could never think why everyone thought it wonderful.

'Everybody finished?' asked Larry, screwing up his papers. 'There's a litter basket over there.'

'Hey,' said Pip, suddenly. 'What do you suppose has happened to Buster and Bingo? They ought to be here by now, surely?'

'Oh, I expect they turned tail and went home when they got too far behind,' said Fatty. 'They probably lost our trail. We won't see them till we get home. I only hope they are behaving themselves.'

A sudden, very familiar noise made them all jump! 'Woof! WOOF!'

'Golly, *that* sounds like them!' said Ern in amazement. 'Where are they? I can't see them anywhere!'

'Wuff – woof!'

'They're both about somewhere!' said Fatty, puzzled. 'But their barks sound a bit muffled. BUSTER! BINGO! Where on earth are you?'

A scrabbling noise came from the big fireplace and the children went over to it at once. An old iron cauldron stood squarely in the middle of the wide hearth, and the barking seemed to come from under there. Fatty lifted up the heavy old thing, and gave a loud exclamation.

'OHO! What have we here? Look, a neat, round trap door! The dogs seem to be under it somewhere. Bets, go and see if there's anyone about whose permission we can ask to pull up the trap door.'

Bets ran to the turnstile and looked all about. There was no one to be seen. She hurried back.

'No, Fatty, I can't see a soul. I expect the turnstile man is away having his dinner – and the artists haven't come back yet, though they've left their easels here.'

'Right. Then we'll have to yank up the trap door *without* permission!' said Fatty. 'Help me, Ern.'

There was now such a loud and excited

barking coming from beneath the trap door that it seemed almost as if there might be half a dozen dogs below, not just two!

'How *did* they get there?' said Larry, watching Fatty and Ern heaving up the trap door. 'They can't possibly have got down through the trap door – so they must have found a way into the hill – and gone up an underground tunnel to Banshee Towers.'

'Oooh – a secret passage!' said Bets, her eyes shining. 'Can we go down it?'

'Here she comes!' said Fatty, panting hard as he and Ern heaved the trap door out of its place. Immediately, the two dogs hurled themselves out, and fell upon Ern and Fatty in rhapsodies of joy, barking, licking, pawing as if they had gone mad.

'Steady on, steady on,' said Fatty, pushing Buster down. 'Buster, will you kindly tell me how you got here?'

'Woof!' said Buster, dancing about happily.

'And how did *you* get here, Bingo,' demanded Ern, whose dog seemed intent on licking every single inch of his face. 'Stop it, Bingo. I shall have to borrow a towel from somewhere soon. Keep your tongue in your mouth for a bit. Oh, goodness, there he goes again!'

Larry was looking down the hole where the trap door had been. He took out a small torch from his pocket and switched it on. He gave a sudden exclamation.

'Look, there are steps cut down from the hearth – almost like ladder steps, going down and down. Where on *earth* do they go to?'

'We might have time to explore a bit,' said Fatty, feeling thrilled to see the steps leading down into the darkness. 'Bets, go and see if we're still the only ones here.'

Bets ran off and then came back, her face rather frightened. 'Fatty, the turnstile man is coming up the hill. He's nearly here. Put the trap door back, quickly!'

Ern and Fatty lifted the trap door into place and then put the heavy cauldron over it. They were still kneeling down by the fireplace when the turnstile man came in, munching an apple. He gave an angry shout when he saw them.

'Quick – pretend we've dropped a coin,'

said Fatty, in a low, urgent voice. 'Look for it, all of you – in the hearth and on the carpet too – quick!'

So, when the puzzled turnstile man ran up, they were all apparently hunting feverishly for a lost coin!

'*Must* find it!' Fatty was saying. 'Simply must. Money is money. Where on earth did it go? Is that it over there, Bets?'

'Oh, so you've dropped some money, have you?' said the man. 'Sure that's all you're up to? Let *me* have a look!' And down he dropped on hands and knees too. He gave a sudden shout, and picked something up.

'I've got it. Here it is!' And he held up a coin in triumph.

'Thanks,' said Fatty, and held out his hand. But the man laughed in his face, and slipped the coin into his trouser pocket. 'Finding's keeping,' he said. 'Now you go off, all of you. You've been here long enough. And how did those dogs get in? You ought to pay for them, you did.'

'Oh, aren't they *your* dogs?' said Ern, in such

a surprised voice that Bets had to put her hand over her mouth to stop a laugh escaping.

'*My* dogs! I should think not. I can't abear them!' said the man, and made as if he were going to kick Buster. Buster growled and showed his teeth and the man backed hurriedly away. 'Go on, now – you clear out,' he said. 'Thursday's my afternoon off, and I want a bit of peace!'

And, very thankfully, the children did clear out, and went to fetch their bicycles, the dogs gambolling round.

'What a bit of luck a coin had been dropped in that hearth sometime, by somebody,' said Ern, as they all mounted.

'Dear Ern, I dropped it there *myself*,' grinned Fatty. 'I knew if that fellow found it, as I meant him to, he wouldn't worry about the trap door any more! Come on now, home everyone. Home, Buster! Bingo! HOME!'

9. HOME AGAIN – AND A GOOD LONG TALK

'Well – that was a rather surprising expedition!' said Fatty, when they were well away from Banshee Towers. 'I feel we have quite a lot to think about. The wailing of the banshee – I don't mean *my* wailing, of course, that wasn't a patch on the old banshee's – my word, *she* could wail all right!'

'Don't remind me of it,' said Bets, with a shudder. 'I just want to put Banshee Towers behind me and ride away home down this hill, as quickly as I can!'

'And then there was that trap door in the hearth,' said Larry. 'And the puzzle of how on earth the dogs arrived underneath it.'

'And *I* didn't like the look of that turnstile man at all,' announced Daisy. 'I thought he looked like a villain.'

'Oh, not as bad as *that*,' said Pip. 'He just

looked bored and bad-tempered – and I must say I would too, if I had a turnstile job on the top of a cold hill in a place where banshees wailed!'

'I'd like to get home and talk about it,' said Larry. 'I don't know what *you* think, Fatty, but it all seems pretty weird to me.'

'A bit of a mystery, you mean?' said Fatty. 'Well, it's about time that the Five Find-Outers had a good juicy mystery to solve, isn't it?'

'Oh *yes*!' said Pip, in delight. 'We've never had one with banshees in before.'

'Well, I could do without banshees, really,' said Bets. 'What about telling the Chief Inspector – you know, Inspector Jenks – he might . . .'

'Bets, we really *can't* tell him silly stories of banshees,' said Fatty. 'They don't *really* exist, you know. They . . .'

'All right – well, what *was* it that we heard this afternoon?' said Bets. 'I don't care what its name is, it was as bad and weird and horrible as any banshee, so there!'

'You're right, Bets. It was pretty awful,' said Pip. 'I didn't like it myself. Real or unreal, that banshee is MOST mysterious. Look out, now, we're coming to a very steep bit. Go as slowly as you can all the way, in case your brakes are weak.'

Away down the hill they sailed in a long line, the two dogs galloping manfully – or 'dogfully', as Bets said – after them. What a day they had had – and how they all longed to be down in Fatty's workroom and talk about it, and make plans to solve yet another mystery! Bets shivered with excitement. There always seemed to be a mystery of some sort when Fatty was around!

Everyone was glad to be in Fatty's cosy workroom, especially the two dogs, who were quite tired out with their long run. Buster flopped down in his basket, panting, and Bingo fell on top of him, too tired to play. In half a second they were sound asleep.

'One great basketful of dog,' said Bets, smiling. 'I'm glad they're such friends.'

'It's nice for Bingo to have a friend like Buster – you know, well-brought-up, like,' said Ern. 'I want Bingo to have good manners. He'll learn from old Buster – real copy-cat Bingo is!'

'No, no,' said Fatty, gravely. 'There you

make a mistake, Ern. Not a copy-cat, surely – a copy-*dog*!'

'Ha ha, funny joke,' said Pip, who was tired, and not in the mood for Fatty's quips.

'I'm thirsty,' said Larry. 'Any orange squash, Fatty?'

'Plenty in my cupboard,' said Fatty. 'And glasses too. And there's some chocolate somewhere. Hurry up and get what you want. I'm longing to discuss the strange happenings of this morning. You know, I think something's going on up there.'

'Up where?' asked Ern.

'Banshee Hill, idiot,' said Fatty. 'Two things puzzle me – that banshee wail – and the hole under the hearth, where that cauldron stands.'

'Well, what's puzzling about the banshee wail?' asked Bets. 'You *said* that's what banshees did – wail and howl and cry.'

'Yes, but you heard what that artist in the black overall said,' went on Fatty. 'He said that the banshee only wailed one day a week! Well, why only *one* day?'

'Perhaps banshees only *do* wail one day a

week,' suggested Daisy. 'I mean, all that awful wailing must be a terrible strain on the throat. I bet *your* throat felt sore after you'd wailed at the top of your voice – you sound a bit husky to me.'

'Well, I'm *not*,' said Fatty. 'I could wail like that for half an hour or more and not feel husky.'

'For goodness sake, don't do anything of the sort,' said Larry. 'You'd have the fire brigade here and the police, and every doctor in the place.'

'Do come back to the point, Larry,' said Fatty. 'WHY does the banshee only wail once a week? There can't be a real banshee there – there aren't such things. It must be somebody faking one – but why?'

'For fun,' said Bets.

'Yes, but why on a certain *day*?' persisted Fatty.

'What on earth does it matter?' said Pip, getting tired of the subject. 'It can wail *every* day of the week, for all I care.'

'Pip, you should have a more alert, enquiring mind,' said Fatty, solemnly. 'You know, that's a fake banshee and I'd jolly well like to find out who's working it and how – and why!'

'I don't want to go up that hill again,' said

Bets. 'I loved the pictures but I hated the wailing.'

'Don't worry, Bets. You needn't go. But *I'm* going,' said Fatty. 'I'm going tomorrow. I tell you, I smell a mystery!'

'Well, you must have the most powerful nose anybody ever had,' said Larry. 'All I can smell is that oil-stove smoking. I suppose your nose is too high and mighty to smell ordinary things like that. Turn down the wick, Ern, you're nearest.'

Ern turned down the wick carefully. 'Fatty,' he said, 'could I come with you if you go to Banshee Hill tomorrow – not to mess about in a mystery, though – just to see those sea pictures again. Especially the one with the high cliffs and the blue sea swirling round it.'

'Oh – the one the French artist was copying,' said Fatty. 'Yes, that was a beauty. All right, Ern, you can come with me – you'll be company – and while you stand and gloat over the pictures, I can do a little snooping. It's just as well I should have someone with me who is obviously there to see the pictures!'

'Oooh, thanks Fatty,' said Ern. 'I hope that banshee doesn't come wailing round me though.'

'It only wails *once* a week, Ern,' said Fatty. 'I'll eat my cap if it wails tomorrow! I'm pretty certain it has its set day, for *some* reason or other.'

'Look, we'd better go, Daisy and I,' said Larry, getting up in a hurry. 'Gosh, I'd quite forgotten our granny is coming to tea. Hurry up, Daisy, for goodness sake. We're going out for the day tomorrow, Fatty, so we won't be seeing you. So long!'

They shot out of the shed door and the others heard them racing up the garden. Pip stood up then, and yanked Bets to her feet. 'Come along, Bets,' he said. 'You look half asleep. Telephone us, Fatty, when there's a meeting again.'

'I should think Bets is tired out with the long bicycle ride,' said Fatty, giving Bets a hug. 'Good-bye, Bets – and don't dream of banshees tonight!'

'I hope I'm not being a nuisance to you, Fatty,' said Ern, when the others had gone. 'Staying here in your shed.'

'No – no, of *course* you're not a nuisance, Ern,' said Fatty. 'Hello – who's this coming? – I seem to know those heavy footsteps.'

'It's Uncle!' said Ern, in alarm. 'He must have

heard that I've not gone home. Fatty, hide me!'

'There's nowhere to hide you,' said Fatty, looking round. 'He'd look in that cupboard at once! Listen now, Ern, I'll lock the door – and when your uncle comes knocking on it, you slip quietly out of the window, see? I'll hand Bingo to you. Hide somewhere and come back when Mr Goon is gone.'

Bang-bang-bang! That was Mr Goon at the shed door. Fatty had quickly turned the key in the lock, so the policeman could not open it. A roar came from the other side.

'Frederick Trotteville, you open this door. I know you've got Ern in there. I saw him through the window. You open this door or I'll go to your father.'

'*Ern*? Ern in *here*, Mr Goon! You must be seeing things!' shouted Fatty, going to the door. 'Wait a minute – it's locked. Shut up, Buster, making that row!'

Buster and Bingo were certainly making a terrific noise. Neither of them liked Mr Goon, and they had recognised his voice at once. Ern was now getting out of the window at the side of the shed. He patted the sill and Bingo came running to him, and leapt into his arms. 'Sh!' said Ern. 'No barking now.' He crept off to where a thick clump of bushes grew, and squeezed into the middle of them.

Fatty quietly shut the window after him and ran back to the door, on which Goon was still angrily hammering. 'Be patient, Mr Goon,' said Fatty. 'The key seems to have stuck – ah – it's all right now – there we are!'

He turned the key smartly, and flung open the door. The angry policeman stormed into the shed at once, shouting at the top of his voice 'Ern! ERN! You come alonga me. You never went home! You disobeyed me! You just wait and see what . . .'

But Goon didn't finish what he had to say because Buster flung himself on him with enormous delight, trying to nip his ankles through the thick trousers.

'GAH!' said Mr Goon, kicking out. 'That dog again! Where's Ern? I saw him, I know I did!'

'Well, have a good look round, Mr Goon,' said Fatty, politely. 'He may be under that stool – or behind the books in the bookcase – or in the dog's basket. Buster, stop that row.'

Goon was quite at a loss as he stood staring round the room. He *had* seen Ern there, he knew he had. It didn't occur to him that Ern had had time to slip out of the window. He glared at Fatty, and glared at Buster, and turned to go. Buster gave a blood-curdling growl, and Goon shot out of the door at top speed.

'You wait!' he shouted, as Fatty shut the door. 'I'll get Ern all right – ho yes, I'll get him!' And away he went, muttering to himself. 'That toad of a boy – too clever by half, he is. Where *is* Ern? Just wait till *I* get hold of him!'

10. BANSHEE TOWERS AGAIN!

When the policeman had gone, Ern crept out of the middle of the bush, and went back to Fatty's shed, grinning. 'Thanks, Fatty,' he said. 'You're a pal! I say, you're sure you don't mind if I go up to Banshee Towers with you tomorrow?'

'Be nice to have your company, Ern,' said Fatty, and meant it! 'Also, you may be useful. You see, I do want to snoop around a bit, and if there are people there, you might be able to take up their attention somehow . . . so that no one will be watching *me*.'

'But how do I take up anyone's attention?' said Ern, alarmed. 'I'm no good at play-acting, Fatty, you know that.'

'Oh, Ern, you can do a sudden bit of tap-dancing – or sing a little song – or pretend to faint,' said Fatty. 'I'll signal to you like this, if I want you to turn people's attention to you, and away from me!'

And Fatty smoothed back his hair three times. 'See? Don't look so alarmed. Nobody will lock you up, or box your ears. They'll just stay still in astonishment, and forget all about me and what I'm doing.'

'All right, Fatty,' said Ern in a mournful voice, and settled down to read one of Fatty's books. 'Coo, the books you've got, Fatty – you must have over a thousand. This one's smashing.'

He was soon lost in the sea story he had found in Fatty's big bookcase. Bingo lay happily on Ern's feet, and Buster sat as close to Fatty as he could. Ern came to the end of a chapter, and looked up in great content. He was perfectly happy. He had a friend, a dog, a good book, and somewhere quiet to read. Ern gave an enormous sigh and went back to his book, thinking how lucky he was to have a clever friend like Fatty.

Next morning, Ern woke up feeling excited. He sat up on the camp-bed in the shed trying to remember the reason for his excitement. Of course – Fatty and I are going up to that Banshee place again – and I shall see those grand pictures, he thought, in delight. 'Bingo – do you hear that? Sh, don't bark too loudly. Nobody must know we're here. I've told you that before.'

Bingo had snuggled down on Ern's feet all night long. He sat up, yawning, wondering when his friend Buster would come. Bingo thought the world of Buster, and copied him in every way he could, even to rubbing his nose with his left paw, instead of his right one. He crawled over Ern's knees and gave him a smacking lick on the nose. Then he rolled over to be tickled.

'Do you know something, Bingo?' said Ern, solemnly, 'Right now I am feeling very, very sorry for all those boys and girls who haven't a dog of their own. They just don't know what they're missing. Now then – that's enough licking. Go and fetch me that towel, so that I can wipe my face. Good dog, then – clever dog! You understand everything I say, don't you? Now, please take the towel back. Very good, Bingo!'

Fatty brought Ern some breakfast, and then disappeared to do a few jobs for his mother. 'I'll be back at ten and we'll set off,' he said. 'We'll take lunch with us – I'll buy it on the way, because

Cook is getting a bit suspicious of the enormous appetite I seem suddenly to have developed. She said this morning that I seem to want enough for *two* people – and she was right!'

They set off just after ten, and Fatty stopped to buy some sandwiches, new currant buns, and oranges. He had already put some lemonade and a cup into his bicycle basket. Ern gave a sudden cry of alarm, as they rode up the village street.

'Fatty – there's my uncle!'

Sure enough, there was Mr Goon, standing at the crossroads, directing the busy traffic with a frown. He couldn't believe his eyes when he saw Ern cycling along with Fatty! 'Stop!' he bawled. 'Ern! You heard me. STOP!'

But, alas, Ern disobeyed the law, and pedalled faster than ever, leaving poor Mr Goon very angry indeed!

'Woof!' said a loud voice, as they pedalled past Mr Goon – and Buster suddenly stuck his head out of a wooden box that Fatty had tied to his rear mudguard! Bingo was in a similar box, on the back of Ern's bicycle, but he was so much afraid of Mr Goon that he didn't dare to venture even the smallest bark, as he passed him. He didn't want to be plucked away from his beloved Ern by the loud-voiced Mr Goon!

'Good idea to take the dogs with us this way,' said Ern. 'I reckon it's really too far for them to run all the way there and back. They seem to like the ride, don't they, Fatty? Gosh, *I'm* enjoying it too.'

As soon as they were out of the town, Fatty burst into song.

> *Up the street*
> *On pedalling feet,*
> *Here we go, Ern and I!*
> *And a song we sing*
> *With a ting-a-ling-ling,*
> *As we both go bicycling by!*
> *Our wheels go round*
> *With a swishity sound,*
> *As fast as the wind we fly,*
> *Through village and town,*
> *Now up, now down,*
> *Here we go, Ern and I!*

Ern almost fell off his bicycle in admiration. 'Coo, Fatty, did you just make that up this very minute – just like that?'

'It suddenly came into my head,' said Fatty, modestly. 'It goes nicely with our pedalling, Ern, doesn't it?' And the two of them sang the 'Bicycling Song', as Ern called it, at the tops of their voices, pedalling in strict time to the rhythm of the lines!

Buster didn't like the singing, and began to bark. Fatty turned round and addressed him. 'No, Buster – you've got the words wrong – *and* the tune as well.'

That made Ern laugh. They pedalled on happily and soon came to the steep hill, up which they had to toil slowly. Banshee Towers glowered at the top as if not welcoming them at all. When they arrived there, the boys put their bicycles into the racks provided in the shed, and sauntered to the turnstile, Buster and Bingo running at their heels.

'Oh – you again,' said the man, grumpily. 'Plus dogs! Didn't I say that *no* dogs were allowed? I'd just like to know how those dogs got into Banshee Towers yesterday.'

'I've no idea,' said Fatty. 'They suddenly appeared. One minute they were not there. The next they were. No one was more surprised than *we* were.'

'They can stay in that shed over there,' said the man. 'But they can't go indoors. See?'

'Right,' said Fatty, paying the money. 'I say, tell me one thing – does the old banshee wail on one special day each week – and if so, why?'

'The legend says that it was on a Thursday that calamity came to the Lord of Banshee Towers,' said the man. 'And so the banshee wails that same day.'

'Oh, so Thursday is always the banshee's great day?' said Fatty. 'Very interesting. Have you any idea where your banshee lives?'

'Don't ask daft questions,' said the turnstile man, losing his temper. 'Go on in and don't come bothering me.'

'Just *one* more question,' said Fatty. 'Tell me, when did the banshee first begin to wail in modern times? It says in the catalogue that she used to wail a hundred years ago – or so the legend went – but hadn't been known to wail since. I saw that the catalogue was printed six years ago. What made the banshee begin to wail again – did she conveniently find her voice six years ago, when the catalogue was printed, and this place was thrown open to the public?'

'Are you trying to say that the banshee isn't real – that she's a fraud?' said the man, angrily. 'Well, you ask the tall, dark man you'll see in the Armour Room today – *he'll* soon put you right. He owns this place, see – and *he* ought to know about the banshee, didn't he?'

'Ah, now that's information worth having,' said Fatty, looking pleased. 'I'll certainly have a chat with the man who owns the place *and* the banshee too. Thanks a lot. What's his name?'

'He's Austrian,' said the man, still very cross. 'Name of Engler. And I hope he wipes the floor with you, you nuisance!'

'Now, now!' said Fatty, raising a finger in reproof, just as if he were a nurse addressing a child. 'Now, now – mustn't be rude. Mustn't lose tempers! Don't want to put you into a corner!'

And with that Fatty marched off to put the

dogs into the shed, leaving a most irritated man behind him, and accompanied by a rather scared, but most admiring, Ern.

'I don't know how you can hold your own like that, Fatty,' he said. 'I really don't. Look, there's the Frenchman we saw yesterday. Wonder how he's got on with the picture he was copying.'

'*Bonjour*,' said Fatty politely to the Frenchman, who was hurrying down the great hall, carrying a rolled-up canvas. 'Finished your picture?'

'Ah, *bonjour*, *mon ami*!' said the Frenchman. 'You come back so soon?'

'Well, my friend here loves the sea pictures,' said Fatty. 'You see, he wants to go into the Navy, so anything to do with the sea attracts him, even if it's only pictures. Won't you show us the copy you made of that grand picture? Is that it you are carrying?'

'Yes, yes – but I must hurry, or I would show it to you,' said the Frenchman, giving a polite little bow. 'Someone awaits me outside. *Au revoir*! We shall meet again if you come often to this place. I am always here!'

He scurried off. Fatty looked after him thoughtfully. Funny little man! He looked round for the owner of the place, the Austrian called – what was it now? – oh yes, Engler. That must be the man over there, in the Armour Room. Tall. Dark. Serious-looking. He looked a hard sort of man. Better be careful of him!

'You go and have a look at your magnificent sea picture, Ern,' said Fatty. 'I'll go and talk to the owner. I want to ask him a few questions about banshees.'

'Right,' said Ern, and wandered off happily round the big room, looking at this picture and that, saving his favourite picture to the last.

He came to it eventually, and stood in front of it, gazing at the great high cliff, the swirling waves, the grim rocks. He stared at the seagulls tossed by the tempestuous wind, and imagined himself in a boat on that angry sea, swept by foaming waves, the wind howling in his ears. Ha – if only *he* could paint a picture like that! It would be almost better than going into the Navy. No – on second thoughts he'd *rather* go to sea.

Ern stood for some time opposite the picture.

Then suddenly a puzzled look came over his face. He stood closer to the picture and peered at the sea from this side and that. He scratched his head. He stood further back. Then he went to one side and stood there, and then to the other side, screwing up his eyes as if he were trying to see something. He shook his head and frowned.

'I'll have to find Fatty,' he said at last. 'It's a puzzle, this is. Can't make it out! Where *is* Fatty? Oh, there he is, talking to that man. Fatty! FATTY! Here, I've got something to ask you!'

11. ERN'S STRANGE DISCOVERY

Fatty had studied the owner of Banshee Towers, and had decided that he didn't look to be the type that usually bought old places just because they were beautiful! He's a sharp businessman, if ever I saw one! thought Fatty. It beats me why he bought this out-of-the-way place. He can't make much money out of visitors, except for a month or two in the summer. I wonder if he owns the pictures as well.

The owner was sitting on the big settee behind which the children had hidden the day before. He was studying a catalogue of some sort, frowning over it. He was big and burly, with great eyebrows and a big nose.

Fatty went up to him, and spoke in his politest voice. 'Excuse me, sir, for interrupting – but I believe you own this magnificent old place?'

'What – er – dear me, you startled me!' said

the man in a very deep voice, with a decidedly Austrian accent. 'Yes, my boy, I own it. But, alas, it was a bad bargain. So few visitors come to see it.'

'I suppose they come because they hope to hear the wailing banshee,' said Fatty. 'We heard it yesterday – a very fine performance, sir. Very fine. Best wailing I ever heard! How is it done, sir?'

'Done? My boy, who knows anything about the poor, poor unhappy banshees?' said the man. 'Who knows how or why they wail?'

'Well, in these days, sir, I expect they wail because their machinery is started up,' said Fatty, unexpectedly. 'I mean – modern banshees are all pretence, aren't they?'

'Certainly NOT,' said the man, angrily. 'You think I am a fraud? You think my banshee does not exist? I own a very fine banshee – poor, poor thing, how she wails! It rends the heart!'

'Let me see now – banshees are supposed only to wail because they want to warn the owner of the place that something terrible is going to happen to him, aren't they?' said Fatty, putting on his most innocent expression. 'You know, sir,

I heard her wailing yesterday, and I hoped somebody would warn you that trouble and unhappiness might be coming to you. Of course, that wouldn't be so if it wasn't a *real* banshee – but simply some kind of machinery, sir – but you are certain it isn't?'

'My boy, I give you leave to go into every room in Banshee Towers, and to look into every hole and corner and cranny there, to see if there is any machinery,' said Mr Engler, solemnly.

'Oh, thank you, sir, that's very kind of you, but I'll take your word for it that you've no machinery hidden in any of the rooms,' said Fatty. 'Let's change the subject, sir. What wonderful sea pictures there are here! What collection are they from, sir? I don't recognise any of them.'

'Well, you seem to be an intelligent boy,' said the man, obviously struck by Fatty's ready conversation. 'So I'll tell you. They are from a famous collection of pictures in Count Ludwig's castle in Austria. He is a cousin of mine, and he has lent me the pictures to attract visitors to Banshee Towers. A truly wonderful collection

– but, alas, few people look at the pictures. Just a few artists come to copy them – and one or two visitors like yourself notice them.'

'They are worth a lot of money, I suppose?' said Fatty.

'Oh yes, yes – thousands of pounds!' said Mr Engler.

'I wonder you dare to risk the chance of some thief coming here to steal them,' said Fatty.

'Now, my boy – use your sense,' said Mr Engler. 'It is not so easy to take great pictures like these from their frames and carry them off unnoticed! Ha, would *you* be able to do it?'

It was at this very moment that Ern decided to go and find Fatty. Mr Engler jumped when Ern's voice came into the room, sounding urgent.

'Fatty! Fatty, here! I've got something to ask you!'

'Excuse me, sir – that's my friend. I'd better go and see what he wants,' said Fatty, surprised to see Ern looking so agitated. 'Thank you for giving me so much information. Very kind of you.'

He went over to Ern. 'Ern! What is it? Now don't blurt it out at the top of your voice, for goodness sake. Come into the hall and tell me quietly.'

'Well, Fatty, you know that sea picture I liked so much – the one I showed you yesterday, with the high cliffs and the swirling sea below?'

'Yes, I remember it quite well. It's still over there,' said Fatty, waving an arm towards it.

'Yes – well, there's something very odd about it today,' said Ern, agitated. 'Come and look.'

'What do you mean – odd?' asked Fatty, surprised, as they came up to the picture.

'Something's gone out of it,' said Ern. 'Something I noticed particularly yesterday, Fatty. It's not there today, straight it isn't!'

'Well, what *was* it?' asked Fatty, exasperated. 'The picture looks *exactly* the same to me!'

'Fatty, I promise you I'm telling the truth,' said Ern. 'I promise you! Now look – see that rock there? – and the sea swirling up to it – and that wave coming up behind? Well, Fatty, *yesterday there was a little red boat painted* on that wave, with two tiny sailors in it. I noticed it particularly, and I thought to myself, well, the artist put in that boat just so's people looking at his picture would realise how enormous the cliffs were, and how grand the sea was, swirling round the rocks. See? If the artist hadn't put a boat there, I wouldn't have known how steep and high the cliffs were, so – so . . .'

'So the picture would have lost some of its grandeur, you mean,' said Fatty, with much interest. 'Ern, this is, as you say, very odd. In fact, most peculiar. *Why* did someone paint out that boat? It must have been the Frenchman who did it, of course.'

'Perhaps he doesn't like boats,' said Ern. 'Maybe he gets seasick. But Fatty, you can't see any marks where he might have washed the boat off the picture, or painted it out with greens or blues! That's what beats me!'

'It certainly is very strange,' said Fatty, extremely puzzled. 'You really *are* quite sure, Ern, that the boat was there yesterday?'

'Well, Bets was with me when we looked carefully at the picture,' said Ern. 'She liked the painting too. I expect she'd remember the boat all right. We'll ask her.'

'Ern, listen – don't mention this to anyone

– not to anyone at all,' said Fatty. 'I can't at the moment think why anyone should remove – or wash out – a boat from a sea picture, but I'd like to think about it before we tell anyone. See?'

'Right,' said Ern. 'Now I'll go and look at some of the others. Maybe *all* the boats have been removed!' But no – those pictures that had boats in them, still had their boats, and their clouds, and their waves. Ern could see nothing missing in them. Nor could Fatty.

'Look – there's the Frenchman who was copying the picture yesterday,' said Ern suddenly. 'He's copying that small one over there now. Let's go and ask him if *he* removed that little boat from the big picture.'

But before they could get to him, Mr Engler had gone over to him, and was in close conversation. Then the two men arose and went into the Armour Room, finally disappearing into a small room beyond.

'No banshee wailing today, Fatty,' said Ern, with a grin, as they walked round the show of sea pictures.

'Not the right day!' said Fatty, and immediately

fell into such deep thought that he didn't hear a word of what Ern was saying to him. *'Not the right day?'* Why was one special day of the week the 'right' day? Fatty didn't believe in the banshee, even though he had felt very scared when it had wailed the day before.

'Ern, I have a feeling I'd like to go and have a look down that trap door hole again,' he said, suddenly. 'You keep watch for me, see, and give a whistle if you see anyone coming. All the artists are gone except that Frenchman, and as far as I can see he's having a good heart-to-heart talk with Mr Engler – goodness knows what about. I wish I did!'

He and Ern went into the Armour Room, and Ern stationed himself in the middle, so that he could watch all doors, and hear anyone approaching from any direction. Fatty went quietly to the great fireplace. He managed to move the cauldron to one side, and saw the trap door underneath as before. He turned to Ern. 'Everything safe?' he said, and Ern nodded. Not a footstep was to be heard anywhere, coming across the stone floors, not a voice echoed.

Fatty pulled up the trap door lid, and peered down. Yes, there were the steps leading downwards. To what? To the banshee – and maybe her machinery? Where was the *lower* entrance to this passage through the hill – the one the dogs must have found and taken to get up to Banshee Towers, and scrabble about under the trap door? It must be a very well-hidden one, somewhere on the deserted hillside!

Fatty wished he dared to go down the steps and see what he could find. But he might be a long time gone, and he couldn't leave Ern behind. Nor did he want to take Ern with him. Neither of them had torches, and it would be dangerous.

He heard a sudden hiss from Ern, and stood up at once. There was just time to shut the trap door and replace the great iron cauldron, so that the trap door lid could not be seen!

Just in time! Footsteps sounded in the little room beyond, and voices. Mr Engler and the artist were coming back! Fatty beckoned to Ern and the two fled into the hall and then through the turnstiles. The turnstile man was not there and, to Fatty's surprise, he suddenly saw him walking out of the hall-entrance with Mr Engler and the artist!

So they are all three buddies, thought Fatty. Well, I don't know what it means, but it means *some*thing! I've got to work all this out, somehow. It's certainly adding up to a mystery of some sort – but I can't for the life of me see what or why or how!

He and Ern went to get the two dogs who, tired of being in the shed, were whining and pawing at the gate. They barked frantically and joyfully when the two boys came up. They hopped into their boxes on the rear mudguards and Fatty and Ern were soon sailing dangerously fast down the steep Banshee Hill.

'I think I'll call a meeting tomorrow,' Fatty said to Ern. 'Something's going on up there that I can't make head or tail of. If we get the others to hear what we have to say and we all talk about it, we might see daylight. Good thing we went up, Ern, or you wouldn't have spotted the missing boat. I'm sure that's a clue to the mystery, whatever it is – but it's just about the most puzzling clue we've ever had! We don't even know what the mystery *is,* or if the clue really belongs to it. Whew!'

12. AN INTERESTING TALK
- AND A GOOD IDEA!

Fatty telephoned Larry and Daisy that night, and also Pip and Bets. He would not tell them why the meeting was being called, and they all felt rather excited. 'Is it a mystery, Fatty? Oh, do say it's another mystery!' said Bets. 'Have you any clues yet?'

'One,' said Fatty. 'And I don't even know what it's a clue *to* – or if it *is* a clue! Tell you all about it tomorrow. Be here at ten, please. Actually, it's a clue Ern found – I didn't even notice it!'

Just before ten o'clock, there came knockings on the door of Fatty's workroom. He had lit the stove, and had set out a variety of biscuits. As Fatty said, 'It's so much *easier* to talk when you've something to eat as well!'

In came Larry, Daisy, Pip and Bets, looking eager and excited. Buster and Bingo gave them a most uproarious greeting, and upset the plate of biscuits.

'Now listen, you two dogs,' said Fatty, sternly, 'I don't know which of you had the bright idea of upsetting biscuits all over the floor, but I tell you this – not *one* biscuit do you have till we've finished our meeting. I know dogs consider it clever to upset plates of biscuits and cats think it is smart to upset milk, so that they can help themselves. But I'm just a bit smarter than you are, see? SIT!'

The dogs sat, eyeing the biscuits mournfully. Bets felt sorry for them, and patted them. 'Do begin the meeting, Fatty,' she said. 'We're LONGING to hear about this new mystery. Is it *really* one?'

'Well, that's what we're going to decide,' said Fatty. 'If it is, we must make our plans to solve it. If it isn't, we just don't bother any more. Now, listen to what Ern discovered yesterday when we went up to Banshee Towers. Ern, would you like to take over and tell what happened?'

'Oh, no thanks, Fatty,' said Ern, uneasily. 'You're the one to talk. There's nobody that talks like you. I could listen for ages. My uncle, Mr Goon, always said you had the gift of the gab, and he's right. You could talk the hind leg off a donkey, you could, or the tail off a horse, or the . . .'

'Well, really, Ern – anyone would think *you* had the gift of the gab,' said Larry, surprised. 'Do go on!'

'No,' said Ern, and subsided. So Fatty took over, and began the tale of Ern's strange discovery.

'Ern went to look at that big sea picture that he and Bets liked so much,' he said. 'Do you remember it, Bets?'

'Oh *yes* – every bit of it. It was lovely!' said Bets.

'Well, describe it,' said Fatty. 'And don't leave even the smallest detail out, Bets. It's important.'

'It was a picture of a stormy sea, with waves lashing against a very high cliff,' said Bets. 'The sky was blue in parts, and white in others. It was so full of spray that it almost made me feel wet.'

'Anything else?' asked Fatty.

'Well no – except that there was a tiny red boat bobbing on a wave,' said Bets. 'When I saw that, I suddenly realised how enormous the cliff was, and I thought the artist must have put it there on purpose – to make the cliff grander and the sea more – well, more magnificent, you know?'

'Bets, that's just what we wanted you to remember – the *boat*,' said Fatty, 'because the boat is the only clue we have. That little boat is no longer in the picture. It's gone. It isn't there!'

There was an astonished silence. 'Well, what's happened to it?' said Pip, at last. 'Did some artist there wash it out – or paint over it? Perhaps he didn't like it?'

'No, he didn't wash it out, it seems,' said Fatty. 'There are *no* marks and *no* erasures. Now, isn't that a peculiar little mystery?'

'It's impossible!' said Pip. 'Perhaps Bets and Ern are mistaken – the little boat must have been in another of the sea pictures. After all, there are masses of them up in that big hall.'

'Yes. *That's* the solution!' said Larry. 'It's obvious! Ern's mistaking one picture for another. There must be *another* picture there, with the little boat in it – there can't have been a boat in the one Ern thinks there was. Yes, I *know* that Bets saw it as well, but she too may have seen it in a different picture, that's all. After all, she didn't go up with you and Ern yesterday. If she had, she would probably have pointed out that it was in a different picture, and even taken you to it.'

'I tell you,' said Ern, exasperated, 'I tell you the boat was in THAT PARTICULAR PICTURE I SAW YESTERDAY AND THE DAY BEFORE. I ought to know! I stood in front of it for ages! I feel as if I could almost paint the same picture myself!'

'All right, Ern, calm down,' said Fatty. 'Now, Find-Outers, any ideas?'

'You're *sure*, Ern, that it's the same picture, and is in exactly the same place?' asked Daisy. 'Same cliffs, same waves, same sky, same frame, everything?'

'Same everything,' said Ern, rather sulkily. 'Goodness knows, I looked at it long enough. It's just the *boat* that is missing – the little tiny boat.'

'Well, I simply don't see any answer to this

particular puzzle,' said Fatty. 'It's certainly a mystery – but rather a silly little mystery, with no rhyme or reason – just a sea picture from which a very small red boat has gone. We must give it up.'

'The smallest mystery we've ever had, and the only one impossible to solve – what a pity!' said Larry.

'I think we *all* ought to pop up to Banshee Towers and have a look round to see if by any chance the picture with the boat has been hung somewhere else,' said Daisy. 'After all, some of the pictures look very alike – they are *all* sea pictures with waves and cliffs and skies and ships. I'd rather like to solve this particular little mystery – not leave it in the air. It's a nice day – we could cycle up again.'

'Yes. Let's do that,' said Pip. 'What do you say, Ern?'

'Good idea,' said Ern. 'I'd like to find my little boat! Let's go now!'

And before long, the six children were on their bicycles, once more on the way to Banshee Towers. A little mystery like this was not going to beat the Find-Outers! They took the dogs too, in the boxes on Ern's and Fatty's back wheels. It was quite a little company, cycling along up the hill to Banshee Towers.

They were there at last – but what a shock! There was a notice up that said 'CLOSED FOR TEMPORARY REPAIRS'.

'Blow! Look at that!' said Ern, in dismay. 'Now we won't be able to find out about the boat.'

It was indeed a blow. 'Panting up that steep hill all for nothing!' groaned Pip. 'Is the turnstile man anywhere about? He's a surly fellow, but he might let us in if we told him we only want to be there for half a minute.'

'I wonder what repairs they are doing?' said Fatty. 'The place seemed in very good order to me.'

'Look, it's probably pipes they are replacing,' said Larry, pointing to a pile of pipes of all sizes. 'Looks as if their water system has gone wrong. These are lead pipes – like we have in our houses at home. Probably the place is damp, and you can't have damp in a picture gallery. Ruins the pictures at once!'

'Yes. You're probably right,' said Fatty, examining the pipes. 'Well, Easter is over, so they won't have many visitors till Whitsun – good time now to do any repairs. Well, what shall we do? Shall we just look round to see if *any*one's about?'

They wandered around, but saw no one. 'What a waste of a morning,' said Larry. 'What can we do now?'

'I tell you what we *could* do, which would be rather fun,' said Pip. 'You remember how the dogs discovered some secret way up the hill, that led to the great fireplace in the Armour Room? They must have found an entrance somewhere on the hill – a cave or a hole of some sort – that had a passage leading to Banshee Towers! Can't we look for that?'

'Well, it *would* be fun,' said Larry, and the others nodded. 'Anyone brought a torch?'

Three of them had torches in their pockets. Good! 'I don't expect there's much chance either of finding where the dogs made their way into the hill, or of getting up any passages ourselves,' said Fatty. 'It was probably nothing more than a large rabbit-hole they found, leading into some underground warren. Anyway, let's have a shot at finding it.'

'The dogs will help,' said Ern, and away they went on their bicycles down the hill with Bingo and Buster racing behind. Halfway down, Fatty leapt off his bike, and called to Buster.

'Buster! Find! Find, Buster!'

Buster stood still with his ears pricked. *Find?* What was he to find? There were no rabbits here. He and Bingo hadn't sniffed the scent of a single one. What *could* Fatty mean?

'Find, Buster! Find the hole you discovered the other day!' ordered Fatty. 'FIND!'

He pointed here and there over the hill. Buster still stood with his ears cocked, his head on one side, trying his hardest to understand what his master wanted. It suddenly dawned on him that there was a hole somewhere – the hole he and Bingo had found – perhaps that was what Fatty wanted? A hole!

He gave a sharp little bark, and ran a little way uphill. He stood there, looking from side to side, sniffing the wind. Bingo came to join him, though he hadn't the faintest idea of what Fatty wanted.

Buster gave another short bark, and ran to the right, and then made for a great bush that overhung a steep part of the hill. Bingo followed, yapping.

'Come on, I think old Buster has understood what I meant,' said Fatty, and he and the others climbed up the hill, soon becoming out of breath, for it was very steep just there. They had carefully hidden their bicycles under some thick bushes, a little lower down.

Both dogs had disappeared! Fatty yelled loudly. 'BUSTER! Where are you? BUSTER!'

Buster appeared by the overhanging bush, and barked. Bingo appeared and barked too. What Buster did, he had to do as well!

'Come on,' said Fatty. 'I think Buster's found what we want! Whew – look here, under this bush – a great hole! I bet Buster thought it was a giant rabbit-hole. I have a feeling that this is where *we* disappear into the heart of the hill. Let's hope we come up in the right place! Follow me, everybody!'

And there they go, one by one. Be careful, Fatty – there may be danger ahead!

13. UP THE PASSAGE – AND A SURPRISING FIND!

The hole was quite a large one, with long grass and some kind of creeping plant growing across the entrance. Fatty, bent double, pushed his way into it, shining his torch in front of him. He could hear Buster and Bingo scrabbling some way ahead, giving little woofs, as if chatting with each other.

The hole became much larger after a few yards, and Fatty was able to straighten himself a little, and make his way more comfortably. He soon saw that the passage he was in was now of rock, not of earth. It was very uneven, and at times the roof came down so low that he had to bend almost double.

Behind him came Bets, then Larry, then Daisy, Ern and Pip being the last two. Larry and Pip held the other torches, which gave a very good light in the black darkness of the strange passage. Ahead were the two dogs, very pleased and excited to think that Fatty and the others were using the passage they had found some days before!

'My word, isn't it steep?' shouted Fatty, and made the others jump – for his voice sounded very strange in the narrow passage – not at all like Fatty's usual voice! It was muffled and mysterious, and had a strange echo.

'Steep-tee-eep!' came the echo. The dogs didn't like it. They stopped, pricked their ears, and whined.

'It's all right, Buster,' said Fatty. 'Only the echo. Carry on!'

'Carry-on, arry-on—on——on!' said the echo, and the dogs barked angrily. That was worse still, of course! The rocky passage was immediately full of wild barks, and the dogs were very frightened indeed. Was this place full of hundreds of dogs? They made their way back to Fatty in alarm, and he patted them, and spoke quietly, trying to defeat the curious echo.

'Now, now – it's all right. Good dogs! VERY good dogs! Go on now – show us the way.'

'Way,' said the echo, also quietly. 'Way-way-waaaaaay!'

After they had all climbed a good while, very glad indeed of their torches, Fatty stopped for a rest. The last bit had been very steep indeed. He waited until the others had come up close, and then spoke.

'We *should* be near Banshee Towers now,' he said. 'You remember that there is a trap door under the old cauldron? – well, that means that any noise we make now may echo up into the Armour Room. So be very quiet, please – just in *case* anyone is there.'

Without a word, and making as little noise as possible, the six went climbing up. Fatty made the dogs keep close to him, so that he could prevent them barking.

But before they came to the trap door, they came to something that surprised them very much! Fatty saw it first, of course, because he was leading. His torch suddenly showed him a big space just in front, and he stopped in surprise. The tunnel had widened out into a kind of underground room – a room with an uneven rocky floor, and equally uneven rocky walls. Fatty was able to stand completely upright. He shone his torch round the underground room in surprise.

He gave a short whistle. 'Whew! What's all this? Quick, everyone, come and look!'

They crowded into the strange rocky room. It was quite empty except for three things: a piece of peculiar-looking machinery – something that looked like a deflated balloon – and a chair!

'What on *earth* is all this?' said Pip, shining his torch on the machinery.

'At a guess I should say it was the machinery that sets the dear old banshee wailing at the top of her voice!' said Fatty.

'Are you sure?' said Bets. 'What's that balloon thing for? Shine your torch on it, Fatty.'

'I should think that this balloon is inflated by a pump worked by that bit of machinery,' said Fatty. 'And then, when it *de*flates, it makes that screaming, wailing banshee noise.'

'But how is it that it's heard all over Banshee Towers?' asked Bets, puzzled.

'Oh, there are probably amplifiers in every room,' said Fatty, who always seemed to know everything. 'You know, things that magnify any sound, and make it tremendously loud. Don't you remember how loud the wailing was when we heard it the other day? And how clear and distinct it was?'

'Oh yes,' said Bets, shivering as she remembered the horrible noise. 'But Fatty, what a peculiar thing to do – to fill the place with wails like that! I should have thought it would frighten people away – not bring them here!'

'Yes. It seems a bit odd when you put it like that, Bets,' said Fatty, fiddling about with the machinery. 'I wonder how this works. What's this wheel for?'

He turned the wheel to the right. Nothing happened. He turned it to the left – and very suddenly indeed, something began to work inside the machinery – clank – click – clonk – click – clunk . . . .

'It's working! Turn it off, quick!' cried Bets, afraid of what might happen. But Fatty didn't. He watched the machine, a little grin on his face.

Oh, Fatty, Fatty, you know quite well what you've done!

The balloon-thing began to move. Buster saw it trembling, and he growled and showed his teeth. Bingo immediately did the same. The balloon grew bigger and bigger – and then came another loud click, and something fell into place and began whirring. The children couldn't see what it was.

'I bet that's the amplifier getting ready to work!' said Fatty, his eyes gleaming. 'We'll hear something in a minute. Don't be scared, little Bets. It's only machinery. Ah – here we go!'

And then, from the now fully-inflated balloon, came a weird, unhappy sound – a wailing that held everyone spellbound, it seemed so human! Bets took Fatty's hand at once, frightened at the strange noise. It sounded so very, very heart-rending.

'It's only a very clever trick, Bets,' said Fatty, in a low voice. 'Just a bit of machinery and a specially fitted-up balloon – and an amplifier to make the wails very loud indeed. All fitted neatly into a most convenient underground hole in a rock. I wonder if Mr Engler is at the bottom of this!'

'Oh Fatty, PLEASE stop the machine!' begged Bets. 'I HATE this wailing. I HATE it.'

Fatty pulled a little lever. The machinery slowed down. The balloon gradually deflated. The wailing grew slower and softer, and then stopped altogether. There was a marvellous silence, and everyone enjoyed the sudden peace. Bets heaved an enormous sigh.

'Oooooooooo! I shall never hear a more horrible noise in all my life than that wailing. Fatty, no real banshee could ever have wailed like that, surely?'

'I should find it very difficult to believe in a real banshee, Bets,' said Fatty, examining the machinery carefully, by the light of his torch. 'I even find it difficult to believe in a man like Engler, who is wicked enough to rig up a thing like this. But unfortunately, *he's* real enough! Well, what do we do now?'

'Fatty, please let's go up through the trap door if we can, and have a look at those pictures again,' begged Ern. 'I do want to see if Bets remembers the one that the boat was in. If she does, I'll know I'm right about it. If she doesn't – well, then there's no mystery. I'm beginning to hope there isn't! What with banshees, and disappearing boats, and hidden machinery, I feel rather sick!'

'Well, don't be sick in here, Ern, there really isn't room!' said Fatty, briskly. 'Right, we'll go up through the trap door – providing nobody's about. But I think that if there had been, we should have had a visitor down here pretty quickly, trying to find out WHY the banshee wailed all on her own! I have a feeling that the place really *is* shut up today.'

Fatty went to an opening in the furthest wall of the strange little rock-room, and shone his torch into it. 'Just as I thought!' he announced. 'Steps! Steps cut into the rock, just like a ladder! I bet it's the steps we saw leading down from that hole in the hearth, where the trap door was!'

The others crowded round him. Yes – there were the steps that they had seen the other day from above!

'I'll go first,' said Fatty. 'Better make no noise,

just in *case* anyone's about. But I feel certain there isn't, or whoever was here would have come rushing to see why the banshee machinery was suddenly working!'

Everyone was silent as Fatty climbed the rocky steps. He soon came to the top, but could see nothing above his head but the trap door lid, set firmly in its place. 'Here goes!' said Fatty, and gave it a push upwards. It upset the iron cauldron standing over it and this fell over on its side with a terrific clatter that scared Fatty almost as much as it frightened the others down below!

He stood at the top of the steps, listening. To his enormous relief, he could hear nothing – no shouts of surprise, no clatter of running feet – nothing! The place must be completely empty. Well, thank goodness for *that*!

Fatty climbed out of the trap door hole and looked round. The place seemed absolutely deserted. Well, now they could examine the pictures to their hearts' content – and maybe solve the mystery of the missing boat!

One by one, he hauled the others up from the hole in the hearth. The dogs were handed up last of all by Ern, and were very glad to scurry around and stretch their legs properly! How they had hated that wailing!

'I want to look at that lovely sea picture,' said Bets, at once. 'Ern, come with me.'

She and Ern hurried through the Armour Room into the great hall where the pictures hung. Yes, there they all were, in their blues and greens, sunshiny, stormy, windy, some of them stretching from floor to ceiling.

'Here's that boat picture,' called Ern, standing in front of it. 'Do you remember it, Bets?'

'Oh *yes*!' said Bets. 'Yes, there was a little red boat that's not there now. I *know* there was one, Ern, it was on this wave here, wasn't it?' And Bets touched one of the waves not far from the bottom of the picture.

'Yes!' said Ern, triumphantly. 'That's *exactly* where it was, Bets. I told you that, didn't I, Fatty? Now Bets has told you too. We can't both be wrong!'

'Fatty, where do you think the boat has gone?' said Bets, really puzzled. 'It doesn't look as if it's been washed out or painted over.'

'A big wave probably caught it and it sank to the bottom,' said Pip, solemnly. 'That's the simplest explanation, Bets.'

'Don't be so *silly*!' said Bets, quite worried over the vanished boat. 'Fatty, I'd like to look at some of the other pictures too.'

But before they could do that, the dogs, who had been wandering happily about together, suddenly stood still and began to growl, their hackles rising on their necks. Fatty shushed everyone at once.

'Get back into the Armour Room, girls. Somebody's coming!' he whispered. 'Hurry up. You'll have to get down the trap door quickly, and run for your lives! We shall be in real trouble if we're found here. Larry and Pip, look after the girls!'

The two girls shot off into the Armour Room with Pip and Larry, and were soon down the steps. They wanted to wait for Ern and Fatty, but Larry wouldn't let them. 'You're in my charge now,' he said. 'Quickly now – get along underground!'

Fatty too went to the Armour Room with Ern,

hoping there would be time for them both to slip down the hole. But there wasn't! He just managed to push the cauldron quickly over the trap door, and step back on to the hearth-rug.

Footsteps came to the door of the room and a voice snapped out, 'Stand where you are! What's all this? How did you get in, you boys! Answer me at once!'

14. PRISONERS - NOW WHAT CAN BE DONE?

It was Mr Engler who stood there, shouting! He looked extremely angry, and his face was very red. Behind him stood the turnstile man, a sneering smile on his face. Buster flew at them, with Bingo behind him, and both dogs were kicked hard by the two men, and howled in pain.

'Call off these dogs, or I'll kill them,' said Mr Engler, pulling a great sword from the wall, where it had been hanging.

'SIT, Buster, SIT, Bingo!' shouted Fatty, his heart cold with fear. To his enormous relief, both dogs sat at once, growling savagely, their hackles still up. Thank goodness Buster had been trained to be instantly obedient, thought Fatty. Bingo, of course, had just copied Buster. How fierce they both looked, showing their teeth, longing to get at these two men who dared to shout at Fatty and Ern.

'Good thing they obey you,' said Mr Engler, still holding the sword. 'I like dogs, or I wouldn't give them a chance. Now, explain your presence here, please. The door was locked – so I presume you came in through one of the windows. I saw that one was open when I came – the one on the first floor. Easy enough to climb up ivy, isn't it? – easy to break into a place. You boys will have to explain all that when you come before the police!'

Fatty was thankful that the man thought they had broken in through an open window. He said nothing. He was certainly not going to explain about the trap door in the hearth! If the man didn't know of it, well and good!

'Oh, don't take us to the police, sir,' blurted out Ern, thinking of Goon's face, if he, Ern, were taken to the police station. 'Please don't. We weren't doing any harm, really we weren't. We were just looking round, like.'

'I've seen these kids before, sir,' said the turnstile man. 'Cheeky lot they are, too. Six of them have been coming up – with these dogs. I *told* them dogs weren't allowed. I was a bit afraid these kids might find out what we . . .'

'Shut up, Flint, you fool!' snapped Mr Engler, clearly afraid that he was about to say something he didn't want the boys to hear. 'Go and begin to load the van, and be sharp about it. I'll deal with what's not ready, and you can fetch it later.'

He turned to the two listening boys. 'I'm afraid you are going to have a very poor weekend,' he said. 'I've decided *not* to hand you over to the police – but to leave you all alone here, without food or drink for two or three days. Just to teach you what happens to lads who break into places! Oh, you needn't think you can get out of the window you so easily slipped in by! I shall tie you up and lock you in this room, and when I come back on Monday – or maybe Tuesday – I'll listen to your apologies and let you go – perhaps!'

'But sir – our parents will be so worried,' began Fatty. 'We haven't done any harm. We apologise *now*. We do really. Don't we, Ern?'

'Ooooh yes,' said Ern, fervently, a little surprised to hear Fatty talking in such a humble voice. Why, Fatty sounded *scared*! First time

I've ever seen him frightened, thought Ern.

'You can apologise when you next see me, and have had time to think what fools you have both been,' said Mr Engler. The turnstile man grinned sarcastically. He was very, very glad to see that 'cheeky boy' as he thought of him, standing there, caught so easily.

'Tie them up,' said Mr Engler, to the turnstile man. 'I'm going to see if Poussin is there. He's about due now.'

Fatty wondered who Poussin was. It was a French name, so maybe it was the French artist. He stood waiting for the turnstile man to tie up him and Ern. 'Got to go and get some rope, if you want me to tie them up,' said the man, turning.

'No. Use those curtain cords,' said Mr Engler. 'I must go and see if Poussin has come. These boys are not to be left alone until their wrists are tied tightly, behind their backs! TIGHTLY, I said, Flint. And DON'T talk to them – else I'll talk to *you*! Do you hear me?'

'Yes,' said Flint, sulkily, and went to tear down the cords that pulled the great curtains open or shut. He had soon tied the boys by their wrists and ankles very tightly indeed.

'You know these cords are too tight,' said Fatty, between his teeth. 'No need to be so brutal.'

'Ha – you're not so funny now, are you!' said Flint. 'Cheeking me out there, you was. Don't feel like cheeking me now, do you?'

Fatty heard another voice – the French artist's. He was in the great hall, with Engler. He was speaking in French, which Fatty understood perfectly. He strained his ears to listen. He was extremely surprised to hear noises of a ladder being dragged along the hall, and set up somewhere. He listened hard. *That* sounded like a knife being used to cut something. What on earth were they doing? Not damaging the pictures, surely!

Then he thought he heard the sound of a brush being slapped over some surface. A brush? A *paint*brush probably. Was the Frenchman painting a picture out there, his easel set up as usual? No, it couldn't be that – he wouldn't *slap* the paint on!

Flint, the turnstile man, finished tying Ern's wrists, and stood back and grinned at the two angry boys. 'Well – happy dreams!' he said. 'And may the rats and mice run all over you tonight! This place is full of them.'

'You wait till we see you again,' said Fatty. 'We'll be handing you over to the police, I hope! What are you all up to? Beats me!'

'You won't see *me* again – I'm off to the States!' said Flint. 'America's the place for me now. We'll soon be off – and the old banshee can wail her head off for us, we shan't hear her!'

He went out, banged the door, and the boys heard the key being turned in the lock. Ern groaned as he lay trussed up on the floor beside Fatty.

'This is a nice how-do-you-do,' he said. 'Good thing the men don't guess we . . .'

'Shut up, Ern,' hissed Fatty. 'They may be listening, hoping we'll give something away. Can you stand up?'

'No,' said Ern, trying. 'Hello, Bingo – pity you can't untie me. Is Buster clever enough to untie *you*, Fatty? Have you taught him things like that yet?'

Buster and Bingo were puzzled and distressed to see Fatty and Ern rolling on the floor, groaning as their cords seemed to get tighter and tighter. They licked the boys' faces, and whined pitifully. Fatty rolled to a settee and by means of using his tied hands, managed to get himself into a sitting position. He then stood up on his tied feet and began to hop to a window that overlooked the yard outside.

He was interested to see a small van there – a plain dark blue one. Flint, the turnstile man, must have just finished loading it, for he was at that moment slamming the door at the back. Then he went to the front, hopped into the driver's seat, and started up the engine. At the same time, a car drove up behind it, and the two drove off together. Fatty quickly memorised the numbers of the van and of the car.

'JBL 333 – and POR 202,' he muttered. 'Gosh, I wish I could write those numbers down – I'll never remember them. Ern, can you remember JBL 333 and POR 202?'

'I don't think so,' said poor Ern. 'I can't think of anything but my wrists and ankles. Fatty, what are we going to do? We'll never be able to get these cords off.'

'Of course we shall!' said Fatty. 'I didn't want to get them off before those fellows went – I was afraid they might come back at any moment.'

'But HOW can we get our hands free?' said Ern. 'The cord's much too strong!'

Fatty hopped across to the wall, where a curious foreign knife hung. He raised his wrists behind his back and placed them so that the cords were against the edge of the knife. Very gently, he began to rub the cords up and down the knife, careful not to press too hard and cut himself.

Ern watched him in admiration. Trust old Fatty to think of something smart! Fatty worked away and finally felt one cord give – then another. He pulled hard, and very thankfully felt the cords loosening and slipping off his hands.

'My word, my hands are all numb and stiff,' he said, trying to bend them this way and that. 'I'll undo yours, Ern, when I can feel some life in my fingers.'

Buster ran to him and licked Fatty's hands,

whining. He knew Fatty was in some kind of trouble and his doggy mind was upset and worried. There didn't seem to be anything at all that he could do for Fatty.

It was some time before Fatty could use his hands, and even then they were shockingly painful. He spent ages trying to undo Ern's cords. He dared not use the knife on them, for his hands were now too numb to use a knife safely.

But at last Ern's cords were undone too. His hands were worse than Fatty's, for Flint had tied them very viciously. Soon their ankles were untied as well, and life began to seem a little brighter.

'Are we going to escape down the underground passage?' asked Ern. 'I don't think I can walk though. My legs are all pins and needles and I can't feel my feet.'

'The girls and Pip and Larry will send help for us,' said Fatty. 'What *I'd* like to do is to get out of this room and wander round some of the upstairs rooms. I have a feeling we might find something interesting there!'

'That fellow locked the door. I heard him,' said Ern.

'I know – but we *might* be able to get to it, and unlock it from *this* side,' said Fatty. He walked unsteadily to the door, and looked at the lock. Then he bent down and looked *under* the door. Ern watched him in interest. What was old Fatty up to now?

'I'm going to use an old trick – one I've used before, Ern,' said Fatty. He went to the table and took a catalogue from the pile there. He tore out the middle pages, leaving only the stiff outer covers. These he took over to the door, knelt down again and pushed them flat underneath it, so that the greater part of the covers was on the other side of the door.

Then he stood up and, with the end of his penknife blade, jiggled the key in the lock until it was in a position for him to give it a push, and send it out on the other side of the door! The key promptly fell out – and there was a little thud as it landed on the floor at the bottom of the door. Buster and Bingo barked loudly. What was happening now?

'Good!' said Fatty, pulling at the piece of stiff cover showing under the door on his side. Carefully he pulled it towards him, oh so gently – and, as the stiff covers came under the door, *the key lying on them came too*! There it was at last, safely on their side of the door. 'Now,' said Fatty, 'We can unlock the door from *our* side, and do a little exploring! Come on, Ern. Can you walk all right?'

15. FATTY DOES A LITTLE DETECTIVE WORK!

Fatty picked up the key that he had so carefully pulled under the bottom of the door. 'Hope I can turn it!' he said, making a face as he put the key in the lock. 'My wrist feels as if it hasn't even the strength to turn a key if the lock is stiff!'

But the key turned easily! Fatty opened the door and peered out cautiously into the picture hall. He knew that he had seen the car and the van go off but he didn't want to run into anyone who might still be in the place.

All was quiet. Buster and Bingo, very much on-guard, stood close by the boys, ready to growl and fly at anyone who might be going to hurt them.

'There can't be anybody here now,' said Fatty. 'The dogs would be growling if there were. Hello – look, there's a step-ladder over there – and a tin of something, with a brush in it. Looks as if somebody's been up to something. You remember we heard a ladder being pulled across the floor, Ern – and the slapping of a brush?'

They were puzzled when they came to the tin. They had expected it to be full of paint, but it wasn't! 'It's some kind of gluey-paste,' said Fatty, dipping his finger into the tin. 'My word – don't get it on your clothes, Ern – it's about the strongest paste or glue I've ever felt. I just can't get it off my finger! Now, what on earth was it used for?'

They gazed at the two sea pictures on each side of the tin. Nothing to help them there – but wait a minute! Fatty suddenly noticed a thin, shining streak of what looked like something sticky down the inner side of one of the frames. He touched it. It *was* sticky!

He was very puzzled. Why had someone used glue of some kind? – had the frame cracked, and needed a little glueing? Pictures weren't *glued* into their frames – they were backed with board, and then the frames were neatly placed over them. Fatty gave it up, putting the strange fact into a corner of his mind to consider later.

'Come on, Fatty, what are you dreaming about, standing there gazing down at that tin of glue, or whatever it is,' said Ern, impatiently. 'I want to get out of this place. So do the dogs!'

Bingo was whining. He didn't like Banshee Towers. He wanted to have a good long run and stretch his legs.

'All right, Bingo, old thing,' said Fatty. 'We'll soon be off and away. I just want to have a little look round – a "snoop" is a better name, perhaps – and see if I can unearth a few of Mr Engler's strange little secrets!'

They went to a big staircase that had a very large board at the bottom with the words 'PRIVATE. NO ENTRY.'

Fatty took not the slightest notice of the big board, but went straight up the stairs. He went rather slowly, and so did Ern, for their ankles were still swollen and painful after the cruelly-tight cords. The dogs raced up before them, barking.

They came to a big room. There was a large desk there, and a smaller one. Pictures and empty frames were stacked all over the place.

There was a great pile of catalogues on the big desk, and a scattering of letters.

'Very interesting,' said Fatty, turning over the canvases on which various pictures had been painted. 'All sea pictures, of course. Look here, Ern – remember this one?'

'Yes, it's a double of the one we saw in the frame by the tin of glue,' he said. 'Can't see any difference! That's a copy, I suppose. Done by that French artist. That's all he did, seems to me – sit there and copy somebody else's pictures! Funny, I should have thought a *real* artist wouldn't want to copy.'

'He might – if he were well paid, Ern,' said Fatty. 'Hello – here's a pile of letters all neatly stacked together and tied with pink tape. Let's have a look and see who they're from!'

'Do you think you ought to look at other people's letters?' said Ern, uncomfortably.

'Oh, I think that after the kind of treatment the spiteful Mr Engler served out to us he really can't complain of anything *we* do!' said Fatty, reading some of the letters. 'In any case, Ern, I intend to give them to Inspector Jenks. He will be very pleased indeed to have them.'

'Coo!' said Ern, astonished. 'I wouldn't say that, Fatty. He might lock you up for taking them. Better leave them here.'

Fatty took no notice. He was absorbed in one or two of the letters. Ern peeped at the heading on each. 'The Hedling Art Gallery, Diddinghame, USA' was one. 'Art Shows Company, New York, USA' was another. 'Grand Pictures Company, Hinkling, USA' said a third. Gracious! thought Ern, What does Fatty think he can find in letters like that!

He peeped down a sheet that Fatty was absorbed in reading, but couldn't make head or tail of it. Just a list of pictures, and prices and artists, thought Ern. He spoke aloud.

'Fatty, I reckon we're just wasting time now. Let's go. Those fellows might come back sooner than we expect – and, anyway, Bets and the others might already be sending help to us, you know. That'd be a waste of time, seeing that we can just walk out and go home when we want to!'

'Right, Ern,' said Fatty. 'Just let me make a list of the Art Galleries listed here that buy pictures from Engler.' He scribbled quickly, and then took a last look round. 'We'll just peep in the room next door first. I have a feeling we still haven't seen quite all I expected to see.'

They went into the next room, a smaller one. Ern stared in surprise. It was fitted up as a very comfortable bedroom! A large wardrobe stood open, showing many clothes hanging there. Thrown across an unmade bed was a dark painting overall, covered with smudges of oil-paint. A book lay on a table beside the bed.

Fatty picked it up. 'At a guess I should say this book was a French one!' he said. He looked down at it and nodded. 'Yes – all about famous Continental pictures – especially pictures of the sea!' Fatty turned to the flyleaf at the beginning of the book. 'And here the owner has kindly written his name – it belongs to that French artist, of course – and here is his address – François Henri Ortalo, 91, Rue Carnot, Paris. Very nice of him to leave it so handy! Interesting to see that Mr Engler has given him such a nice room to live in, too. He must be very useful to him!'

'Oh, do stop messing about with books and letters!' said Ern, despairingly. 'I want to go! I hate this place. At any moment I expect to hear that awful banshee wail.'

'All right, Ern, we'll go,' said Fatty, scribbling quickly again in his notebook. 'I think we'd better make ourselves scarce, anyway, in case Mr Engler pops back again through the front door. I don't feel inclined to meet him again today. I don't like his manners!'

'He's a beast,' said Ern. 'My ankles still feel as if I've been running for miles, they ache so, where they were tied.'

'Ah well,' said Fatty, snapping shut his notebook. 'We'll soon forget our wrists and ankles. Actually I'm feeling rather excited. I think I've now got the whole mystery wrapped up very neatly indeed!'

'You're boasting, Fatty!' said Ern, disbelievingly. 'What about the little painted boat that disappeared from that picture downstairs? I bet you don't know how *that* happened?'

'Well, we'll see,' said Fatty. 'I really think I'm beginning to see daylight! We'll go home now and find the others and tell them what we've found. Let's see – they had to escape down that underground passage in the hill – and find their bikes – and then ride home.'

'Well, unless they stopped on the way to have ice creams or something, they will be home before us,' said Ern.

'They'd hardly stop for ice creams when they knew we were in trouble!' said Fatty.

'No, I forgot that,' said Ern. 'Come on – let's go downstairs, slip out of the front door with the dogs, and run down the hill to where we left our bikes underneath that bush.'

They went down the stairs with the two excited dogs, both wagging their tails madly, though, as Ern pointed out, Bingo's tail *waved* rather than wagged, it was so very, very long!

They opened the front door and slipped out, shutting it quietly behind them. They made their way cautiously down the hill, keeping close to the hedges, half-afraid of seeing Mr Engler and his companions somewhere about. The two dogs, sensing that all was not quite right with their masters, pressed close to their heels, and didn't even attempt to go sniffing for rabbits.

At last they came to where they had left their bicycles, hidden in bushes. They looked round for the bicycles belonging to the other four, but they were gone.

'Good – then they got down the banshee passage safely,' said Fatty. 'They can't really be very much in front of us now – we were pretty quick down that hill!'

They were soon riding fast down the rest of the hill, the dogs bumping in their boxes behind. It was a miracle that they didn't fall out, for the boys went so fast.

'What do we do when we get back?' shouted Ern. 'I hope you won't go and report everything to my Uncle Goon. I wouldn't like that. You know I'm in trouble with him!'

'Don't worry, Ern. We hold all the winning cards now,' shouted back Fatty, comfortingly. 'I rather think we ought to go over Mr Goon's head, and get in touch with Chief Inspector Jenks. We know him quite well enough. This is a bit too big a thing for a village policeman to handle.'

'Luvaduck!' said Ern, in awe. 'But won't the

Chief Inspector think it's a bit cheeky of us to telephone him? I mean, he's a Big Noise, he is.'

'We'll get back to my shed first,' said Fatty, freewheeling very fast. 'And find out where the others are. They can't have been back very long. My word, Ern – I'm beginning to feel excited. I'm seeing daylight! The mystery is dissolving – everything FITS!'

'Go on, Fatty!' said Ern, disbelievingly. 'It's just a muddle to me, straight it is! Fits! The only fits *I* know are the ones I'll have when my uncle gets hold of me! Oooh, Fatty, go slower – old Bingo nearly shot out of his box just then. FATTY!'

16. A HORRID SHOCK!

Fatty and Ern arrived at Fatty's home safely, much to Buster's relief. Part of the road had been so bumpy that poor Buster had found himself wishing he had sharp cat-claws to hold on with, instead of his own blunt ones! He had decided that he didn't want to go bicycling with Fatty ever again. Bicycling and dogs didn't really go very well together!

He and Bingo jumped gladly out of the boxes tied on to the back mudguards, and Buster went to see if anyone had put something good into his enamel bowl. Ah – kind old Cookie! She had filled his bowl with some nice fresh meat. Bingo rushed up too – and, hungry as he was, Buster remembered his manners, and allowed Bingo to share.

'Good, Buster. I'm pleased with you,' said Fatty. 'We'll buy a good dollop of meat for Bingo, and I'm sure he'll share his with you too. Now you two dogs stay out here.'

He opened the door of his shed. No one was there! 'Where are the others?' he said, looking round. 'Gosh – I hope they're all right. What's happened to them? We certainly didn't pass them on the way!'

'Perhaps one of them had a puncture,' said Ern – and as it happened, he was quite right! Larry's front tyre suddenly went flat, and he and the others had stopped at a little opening in a nearby wood, while Larry mended the puncture.

Ern and Fatty had actually cycled past them, and hadn't even seen them, or heard their shouts!

'You simply *whizzed* by,' complained Larry, when at last he and the others arrived at Fatty's workroom. 'We yelled and shouted, but you were gone – psssssst! – like that! Sixty miles an hour, and the two dogs bumping up and down like apples in a basket!'

'Fatty, are you all right? What happened when we left you?' said Bets. 'I was so afraid those men might hurt you!'

'Oh, *we* were all right,' said Fatty, hurriedly

pulling his coat sleeves down as far as they would go, to hide the painful red lines round his wrists. 'We found out a whole lot of interesting things, Bets. We must have a meeting at once!'

But before they could really settle down to it, someone came knocking at the shed door, opened it and looked in. 'Frederick, are you there? There's someone on the telephone for you.'

'Oh, Mummy, can't you say I'm busy or something!' said Fatty, exasperated. 'We're JUST starting a most *important* meeting. *Really* important.

'All right, dear. I'll go back and tell Chief Inspector Jenks what you say,' said his mother, and shut the door.

But Fatty leapt up with a yell. 'MUMMY! Wait! You didn't say it was Inspector Jenks! Mummy, I'm coming straightaway!'

Ern looked round at the others, as Fatty shot out of the door at top speed, Buster at his heels. 'I bet the Inspector's heard of our discoveries at Banshee Towers,' he said, pleased. 'I expect he wants to ask Fatty a whole lot of questions. Funny how old Fatty always seems to get in on things first, isn't it? My word, you wait till Fatty tells you what we discovered this morning!'

Fatty ran all the way up the garden to his house, his mind going over likely reasons for the Chief Inspector's telephone call.

Probably he's heard about the Banshee Towers' goings-on – the wailing banshee, for instance – and maybe he's suspicious of Mr Engler's doings. Well, I can certainly give him some up-to-date information, thought Fatty, feeling pleased.

He ran to the telephone and picked up the receiver. 'Chief Inspector Jenks? Frederick Trotteville here, sir. Sorry to keep you waiting.'

'Frederick, I'll come to the point at once,' said the Chief. 'I'm sorry to say I've had a serious complaint about you. I expect you have a perfectly good explanation, and I sincerely hope you have.'

Fatty felt most alarmed. 'What's all this about, sir?' he asked, bewildered.

'Well, actually there are *two* complaints!' said

the Chief. 'One, *not* very serious, from Mr Goon, about Ern who, he says, was put in his charge by Ern's mother and who has run away and is being harboured by you in your shed.'

'That's quite right, sir,' said Fatty, at once. 'And I'm sure you won't blame me, sir. Mr Goon went for poor old Ern, and he . . .'

'I'm afraid Ern will have to go *back* to Mr Goon,' said the Chief. 'It's his mother's wish – and parents do have *some* rights, you know.'

'All right, sir. I'll see to it,' said Fatty, feeling very, very sorry for Ern.

'The second complaint, Frederick,' said the clear voice down the telephone, 'the second complaint is much more serious. It's been put in by a Mr Engler, the owner of Banshee Towers. He accuses you of breaking into the Towers, with another boy, whose name he doesn't know – and there are also two dogs complained of. Apparently dogs are not allowed inside, and you were told this – and yet you were found there with a *couple*! Whose is the second dog?'

'Ern's,' said Fatty, in a small voice. His heart was sinking down and down and down.

'ERN'S! I didn't even know he *had* a dog!' said the Chief.

'Yes, sir, he has. Called Bingo,' said Fatty.

'What on *earth* were you and Ern and two dogs doing wandering about Banshee Towers?' demanded the Chief. 'Apparently it was closed for the day, and the doors were locked. Frederick, surely you *didn't* break in anywhere?'

'Well, not exactly *break* in, if you mean smash locks or windows or anything like that,' said poor Fatty. 'We certainly did *get* in – we . . .'

The Chief gave a deep groan. 'You are a very, very foolish boy, Frederick. You have played right into this fellow Engler's hands. He is a smart, spiteful, clever crook. We've been trying to pin something on him – and now you've messed things up by putting yourself in *his* hands. Frederick, I simply do not know how I'm going to get you out of this fix.'

'I know he's a crook, sir,' said Fatty, in a small voice. 'We were trying to catch him out, sir – that phoney banshee wailing, for instance, and . . .'

'*You* knew he was a crook!' said the Chief, very surprised. 'How on earth . . . look here,

Frederick, I'd better come round and see you. I simply never know what you are up to. The sooner you grow up and join the police force so that I can *really* keep my eye on you, the better. Stay at home till I come. That's an order, see?'

He slammed down the telephone, and Fatty put back his own receiver, most surprised to find his hand shaking. Gosh, this wasn't funny at all. What in the world would his father say?

I suppose I must be getting a bit too big for my boots, said Fatty to himself. My word, I've never heard the Chief go off the handle like that before! Did I feel like a worm? Yes, I certainly did. I only wish I had a nice, deep hole to go to!

He called to his mother. 'Mummy! The Inspector will be along in a little while. Will you tell him we're down in my shed, please?'

Then away he went, hoping that his mother wouldn't call him back and ask him awkward questions. He opened the door of his shed, and went in.

'You look gloomy, Fatty. What's up?' said Bets, at once. Fatty sank down dramatically into a chair, sighed, and passed his hand over his forehead.

'Well, I rather think I may have to go to prison – or to borstal or somewhere,' he said. 'Old man Engler has put in a complaint about me – charged me with breaking and entering Banshee Towers. And Mr Goon has *also* put in a complaint – that when Ern ran away, I "harboured" him.'

'You never harboured me!' said Ern, who hadn't the faintest idea of what 'harbouring' really meant. 'I'm not a ship! You just gave me board and lodging, Fatty – let me stay here in your shed.'

'Well, that's another way of saying that I "harboured" you – gave you shelter,' said Fatty.

Ern jumped up at once. 'I'll go back to my uncle's then,' he said. 'I won't let you get punished because you've been kind to *me*, Fatty! That's not fair!'

'Sit down, Ern,' said Fatty. 'We can't do anything for the moment. Chief Inspector Jenks is coming along here soon. I'll have to wait for him. I'd like you all to stay, though.'

'Is my uncle coming too?' said Ern, fearfully.

'I don't think so,' said Fatty. 'Gosh, wouldn't *I* like to put in a complaint about your *uncle*, Ern? In fact, I can think of several complaints I could put in.'

'Nothing to what *I* could think of,' said Ern, gloomily. 'Shouting at me and almost deafening me. Pushing me around. Taking my . . .'

'Listen – someone's coming,' said Fatty, his ears even sharper just then than those of the dogs. 'I heard a car draw up outside our front gate, I'm sure.'

'You couldn't have, Fatty!' said Larry. 'It's right down the garden, and . . .'

But just then the two dogs set up such a loud barking that nobody could hear anyone speak. 'SHUT UP!' shouted Fatty, making a dive for Buster. 'Do you want to be had up for creating a noisy disturbance, Buster! Ern, get hold of Bingo. They both seem to have gone mad.'

A loud knock came at the shed door, and the two dogs almost barked the place down. Then the door opened and there stood Chief Inspector Jenks, tall, burly, keen-eyed – but not smiling as he usually was. He looked round the little company.

'Oh, so *all* the Find-Outers are here, are they?' he said, and smiled. Fatty was most relieved to see that smile. Perhaps the Inspector wasn't going to be too hard on him after all.

'Well, little Bets, so you're here too, are you?' said the Chief Inspector and patted her head. She caught hold of his hand.

'Inspector Jenks, you won't take Fatty to prison, will you?' she said, in a suddenly choky voice. 'He's just been working hard on a mystery, that's all. We all have.'

'Cheer up, Bets – I couldn't take him if I tried!' said the Chief. 'He's not old enough. Still a kid, you know – bit too big for his boots sometimes, that's all. Well, now, how's everybody? My word, here's a new dog. What's your name?'

'Bingo,' said Ern, with such pride in his voice that everyone smiled. 'He's *my* dog, sir. My very own. You should see him play with Buster here – they're a pair, they are.'

'He's a nice dog, Ern,' said the Chief, and

patted Bingo, who immediately rolled over on his back in delight. 'I gather your uncle doesn't like him. I can't imagine why.'

'Nor can I, sir,' said Ern. 'Sir, you won't let my uncle take him away from me, or anything like that, will you?'

'We'll talk about you and Bingo later,' said the Inspector, 'and see what can be done. It's Frederick here I'm worried about. This man, Engler, Frederick, certainly has a sound complaint against you. What do you know about him?'

'I know a great deal,' said Fatty. 'And very surprising it is, sir. The others don't yet know all the things I know – *they'll* be surprised too! I rather think you'll turn your attention to Mr Engler, sir – and one or two others – when I've finished telling my story!'

Inspector Jenks looked most surprised. He sat back comfortably in his chair.

'Tell your story, Fatty,' he said, in a much more friendly tone. 'I'm ready – no embroidery, mind – just the plain facts – ones that you are absolutely sure of!'

Buster sat up straight, and Bingo sat up straight too. They were going to listen with as much interest as everyone else.

'Well, sir,' said Fatty, in a very serious voice. 'It all started with the disappearance of a tiny boat in a big picture . . .'

17. FATTY SOLVES THE MYSTERY!

There was dead silence in the shed, as Fatty told the story of the banshee mystery.

'It all started with the disappearance of a tiny boat in a big picture in the picture gallery at Banshee Towers,' he began.

'A boat in a *picture*!' said the Inspector, astonished.

'Yes, sir. You see, we thought we'd make a few expeditions these holidays, and that was one of them – to Banshee Towers, to see the lovely sea pictures there,' went on Fatty.

'It was Ern and I who *really* wanted to go,' said Bets.

'So we all went up on our bikes, and paid to go in. We had a look round – the pictures were grand,' said Fatty, 'and Ern here stood for ages in front of a very big one . . .'

'Smashing, it was!' said Ern, taking up the

story. 'And it had a tiny red boat, sir, painted on a wave near the bottom of the picture.'

'Well, what about it?' said the Inspector.

'Well, sir, we went again the next day, and I went to look at that picture again – and the boat was *gone*!' said Ern. 'And it wasn't painted out or anything, it just wasn't there.'

'Strange,' said Inspector Jenks. 'You must have made a mistake – looked at another picture perhaps?'

'No, sir – Bets here can say the same as me,' said Ern, and Bets nodded.

'That was the beginning of the mystery,' said Fatty. 'I sort of smelt something fishy from that very moment. I didn't much like the turnstile man, and I certainly didn't like the owner of the pictures, a man called Mr Engler. And I didn't much like one of the artists there, a Frenchman.'

'Oh – there were artists there, were there?' said the Inspector. 'Copying the pictures?'

'Yes, sir – but not awfully well, in my opinion,' said Fatty. 'Except the Frenchman, sir – honestly, he was very, very good. He wasn't very nice though – but he was a *real* artist, sir, the others were only art students from some art school.

'It said in the catalogue, sir, that the pictures there belonged to a Count Ludwig, of Austria, who had lent them to this Mr Engler to show in his gallery. Mr Engler is an Austrian too, I believe. The artists were copying them just for practice, or to sell as copies afterwards. They were most of them awful – I wouldn't have given a penny for any of them!' went on Fatty.

'Frederick, you may as well know that we have reason to believe Engler is a crook,' said the Chief. 'Please tell me straight out if *you* have any reason to believe he is, and if so, WHAT REASONS? This is as important for you, as for me.'

'All right, sir, I can give you plenty of reasons,' said Fatty, briskly. 'I'm pretty sure that what he does is to get that French artist to copy the pictures he has had lent to him from various art galleries all over the place. Then he takes the original picture out of its frame, and rolls it up – and sticks the finished copy in its place – and I must say that François Ortalo makes some wonderful copies!'

'He sells the originals somewhere, for a large sum of money, of course,' said Inspector Jenks. 'Just what we suspected – but couldn't prove!'

'Well, you can prove it now, sir,' said Fatty. 'That French artist made a big mistake when he copied that fine sea picture that Ern and Bets loved – he forgot to put that tiny boat into the copied picture! That's the *only* difference that Ern and Bets could see in the two pictures!'

'A very, very small omission!' said Inspector Jenks. 'One that might have gone unnoticed for years – in fact, it might *never* have been spotted. I don't think anyone but sharp-eyed children would notice and remember a tiny boat so clearly! Ern, I congratulate you! You may be the means of catching a very clever and remarkable swindler!'

Ern went as red as a beetroot, tried to say something, and couldn't.

'Of course,' went on the Inspector, 'we want to know quite a few more things, before we can charge this rogue with stealing. Perhaps you can tell me some of them, Frederick?'

'Well, I don't know, sir,' said Fatty. 'I *can* tell

you a few things, though. The Frenchman's *real* name and address, for instance. I found it in a book when I – er – broke into his bedroom.'

Everyone stared at Fatty in surprise. 'What's his name? – quick, give it to me,' said the Chief, opening a notebook.

'His name is François Henri Ortalo of 91, Rue Carnot, Paris,' said Fatty. 'He knows all about the famous pictures of Europe. I found his name in a book about them.'

The Chief gave a little whistle. 'Oho – so François Ortalo has turned up here, has he?' he said. 'I wouldn't like to say how many different countries want him for swindling people over pictures. Good work, Fatty! Anything else?'

'Well, I know which art galleries in America *buy* the original pictures,' said Fatty, and gave Inspector Jenks the list he had written down that morning in the office at Banshee Towers.

'Bless my soul!' said the Chief, hardly able to believe his ears. 'Am I dreaming? We've been looking everywhere for this information. How in the world do you know this?'

'Well, I just *happened* to see Mr Engler's office

desk,' said Fatty. 'And I just glanced at a few things, sir.'

'I can only hope, Frederick Trotteville, that when you are grown-up, you will join the police force and not the ranks of the burglars!' said the Inspector. 'I suppose you do know that you had no right to go snooping in that fellow's desk, rogue though he is!'

'Well, I wasn't sure, sir,' said Fatty, with a twinkle in his eye. 'But Ern here was rather shocked, weren't you, Ern?'

'Well, yes, I was,' said Ern. 'But then I didn't know that Fatty was getting information to pass on to *you*, sir.'

'Is there really a Count Ludwig, sir, who lends these pictures to Mr Engler?' asked Fatty.

'Oh, yes,' said the Inspector. 'And he must be a poor judge of art – because although Engler never sends him back his valuable original pictures, but only dud copies, he has apparently never noticed the difference!'

'Then he won't notice that the tiny little boat is missing when he gets the copy?' said Bets, amazed.

'He certainly won't,' said the chief. 'You are much smarter than he is, little Bets! And Ern too!'

'Can you charge Mr Engler – and the artist – and perhaps the turnstile man – with robbery and swindling?' asked Fatty.

'It's difficult,' said the Inspector. 'I'd feel safer if I could find out how he gets the original pictures safely out of the art galleries he shows them in – such as Banshee Towers, for instance. It isn't easy to smuggle big pictures out of a place, you know – or into one, for that matter. It's been really puzzling us. We've watched and watched that fellow, not only here but in other places too – and we've never been able to lay our hands on any pictures being smuggled out or in!'

'Oh, that's easy,' said Fatty. 'I guessed that early on, sir.'

'Fatty! You never told us! *How* did they get the pictures out?' said Larry, astonished.

'Do you remember that there were always lengths of fat lead pipes about – supposed to be for repairs?' said Fatty. 'Well, I went and snooped down one and I saw something tightly rolled up in it – I couldn't imagine then what it was – but now I'm absolutely certain that it was a rolled-up canvas – a picture off the walls. It wouldn't be missed, for a copy would be immediately slapped into place!'

'FATTY! Remember that ladder this morning – and the cutting sound we heard when we were locked in that room – and the slapping of a brush?' almost shouted Ern, half-leaping from his chair. 'That was what they were doing then! They climbed up the ladder to cut the picture out, then they slapped some sort of gluey-paste on the empty space, and stretched the copy over it – it stuck almost at once, of course.'

'Yes. I remember,' said Fatty. 'You're quite right, Ern. You've been pretty clever over this.'

'Why didn't you tell us all these things?' said Bets.

'Well, I wasn't quite sure how everything fitted,' said Fatty. 'You know, it was a bit like a jigsaw. I couldn't see the whole picture, or know what it meant, till I'd found *every* bit of the jigsaw. It wasn't till this morning that I found the last piece – the pipes in the shed! Then at last I knew how they managed to get the pictures out without anyone guessing!'

'You've done remarkably well, Fatty. But I rather fear the men have smelt a rat and gone,' said the Chief, shutting his notebook. 'Someone must have tipped them that we were on the watch. They went away in a blue van and a car, apparently. The man we had on watch unfortunately wasn't quick enough to take the numbers. So I fear we can't set up road blocks anywhere, or issue a general warning to the police. We *have* to know the registration numbers of the vehicles.'

'Oh those – I nearly forgot,' said Fatty. 'I saw the numbers this morning. Now – let me see – yes – one was "Pair of Rogues", and . . .'

' "Pair of Rogues" – *that's* not a car number!' said Larry.

'And the other was "Jolly Bad Lot",' said Fatty. 'Yes – POR 202 and JBL 333, sir. POR for "Pair of Rogues!" and JBL for "Jolly Bad Lot". Easy way to remember those vehicles, sir – the letters described the occupants so well!'

'Well, I won't say what a marvel I think you

are, or you *might* get a swelled head,' said the Inspector, jotting down the numbers at once. 'Do you happen to have memorised the number of *my* car in the same way, Fatty?'

'Yes, sir. Your car number is VGF 888,' said Fatty, promptly. 'Er – VGF stands for "Very Good Fellow", sir.'

'Well, I'm glad to hear *that*,' said the Inspector, getting up. 'Thanks, Fatty, thanks, Ern. We can now pin down those three rogues, and put them somewhere where, I am pretty certain, they will not see many beautiful pictures!'

'What about Mr Engler's complaint about me, sir?' asked Fatty. 'You know – breaking and entering into Banshee Towers. Actually we didn't *break* in, sir – we came up that underground passage.'

'Hm, well, in the circumstances, considering that you have given me so much help in this case, Frederick, I shall cross out that complaint in my books,' said Inspector Jenks, with a very broad smile indeed. 'And you needn't worry about Mr Goon. I am going straight up to the police station to tell him of the unexpected – and really astonishing – help you have given me this morning. I must say that I think the Five Find-Outers are remarkably good detectives!'

'What about Ern?' asked Bets, anxiously. 'Will it be *safe* for him to go back to Mr Goon's?'

'QUITE safe,' said the Inspector. 'I shall tell him that his nephew Ern was clever enough to spot what is probably the only clue in existence that could lead to the arrest of a smart rogue like Mr Engler. Well done indeed, Ern!'

And with that, out went the Inspector, murmuring something to himself. 'Let's see now – my car's number is VGF – and Fatty said it stood for "Very Good Fellow". Hm – I just wonder what *else* Fatty makes those letters stand for, when I'm *out* of favour. He's certainly worth watching is Frederick Trotteville!'

18. YOU NEVER KNOW WHAT OLD FATTY IS UP TO!

Mr Goon was amazed to hear what Inspector Jenks had to say. He simply couldn't believe his ears.

'All those pictures copied, and the originals *sold*! That fellow Engler must have made a fortune. And you say Ern – ERN, my nephew, was the one that spotted the first clue! I'd never have thought it of Ern, never.'

'Well, Goon, I shouldn't be surprised if your nephew doesn't make a very fine police officer in some years' time,' said Inspector Jenks, briskly. 'It's a pity you scared him so much, and he ran away. He might have been of some use to you.'

'Yes, sir. I sort of lost my temper,' said Mr Goon. 'I'd like him back, sir. If he's going to be as brainy as you think he is, well, I wouldn't mind teaching him a few things myself, sir, that might be useful to him later on.'

'*That's* the way to talk, Goon,' said the Chief, getting up, and clapping the policeman on the back. 'Youngsters nowadays have some fine stuff in them, you know. As for that boy, Frederick Trotteville – well, I pity all the rogues and swindlers and thieves in a few years' time. Once Frederick gets those brains of his to work, they won't have a chance!'

'I think I'll go down to the Trottevilles' house, and have a word with Ern,' said Goon, getting up. 'His mother's been after me about him, when she heard he wasn't here. Very angry she was – not with Ern, but with *me*. Just like her sauce!'

'Ah, you just tell her how clever Ern has been – that will calm her down,' said the Inspector. 'Well, good-bye, Goon. I'll let you know when we catch those swindlers. You'll have Ern back, of course, and no hard words said on either side. And by the way, what a VERY nice, well-behaved dog he has, hasn't he? Even SITS when he's told. I'm sure you'll enjoy having Bingo back, too, Goon!'

He departed, leaving Mr Goon feeling rather like a pricked balloon, with the air slowly departing from him. Well, he'd better go down and see those 'Find-Outers' as they called themselves. Silly name – but no doubt about it, somehow or other they *did* solve mysteries, and find out extraordinary clues.

Maybe it's silly of me to go against them, thought Goon, frowning. Be better if I was more friendly, like, then they'd tell me things. That Ern now – whoever would have thought he had a brain in his head? I can't believe it!

He set off on his bicycle to ride to Fatty's house, keeping a sharp look out for dogs. It was a curious thing, but as soon as dogs saw Mr Goon riding majestically down the road on his old bicycle, they seemed to have but one thought in their doggy minds, and that was to race out into the road at top speed, barking at the top of their voices, and leap at poor Mr Goon's ankles, as his feet went up and down on the pedals.

Down in the shed, no one guessed that Mr Goon was coming. They were all talking about their adventures in Banshee Towers. 'THE most exciting part was where we set off the wailing banshee machinery,' said Larry. 'My word, that was a clever stunt of Mr Engler's, wasn't it?'

'I *wish* we had that machinery here,' said Fatty. 'What a shock everyone would get in the middle of the night!'

'Well, if you particularly *want* to give your neighbours a shock, *you* don't need banshee machinery!' said Pip, giving Fatty a friendly punch. 'All you need is your own frightful wail – you're as good as any banshee, Fatty. My word, when you wailed in that Armour Room, the first day we were there, I nearly died of fright!'

'There's only one part of the mystery we didn't solve,' said Larry. 'And that was why the banshee apparently chose Thursday for its weekly wail. Why Thursday?'

'Well, apparently there really *wasn't* any mystery about that,' said Fatty. 'And I needn't have bothered my head over it. Thursday is the turnstile man's half-day off – so he used to set the machinery going to clear everyone away early! Then he'd be able to shut up the place and get off in good time. And I've no doubt that the French artist used to do a bit of packing up then

– carefully putting the pictures into those lead pipes, ready for collection.'

'Sh! Someone's coming,' said Bets. 'Oh, Fatty – it's Mr Goon. Whatever is *he* here for?'

'To complain about me "harbouring" Ern, I suppose,' said Fatty, hurrying to the window at the back of the shed. 'Look, I'm not seeing him this morning. I might be a bit rude if he starts saying anything nasty about old Ern. Now you others tell him that Ern's been marvellous, and that even the banshee must have been pretty scared of Ern, and . . .'

Bang-bang! That was Mr Goon knocking at the shed door.

Fatty immediately leapt out of the window with Buster. 'If you have any trouble with Mr Goon, don't let it worry you,' he said, popping his head through the window. 'I'll be listening out here, and I'll come to your help at once.'

Larry then opened the door, and there stood Mr Goon, not looking nearly so fierce as usual. He stepped in, and to everyone's immense astonishment, smiled and nodded.

'Good morning, Mr Goon,' said Bets,

politely. The others muttered a greeting too.

'Well, well,' said Mr Goon, in an unexpectedly hearty voice. 'Here you all are – oh, except Frederick. I – er – came to congratulate him – and you all – on helping to solve the mystery of Banshee Towers. Ern, I hear that you were quite clever at spotting a very important clue.'

Ern blushed bright red at this compliment, and couldn't find a word to say. There was an awkward silence. Bingo broke it by suddenly giving a loud bark, and rushing at Mr Goon's ankles.

Mr Goon gave a sickly smile, and tried to push him away. 'Bingo,' said Ern, suddenly, in a stern voice. 'Stop that! SIT!'

And Bingo meekly sat down at once, though he still looked longingly at Mr Goon's ankles!

'Ha – well-trained dog that,' said Mr Goon, surprised. 'Er – I'll be quite pleased to have him back again, Ern. Bring him with you when you come.'

There was another awkward and astonished silence. Ern broke it. 'Do you really want me to come back, Uncle – and Bingo here, too? He's not a bad dog, just a bit excitable at times, but he's not much more than a pup.'

'Oh, he's a fine dog,' said Mr Goon, in a hearty voice. 'Very fine. Obedient, too. My word, he must have scared that old banshee! Ha ha ha!'

Nobody else laughed. They were all still a bit wary of their old enemy.

'Of course, you know,' said Goon, 'that banshee business is a bit of a fraud. The sort of thing that Frederick would make a lot of. It's said to wail, I know, but *I've* never heard it whenever I've been near the Towers! Ho ho – I bet it wouldn't dare to raise its voice if it saw *me* anywhere near!'

'Well, *we* heard it all right,' said Bets. 'It sounded like – oh, let me see . . . like . . .'

And then, from outside the window, came a little wail. Just a very little one at first. Then it became louder and pitched higher in tone, and soon the little room was full of the most heart-rending, eerie wailing that Goon had ever heard. Bets jumped at first – but she and the others knew at once that it was only old Fatty showing the disbelieving Mr Goon what a banshee's wail was like!

'Pretend to be scared!' whispered Larry to the others – and at once they clutched one another, and looked so frightened that Mr Goon felt as if *he* wanted to clutch at somebody too!

Bingo was terrified, and rushed round the room, yelping at the top of his voice, trying to find where the weird noise was coming from. What with the wailing and the barking, and everyone's frightened looks, Mr Goon was scared out of his life.

'Eeee-oooooooo-oh-oh-oh, eeeeeeeeeeeeee!' wailed Fatty, enjoying himself thoroughly outside the window. Buster began to yelp as soon as he heard Bingo barking, and when Fatty began another set of wails, Mr Goon could stand it no longer.

'I'll get help!' he panted. 'Someone's in danger!' And out of the door he rushed, and up the garden.

It was most unfortunate that Fatty's mother and the old cook were picking early daffodils in the garden just then. They heard the wailing too, and stood upright at once, listening in fright.

'One of the children has been hurt!' said Mrs Trotteville. 'Oh, what terrible screams and wails! Quick, we must see what's the matter.'

So down to the shed they rushed at top speed, just as Mr Goon was racing up the path as if wild tigers were after him! They met at a corner, and Mr Goon was knocked flying by the plump cook. He sat down heavily in a bed of mint, looking most astonished.

'What's happened, what's happened?' cried Mrs Trotteville. 'Has the shed stove fallen over? Has there been an accident?'

But Mr Goon had no breath to reply. He just went on sitting in the mint, panting loudly, hoping that a banshee wouldn't suddenly appear before him. Poor Mr Goon!

Mrs Trotteville and the cook ran to the shed, feeling very anxious indeed. But what in the world was this noise they heard *now*? No wailing – but shrieks of laughter!

'Ha ha ha ha! Oh, I never thought Mr Goon could run like that!'

'Ho ho ho! Good old banshee!'

'Ha ha, ho ho, he he, ho ho . . .' The laughter

went on and on, and didn't stop even when Mrs Trotteville walked into the shed, and gazed round at everyone in indignation.

They had all collapsed into chairs or on the floor. Fatty had climbed back into the room through the window, and was wiping tears from his eyes. He had no breath left to be a wailing banshee any longer! Buster and Bingo had gone completely mad and were barking and tearing round and round the room non-stop.

'FREDERICK! WHAT IS ALL THIS?' demanded Mrs Trotteville in a very cross voice indeed. She poked at Fatty with a hard forefinger, as he lay collapsed in a chair.

'Oh, Mummy, don't. You know I'm ticklish,' said Fatty. 'Mummy, I was only being a banshee. Why are you so cross? It's not against the law to wail like a banshee, is it?' And off he went again into another roar of laughter.

'I shall fetch your father,' said his mother, astounded at Fatty's behaviour. 'I really do not know what has come over you all – or Mr Goon either!'

'Mr Goon – what's he doing that's upset

you, Mother?' asked Fatty at once.

'He's sitting down in the very middle of my mint bed, if you want to know,' said his mother. 'And serve him right too – rushing straight into us like that.'

'Sitting down in the *mint* bed, Mummy! Oh, this is too good to be true!' said Fatty. 'Mummy, do you mean to say you pushed him over? – oh, Mummy, you'll be put into prison if you do things like that. Poor, poor Mr Goon – he'll smell of mint for weeks!'

'Oh, Fatty, please don't make *me* laugh, too,' said his mother, feeling a sudden desire to join in the merriment. 'I don't know *what* to do with you, Fatty. You're a bad lot. Go and help Mr Goon out of my mint bed. I'm sure the poor man is still there!'

Yes – there he is, listening in amazement to the laughter coming from Fatty's shed!

'What's happening now? How is it something *always* happens when that boy is about?' he grunts. 'Pooh, what a smell of mint! One of these days, Frederick Trotteville, I'll get the better of you! You see if I don't!'

Well, we'll see next time there's a mystery to solve, Mr Goon. But don't be too sure of yourself, will you? You just NEVER know what old Fatty is up to!

THE MYSTERY OF THE MISSING MAN

OTHER ENID BLYTON COLLECTIONS

The Magic Faraway Tree Collection

The Wishing-Chair Collection

The O'Clock Tales

The Magic Folk Collection

St Clare's: The First Year

The Early Years at Malory Towers

The Chimney Corner Collection

CONTENTS

1. FATTY'S NEWS

'I'm going to buy some Easter eggs,' said Pip, at breakfast-time. 'Are you coming too, Bets? Then we might go and call on old Fatty.'

'Oh yes – let's!' said Bets. 'I've only seen him once since he came back from school, and then he was with Mrs Trotteville and we couldn't say much.'

'We'll call in and tell Larry and Daisy to come too,' said Pip. 'We might go and have buns and coffee at the café. Mummy, do you want anything in the village?'

'No, unless you'd like to buy yourself an alarm clock,' said Mrs Hilton, buttering her toast. Pip stared.

'What for?' he said. 'I've got a watch.'

Bets giggled. 'You mean he might get up in time for breakfast then, Mummy!' she said.

'Ha! Funny joke,' said Pip. 'Anyway, no alarm clock would wake *me* if I'm really asleep. Besides,

1

Mummy – I've only just come back from a very, very hard term's work, and as for the exams last week, well I bet *you* wouldn't get top marks any more than I shall. I've not slept well for weeks, worrying about my marks.'

'I suppose that means that you'll be somewhere near the bottom again,' said Pip's father, putting down his morning paper for a moment. 'Well, we shall know the worst in a few days' time when your report comes.'

Pip changed the subject quickly – a trick which he was very good at. 'Dad, what do you want for Easter?' he asked. 'I did think of getting you a new wallet – and Mummy, I suppose you wouldn't like a marzipan egg, would you? I know you like marzipan, and . . .'

The trick worked. Both his parents had to smile. His mother tapped him on the hand. 'All right, all right, we won't mention reports till after Easter. And yes, I *do* like marzipan. Now, do you want to finish the toast? – because, if so, I'll leave you to it. Bets, remember to make your bed and dust your room before you go out. AND – please don't forget that dinner is at one o'clock *sharp*.'

The telephone rang as Mrs Hilton left the table. She went into the hall to answer it and called back into the room almost at once.

'It's Fatty – he wants to speak to one of you. You go, Bets, you've finished your meal.'

Bets flew to the telephone. 'Hello! Hello, Fatty!'

'Hello, little Bets!' said a warm, lively voice on the telephone. 'What about meeting somewhere this morning? I've got a spot of Easter shopping to do.'

'Oh *yes*, Fatty!' said Bets, eagerly. 'Pip and I were just thinking the same. Let's meet at the café, shall we – for buns and coffee? Say at quarter to eleven.'

'Right,' said Fatty. 'Will you tell Larry and Daisy, or shall I?'

'We will,' said Bets. 'Have you got any news, Fatty? Anything exciting happening?'

She heard Fatty's laugh at the other end of the phone. 'What do you mean? You surely don't think I've got a mystery up my sleeve already? Not a hope! As a matter of fact, I'm rather fed-up about something. Tell you when I see you. So long!'

Bets put down her receiver, and went to tell Pip. He was eating the last piece of toast and was alone in the room. 'My word!' said Bets, eyeing the toast, 'I never in my life saw so much marmalade spread on a small bit of toast.'

'Oh, shut up,' said Pip. 'You wait till you go to boarding-school – you'll know how nice it is to get home and not have to share the marmalade with about twenty others at your table. What did Fatty say?'

Bets told him. 'Fine!' said Pip. 'Well, you hurry up and make our beds, and . . .'

'You jolly well make your own,' said Bets, indignantly, and went out of the room. She went up the stairs two at a time, feeling happy. Holidays were good – she wasn't all alone then, the only one going to a day-school. All five of them were together – and Buster, Fatty's little Scottie too – that made six.

Pip and Bets called for Larry and Daisy at half past ten, and all four made their way to the village and went to their favourite little café. Fatty wasn't there yet, so they sat down and ordered currant buns with butter, and hot coffee. 'With plenty of milk,' said Larry, 'and you needn't put in the sugar. We'll help ourselves.'

Fatty was five minutes late. He arrived on his bicycle, with Buster running beside the pedals. He came in, grinning as usual, and swung Bets out of her chair and up in the air. Then he put her down with a groan.

'No, I won't be able to do that much longer, Bets. You're growing too big! My word, you're a weight.' Fatty helped himself to a bun. Then he sobered up and looked thoughtful. 'I've sworn to get fit these hols,' he said. 'I can smash tennis balls over the net all right, and place them as cunningly as the next man – and I can take a cannon-ball service without blinking an eyelid – but it's this running about the court that gets me. I puff like an old man.'

'Well, you'll just *have* to practice then, Fatty,' said Bets, feeling very sympathetic. 'We'll all help you.'

'I'm going to do cross-country running each day – or I might do it at night, when there's not so much traffic,' said Fatty. 'You've seen guys tearing along all by themselves in white shorts and singlets, haven't you? Grim and aloof and determined. Well, *I* shall be grim and aloof and determined.'

'Fatty, you said on the telephone this morning that you were fed-up about something,' said Bets, remembering. 'What did you mean?'

'Oh, yes,' said Fatty, absentmindedly helping himself to a lump of sugar from the basin. 'Well, it's this – there's some kind of peculiar conference going to be held here in Peterswood after Easter – next week, I think – and one of the members is going to stay with us – he's a friend of my father – he went to school with him or something.'

'Well – but why are you fed-up about *that*?' asked Larry. 'You won't need to entertain him, surely? He'll be some old fogey who spends his days at the conference, won't he?'

'Oh yes, but he's bringing his awful *daughter*,' said Fatty. 'At least, I've never seen her, but I bet she'll be awful. Mummy says she's an only child, and that her mother died when she was two, so she's been brought up by her father. And *I'm* supposed to entertain her.'

There was a horrified silence. 'Gosh!' said Pip at last. 'That *is* bad news. Either we've got to do without your company these hols, Fatty – or you've got to bring the girl with you wherever we go.'

'That's just about it,' said Fatty, gloomily, and took another bun.

'When's this girl coming?' asked Bets. 'I do think it's too bad, Fatty. Why should *you* have to entertain her? Why can't your mother?'

'Well, you know how busy my mother is, with committees and things,' said Fatty. 'She rushed off to something or other this morning and said, "Well, Frederick, I know I can depend on you to make Eunice feel at home – and don't forget to meet her and her father on the eleven-fifty train . . ."'

'*Eunice*!' said Daisy. 'Goodness, what an unusual name. But, look at the clock, Fatty – you won't be in time to meet them – it's quarter to twelve already!'

'Oh, my goodness!' cried Fatty, leaping to his feet. 'I must go. No, it's all right. That clock's fast. What about you all coming with me to the station and seeing what our dear Eunice is like? Come on!'

They paid the bill hurriedly and went out of the little shop, all looking gloomy. Yes, no wonder Fatty felt fed-up. Blow Eunice – she would spoil everything!

2. EUNICE

They hurried up the road, and past the Town Hall. 'Look, that's where the conference is going to be,' said Larry, pointing to a large notice. 'Four meetings next week – and look, it says, "All Coleopterists are invited to attend". Whatever are Coleopterists?'

'Colly-what?' asked Bets. 'Fatty, what are these colly-people?'

'Owners of collie dogs?' suggested Pip. 'Or growers of cauliflowers?'

'Or sufferers from colly-wobbles?' said Daisy, with a laugh.

'Idiot,' said Fatty. 'They're ... hello, look out – here's Mr Goon on his bicycle.'

Mr Goon bore down on them, his uniform almost bursting at the seams. He was not at all pleased to see the Five, and even less pleased to see Buster, who immediately flew at his ankles. Goon glared at him.

'That dog!' he said in disgust. 'Call him off! So you're back again for the holidays, are you? Well, no meddling in what isn't your business, see? I'm going to be busy the next week or two, what with a Fair coming here, and that there conference of colly – colly – er . . .'

'Collie dog breeders?' suggested Fatty, innocently.

'Oh, so that's what they are, is it?' said Goon, with displeasure. 'Bringing a whole lot of dogs with them then, I shouldn't wonder. Dogs! As if we hadn't got enough running about in this town! You'd better keep that dog of yours on the lead, if there's collie dogs wandering about,' he said. 'Vicious, some of them are – and they'd make mincemeat of that dog of yours.'

And away sailed Goon on his bicycle, feeling very pleased at having ticked off the five children. Buster sent a volley of barks after him.

'Don't say such rude things, Buster,' said Fatty, gravely. 'Remember that other dogs are listening.'

Bets giggled. 'Oh, Fatty, whatever made you tell Mr Goon about Pip's silly idea of collie dog breeders? He'll be watching out for collie dogs everywhere!'

'Anyway, what *are* Coleopterists?' asked

Daisy. 'Don't you know, Fatty! I thought you knew everything.'

'Of course I know,' said Fatty, wheeling his bicycle along more quickly, as he caught sight of a clock. 'Coleopterists are lovers of beetles.'

This announcement was greeted with exclamations of utter disbelief.

'Liar! Nobody loves beetles! Ugh!'

'Fatty, we're not as stupid as Mr Goon.'

'Think of something better than that, Fatty!'

'All right, all right,' said Fatty, amiably. 'I can think of plenty of things. But that happens to be the truth.'

'As if anyone would hold a conference about beetles!' said Pip, scornfully. 'I'll ask your father's friend about it!'

'Right. You ask him,' said Fatty. 'Hey, that was the train whistling – hurry up. My mother will be furious if I'm late meeting Mr Tolling and his dear little Eunice.'

'How old is she?' panted Bets, trying to keep up with Fatty.

'I don't know,' said Fatty. 'You'll soon see. Here we are – just in time. Phew! Watch my bike for me,

Pip – I'll go on to the platform and meet father and daughter!'

He flung his bicycle against the station wall and ran inside hurriedly as the train pulled in to a standstill, the engine humming in a way that Buster could not bear.

Fatty smoothed back his hair and waited to see whether a man and a girl got out of the train. He soon saw a very small man with a dark beard and large glasses fussing over two suitcases. With him was a girl, rather taller than the man – a stout, rather shapeless girl with two very long plaits hanging down her back. She wore school clothes – a dark blue belted overcoat, and a dark blue felt hat with a coloured band and a badge on the left-hand side.

Her loud, clear voice came to Fatty as he stood waiting. 'No Dad, we don't need a porter – you can take your small case and I'll carry the large one. We're sure to be able to get a taxi.'

'Where did I put the tickets?' said her father, diving into one pocket after another.

'You gave them to me,' said the girl in her clear, competent voice. Fatty felt horrified. Was this hefty, bossy girl going to be his constant companion for at least a week? He watched her take the tickets out of a strong leather purse, and then put it safely away again. She looked all round.

'Wasn't somebody going to meet us?' she said. 'Well, I do think . . .'

Fatty didn't know what she was about to say, as he rushed up to the two of them, but he could guess. He smiled politely.

'Er, are you Mr Belling, sir? I'm . . .'

'No, my name's not Belling,' said the small, bearded man. 'It's Tolling.'

'Oh gosh – sorry,' said Fatty, who had quite honestly made a slip. 'I suppose – er – well – bells toll, you know, so I . . .'

'It's all right,' said the girl. 'I'm used to that silly joke, but my father isn't – so don't address him as Mr Belling, or Jingling, or Tingling – he just won't understand, and it's such a waste of time explaining to him what it means.'

Fatty was quite taken aback. 'Er – I'm Frederick Trotteville,' he said, and put out his hand to take the suitcase from Mr Tolling.

'Well, if I wanted to be funny, like you, I'd

address you as Frederick *Canter*ville,' said the girl, and gave him a sudden grin. 'No, don't take my suitcase, I can manage it, thanks. But be careful of Dad's case – it's full of beetles!'

Fatty looked down at it anxiously and was relieved to see that it was well strapped. He didn't fancy the idea of dead beetles spilling over the platform.

'I'll get you a taxi,' he said.

'Put *Dad* into a taxi with his beetles,' said the girl. 'By the way, I'm Eunice – Eunice Tolling, *not* Belling. I don't want to go in the taxi – they make me car-sick. I'd rather walk, if it's all the same to you. You can put this other suitcase into the taxi too.'

'Yes, Mam,' said Fatty, feeling as if he were under orders. He called the one and only taxi there and helped Mr Tolling into it. He insisted on having his beetle suitcase on his knees. Fatty put the second one on the floor, and then gave the driver his address. The taxi sped out of the station and Eunice heaved a sigh of relief.

'Well, that's Dad safely settled,' she said. 'What time is it – about twelve? Is there anywhere near for me to have a bun or something? I'm famished. We had breakfast at seven o'clock.'

'Er – well, yes,' said Fatty, and caught sight of the other four grinning at him nearby. 'Wait a minute, though, please. I want to introduce you to four friends of mine – Larry, Pip, Daisy – and Bets.'

'Hello,' said Eunice and gave them all a swift look. 'And I suppose this Scottie is your dog? He keeps on getting under my feet – can you make him walk to heel?'

'Heel, Buster,' said Fatty, in a strangled sort of voice, in the midst of a dead silence. Buster obediently came to heel and sat down, looking rather surprised. Not one of the others could find a word to say. They simply stared at Eunice, and then fell in behind her and Fatty, looking at one another slyly. What a girl!

'Er – Eunice wants something to eat,' Fatty informed the others behind him. 'Pity we've just had our elevenses. Where shall we take her?'

'There's a tea shop or something over there, look,' said Eunice, pointing to a rather expensive coffee shop which the children did not as a rule go to, because of the very high prices.

'That's too expensive for us,' said Daisy. 'They charge a fortune just for . . .'

'Oh well, *I'll* pay,' said Eunice. 'I must say I like the look of those chocolate éclairs. Come on, I'll pay for you all.'

'Well, we've just *had* buns and coffee,' said Daisy. 'We don't want any more to eat. And Fatty was with us.'

'Who's Fatty?' asked Eunice in surprise. 'Oh, you mean *Frederick*. How rude! If that's his nickname, I won't use it. Frederick, I shall call you by your proper name, if you don't mind.'

'Er – no, I don't mind,' said Fatty, signalling to the others to go away and leave them. He felt that he might be able to manage this awful girl better by himself without the others staring and giggling.

'Well, we'd better go,' said Larry, reluctantly. This girl was dreadful, but it really was fascinating to see how she treated Fatty. Why, he had hardly got a word in! And to think she was going to stay in his home!

'So long,' said Fatty curtly, and jerked his head violently to make the others understand that he wasn't going to put up with them a minute longer. Grinning at him like that!

They stood and watched Fatty and Eunice going through the shop door and finding a table. They gazed while Eunice signalled to a waitress and gave a lengthy order. They watched two plates of cakes and pastries being brought, and what looked like a cup of frothy drinking chocolate – yes, and one for Fatty too!

Eunice was talking nineteen to the dozen! She could talk and eat at the same time, which was bad manners, but very interesting to watch. Fatty looked thoroughly miserable. He kept trying to interrupt, but Eunice was like a steamroller – and her conversation rolled over him without a stop.

'Poor old Fatty – fancy having to sit and listen to that awful girl all the time,' said Bets, sympathetically.

Fatty couldn't bear to sit there in dead silence and watch Eunice devour all the pastries. If he could have talked himself, and aired his opinions as he generally did, it wouldn't have been so bad. In self-defence he took an éclair – and another – and another.

'Oh, *Fatty*!' said Daisy, still gazing through the window. She turned to the others. 'Come on, let's go. If he catches sight of us, he'll be furious. We'd better go home.'

Sadly they went down the road. Bets was almost in tears. 'It wouldn't have been *quite* so bad if Eunice had been nice,' she said. 'But how CAN we let her go about with us? – and yet we can't desert poor Fatty and leave him alone with Eunice all the time. It really *is* a problem!'

3. FATTY ESCAPES

Larry and Daisy went to tea with Pip and Bets that afternoon. Not a word had come from Fatty, not even a telephone call. But, in the middle of tea, they heard someone coming up the drive.

Bets flew to the window. 'It's Fatty!' she said. 'Fatty – in white shorts and singlet and running shoes! He's panting like anything. I suppose he's trying to work off all those éclairs!'

Pip yelled out of the window. 'Come on up to the playroom. We're having tea.'

Fatty went in at the garden door and ran panting into the hall. He met Mrs Hilton coming out of the drawing-room with a friend. She gave a scream.

'Good gracious – what ....! Oh, it's you, Frederick. Have you come to tea in *that* get-up? Well, really!'

'Sorry, Mrs Hilton, I'm just doing a little

cross-country running – in training, you know,'
panted Fatty, and escaped thankfully up the stairs.
The others were waiting for him eagerly. Bets gave
him a hug.

'Oh, you're soaking wet,' she said. 'Is it raining?'

'No. I'm just hot with running,' said Fatty, and
sank with a groan into a comfortable chair.

'I thought you weren't going to start till after
Easter,' said Daisy.

'I wasn't. But I HAD to get away from Eunice
somehow!' groaned Fatty. 'And this was the best
excuse I could think of. She talks non-stop – she
lays down the law to me – to ME, imagine that!
And she follows me about wherever I go. She even
came knocking at my bedroom door this afternoon
to borrow a book – and then she sat herself down
by my bookcase and wouldn't *go*.'

'You should have *pushed* her out!' said
Bets, indignantly.

'I should think that if it came to pushing, Eunice
might send old Fatty flying,' said Larry. 'She's . . .'

'Oh well – if you're going to make insulting
remarks like that, I'm going,' said Fatty, quite
huffily, and got up. Daisy pushed him down again.

'You *are* touchy!' she said. 'Don't you let that girl get under your skin! You tell her a few things.'

'I would, if she'd stop to listen,' said Fatty. 'Hey, is that tea I see on the table? I'm so thirsty I could drink the whole teapotful.'

'You'll only put back all the weight you've lost from your running,' said Daisy. 'Still, you'll have to feed yourself up if you've got to cope with Eunice for a week! Pass him the chocolate biscuits, Pip.'

'I shouldn't be weak enough to take these,' groaned poor Fatty, taking three. 'I know I shouldn't. But, honestly, I shall be worn out in a few days – I shall be a shadow of myself.'

'That's what I said,' agreed Daisy, pouring him out a milky cup of tea and putting three lumps of sugar in it. 'But Fatty, seriously – what *are* we going to do about Eunice?'

'Don't ask *me*!' said Fatty, nibbling at a biscuit with enjoyment. 'The worst of it is, Mummy *likes* her!'

There was a surprised silence.

'But why?' said Daisy at last. 'Mothers do sometimes like children we don't like, we all know that – we have to ask them to our parties! But how *can* your mother like Eunice?'

'She says she's so sensible and reliable and helpful,' explained Fatty. 'She unpacked the big suitcase and put everything away neatly in the drawers of their two rooms – and then she went to the kitchen and asked Jane to be sure and not move her father's beetle case, not even to dust it . . .'

'What did Jane say to that?' asked Pip, with interest. Jane was not at all friendly towards beetles, spiders or moths.

'Oh, she went up in the air at first, thinking the beetles were live ones, but she calmed down when she heard they were dead,' said Fatty, with a laugh. 'And then Eunice went back to Mummy and asked her the times of every meal, so that she could be sure that her father was punctual – and she offered to make her bed each day and her father's, and to do the rooms too, if it wouldn't upset Jane.'

'Gosh, what a girl!' said Larry. 'I can't see *Daisy* doing all that. No wonder your mother likes Eunice.'

'She thinks she's the cat's whiskers, *and* the cat's

tail too,' said Fatty, absentmindedly taking a slice of cake. 'She says Eunice has the most beautiful manners, and will be *so* nice to have in the house, and is *so* sweet to her father, and . . .'

'Well, if your mother's so keen on her, perhaps they'll pal up together after all, and you'll be free to be with us,' said Pip, cheering up.

'Not a bit of it,' said Fatty. 'Mummy kept saying how nice it was for *me* to have a girl in the house, as I'd no sister, and all that sort of thing. And how we could do things together – go for walks – and go to the Fair when it comes – and I could show Eunice my shed at the bottom of the garden – fancy showing *her* that! I was furious when Mummy even *mentioned* my shed. I was planning to keep it as a sort of hideaway when I couldn't stand Eunice a minute longer.'

Fatty paused for breath. The others looked at him with great sympathy. Usually Fatty never turned a hair, thought Larry – not a hair – whatever happened. 'Did you put on that get-up and go out running to get away from Eunice?' he asked, with a grin.

'You know I did,' said Fatty. 'I waited till Eunice

was telling Mummy all about the goals she shot last term in hockey and then I murmured something about getting a bit of training done, shot upstairs, and put on these things, and went out of the garden door like a streak of lightning.'

'Let's hope Eunice doesn't think of trotting along with you,' said Larry, with a grin. 'It might occur to her to train too!'

'Don't *suggest* such a thing!' said Fatty, in horror.

'Well, what are we all going to do about it?' asked Daisy. 'It's quite clear that we can't leave you to Eunice, Fatty – you'll be as limp as a rag before Easter is over. Let's see, it's Easter Sunday tomorrow. Then Easter Monday – we could all go to the Fair together, couldn't we?'

'We could,' said Fatty, looking pleased. 'It's really decent of you to let that awful girl inflict herself on you – but it will just about save my life! I'll *have* to put up with her tomorrow, but I'll arrange something for Easter Monday.'

'When does the beetle conference begin?' asked Pip. 'Tuesday?'

'Yes,' said Fatty. 'And Mr Belling – I mean Tolling – has asked me to go! He has given me a ticket to take me to every single meeting if I want to go. Imagine me sitting there listening to beetle-talk!'

'Won't Eunice go?' asked Larry.

'No. She says she knows all she wants to know about beetles – and I believe her!' said Fatty. 'I think she must know as much as her father – she helps him with his specimens.'

'Ugh!' said Bets, and shivered. 'I don't mind beetles when they're ladybirds, or those dear little violet ones that scurry through the grass . . .'

'I don't mind beetles at *all*,' said Pip. 'But I don't want to be a colly – er – colly – what was it?'

'Coleopterist,' said Fatty. 'Ha! You didn't believe me when I told you they were beetle-lovers! I've a good mind to go to one of the meetings just to see what a collection of beetle-lovers is like.'

'I thought Eunice's father looked rather like a little black beetle himself,' said Bets. 'Quite a *nice* one – rather helpless, you know – as if he might lose his way if he ran through the blades of grass . . .'

The others laughed. A bell rang loudly just then, and Fatty sat up straight. 'The telephone! If that's Eunice, you're not to say I'm here – OK?'

But it was Mrs Hilton who answered the phone, and then called up the stairs.

'Frederick, that was someone called Eunice Tolling,' she said. 'Frederick, are you there? Eunice wants to speak to you.'

But Fatty was at that very moment climbing down the tree outside the playroom window. 'Tell your mother I've gone – she *must* say that or Eunice will come along here,' he hissed.

'Fatty's left, Mummy,' called Bets. 'He's just gone home.'

'Well I thought I heard his voice just a minute ago,' said her mother, surprised. 'He must have left very suddenly!'

'He did,' admitted Bets with a chuckle, and went back to the playroom before any more awkward questions could be asked. She ran to the window. She could just see Fatty speeding out of the front gate.

'Poor old Fatty!' she said, watching him. 'It's the first time anyone has ever got the better of him. Well, I expect it will come to a stand-up fight, sooner or later!'

Fatty trotted round Peterswood Village, in

no hurry to get back home. Could he slip in the kitchen door? Eunice might be keeping an ear open for the garden door!

He circled his house and garden, and went in at the little gate that led out from the very bottom of the garden into the lane. His shed was near there, and he would make sure that it was well and truly locked as he passed. It would never do to let Eunice pry into all his secrets there. Then he would slip through the garden and up to the kitchen door and get in that way.

He looked at his shed as he passed, and tried the door. Yes, it was locked – and nobody but him knew where the key was. Good. Now, was it safe to go into the house?

He crept up the path to the kitchen door, and listened outside. He could hear the kitchen radio going. Good, Jane and Cookie were there – he could easily slip through and upstairs. They never minded!

He opened the door quietly, went through the scullery and into the comfortable kitchen. To his utter horror, Eunice was there, doing some ironing and talking to the two maids. She looked up in surprise as he came creeping in.

'Oh, it's you! Why did you go out running without telling me? I'd have liked to come with you – I'm a very good runner. Don't go alone another time, I'll keep you company, Frederick! Please don't be afraid of asking me – I'm willing to do anything for you, it's so kind of your mother to have us here like this!'

'Er – I'll just go and change,' said poor Fatty, quite horrified, and fled before Eunice could say another word. Have her with him when he went running? Good gracious, what a truly horrible idea!

4. THE DIRTY OLD TRAMP

Easter Sunday was a glorious day. The Trotteville family and the Tollings went to church, and Fatty reflected that at least Eunice couldn't talk at church. Unfortunately she could sing though, and almost deafened Fatty who had to sit next to her.

He was also very much embarrassed because of the surprised looks of the congregation at this unexpected addition to their singing powers. Everyone seemed to be turning round and staring. Very bad manners, thought Fatty severely – but Eunice loved it, and sang serenely and powerfully on, basking in the stares of the people around her.

Fatty cast about in his mind to think how to get rid of Eunice that afternoon. He knew that his mother and father – and probably Mr Tolling – would retire to have a nap. Could he say that he wanted to work? No, his father would certainly not believe that. Could he say he was tired and wanted to go and rest?

'No! Mummy will feel my head and see if it's hot, and think I'm sickening for something,' groaned Fatty. 'I think I'll go down to my shed. I won't tell Eunice. I'll just slip off down there. I'll take my book, and I might perhaps practise a bit of disguising. I haven't done any for ages, not since I went back to school last term.'

Fatty waited until the grown-ups had retired to have a nap. Eunice was busy writing a letter. Fatty sat as quiet as a mouse in a corner, hoping that she wouldn't notice if he slipped out. But as soon as he stood up quietly, she lifted her head and swung back her long plaits.

'Where are you going, Frederick?' she asked. 'I won't be long finishing this letter, then we'll have a walk or a game of something.'

Fatty saw a ray of hope. 'I'll take your letter to the post for you,' he said. 'Chuck it across when it's finished. There are two of Mummy's I'm going to take.'

'Oh, thanks – if it's not a bother to you,' said the ever-polite Eunice and went on scribbling.

With relief, Fatty saw her blot the letter, put it into an envelope, address it and stamp it. He got up at once.

'Thanks,' said Eunice. 'I'll think about something for us to do, while you're gone.'

Fatty shot out of the room and out of the garden door. He shut it firmly behind him. He was *not* going back through that door for quite a long time – he was going down to his shed when he came back from the post – and there he was going to stay!

He ran to the post, and then circled the house and garden till he came to the little gate again at the very bottom. He slid through it, shut it, and made his way cautiously to his shed. Really! he thought, it's disgraceful to think I've got to skulk about in my own garden like this!

He unlocked his shed door and went in. He locked it again, and sat down with a sigh of relief. Now he could be alone till teatime at any rate – and if he could be really stern with himself, he could miss tea, and not go indoors until the evening meal. I could say I missed tea because I'm slimming, thought Fatty.

He began to pull open the drawers of the old

chest he had there, looking at his store of disguises
– dirty old coats and trousers, torn pullovers and
cardigans – a butcher's boy outfit – a telegram
boy's suit – and an old skirt and shawl and blouse
that he had used when he had last pretended to be
a gypsy woman!

He thought about Eunice as he examined
everything. He began to have an uneasy feeling
that she would not sit down quietly and wait for
hours for him to return from posting the letters.
She would smell a rat! She might even go and look
for him!

And if she asks Mummy or Jane where I could
be, they'll very likely say I'm down here! thought
Fatty in sudden horror. Gosh – I never thought of
that! I'd better dress myself up in something – some
disguise, in case Eunice comes snooping along to
my shed. I will NOT have her in here, pulling open
the drawers, and messing about with all my things.

He decided that it would be easiest to make up
as an old man. He had a wig and beard, and it was
easy to paint wrinkles. He could slip on the dirty
old flannel trousers hanging on the nail, and put on
a ragged old mackintosh.

It didn't take Fatty very long, and he really enjoyed himself. He peered at his face in the mirror when it was complete with beard, moustache and wig. He drew very thick eyebrows, and grinned at himself.

'You do look a rogue!' he said. 'I shouldn't like to meet *you* in the dark!'

He put on the old trousers and the mackintosh, and actually put an old pipe into his mouth to complete the disguise. Fatty never left out any details if he could help it.

Then, chewing on the pipe, he sat down in the old chair there to read a book. He sighed with relief. Now he would have at least two hours' peace – and more if he could stop himself from going in to tea.

He grinned when he thought of Eunice sitting waiting for him, thinking up all kinds of plans, wondering why he didn't come back. Well, maybe she would be sensible and lie back in his mother's comfortable armchair and go to sleep – if she ever *did* go to sleep. Fatty felt it was very doubtful that she ever *really* slept soundly – she probably slept like Buster, with one ear open.

He suddenly remembered that Buster was still shut up in his bedroom. Blow! Why hadn't he gone and fetched him before he went to the post? Now Buster might begin to whine and bark, and wake everyone up!

That was exactly what Buster did do. He waited patiently in his basket up in Fatty's bedroom for some time. He heard Fatty going out to the post, and he waited with ears pricked to hear him come back.

But Fatty didn't come back. He had gone to his shed. Buster grew anxious and impatient. He whined very softly. Then he barked – not a very loud bark, for Buster was sensible enough to know what Sunday naps were, and the house was full of Sunday – he knew that!

He ran to the door and scraped at it, whining again. Then he gave a sharp bark.

Someone came up the stairs at once. It was Eunice, of course. She, too, had waited and waited for Fatty to come back, and was beginning to feel annoyed. She liked Fatty very much, and felt that she had made a great impression on him. He was not rude and snappy to her as so many other boys had been.

Eunice had heard the whining and barking, and had been afraid that the sleepers upstairs would awake. That's Buster! she thought. I'd better go and quieten him. I do wonder where Fatty is – it's too bad of him to be so long.

She stood outside Fatty's door and knocked gently. Buster answered by an eager little whine. He didn't like this girl Eunice very much, but he was quite willing for her to let him out of the bedroom. Then he would go and find Fatty!

Eunice opened the door and grabbed Buster as he squeezed out. 'Sh!' she said. 'Don't bark. Bad dog! You mustn't make a noise.'

Buster was so surprised to hear himself being called a bad dog that he stopped and looked at Eunice to see if she really meant it. She took hold of his collar, looked into the room, saw his lead and slipped it on.

Buster was very cross. How dare this girl put him on the lead when he wanted to go and find Fatty!

'Come on,' whispered Eunice. 'I'll take you for a run round the garden till Frederick comes back! Hush now!'

With a protesting whine, Buster allowed himself to be taken downstairs and out of the garden door. All right, he would soon find Fatty! He was sure he could smell him somewhere!

To his annoyance, he could not get away from Eunice. She had strong hands and no amount of pulling on Buster's part made any difference. She would not set him free!

Buster felt suddenly sure that Fatty was down in his shed. He dragged at the lead and pulled Eunice down the garden. There was the shed – and Buster flung himself on the door, barking. Wuff, wuff, wuff, wuff! Let me in! Wuff, wuff!

Fatty was pleased, and was just about to get up and let Buster in, when he heard Eunice's voice!

'Bad dog! Be quiet! You'll wake everyone up! The door's locked, so Frederick is not in there. Come away, I tell you!'

Fatty crouched down in a corner in horror. So that awful girl had tracked him down here – with Buster too! If he knew anything about Buster, he would bark the place down now that he knew Fatty was in the shed – as he most certainly did!

Buster proceeded to bark his head off! He yelped

and barked and scratched at the door, and even growled at Eunice when she tried to drag him away.

'There's nobody *in* there,' she kept saying. And then her voice suddenly changed. 'Or *is* there? Perhaps someone is hiding in Frederick's shed – someone who has no business to *be* there!'

Fatty crouched even further back as he saw Eunice's face peering through the window. 'Buster! I can see someone's foot!' he heard her say in an excited voice. 'I believe there *is* someone there!'

She went to the door and peered through the keyhole – and immediately opposite her, she saw what she took to be a dirty old tramp, smoking a pipe. She gave a loud scream!

'What are you doing in there? Come out at once, or I'll set this dog on you!' she yelled.

Fatty was simply horrified. He couldn't *imagine* what to do! And then Eunice spotted someone walking along the lane nearby, and shouted loudly once more.

'Help! Help! There's someone hiding in this shed. Help!'

Then, to Fatty's utter horror, he heard Mr Goon's voice. Mr *Goon*! What bad luck that his beat should have led him there just at that time.

The policeman lost no time in coming in through the gate. 'What is it, Miss? Who's in there?' he asked. 'Keep that dog off me, please!'

'Look inside that shed,' said Eunice. 'There's a horrible old tramp there – smoking! He may set the place on fire!'

Goon peered through the keyhole and made out the dirty figure crouching in a corner. Then Buster suddenly went quite mad and ran at the policeman's ankles.

'*Keep* that dog off me, will you!' shouted Goon, commandingly. 'And you in there – you come out! This is private property, this is!'

There was nothing for it but to come out. Fatty had no wish for Goon to break down the door, as he quite meant to do. All right, he would unlock the door and make a dash for it and trust Buster to keep Goon away!

5. TWO EXAGGERATORS

'Oi'm a-comin', Oi'm a-comin',' croaked Fatty, stumbling to the door. 'Keep that dog off me!'

'Here, girl – let the dog pounce on the fellow when he comes out,' ordered Goon. 'He'll catch him for us and make things easy. Look out, now, he's unlocking the door – the sauce of it, locking himself in like that!'

The door opened very suddenly indeed, and the old man inside rushed out. He lunged at Goon and almost bowled him over, big as he was.

'Buster, go for him, go for him!' cried Eunice in excitement. 'Get him – he's a tramp, he's no business there. Catch him!'

Buster, mad with excitement at seeing Fatty again, leapt all round him in delight, barking loudly. Eunice and Goon quite imagined that he was attacking the old man, and were surprised that the old fellow didn't yell for the dog to be called off.

'Hey, he's escaping!' cried Goon, as he realised that the tramp was halfway up the garden, the dog still barking round him. 'I'll go after him – you keep back, Miss, he's a dangerous fellow.'

But Fatty had too big a start and was now out of the front gate and racing for dear life down the road. Goon marvelled that an old man could run so fast.

By the time that Goon had got to the first corner, Fatty had entirely disappeared. He had run into the garden of the house there, gone right down to the bottom, leapt over the wall and made his way back once more to the little lane right at the bottom of his own garden. He and Buster stood there, panting and listening. Buster licked Fatty's hand feeling very happy.

'They've come back – they've gone into the house, Buster,' said Fatty at last. 'Now they'll wake up Dad and Mum and tell them fairy tales about an old thief of a tramp lying in my shed. Blow them!'

He slid into his shed, took his own clothes and slid out again, locking the shed behind him. He put the keys into his pocket. Then he crept up the garden to the kitchen door. He peered in at the window. Good – only Jane and Cookie were there, looking rather startled as they listened to something going on out in the hall.

That's Mr Goon and Eunice there, I suppose, thought Fatty, exasperated. Well, I *must* change out of these things somehow – but where? I daren't go in yet.'

He decided to change them under a tree, but first he peered in at the hall window to see what was going on. His father and mother and Mr Tolling were all there, and Mr Goon was trying in vain to get a word in – but Eunice was in full spate, describing at great length all that had happened.

'He was FIERCE, that tramp!' she cried. 'As strong as ten men, Mr Goon here said. Buster was very brave, he barked and bit – and the tramp kicked out at him like anything. Oh, if only Frederick had been there, this would never have happened. He would have turned that fellow out at once.'

'Here!' said Mr Goon, indignantly, breaking in at last. 'What do you mean? If *I* couldn't get him, nobody could. I tell you . . .'

'A-a-a-a-ah!' suddenly screamed Eunice and

pointed to the hall window, through which Fatty was peering, enjoying the whole scene. 'There's that tramp again. Quick, Mr Goon!'

Everyone raced out of the front door as Fatty neatly slipped in at the side door. He shot upstairs at top speed, and into his bedroom, with an excited Buster.

'Not a word, Buster,' he said. 'Not a bark, please. Just let me get changed!'

He stripped off the old clothes at top speed, and stuffed them into a cupboard. He cleaned his face, and removed whiskers, moustache and beard. Then he washed his hands and sank down into a chair with a sigh.

'Whew! What a joke, Buster! I wonder if they're all still chasing that old tramp. Disgusting old fellow, wasn't he? No wonder you barked at him!'

He sat and waited for a while but nobody came back, so he decided to go downstairs, and out into the road, and wait there. Then he would walk briskly up as if he had been out for a stroll, and pretend to be most surprised to see the others.

It all went off beautifully. Fatty strolled up with Buster just as a very disgruntled Goon came back with an equally disappointed Eunice, and a very annoyed trio of parents.

'What nonsense!' Mr Trotteville was saying. 'I don't believe there *was* any tramp there – just this girl's imagination! And you believed her, Goon! On a Sunday afternoon, too!'

Goon was red and angry, and Eunice was white-faced and furious, but had enough manners not to argue. They suddenly saw Fatty strolling along and shouted to him.

'Frederick! Where have you been?'

'You seen a nasty-looking tramp, Frederick?' asked Goon. 'Whiskers and all? He was down in your shed – smoking his pipe too. Might have set the place alight!'

'A tramp – with whiskers?' said Fatty, sounding extremely surprised. 'Where is he? Quick, I'll set Buster on him!'

'That dog's already *been* at him,' said Mr Goon, exasperated. 'Must have bit his trousers to pieces – barking and snarling. I wonder he's got any ankles left!'

'Well, Mr Goon, I think we'll not bother any more,' said Mr Trotteville, firmly. 'The man's gone and we can't do anything about it. Come in, Eunice – you can't do anything either.'

'What a thing to happen – on a Sunday too!' said Mr Tolling, looking rather white. 'A good thing you happened to be about, Constable. Tramps hiding in garden sheds! Was anything stolen?'

'We'll leave that to Frederick to find out,' said Mr Trotteville, beginning to look exasperated. 'Anyway, he only keeps a lot of rubbish there.'

Fatty said nothing to that. He was not at all anxious for his father to see what he *really* kept in his shed! All kinds of disguises, sets of grease-paints for making up his face, dreadful false teeth to wear over his own, cheekpads to alter the shape of his cheeks, false eyebrows, moustaches, beards – good gracious, Mr Trotteville would certainly have been amazed to find so many peculiar things!

'Frederick, perhaps we'd better go down to your shed and have a look round to see if that tramp took anything,' suggested Goon, who thought this might be a very good opportunity of seeing exactly what Fatty *did* keep in his shed. Goon had a shrewd idea of the contents, and it would have been a real feather in his cap if he could have poked round into every corner. Ha! He'd find a few of that boy's secrets then!

'Oh, I can easily look myself,' said Fatty. 'And I wouldn't dream of bothering you any further, Mr Goon. You go home and finish your Sunday nap.'

Goon went red. 'I'm on duty,' he said, 'and a good thing for you I was too! If I hadn't come by when I did, that there tramp might have stolen half your things and set your shed on fire!'

'I bet he wasn't smoking,' said Fatty, who knew quite well that he, Fatty, had only had an unlighted pipe in his mouth.

'You don't know anything about it!' said Eunice. '*I* saw him, not you – and he was smoking like a chimney – wasn't he, Constable?'

'That's right, Miss,' said Goon, thinking that Eunice was someone after his own heart, willing to exaggerate to make a story more exciting! 'A very nasty-looking piece of work, he looked – no wonder the dog went for him.'

'Good old Buster,' said Fatty, bending down to pat the little Scottie, and to hide a grin. Well, well, what a couple of exaggerators Goon and Eunice were! It was really a pity he couldn't tell them that *he* was the dirty old tramp!

The others had all gone indoors now, and Fatty decided that he had had enough of Goon and would go in too. He debated whether to bicycle up to Pip's and tell him about the tramp episode, but decided that he'd better not. Eunice might follow him there!

'Come on indoors,' he said to Eunice. 'It must be teatime by now.'

Eunice followed him in and, to Fatty's disgust, she insisted on telling him again and again how she had peered through the window and keyhole of his shed, and had spotted the tramp, and how she and Goon had gone for him when he came out.

'I don't know why you *wanted* to go and spy into my shed,' said Fatty at last, so tired of Eunice that he decided to be rude. Perhaps she would go off in a huff then. That would be fine.

'I was *not* spying!' she said angrily and, to Fatty's delight, took herself off at once. She marched out of the door and stamped up the stairs to her room. Fatty immediately shot out to the kitchen with Buster, collected some cakes and scones and biscuits from the tea tray, and raced off again.

Eunice won't come spying into my shed again today, he thought. I can take these down there and eat and read in peace. I only hope Mr Goon doesn't come snooping round. What a life – Eunice always about, and Mr Goon popping up whenever he's not wanted.

He let himself into his shed, locked the door behind him, and sat down. He found his book and began to munch. It was only when he had eaten two-thirds of what he had brought that he remembered he was slimming. And so, when Eunice, who seemed to have forgotten that she had been offended, suggested after supper that they should have a game of chess, Fatty mournfully shook his head.

'Nothing I'd like better than to beat you at chess, Eunice,' he said, 'but . . .'

'Beat me! You couldn't!' said Eunice. 'I'm champion chess player of my school!'

'How strange – so am I,' said Fatty, quite truthfully. 'But I'm now going for an hour's run down by the river and back.'

'What – in the dark?' said his mother. 'Really,

I think you are overdoing this running business, Frederick!'

Fatty thought so too – but the idea of a solemn evening playing chess with a fiercely-brooding Eunice was too much for him. Sorrowfully, he went off with Buster to change into running shorts, and was soon loping along by the quiet river, with Buster at his heels. What a life!

6. CHIEF INSPECTOR JENKS HAS SOMETHING TO SAY

On Easter Monday morning, just as Mr Goon was finishing a large breakfast of fried bacon and three eggs, a long shiny black car drew up outside his house. Mr Goon caught sight of it as he was about to attack his third egg, and his mouth fell open even wider.

The Inspector! Now what does he want with me this morning! thought Goon, and hurriedly did up his tunic and ran to brush his hair. He called to the housekeeper in the kitchen in his most urgent voice.

'Mrs Boggs! Ask whoever it is into the office, quick!' Just as he spoke, there came a peremptory knock at the front door, and Mrs Boggs flew to open it.

Outside stood a tall Inspector of Police – Chief Inspector Jenks – with keen sharp eyes and an impatient look about him. Mrs Boggs showed him

48

into the office. 'Mr Goon will be along at once, sir,' she said, and almost dropped a curtsey as she backed from the room.

Goon came in at once, looking much tidier. 'Good morning, sir,' he said. 'Er – this is an unexpected visit.'

'Goon,' said the Inspector, abruptly, 'there's a dangerous man somewhere in this district. An escaped prisoner, violent, and up to every trick there is. Known to be clever at disguises. Now, there's a Fair at Peterswood, a likely place for a fellow like this to make for. I want you to keep your eyes open and report to me at once if there's anyone you're in the least suspicious about. I'll send men over immediately to watch whoever you report on.'

Goon swelled up at once with importance. 'Yes, sir,' he said. 'Er – would it be a good idea to go to the Fair *out* of uniform, sir? You know I took a special course at the police school, sir – disguises and all that.'

'Well,' said the Chief, looking at Goon doubtfully, 'you can try it, I suppose. Now, here are a few details of this fellow we want.' He laid some notes down on the desk and Goon looked at them with interest.

'Medium height, sharp-eyed, scar over rather thin mouth, which a moustache, real or false, could hide. May wear false whiskers ...' Goon stopped, as an astonishing idea came to him. He stared in excitement at the Inspector.

'I saw this man yesterday!' he said excitedly, and actually poked the Chief in the chest. 'Yes, I did – whiskers and all!'

'Where?' asked the Chief, sharply.

'And he was violent too – *very* violent!' went on Goon. 'Kicked and flailed his arms about, and strong as I am, I couldn't hold him.'

'WHERE was this man?' demanded the Inspector again, but Goon couldn't be stopped.

'And sharp-eyed too – eyes like gimlets, he had. And a moustache as well and, now I come to think of it, he might have had a scar under it. Bless me, if he wasn't the man!'

'GOON,' said the Chief, in a dangerous voice. 'Kindly stop gabbling and listen to me. WHERE was this fellow?'

'Er – well, sir – funny thing, sir, but he was in

that Frederick Trotteville's garden, down in his shed,' said Goon. 'I was called in by a young lady staying there, sir. Buster, that Scottie, he went for the old tramp fiercely, and must have bit his ankles to the bone. Real savage he was, sir.'

'Was Frederick Trotteville there too?' asked the Chief. 'Couldn't *he* catch the man? He's usually pretty nippy at that kind of thing.'

'Well, if that fellow could have been caught, *I'd* have caught him,' said Goon, huffily. 'Actually, Frederick didn't come along till too late. I'd done the dirty work before he turned up.'

'I see,' said the Inspector, thoughtfully. 'I think I'll go along and see what Frederick thought of this fellow.'

'He didn't see him, sir,' said Goon. 'I told you, he came along too late.'

'Yes, I heard you,' said the Chief, curtly. 'All right. Study those notes, Goon, and keep your eyes skinned. That fellow has been seen here – and we know he's got friends nearby who might fix him up with some disguise. He's not a fellow who'll hide away. He'd take a delight in mixing with people somewhere and watching the police trying to find him.'

'Ho – then I'll certainly disguise myself,' said Goon. 'Supposing I put on my . . .'

But the Inspector was already striding out to his car, and Goon was left muttering to himself. 'To the Trottevilles' house,' ordered the Inspector, and the big car slid smoothly away. It turned in at Fatty's drive and stopped beside the front door. The Inspector got out and rang the bell.

'Is Frederick in?' he asked, when Jane came to the door.

'Oh, good morning, sir,' said Jane. 'Yes, I think so. He was just going out. Come in, sir, and I'll call him.'

The Chief Inspector stepped in, and was shown into Mrs Trotteville's pretty drawing-room. Then came the sound of hurried footsteps down the stairs and Fatty appeared, dressed in running shorts and white singlet. The Chief looked surprised.

'Hello, Frederick – in training for something?' he enquired.

'Yes, sir,' explained Fatty. 'I've a chance of getting into the First Tennis Team next term. Nice to see you, sir!'

The Inspector came straight to the point. 'Frederick, I've just come from Goon,' he said. 'I went to see him to ask him to look out for someone for me – and he immediately started a peculiar story about a tramp he'd found down in your shed.'

Fatty felt himself going red. 'Yes, sir,' he said. 'Er – what else did he tell you?'

'Oh, I got a good many details from him,' said the Chief, drily. 'According to him, this fellow was extremely violent, had very sharp eyes, like gimlets, and a moustache, probably with a scar under it – and Buster flew at him and bit his ankles to the bone. The tramp's ankles, not Goon's.'

'Did he say anything else, sir?' asked Fatty, cautiously.

'He did say that you turned up too late to help him,' said the Inspector. 'Exactly what do you know about this violent tramp who was hiding in your shed? I thought you always kept it locked.'

'You think I was that tramp, sir, don't you?' said Fatty, looking the Chief in the eyes.

'It certainly had occurred to me,' said the Chief, looking straight back at Fatty.

'All right,' said Fatty, with a sigh. 'Yes, I was the

tramp. But it was only a joke, sir. I didn't even know Mr Goon was anywhere near. A friend of ours, staying here, peeped into my shed and saw me there, looking like a tramp – I was in disguise, of course – and screamed for help. And Goon came in, and I got away. Buster didn't go for me, of course, he was just excited to see me and leapt all round me as I went. Er – Mr Goon exaggerated a bit, I expect.'

'Yes, I guessed as much,' said the Inspector, a twinkle in his eye. 'You were extremely strong and violent, according to him – he quite thought you were the man we're after.'

'I suppose – I suppose you wouldn't care to tell me about this man,' said Fatty, hopefully. 'I mean, I might be able to help. You never know.'

'I'll leave you a copy of the notes I left with Goon,' said the Chief, and he took a sheaf of papers from his pocket and extracted two or three pages from them. 'Better not tell Goon that you know about this man – but keep your eyes open for anything out of the way this next week. The Fair's on – and there's a conference of some sort on too – so the place will be full of strangers.'

'Oh, thanks, sir,' said Fatty joyfully, as he picked up the notes. 'Thanks a lot. This is right up my street! I'll do my best. I can tell the others, sir, can't I? You know they can be trusted too – we've done quite a lot to help you in the past, haven't we?'

The Chief laughed. 'Yes. So long as you give the orders to the others, and they obey you, that's all right. But remember, Frederick, this fellow is dangerous – all I want you to do is to keep your eyes and ears open and pass on anything you hear that might be of value. You've got a way of picking up information – in fact, I might almost say you've got a gift for it!'

'Thanks, Chief,' said Fatty, pleased, and saw him politely to the front door. As soon as he had shut it, Eunice came running up to him.

'Who was that, Frederick? It was a Chief Inspector, wasn't it? What did he want to see you for? Was it about that tramp yesterday?'

'Yes, mostly about him,' said Fatty, guardedly. He wasn't going to let Eunice know what else the Chief had told him.

'Well, I do think you might have called *me*,' said Eunice, indignantly. 'After all, *I* found him – and *I* called the policeman – and *I* tried to catch him.'

'Well, the Chief got all the information from Mr Goon, I expect,' said Fatty. 'Now I must start on my training, Eunice. Sorry to have to leave you to yourself.'

'I'll come too,' said Eunice, but at that moment Mrs Trotteville came in and, to Fatty's relief, made it impossible for Eunice to go with him, by asking her if she would mind arranging the flowers.

Eunice, always good-mannered with her elders, agreed at once, and Fatty fled in delight. He meant to go and tell the others the exciting news he had, and he waited until Eunice was safely in the garden and then flew to the telephone.

He rang Pip's number, but it was engaged. Blow! He rang Larry's and, to his relief, Daisy came to the phone.

'Daisy! Listen, there's a mystery looming up!' said Fatty, delightedly. 'A smasher! The Chief Inspector has just been here, and he wants our help. Can we meet at your house in ten minutes' time? We can? Good. Ring Pip for me will you, and get him and Bets along too?'

He rang off, smiling, but as he turned he heard

a reproachful voice. 'Frederick! You said the Chief came about that tramp. What *did* he come for? And what's this about a mystery? I do think you might tell me.'

It was Eunice who had come in at the garden door with some daffodils. She had heard every word!

'Sorry. Can't stop, Eunice!' said Fatty, and ran straight out of the front door, Buster at his heels. He had meant to change back into his trousers, but he felt that Eunice would probably follow him right up to his room and harangue him there about their 'mystery'.

So away he fled to Larry's, still in his running things, leaving a very angry Eunice glaring after him. How *maddening* that she had overheard him on the telephone!

7. IMPORTANT MEETING

Larry and Daisy were in their summerhouse waiting for him. Pip and Bets had not yet arrived. They were surprised to see Fatty in running shorts again.

'Hey, do you *live* in those?' said Larry. 'I'd better get you a coat. You'll shiver out here. The wind is blowing straight into the summerhouse.'

Pip and Bets arrived almost immediately, and the five, with a happy and interested Buster, held a most interesting meeting.

Fatty first of all told them the story of how he had escaped from Eunice the day before and gone down to his shed and practised a little disguising.

'I put on the tramp rig-out,' he said. 'Whiskers and all. So, of course, when Eunice came peeping in at the window and the keyhole, she got a bit of a shock, and yelled for help!'

They all laughed. 'Serve her right for snooping,' said Larry. 'Go on.'

'Well, who should come to her help but old Goon, who was walking down the lane nearby, on his Sunday beat,' said Fatty. 'So you can guess I had a bit of a do getting away. Buster nearly went mad with excitement and jumped all over me and rushed off beside me – and Mr Goon and Eunice thought he was attacking me – Goon said he must have bitten my ankles to the bone!'

'But they *didn't* catch you, did they?' said Bets, anxiously.

'Of course not,' went on Fatty. 'Anyway, it happened that the Chief Inspector went to see Mr Goon about some dangerous fellow – an escaped prisoner – whom he thinks is hiding somewhere in Peterswood – and old Mr Goon told him all about the tramp he'd chased out of my shed, and said he was sure he was the prisoner, hiding there!'

There was such uproarious laughter over this that it was some time before Fatty could go on. 'Do shut up,' he begged. 'You'll bring your mother out here, Larry – she'll think we're planning something awful.'

'All right, but it's very funny,' said Larry. 'What next?'

'Well, as you can imagine, the Chief wasn't as idiotic as Mr Goon,' said Fatty. 'He guessed at once that the old tramp was me, and came to tackle me about it.'

Everyone gazed anxiously at Fatty.

'Was he angry?' asked Bets.

'No. Of course not. Can't I practise disguising myself down in my own shed if I want to?' said Fatty. 'Of course I can! But, you see, the Chief had to let the cat out of the bag – he had to tell me about the man that Mr Goon thought I was! And I pounced on that at once, and asked if we could help in any way. And he said we could!'

'Great!' said Pip, thrilled. 'Then we've got another mystery to get our teeth into. Well, perhaps not quite a *mystery* – but something very like it! Do you know anything about this man?'

'Yes. Look,' said Fatty, and put his notes down on the summerhouse table. 'Here are the particulars. And here are photos of the man too – front face and side face. But he'll be in disguise – he's clever at that, apparently – so the photos won't be *much* good.'

They all stared down at them. The man had

very sharp, intelligent eyes under dark brows, an ordinary nose, and thin mouth, and over it, under the nose, a thin, curving scar. Fatty pointed to it.

'He'll have to hide *that*,' he said. 'And that probably means he will be wearing a false moustache until he can grow one. He may even wear a beard too, to hide his rather weak chin.'

The man's hair was thick and straight. 'He could wave that – or have it permed,' said Fatty. 'Or perhaps have it thinned so that he looked a bit bald. You never know.'

'Well, if he can do all those things to himself, I don't see what use these photos are,' said Daisy.

'His hands are a bit knobbly, look,' said Pip. 'I bet he'll wear gloves to hide those!'

'Except that plenty of people have knobbly hands,' said Bets. 'Our gardener has, for instance. Very knobbly.'

'Has he any likes or dislikes?' asked Daisy.

'Apparently he is fond of cats,' said Fatty. 'And, dear me, look – here's an odd thing I didn't notice before. He is interested in nature, but especially in *insects*. A-HA!'

'What's the A-HA for?' asked Pip, surprised.

'Interested in *insects* – and he's known to be in *Peterswood*,' said Fatty. 'Doesn't that ring a bell, my dear Fatheads?'

'Oh, you mean the conference of Colly-something,' said Larry, remembering. 'Yes – yes, there may be something in that. You mean, he may get himself up as a colly-something – a beetle-lover – and go and sit solemnly in the meetings at the Town Hall, while everyone is looking for him elsewhere.'

'Well, it does sound a bit far-fetched,' admitted Fatty. 'But we can't afford to miss any possible clue. It might be the best possible hiding-place – meetings for beetle-lovers! Whoever would think of looking for an escaped prisoner there? With thick glasses to hide his sharp eyes . . .'

'And the kind of hat and muffler and thick coat that Mr Tolling wears,' said Bets. 'Honestly, I couldn't help thinking *he* looked as if he was in disguise when we saw him at the station – moustache and beard and all!'

'Well, we've got a difficult job on,' said Fatty, sounding pleased as he gathered up the papers. 'But we're going to have some fun! And remember, Goon is also on the look out for this fellow, and whatever we do we mustn't let him spot him first!'

'Good gracious, no!' said Daisy. 'By the way, what height is the man? Tall? Short?'

'Medium,' said Fatty. 'But we must remember that he can make himself taller by wearing higher heels, or shorter by stooping. Inspector Jenks said he was very good at disguising himself. Now, we must make plans.'

'Yes. Let's,' said Bets. 'And we mustn't let Eunice know a thing.'

'She overheard my conversation with Daisy, on the telephone,' said Fatty, frowning. 'Just like her! She was very inquisitive as to why the Chief had come to see me this morning, of course – and angry because he didn't see *her* about the old tramp. Little does she know that he was only me, down in that shed!'

'Well, we'll certainly have to be careful when Eunice is about,' said Larry. 'Now, how are we going to set about this mystery, Fatty? Let's think.'

'Well, it's obvious that the fellow must mix with plenty of other people, where he would go unnoticed,' said Fatty, considering. 'He probably wouldn't want to take a room in a hotel – or in a boarding-house. He would know that the police would make enquiries at all those. No, *I* think there are two places to look for him.'

'What are they?' asked Bets. 'The Fair is one, of course.'

'And the Coleopterist conference is the second,' said Fatty. 'I'm sure of that.'

'But we can't get into any of their meetings,' objected Daisy. 'We're none of us colly-whatever-you-said.'

'*I* can get in,' said Fatty. 'Eunice's father gave me tickets for every meeting! He gave Mummy and Dad some too – so we can go to any meeting we like!'

'Well, *I* don't want to,' said Daisy, decidedly. 'Ugh – beetles crawling about all over the place.'

'Don't be an idiot. If there are beetles on show, they'll be stuck in rows in cases,' said Larry. 'Won't they, Fatty? As dead as door-nails!'

'Yes. But I expect that all that will happen at the meetings is that the Chief Coleopterists will get up and make long, long speeches,' said Fatty. 'They might perhaps chat together at the end of each meeting. It will be very, very dull for any of us whose job it is to attend one in order to examine the Coleopterists to see if any of them resemble the escaped prisoner.

'Bags I don't,' said Daisy, promptly. 'I'd rather go to the Fair.'

'Oh well – we'll *all* go there,' agreed Fatty. 'Actually, I thought we'd go this afternoon. The Coleopterist conference doesn't begin till tomorrow, anyway. So what about a visit to the Fair and mixing business with pleasure?'

Everyone thought that this was a very good idea. 'But what about Eunice?' said Bets, anxiously. 'Will she have to come too?'

There was a moment's silence and then Fatty gave a heavy sigh. 'I don't see any way out of that,' he said. 'Mummy will expect me to take her, and she'll kick up an awful fuss if I try to get out of it. Blow!'

'We'll try and take it in turns to be with her,' said Larry, generously. 'You're the brightest one of us all, Fatty, so you're more likely to spot anyone like the man we're after – and if this afternoon you see anyone you particularly want to examine, or follow, or talk to, just give me one of your winks, and I'll take charge of Eunice at once.'

'Well, thanks,' said Fatty, relieved. 'I must say she would rather cramp my style if she stuck to me like a leech all afternoon. And remember, not a word in front of Eunice about this business. If anyone is careless enough to drop a hint without meaning to, they'll have to retire from this mystery altogether.'

This was a truly awful threat, and Bets felt quite scared. She decided that it would be best if she hardly spoke at all when Eunice was near. Fatty grinned at her serious face.

'It's all right, young Bets. You won't let us down. You never have yet. The one I'm really afraid of is Buster. He's been listening to us with pricked ears the whole time. Buster, don't you dare give anything away to that girl, will you?'

'Wuff!' said the little Scottie, joyfully, sensing that the solemn meeting was at an end, and that Fatty was relaxing. He rolled over for his tummy to be tickled.

'Well, where do we meet?' asked Daisy. 'Gosh, look, there's *Eunice*! She's tracked us down!'

'And she thinks I'm miles away running for all

I'm worth!' said Fatty, horrified. 'Quick, go out of the summerhouse, all of you, and leave me here. Take the girl indoors and stuff her with biscuits, or something. She's always willing to eat.'

Hurriedly the others went out of the little summerhouse to meet a rather sulky Eunice. 'Hello!' she said. 'Where's Fatty? His mother said he might be at Pip's, so I went there, and Pip's mother said you were all meeting here, so I came on here.'

'Welcome!' said Larry, with a much-too-bright smile. 'Come indoors and have a snack. I hope you like gingerbread biscuits. Wherever can old Fatty be? I hope he won't wear himself out, running for miles and miles – *do* come in, Eunice! This way!'

8. A LITTLE ABOUT BEETLES

Fatty, left by himself in the summerhouse with Buster, stayed there for some while, fearing that he might be seen by the sharp-eyed Eunice. But then, as the coast seemed quiet and clear, he stepped out briskly, made his way to the side gate, and disappeared into the road.

Only Bets saw him go. She was watching the gate, knowing that he would probably slip out there when he thought it was safe. She went quickly out of the room, ran down the stairs and out into the garden. She tore after Fatty, shouting.

He turned, and when he saw it was only Bets, he stopped. 'What is it?' he said, as she came running up out of breath. 'Don't tell me Eunice saw me!'

'No, she didn't,' panted Bets. 'But we didn't arrange what time to meet this afternoon at the Fair, or where.'

Fatty considered. 'I should think three o'clock would be a good time,' he said. 'There will be heaps of people there then, and the man we're looking for would probably think it safe to be there. He may possibly have taken a job at the Fair, you know.'

'Yes. So he might,' said Bets. 'Perhaps that's how it was that he has been seen here.'

'You go back to the others,' said Fatty, giving Bets a pat. 'Don't say you've seen me, of course.'

'What are you going to do?' asked Bets. 'You aren't *really* going to go running, are you?'

'Yes. I am,' said Fatty. 'Buster and I will now race at a good speed round the county of Bucks. So long, young Bets!'

Bets watched him set off at a steady trot, with Buster at his heels. She went back to the others, wondering if they had thought of any way of getting rid of the loud-voiced Eunice.

Fatty really did have a long run that morning. For one thing, it was a lovely April day, and for another he quite enjoyed stretching his legs and running so steadily. He ran by the river mostly, and then turned when he got to Marlow, and went back again.

Jog-jog-jog, jog-jog-jog. Fatty's alert mind ran as steadily as his feet all the time he jogged along. Why had that escaped prisoner come to Peterswood? Had he friends there? Where was he sleeping at night? Was he dossing down behind some haystack or in somebody's garden? What work was he doing? He had to get money to keep himself, presumably, unless he had friends to help him. The Fair was certainly the likeliest place to look for him.

He came to Peterswood, turned up from the river into the road that led to the village, and jogged up it. He glanced at his watch. Yes, he had made good time. He turned the corner abruptly and was almost knocked down by a bicycle.

'Hey!' said Mr Goon's familiar voice. 'What you doing? – you almost knocked me off my bike.'

'Well, you nearly knocked *me* down!' said Fatty, jogging on without stopping. Goon swung his bicycle round and followed him, riding beside him, much to Fatty's annoyance.

'What's the idea?' asked the annoying Mr Goon, pedalling along, keeping out of Buster's way – though by this time Buster was far too tired to snap at anyone's ankles, even Goon's.

'What's *what* idea?' said Fatty. 'Haven't you ever seen anyone running before?'

'Yes. But what have you suddenly *started* it for?' asked Mr Goon, wondering whether this outbreak of running had anything to do with hunting escaped prisoners.

'To get fit,' said Fatty. 'And it wouldn't be a bad thing if you did the same, Mr Goon. Think how easy it would be to chase tramps and people like that if you were really in training, and could run fast!'

'You seen any more of that old tramp in your shed?' asked Mr Goon.

'No. Have you?' said Fatty and ran to a stile, climbed over it and jumped down into the field. He was tired of Mr Goon.

There now – I wanted to find out if the Chief had gone and told him anything about that escaped prisoner, thought Goon. I don't want that big boy messing about looking for him, always turning up everywhere. Drat him!

Eunice came home in time for lunch, having spent what she considered to be a very pleasant morning with the others. Fatty wondered if *they* had found it quite so pleasant! He himself had arrived back at twelve o'clock and had spent the rest of the morning in peace and quiet, down in his shed, looking through all his belongings there, in case a sudden disguise should be needed.

'We're all going to the Fair this afternoon,' she announced to Fatty, as soon as he came in to lunch, looking spick and span in grey trousers.

'Good,' said Fatty, politely.

'But I warn you – don't try throwing any rings at the hoopla stalls,' said Eunice.

'Why not?' asked Fatty, surprised.

'Well, because they're a fraud,' said Eunice. 'The rings are made just *too* small to fit over anything – anything decent that is, I mean – it's no good throwing for a clock or anything like that – you'd never get it.'

'Rubbish,' said Fatty, who considered himself very good at hoopla. 'I've often won things at hoopla stalls. *You* probably don't win anything because you're not good at throwing.'

Mr and Mrs Trotteville came in with Mr Tolling. He beamed round through his thick glasses. 'Well! And how have you two been getting on together this morning? I hope you've played together nicely.'

'Father! DON'T talk as if we were seven years old!' said Eunice. 'As a matter of fact, I've hardly *seen* Frederick this morning.'

'Oh, Frederick, didn't you look after Eunice?' said his mother. 'She's your guest, you know.'

'I've been cross-country running,' said Fatty. 'Eunice was with the others. Mummy – do I look any fitter?'

'Well, no,' said his mother, looking at him carefully. 'And I don't suppose you *will* be as long as you eat so many potatoes, Frederick. Look how many you've taken – five!'

'Gosh, so I have,' said Fatty, quite startled. 'And I only meant to take two.' He put three back, looking rather gloomy.

'I'm much looking forward to my first conference at your Town Hall tomorrow,' said Mr Tolling, taking quite a lot of potatoes himself. 'Some very distinguished people will be there.'

'Who?' asked Fatty, politely.

'Well, there will be William Wattling,' said Mr Tolling. 'He is *the* expert on the Cross-Veined

Three-Spot Mackling Beetle of Peruvia. A wonderful man – truly wonderful. He spent one whole week lying outside this beetle's hole, in the middle of a swamp.'

'Good heavens! I wonder he's alive to tell the tale!' said Mr Trotteville, startled at this revelation of what a beetle-lover would do.

'And there's Maria Janizena,' said Mr Tolling, enjoying himself. 'Now *she's* a marvel, she really is. Believe it or not, she found a batch of eighty-four eggs belonging to the Skulking Hunch-Beetle of Thibet, and hatched every one out herself.'

'What! Did she sit on them?' said Fatty, sounding amazed.

'Now, *Frederick*,' said his mother. However, Mr Tolling apparently saw nothing but complimentary astonishment in Fatty's question, and went on solemnly.

'No, boy, no – of course not. She merely put the eggs in a warm cupboard, but the astonishing thing was that when the eighty-four eggs hatched out, there were 168 young beetles – not eighty-four. Now what do you make of that strange fact?'

'All twins,' said Fatty, solemnly, and was most

gratified to hear Eunice give a loud guffaw and his father chuckle loudly.

'Shall we change the subject?' asked Mrs Trotteville. 'I keep thinking I see beetles in the cabbage.'

'Really, Mrs Trotteville?' said Mr Tolling, full of immediate interest. 'Where? I must examine them.'

Now it was Fatty's turn to roar, and poor Mr Tolling looked bewildered.

'Father's no good at seeing a joke,' Eunice informed the company. 'Are you, Father?'

'Who else will be at the conference?' asked Fatty. 'Will they *all* be experts?'

'Most of them, my boy, most of them,' said Mr Tolling. 'We would not welcome any novices at our meetings. I think I may say that every one of us there will have a large knowledge of the Coleoptera as a whole.'

'And do *you* know everyone?' asked Fatty, thinking that if Mr Tolling *did* know all these learned beetle-lovers, he could most certainly point out to Fatty anyone he did not recognise – and that might be a most suspicious person – you never knew!

'No, my dear boy, I don't know all of them,' said Mr Tolling. 'I have the list of all those who are going to attend the meeting, here in my wallet – and I know perhaps half of them.'

'Could I see the list sometime, sir?' asked Fatty, eagerly. If he went to the meetings and saw someone like the escaped prisoner, he could check him on the list – and if he was not down on it, well, that would be very suspicious indeed!

'Yes, Frederick, certainly,' said Mr Tolling, most gratified to think that Fatty should show such interest. 'I take it that you will like to come to one or more of the meetings? I can vouch for you, of course, at the door. No strangers are allowed in, unless vouched for.'

That was really interesting news. It looked as if any checking-up would be fairly easy. Fatty took the list of names from the obliging Mr Tolling with warm thanks. 'And I'll certainly be coming to some of the meetings, sir,' he said, much to the amazement of his parents. 'The Coleoptera are most interesting – *most* interesting! Mummy, do you remember those two stag beetles I had when I was at kindergarten – the ones that kept fighting each other?'

Mr Tolling looked pained, and Mrs Trotteville frowned at Fatty. Really, this was going too far. She couldn't understand why Fatty was playing up to the very boring Mr Tolling in this way. Fatty saw her frown and changed the subject in his usual cheerful way.

'We're all going to the Fair this afternoon!' he said. 'Mr Tolling, you come too – it'll be a change from beetles. Come and ride on the roundabout.'

'Well,' said Mr Tolling, most surprisingly, 'I think I will! It's years since I went to anything but meetings – yes, Frederick, I'll accept your kind invitation with pleasure!'

Whew! What a shock that was for Fatty!

9. FUN AT THE FAIR

Larry, Daisy, Pip and Bets were extremely surprised when they saw Fatty coming to meet them at the Fair, accompanied by Mr Tolling. It was bad enough to have Eunice, but here was her father too! Whatever could Fatty be thinking of?

'Sorry,' said Fatty, when he got Larry to himself for a moment. 'I just asked him to come for a joke – pulling his leg, you know – and he accepted! You could have knocked me down with a feather – or a beetle!'

'You really are an idiot,' said Larry, in disgust. 'Now we've got to drag the two of them about with us. And did Mr Tolling *have* to come to a Fair dressed like that – in town clothes, all muffled up as if it was a winter's day? He looks strange enough, anyhow, with his beard and thick glasses. Honestly, we'll be laughed at wherever we go.'

'I tell you, I'm sorry,' said Fatty, annoyed. 'How

was *I* to know he'd say he'd come? Shut up about it and let's go round the Fair. And look out for you know what.'

The Fair was quite an ordinary one, with a roundabout, swings, hoopla stalls, a shooting range, cake and sweet stalls, and various small side-shows. The little company walked round it, trying their luck at the hoopla, where Eunice proved most annoyingly right. Nobody's rings fell completely round anything.

'I told you so,' she said, which impelled Fatty to waste more money trying to prove her wrong.

'There you are!' she said. 'I *told* you the rings are too small. They always are!'

'Here, Miss – don't you say things like that!' said the boy in charge. 'It's just that you ain't got the right knack of throwing, see? You watch *me* do it!'

And he climbed out of his stall, took a handful of rings and proceeded to throw each one round something – a teapot, a clock, a vase, and a box of chocolates. He grinned at Eunice's crestfallen face.

'Easy when you know how,' he said. 'Have another go.' But nobody would!

Mr Tolling appeared to enjoy himself extremely.

He tried the hoopla. He bought sweets and even sucked them himself. He went on the little Dodgem cars with Eunice, and put up bravely with her desire to bump violently every car in sight.

'Can't get rid of him,' sighed Fatty to Daisy. 'Have you seen anyone *interesting* – you know what I mean, don't you?'

'Yes. But I haven't,' said Daisy. 'Look. Let's go in here – where that clown is calling out something about boxing. If it's clowns boxing, it ought to be funny.'

It wasn't. It was merely a boxing ring into which anyone could step to box with a stalwart youngster called Champ Charlie. Daisy was not in the least interested in boxing and Fatty took her out again, laughing at the clown's antics as he did so. Then his face suddenly changed and he stared hard. Daisy wondered why, and she gazed at the clown too, with his painted face and white-gloved hands.

Fatty took Daisy off and they went behind a tent. 'That clown!' said Fatty. 'Did you see his painted face? There was a big red line all over the space between his mouth and nose – where the escaped prisoner is known to have a noticeable scar?'

'Oh, Fatty, yes!' said Daisy. 'And his hands were gloved. They might be very knobbly for all we know.'

'And his eyes were sharp, roving everywhere, did you notice?' said Fatty. 'We can't see what kind of hair he's got because he had a clown's close-fitting cap on. He was about medium height too. I say – I just wonder!'

'Well, he's our first suspect,' said Daisy. 'We may find two or three more! Let's have one more look at the clown and then we'll go somewhere else. I don't know where the others are, but that doesn't matter. Come on.'

They went to have a good look at the clown again. He was calling out in a raucous voice, 'Come on in, folks – see some fine boxing! Come on in. See Champ Charlie knock 'em all out.'

Yes, his thickly-painted mouth would certainly hide any scar above it, and his eyes were as sharp as needles as they raked the crowd for possible customers. Fatty pulled Daisy over to the stall opposite, which sold cups of tea.

'Cup of char, mate?' said the man there, and Fatty nodded.

'It's all right. He means tea,' said Fatty, seeing

Daisy's mystified look. He spoke to the man who was pouring out the tea.

'I seem to have seen that clown over there somewhere else,' he said. 'What's his name, do you know?'

'I don't,' said the man, handing the cup. 'I never saw him before. He's just called Bert.'

'Does he travel with the Fair?' asked Fatty.

'How do I know?' said the man, turning to another customer. 'Ask him yourself.'

Fatty didn't want to. He decided that it would be best to go to the Fair the next morning, when there would be fewer people, and try to get into conversation with the clown when he wasn't so busy. He might find him out of his clown-costume then, and without his paint.

'Come on, Daisy,' he said, seeing that she didn't like her tea. 'Pour it away. I only wanted to get it to make an excuse to ask the man about that clown.'

'I know,' said Daisy. 'Look, let's go into the shooting range and look round there.'

They went in, passing an old woman sitting on a chair, who tried to sell them tickets, and watched some young men shooting at ping pong balls that bobbed up and down on little jets of water. Daisy nudged Fatty and nodded towards a man who had just come in, and was taking over from the boy who had been handing out the rifles.

Fatty was startled. At first sight, the man looked very like the photograph of the escaped prisoner – sharp eyes, dark brows, thick dark hair. He was burnt very brown.

Fatty pushed Daisy outside. 'It isn't the fellow we're looking for,' he said, regretfully. 'There's no scar above his mouth – at first I thought his sunburn might have been painted on to hide it, but it isn't.'

'And his hands weren't knobbly,' said Daisy. 'I looked at them specially. They're smooth, almost like a woman's hands.'

'Anyway, if he *was* the fellow we want, he wouldn't go about openly like that with no disguise,' said Fatty. 'It's just a fluke that he's like him. We can wash him out.'

'Let's just look into the shooting range *once* more,' said Daisy. They went back to it, passing the old woman sitting on a chair outside. She called to them in a cracked voice. 'Take a shot, young sir, take a shot!'

'No, thanks,' said Fatty, and looked in at the shooting tent again. No, the man there was definitely too young to be the escaped prisoner and, as Daisy said, his hands were very smooth. Fatty knew from experience that while it was possible to alter and disguise a face very easily, it was exceedingly difficult to disguise hands.

'Spare a copper, young miss,' said the cracked voice of the old woman. Daisy looked down and pitied the poor old creature. Her face was screwed-up and full of wrinkles, though her eyes were still lively. She had a filthy shawl pulled over her head, and her skinny, bony hands clutched the roll of tickets.

Daisy nudged Fatty as they went by. 'What a pity that man in there didn't have knobbly hands like that old woman!' she said. 'We'd *really* have thought he might have been the man we want!'

'We shall get knobbly hands on the brain soon,' said Fatty. 'Let's go and find the others. But hey, look – DO look, Daisy!'

Daisy looked where Fatty nodded, and saw a fat

red-faced man watching the swings. He had a red moustache and a little red beard. He wore no collar, but a dirty blue muffler instead, and a blue cap pulled right down over his forehead. His tweed coat was too tight for him, and his grey flannel trousers a little too short. Altogether he was a figure of fun, and passers-by laughed when they saw him.

'Do you know who that is?' said Fatty in a low voice to Daisy. She shook her head.

'Oh, Daisy, Daisy – you'll never make a detective!' said Fatty, disappointed. And then Daisy gave a little squeal and turned laughing eyes on Fatty.

'Sh!' said Fatty, warningly, and guided Daisy away to a distant corner, where she laughed loud and long.

'Oh, Fatty, it was *Mr Goon* in disguise!' she giggled. 'Oh, do let's find the others and see if they've spotted him. Oh dear, *why* does he make himself so very, very conspicuous! Fancy trailing a suspect in that get-up – he'd be noticed at once! Oh, that red moustache!'

They saw the others in the distance and ran

to join them. As soon as they came near, Larry called out. 'Have you seen Mr Goon? We nearly died of laughing!'

'Yes, we saw him,' said Fatty. 'What a sight! Hey – let's go and ask him the time, or something! We won't let on that we know him. He'll be so pleased to think we haven't seen through his disguise!'

'Yes, quick, come on while he's still over there!' said Pip. 'I'll go up and ask him the time first – then you can go and ask him something, Bets – and then Larry. Quick!'

They wandered near Mr Goon, who was now watching the Dodgem cars with much concentration, his cap almost hiding his eyes. Pip went up to him.

'Please, sir, could you tell me the time?' he said. Goon looked surprised when he saw that it was Pip, and then grunted. 'Four o'clock or thereabouts,' he said, putting on a very deep voice, which made Pip jump.

'Thank you, sir,' said Pip, and went back to the others, chuckling.

Goon obviously felt pleased that his disguise was apparently so good. He even wandered nearer to where the children stood watching the roundabout.

Ho, he thought, they didn't know it was he, Goon, who was there keeping a sharp eye on them! He walked past them, whistling. Bets ran after him.

'Oh, please,' she said, 'do you know what time the Fair closes?' Goon cleared his throat and put on his deep voice again.

'About half past ten,' he said, and then feeling his moustache coming loose, he put up his hand hurriedly to press it back. Bets gave a sudden giggle and fled.

Larry tried next. He walked close to Goon, pretended to pick something up from the ground and looked at it. Then he turned round. 'Have you dropped this button, sir?' he asked. As it was one that Daisy had hurriedly twisted off her red dress, it obviously wasn't Goon's!

Goon cleared his throat again. 'No, my boy, it is not mine,' he said. 'Er, are you enjoying yourself?'

'Oh, very much, sir, thank you!' said Larry – and then up came Fatty.

'Please, sir, I'd like to know where you got those policeman's boots you're wearing?' he said sternly. 'I mean, I hope they're not stolen, sir.'

'You toad of a boy!' said Goon, reverting to his

own voice. 'You *would* say a thing like that. Clear orf!'

'Good gracious – it's *you*, Mr Goon!' gasped Fatty, looking quite flabbergasted. 'Well now, who would have thought it!'

'I said, "CLEAR ORF!" ' thundered Mr Goon, much to the surprise of everyone nearby. And Fatty 'cleared orf', laughing till the tears came into his eyes. Poor old Goon!

10. MR. TOLLING LOSES HIS WAY

'Where's Eunice?' said Fatty, when he and the others had finished laughing. 'Has she gone home?'

'No. She wanted to go in a swing with her father, so we left her to it,' said Larry. 'Honestly, Mr Tolling is a surprise! He's trying everything!'

'Where is he now?' asked Fatty.

'I expect they've gone to the roundabouts,' said Daisy. 'I heard Mr Tolling say he'd like to. Goodness – he won't be fit to face the beetles tomorrow!'

'There they are, look,' said Pip, as they strolled near the roundabout. It was going on its circular tour for the ten-thousandth time, churning out its old-fashioned tune.

'Not many people on it,' said Fatty. 'Only about seven or eight. What about us having a ride? Look, it's slowing down.'

Everyone got off except for one person. That was

Mr Tolling. Eunice called to him, 'It's stopped, Father!'

'I'm having another go,' said the surprising Mr Tolling. He was clutching the tall neck of a giraffe, and looked very peculiar, sitting on the big wooden creature in his dark town clothes.

'All right. But it makes me feel sick,' said Eunice. 'You go on alone. Oh – here are the others. Are you going on the roundabout, Frederick?'

'We thought we would,' said Fatty, and paid for everyone. 'Sure you won't, Eunice? Right! Get on, everybody! Choose some kind of animal to ride!'

Mr Goon wandered over to the roundabout. He looked keenly at the roundabout boy, as if wondering if *he* might be a disguised prisoner. Then he looked sharply at a man going by wheeling a barrow.

'He's feeling very important, wearing a disguise and peering at everyone,' said Larry to Daisy. 'I can't say his disguise is a very good one. He looks *exactly* what he is – a policeman in disguise!'

They gazed at him, and then saw him give a slight start, as if he were surprised. He was looking at the roundabout, staring hard at Mr Tolling.

Why is he staring at Eunice's father? wondered

Daisy. She leaned over to where Fatty was riding an absurdly large duck that rose and fell as soon as the roundabout began. 'Fatty, look at old Mr Goon. He's staring at Mr Tolling as if he's seen a ghost.'

Fatty looked at Goon and then at Mr Tolling. 'Well – he's never seen Mr Tolling in outdoor clothes before,' he said, 'and honestly he looks a bit strange, doesn't he? Perhaps old Mr Goon thinks he's the escaped prisoner!'

'Oh, *Fatty*! I believe he really *does* think that!' said Daisy, with a little squeal of laughter. 'He can't take his eyes off him!'

Fatty gazed at Mr Tolling again. He suddenly saw why Mr Goon might possibly be thinking that Eunice's father was the man they were looking for! Yes – the right height – a moustache and beard – intelligent eyes – knobbly hands. Good gracious, he couldn't *be* the escaped prisoner, could he?

Fatty pulled himself together. Don't be an idiot! he said to himself. You know full well he's your father's friend and Eunice's parent. But, gosh, I might have thought the same as Mr Goon is thinking, if I didn't *know* who he was!'

The roundabout had now begun its usual

journey, and the raucous music rang out all over the Fair. Every time that Mr Tolling and his giraffe came round in front of Mr Goon's eyes, the policeman stared and stared. Fatty began to laugh.

Now what would Goon do? Arrest poor Mr Tolling? Oh no, that would never do. Eunice would be really shocked and upset.

The roundabout slowed down again, and at last stopped. Mr Tolling was on the opposite side to Mr Goon and got off there. He called to Eunice, who was nearby waiting for him.

'I'm going back now. I told Mrs Trotteville I'd be in to tea, and I see it's late. You go back to your friends, Eunice.'

Eunice went off at once to join the others, who were now all getting off the roundabout. Fatty looked for Mr Goon, who was nowhere to be seen. And then he spotted him. Yes, there he was, trailing Mr Tolling across the Fair towards the gate. Good gracious, so he really *did* think that Mr Tolling was the escaped prisoner!

'Hey!' said Fatty, pulling Larry and Daisy aside from Eunice and the others. 'Hey – I think old Mr Goon has somehow got the idea that Mr Tolling is the man we're after! I'll follow him to see what happens, and you two stay here with the others. Mr Goon might notice *three* of us behind him – I'll see that he doesn't spot *me*! I may have to rescue Mr Tolling from the clutches of the law!'

Daisy laughed. 'All right, you follow them. I'll go back to the others, but we won't say a word to Eunice, or she'll be after you like a shot.'

Fatty started off across the Fair field, and soon saw Goon not far in front of him. There wasn't much fear of the disguised policeman looking round and seeing Fatty, because he was obviously so intent on his own prey. Mr Tolling was hurrying along – he must be hungry for his tea, thought Fatty!

And then Mr Tolling unfortunately lost his way! He took the wrong turning, and went off towards Maidenhead instead of Peterswood. Fatty felt cross. Now they would go miles out of their way!

Mr Tolling suddenly realised that he was on the wrong road and stopped. He looked up and down the street, hoping to see someone from whom he might ask the right way. He was short-sighted, and peered into the distance, delighted to make out someone at last. It was Mr Goon, of course, sauntering up behind him.

'Oh, pardon me, but could you please put me on the right road to Peterswood?' said Mr Tolling, politely. 'I seem to have taken the wrong turning.' He gazed up at Goon in surprise. What a peculiar-looking person!

Goon stared down at him most forbiddingly. Was there a scar under that moustache? 'I'll take you back on the right road myself,' said Goon. 'We'll, er – have a little conversation on the way.'

'Oh, you don't need to come *with* me,' said Mr Tolling, feeling quite alarmed at Goon's fierce gaze. 'Just tell me the road to take.'

'This way,' said Goon, almost as if he were taking someone off to prison. He actually took firm hold of Mr Tolling's arm. But Mr Tolling shook it off angrily.

'If you behave like this I shall report you for harrassing me!' he said. 'You must be one of those fellows from the Fair.'

'Here, that's enough!' said Goon, annoyed. 'All right – go by yourself if you want to! That's the way, see?'

Mr Tolling went on by himself, turning round every now and again to see if Goon was following him. He was most annoyed to find that he was. Awful fellow with his silly red moustache and beard! Surely he didn't mean to rob him?

Goon kept quite close behind him, and Mr Tolling hurried a little, trying to get rid of him. Goon hurried too. Fatty, who had kept well out of sight, grinned as he saw what was going on. Poor Mr Tolling – he must be very fed-up with Goon on his heels all the time. He decided to rescue him.

He came out from behind a bush with Buster as Mr Tolling passed, and hailed him. 'Hello, sir! What are you doing here? We thought you'd gone home.'

'Oh – Frederick – I'm so pleased to see you,' said Mr Tolling, delighted. 'I took the wrong road. I asked that fellow behind there to tell me the way, and he was most unpleasant – most familiar too. I half thought he might be thinking of robbing me!'

'Don't worry about that,' said Fatty, comfortingly and, to Goon's amazement, he took hold of Mr Tolling's arm. Goon, of course, still had no idea that it was Mr Tolling in front of him, and he could not imagine why Fatty appeared to be so friendly with him. Then a very worrying thought crossed his mind. Of course! Fatty must have the same idea as he, Goon, had – he probably thought that that fellow might be the man they were both looking for! The Chief Inspector must have told Fatty about him when he went to see him about that tramp.

He followed them both, annoyed to see that Fatty was on apparently such friendly terms with the man. Was he questioning him – finding out all about him? Goon went a little closer, afraid that Fatty was finding out all that he, Goon, ought to know. Where were they going, anyhow? Would Fatty take the man right to where he was hiding, supposing that he *was* the escaped prisoner? That would be too good to be true, but Goon didn't want that. He didn't want Fatty interfering at all!

To his enormous surprise, Fatty turned down the road that led to his own home! He and the man now appeared to be the best of friends. Goon hurried right up to them, and joined them. Mr Tolling looked at him with dislike.

'What do you want, fellow?' he said. 'Why are

you trailing behind us like this? I shall report you if you aren't careful!'

Fatty chuckled. Goon glared at him. 'Where are you going?' he demanded.

'Home,' said Fatty, looking mildly surprised. 'Where are *you* going?'

'Who *is* this man?' said Mr Tolling, puzzled and exasperated. 'I'm tired of him.'

'So am I,' said Fatty, and took Mr Tolling's arm again. 'Come on – we're almost home.'

Goon followed, frowning. Surely Fatty *wasn't* going to take this fellow to his own home? Toad of a boy! Always leading him a dance!

Fatty came to the front gate of his house and held it open politely for Mr Tolling, who went through thankfully. Goon stared, astounded. What *was* all this?

'You've a very short memory, Mr Goon,' said Fatty, as he closed the gate. 'Don't you remember Mr Tolling? You saw him yesterday, when you were called in about that fellow you thought was a tramp – the one down in my shed, you know. You didn't recognise *him* either, did you?'

Goon stared after Fatty as he and Mr Tolling

went up the drive to the front door, his head in a whirl. Good heavens, yes – of *course*, that was the fellow he had seen with Mr Trotteville yesterday – only he looked so different in his outdoor clothes! And what did Fatty mean about that tramp? Why should he, Goon, have recognised that dirty old fellow?

It suddenly dawned upon poor old Goon that he should indeed have recognised the tramp! It must have been Fatty himself! And he had told the Chief Inspector a lot of nonsense about him – how strong and violent he had been – and how that dog Buster had bitten the tramp's ankles to the bone – and – and . . .

Goon gave a deep groan and went slowly to his own house. So *that* was why the Inspector had wanted to go and ask Fatty all about the tramp. *He* had guessed it was Fatty all the time. Another bad mark for Goon! 'Pest of a boy!' muttered Goon to himself, as he let himself in at his front door. 'He knows about that escaped prisoner too – and if I don't look out, he'll spot him before I do. That's what they were all at the Fair for!'

Poor Goon – he was so upset that he couldn't

even eat his tea. That boy, if only he could get his hands on him!

11. FATTY HAS TROUBLE
WITH EUNICE

Fatty and Mr Tolling were extremely late for tea, which had been cleared away. Mr Tolling apologised profusely, and Jane brought in some fresh tea, complete with hot scones and chocolate cake.

Fatty was glad that he had brought Mr Tolling home. Nobody would have *thought* of bringing Fatty tea if he had arrived when it had been cleared away – but now here was a perfectly splendid tea, all because of Mr Tolling and his apologies.

Mr Tolling described his adventures at the Fair, and then how he had been followed home by what he called 'a half-mad, very nasty-looking fellow with no manners at all'. Fatty grinned. He wished that Goon could have heard that!

Eunice arrived much later, having been given tea by Larry at the Fair. She was cross that Fatty had gone off home without her.

'Well, I saw your father in difficulties,' said

Fatty. 'And I felt I *must* see him home. He had lost his way.'

'Well, really, Father,' said Eunice. 'You'll lose yourself on your way to bed one of these days!'

'Hadn't you and Eunice better have a nice game of chess?' said Mrs Trotteville, to Fatty's horror. Before he could think of an excuse to say no, Eunice had arranged everything in her maddeningly competent way, getting the chessboard out and setting out the men.

'Ha – two school champions,' said Mr Trotteville, with interest, and put down his paper to watch. But he soon became bored, for Eunice took at least twenty minutes before she made a move. Fatty was a much quicker player, and he soon grew bored too, and began going over all the happenings at the Fair in his mind.

That clown, he thought, we must certainly find out about him. And that boy in the shooting range who was so like the photo of the escaped man. Does *he* come into the picture anywhere? I can't see how. Well, tomorrow morning I'll go to the Fair again and talk to that clown – and in the afternoon, I'll go along to the Coleopterist meeting, and just have a good look round there.

'Your turn, Frederick,' said Eunice, impatiently. 'You're not paying attention.'

Fatty made his move at once, and Eunice again fell into a kind of trance, gazing at the chessmen intently. Poor Fatty became more and more bored. Chess was always a slow game – but this was dreadful!

Mr Tolling began talking about the Fair again, and how he had enjoyed it. 'There was only one thing I forgot to go and see,' he said. 'And that was the flea circus. How anyone can ever be fond enough of insects to train fleas to perform tricks I simply do not know!'

'Good gracious! I'd rather walk ten miles than go near a flea circus!' said Fatty's mother, horrified. 'Are fleas really clever enough to be trained, Mr Tolling? And do people ever train beetles?'

'Fleas are highly intelligent,' said Mr Tolling. 'Beetles vary. Now the *most* intelligent beetle known is found in the Atlas Mountains at a height of two thousand feet. It actually sews leaves together to . . .'

But why the beetle sewed leaves together Fatty

didn't hear, because an idea had suddenly flashed into his mind.

A *flea* circus! he thought. Of course – the fellow we're after is keen on insects. *He might be looking after the fleas!* Gosh, I never even knew there was a flea circus at the Fair! I must certainly go to it tomorrow, and have a look. I wonder if the others knew about it. As soon as I've made my next move, I'll go and telephone Larry.

Eunice at last made a move, and Fatty at once made his. Eunice frowned. 'You ought to think longer,' she said. 'No good chess player plays quickly.'

'I have plenty of time to think out my moves while you're thinking out yours,' said Fatty. 'That's more than enough time, my dear Eunice. As for trying to tell me I'm not a good player, you just wait till you're well and truly beaten – then you'll know who's the good player! Excuse me a moment, I have to go and telephone.'

Eunice was not pleased. She bent her head over the chessboard again, determined to beat Fatty. He went out into the hall and looked round and about cautiously. Nobody appeared to be within listening range.

He was soon speaking to Larry. 'I say, Larry, thanks for giving Eunice tea. I had a funny time going after Mr Tolling. Listen. I can't talk loudly, so glue your ear to the receiver.'

He told Larry how Mr Goon had followed poor Mr Tolling and scared him, and how puzzled and exasperated Goon had been when he, Fatty, had taken Mr Tolling right in at his front gate. Larry roared.

'You always get the exciting bits, Fatty,' he said. 'What about tomorrow? Do we all meet at the Fair again – to see that clown?'

'Yes – and guess what? – did you know there was a flea circus there?' asked Fatty. 'I didn't.'

'Oh yes, I saw a notice up,' said Larry. 'But, gosh, Fatty – you don't want to go to a *flea* circus, surely! Why, even Buster hates fleas.'

'Larry, think back to those notes about You Know Who!' said Fatty, lowering his voice. 'Remember what he liked?'

'Yes. Cats,' said Larry. 'There wasn't anything about liking fleas though. I'm sure there wasn't.'

'I know, but there was a bit about being interested in *insects*,' said Fatty.

'Oh my goodness, yes!' said Larry. 'Of course. I just thought of butterflies or moths or beetles or bees – not fleas. Well, we'd better visit the flea circus tomorrow then. There may be a clue there.'

'Yes. Meet at the crossroads by the bus stop at ten o'clock,' said Fatty. 'Tell Pip and Bets, will you? I must get back to my game of chess. At the rate we're playing it, I probably won't be able to meet you at ten tomorrow! Good-bye.'

He put down the receiver and went back to the chessboard. Eunice had just made a move. To Fatty's horror, he saw that it was an extremely good move – a master move, in fact – and that if he didn't think really hard, he might find himself checkmated.

So for the next ten minutes he forgot all about clowns and flea circuses and Fairs, and frowned over the chessmen. However, he need not have worried, because in the end Buster brought the game to a very sudden finish.

The Scottie had been lying quietly under the little chess table when he thought he heard the scratch-scratch-scratch of a mouse in the wainscoting nearby. He pricked up both ears, and turned his head towards the noise. To his joy, the mouse actually came out of a small hole and ran across the room.

Buster leapt up in excitement and upset the chess table! All the pieces were scattered on the floor, and Eunice shouted in exasperation. 'What did he want to do that for? Just as I had got you into a hole, too, Frederick. Two more moves and I would have checkmated you!'

'You wouldn't,' said Fatty. 'Buster, stop barking, you idiot. You'll bring Mummy in here.'

'I shall put all the pieces back again on the board,' said Eunice, firmly. 'I remember where they were – and we'll go on playing.'

Fatty groaned. He had never been so tired of a game of chess before.

'What made Buster upset the table like that?' said Eunice, severely, picking up the pieces.

'Didn't you see the mouse run across the room?' asked Fatty. 'It ran right by your chair. Buster saw it and . . .'

'What? A *mouse*?' said Eunice, with a shriek. 'Oh *no*! I can't *bear* mice. Is it still here?'

'Bound to be,' said Fatty, pleased to see that the

bold, confident Eunice was trembling all over. Well, well – who would have thought it! Not even little Bets was afraid of mice! 'It was a pretty big mouse too – look, Buster is sniffing round your chair again.'

Eunice gave another shriek and disappeared out of the door at sixty miles an hour. Fatty heaved a sigh of relief and immediately put the chessmen away in their box, then hid them at the back of his mother's sewing cupboard.

'And there they can stay till Eunice has gone,' he decided. 'Don't catch that mouse, Buster. It just about saved my life!'

The evening passed unexpectedly peacefully after that, because after supper had been cleared away, Mr Tolling announced that it would be nice to have a game of bridge.

'Eunice plays a wonderful game,' he said to Mrs Trotteville. 'She and I will take you and your husband on, Mrs Trotteville. I am sure that Frederick will not mind being left out.'

Fatty was only too pleased! He wanted to think over the next morning's plans. He had almost decided that he would go to the Fair in some kind of disguise. It would be easier to mix with the Fair people then, and ask a few questions, and keep his eyes and ears open. He slipped down to his shed as soon as the four others were sitting quietly over the bridge table, Eunice, as usual, laying down the law to everyone.

He locked himself into his shed, drew the old curtains over the windows, and lit his oil-lamp. Now, what about tomorrow's disguise?

I'll go dressed as a youth who wants a job with the Fair, he thought. I'll put a lot of sunburn colouring on my face, and I'll wear false teeth over my own teeth in front – yes, and I'll walk with a bit of a limp. I bet none of the Fair people will think I'm anything to do with the party of children who visited the Fair only this afternoon!

He spent a pleasant hour sorting out the clothes he meant to wear – a very disreputable pair of flannel trousers, with stains all down the legs – a coat that had once belonged to a gardener, and which Fatty had bought from him – a pair of broken-down old shoes, bright yellow socks, and an extremely dirty shirt, striped in what once had been bright colours.

'Yes,' said Fatty, looking at them. 'You'll do fine! I'd better rub dirt into my fingernails too. I forgot that once, and it gave me away! And where's that dirty old handkerchief? I'll put that into the coat pocket.'

He decided to get his mother on his side the next morning, so that she could give Eunice some job to keep her busy. Fatty felt that he really couldn't cope with Eunice any more. It would be too difficult to slip down to his shed and disguise himself if she was about.

So he took Mrs Trotteville into his confidence that night. 'Mummy, *do* you think you could give Eunice a job to do for you tomorrow morning?' he asked. 'I'm doing something special with the others, and it's not really fair on them to drag her about with us *all* the time. They were awfully good to her yesterday.'

Mrs Trotteville sympathised with Fatty just then, because she had become very tired of Eunice at the bridge table that evening. Eunice had had remarkably good cards, and had won every game. She had then proceeded to give the others a most competent lecture on how the game of bridge *ought* to be played, and Mrs Trotteville had suddenly longed to slap her.

So she could quite see Fatty's point about keeping her busy the next day. 'Yes, of course, Frederick,' she said. 'I'll ask her if she will take round the Parish magazines for me – I'm sure she will be thrilled to go round the village with them and tell everyone how to keep their gardens tidy or how to train their dogs!'

Fatty laughed and gave his mother a hug. 'Thanks!' he said. 'All the same, I wouldn't put it past Eunice to deliver all the magazines at top speed, and then come racing after us to see what *we're* doing!'

'You'd better put a mouse into your pocket,' said his mother, much to Fatty's amusement. 'You'd be *quite* safe then!'

12. FATTY AND BERT THE CLOWN

Fatty really enjoyed himself next morning down in his shed. He waited until Eunice had started off with the bundle of Parish magazines and then he began his disguising, whistling quietly to himself.

He gave himself a very sun-tanned face indeed. 'As sun-tanned as the boy in the shooting range!' he said. He then stuck on some shaggy eyebrows over his own, which gave him rather a forbidding expression. He ruffled his hair so that most of it stood up on end.

He dug his fingers into some dark earth just outside the shed and got his nails extremely dirty, and his hands too. Then he dressed himself in the old clothes, and finally put in the prominent false teeth. He looked in the glass and grinned, half-startled himself to see the big teeth that stuck out over his lower lips.

'You'll do,' he said. 'What's your name, now?

Bert? Sid? Alf? Yes, Alf, I think. Come on, Alf, it's time you went to make your enquiries at the Fair.'

He slipped out of the shed, went to the little gate that led into the lane at the bottom of the garden and looked out. No one was about. He could go in safety.

He put his hands in his pocket and slouched down the road, whistling as best he could through his prominent front teeth. He had had to leave Buster behind, for Buster following at his heels would certainly give him away!

He had one very bad moment when he passed the gate of a house not far from his own. Someone came hurrying out and bumped into him. Fatty was about to raise his cap and apologise when he remembered that he was Alf. And then, to his horror, he saw that it was Eunice who had bumped into him. Some of her magazines had fallen to the ground.

'Well, you might at least say you're sorry, young man!' she said. 'And can't you pick those up for me?'

'Pick 'em up yourself,' mumbled Fatty, and ambled off, grinning at the look on Eunice's face.

She hadn't had the slightest idea who he was. His disguise must be quite perfect!

Eunice stared after the slouching youth in disgust. 'Dirty, ill-mannered lout,' she said, and picked up her magazines. 'I'd like to box his ears!'

Fatty made his way to the crossroads where he had planned to meet the others. Ah, yes – there they were, waiting. Good. They were looking down the road for him, but not one of them recognised him as he came shambling up, hands in pockets. He went right past them, grinning to himself.

He sat down on the bus stop seat. 'Got the time, Mister?' he called to Larry.

'Almost ten,' said Larry.

There was a pause, and the others began to talk among themselves. 'I hope he's got rid of Eunice,' he heard Larry say. He called out to him again.

'Got a fag, Mister?'

'No,' said Larry, shortly.

'When's the next bus?' asked Fatty. ''Arf past ten, ain't it?'

'There's a timetable there,' said Pip, pointing to one. They all looked at the youth in disgust. Goodness, what a lout!

'He probably belongs to the Fair,' said Daisy, and that made Fatty chuckle to himself. Then he heard the bus rumbling round the corner and stood up. The others gave a despairing look down the road. 'Fatty's missed the bus,' said Bets, dolefully. 'What do we do? Wait for the next one and see if he turns up?'

'No need to do that,' said Fatty aimably, in his own voice. 'We'll all catch this one. Come on!'

He roared at their amazed faces. They were so astonished that they almost missed the bus, for they stood rooted to the ground! Fatty had to hustle them in.

'Say nothing,' he hissed. 'Don't speak to me in the bus. I'll find some way of talking to you at the Fair.'

The other four sat silent in the bus, quite overcome by Fatty's surprising appearance. Bets shot sidelong glances at him. Never, never would she have thought that it was Fatty sitting alongside her. *Was* it? Well, it must be, because of his voice. How clever he was!

They all got off at the Fair and went in at the gate. 'You can follow me around,' said Fatty, in a low voice. 'Keep your eyes and ears open. I'm going to find the clown first.'

He went on in front of them, and they followed. He came to the little boxing tent and looked for the clown, but there was no one there. The tent was empty, except for the little boxing ring.

'Who are you looking for, mate?' said a boy, passing by, carrying a bucket of water.

'Bert,' said Fatty, remembering the clown's name. 'The clown, you know.'

'He's gone to have a tooth out,' said the boy. 'He'll be back in a few minutes. He was half-mad with toothache in the night.'

'Right. I'll wait,' said Fatty, and sat down on the grass. The other four heard all this, and wandered off, keeping a watch in case Bert came back.

Nobody recognised Bert when he did come back for he was not in his clown-suit. He had a shock of thick dark hair, and the whole of his face, except his sharp eyes was covered by a dirty scarf. He came to the boxing tent and was just about to go inside when Fatty spoke to him.

'Hey? You Bert the clown?'

'Yep,' said Bert, from behind his scarf. 'What's

biting you chum? You waiting for me?'

'Yep,' answered Fatty. 'I . . .'

'Oh – then you'd be the boy old Dicky said he'd send along to help me,' said Bert.

'Yep,' said Fatty, thankfully. This was a bit of luck! 'What do I have to do?'

'You good at figures?' asked Bert, his face still hidden by his scarf. 'Here, I'll show you what kind of figures you'd have to keep. I'm no good at head work, I'm not.'

He disappeared into the tent and came out with a small accounts book which apparently showed the takings for each day. Fatty glanced at the hand that held it out to him. *What* a knobbly one! All bones. A little feeling of excitement crept up his spine.

If only I could see his face now he hasn't got on any paint, I'd know then about the scar, thought Fatty, pretending to go through the account book. His hair's right – and his eyes and eyebrows – and his height. How can I get him to take off that scarf?

He handed back the book. 'Reckon I could keep them figures for you OK,' he said.

'When could you start, chum?' asked Bert.

'Tell you later on,' said Fatty. 'I got to go and see a bloke about another job first. That do?'

'OK by me,' said Bert. 'Long as you let me know today.' He was about to go into the boxing tent when Fatty spoke to him again.

'What you done to your face?' he said. 'Got a cold or something?'

'No,' said Bert. 'Had a tooth out, that's all, and the dentist said I'd better keep my face covered up with this cold wind about.'

'Was it a bad tooth?' said Fatty, with much sympathy in his voice.

'Pretty bad,' said Bert. 'Right in the front too. Good thing I haven't got teeth that stick out like yours, or the gap would show like anything!'

'Let's see it,' said Fatty. 'I bet it won't notice much.' Bert promptly pulled down his scarf and opened his mouth. He pointed to a gap in his top teeth. 'See? That's where he took it out. Had a root as long as a tree's!'

But Fatty was not looking at the teeth – he was looking for a thin, curving scar just above the mouth! He stared hard.

There was no scar there! Not even the sign of

where one might have been! Fatty was bitterly disappointed, for he really had thought that the clown was the man he wanted.

'Nasty place,' he said. 'I reckon it will soon heal though. Well, so long!'

He could see the four others nearby, all gazing as hard as they could when the clown pulled off his scarf. He walked by them. 'No go,' he said out of the side of his mouth. 'He's not the man. Everything fitted except the scar!'

'Let's go to the flea circus now,' said Larry to the others in a loud voice, meant to reach Fatty's ears. And off they all walked, passing Fatty on the way. They went in the direction pointed out by a wooden hand that had 'Flea Circus' painted on it.

But the flea circus was not yet open. A flag flew at the top of a fairly big tent, with 'Fangio's Famous Fleas' printed across it. Fatty peeped inside.

There was only an old woman there – the same old woman who had been sitting in a chair outside the shooting tent the day before. She was over by a table that held big glass cages, gazing intently into them.

'Afternoon, Ma,' said Fatty, and the old lady

jumped at the sound of his voice. She turned her wrinkled face to him, pulling her dirty shawl over her head. 'Is the flea circus open, Ma?' asked Fatty. 'There's some kids here want to see it.'

'My daughter ain't here yet,' said the old woman, in her cracked voice.

'Oh, does *she* run the flea circus?' asked Fatty. 'Who's Fangio then?'

'He was her father,' said the old woman. 'Dead now, though, so she runs it herself, Lucita does. Wunnerful creatures, them fleas. You can make 'em do anything you want to. And strong! Why, you should see what a load they can pull in this little cart!'

'Pull a *cart*! Surely fleas can't pull a *cart*!' said Larry, coming right into the tent. 'Can we see the cart?'

'Yes, you come in,' said the old woman, her face wrinkled up into what Larry supposed was meant to be a smile. *How* wrinkled she was – he wondered if she was a hundred years old! The untidy hair sticking out from under her shawl was white – a dirty white, it is true – but it would have been snowy-white if it had been clean.

'Are you Mrs Fangio?' asked Daisy.

'That's right,' said the old woman. 'Come to help my daughter and my son at the Fair. My son's over at the shooting tent.'

Fatty remembered the son. So did they all! He had been so very like the photos of the escaped prisoner – except that he had no scar above his mouth, and his hands were not knobbly or bony.

'You see here now,' said the old woman, eagerly. 'Here's the little cart – and here's a crane the fleas work – and they can roll this little barrel along.'

'How amazing!' said Daisy. 'But where are the fleas? I hate fleas but I must say I'd like to have a look at such miraculous ones!'

'I'll show you!' said the old woman, but before she could even undo the tiny cages where the fleas were kept, an angry voice called loudly, 'Didn't I say you weren't to touch them fleas? You just keep your hands off them!'

13. FATTY ASKS A QUESTION

Everyone turned round at once. A girl stood in the doorway, a dark-haired, sharp-eyed, young woman. Her thin mouth looked sulky as she stared at the little company.

Now where have I seen her before? thought Fatty at once. She reminds me of someone. Where *have* I seen someone like her?

The girl came into the tent, scowling. 'Clear out,' she said to the children, and then turned to Fatty, evidently regarding him as belonging to the Fair, 'Clear those kids out. We

don't allow anyone in the tent when there's no show on. Them fleas are valuable.'

She then turned on the old woman. 'Didn't you say you'd keep your hands off of them fleas?' she said. 'Interfering again, I suppose! You let them be, they're mine.'

'You shouldn't ought to talk to your old mother

121

like that,' said the old woman, darting a fierce glance at the young woman. She opened her mouth as if to make a sharp retort, looked at the children standing near the doorway, and thought better of it.

'Want any help here?' said Fatty, still wondering who it was that the girl reminded him of.

'Well, *she's* supposed to keep the tent clean,' said the girl, with an angry look at the old woman. 'But you can sweep it out if you want. I'll pay you.'

'But are you sure your mother won't mind?' said Fatty. 'I don't want to do her out of a job.'

'I've got another job tomorrow,' cackled the old woman. 'You can have this job, young feller, and I hope you don't feel the edge of that girl's tongue as often as I do! Fleas! I could manage fleas better than she can, before she was born.'

'Oh, get out,' said the young woman. 'And don't go near Josef. He's in a vile temper today.'

What an unpleasant family! thought Fatty, taking a broom from the back of the tent and beginning to sweep the littered ground. 'Who's Josef?' he asked.

'My brother. Over at the shooting tent,' said the girl. 'He's my twin.'

Fatty stopped sweeping and looked at her. Of *course*! That was who she reminded him of – the young man over at the shooting tent, the one who was so like the escaped prisoner. The same sharp eyes, dark brows, the same springing dark hair, thin mouth and sulky look. So they were twins – that explained the likeness!

'Got any more brothers or sisters?' he asked, wondering if perhaps there was another brother who might be the man he wanted.

'No. Josef and I are all that's left of our family,' said the girl.

'And your mother,' said Fatty, sweeping hard.

'Oh, her – yes,' said the girl, who obviously had no love for the old woman.

'Do you sleep here in this tent?' asked Fatty. He could not see any bedding and he wondered what the girl and her brother did at night.

'No! We have a caravan, down in Barker's Field,' said the girl. 'There's a crowd of them there. Want to know a lot, don't you? You new to the Fair?'

'Yes,' said Fatty, truthfully. 'Always had a liking for Fairs, so I came here to look for a job. I wouldn't mind working in a circus, either – especially with animals.'

'Well, keep off lions and tigers,' said the girl. 'They'll flash out their paws at you for nothing when you pass them – and maybe scar you for life!'

'Talking of scars,' said Fatty, 'did you ever meet anyone with a scar curving above his upper lip?'

'And what do you mean by *that*?' said the girl, and she gave Fatty such a glare that he was astonished. 'Go on, what do you mean by *that*?'

'Nothing,' said Fatty, surprised.

'You clear out,' said the girl, and held out a coin. 'And don't come back here.'

'But why – what have I said to upset you?' asked Fatty. 'I didn't mean . . .'

'Clear out or I'll have Josef run you out,' said the girl crisply, and Fatty decided that it was best to go, and go quickly. He went out of the tent, looked round for the others, and gave them a brief nod. Then he made for the gate, and went out. He waited outside for the four to come along.

'I do wish we could have seen those performing fleas,' said Bets, as she came up. 'Hello, Fa . . .'

'Sh!' hissed Fatty, and Bets went red,

remembering that Fatty must never be recognised when in disguise.

'We'll catch the bus back,' said Larry, and they all made for the bus stop, Fatty a little way behind, as if he did not belong to them.

The top of the bus was empty when they got on, so they all trooped upstairs. 'Anything interesting, Fatty?' asked Larry.

'I don't know. I *think* so,' said Fatty. 'We won't talk here. All come down to my shed, please; we'll meet there. I want to talk something over.'

Fatty leapt off the bus as soon as it stopped and made his way to the lane at the back of his garden. He slipped in through the little gate there and went cautiously to the nearby shed. Was Eunice anywhere about? She didn't appear to be. Good!

The others soon joined him, and he locked the door. 'What's up, Fatty?' asked Larry. 'Oh, blow – there's Buster outside – he must have heard our voices. I'll let him in.'

Having let in the excited little Scottie, they all settled down again, and looked expectantly at Fatty.

'It's something that girl said – the girl who owns the fleas,' said Fatty. 'First of all, I must tell you that she's twin to that fellow in the shooting tent – the one we thought was so like the escaped prisoner.'

'Oh, I *thought* she reminded me of someone,' said Bets. 'Of course, that's who it was. Go on, Fatty.'

'Well, I was sweeping the tent out for her, and talking,' said Fatty, 'and I happened to say that I'd like to work with animals, in a circus, and she said, "Well, keep off lions and tigers. They'll flash out their paws at you for nothing when you pass them, and maybe scar you for life." And *I* said, quite casually, "Talking of scars, did you ever meet anyone with a scar curving above his upper lip?"'

'And what did she say then?' asked Pip.

'She said, "And what do you mean by *that*?"' said Fatty, 'and gave me such a glare. Then she said, "You clear out and don't come back here." Just like that.'

There was a silence. 'What did she mean?' said Daisy, puzzled.

'That's what *I* want to know,' said Fatty. 'My question disturbed her – maybe even frightened her. Why?'

'Because she jolly well *does* know someone with

a scar above his upper lip!' said Larry. 'That's why!'

'Exactly,' said Fatty. 'Now you see why I wanted to have a talk about it.'

'My word, yes, we've got to get to the bottom of this,' said Larry, excited. 'If she does know someone with a scar like that, it's obviously the escaped prisoner. Well, he's not at the Fair. We've pretty well seen everyone closely now – so where is he?'

'Where does that girl live?' asked Pip. 'In the Fair?'

'No, in a caravan that stands with a good many others in Barker's Field,' said Fatty.

'Would she be hiding this fellow, do you think?' asked Larry. 'In her caravan, perhaps? Would he be another brother?'

'No. She told me that she and her twin are all that's left of her family,' said Fatty. 'Except that ugly old mother, of course. But yet, she and her brother are so like the photo of that man, aren't they? I wonder if the Chief Inspector knows if there's another brother?'

'You could easily find out,' said Pip. 'Wait – doesn't it say in those notes you had?'

Fatty took them out of a drawer and the five of them examined them. 'Yes, it says here, "Family. No brothers or sisters. Father and mother dead. One uncle, dead. No children." '

'Well, that girl and her twin *can't* be his brother or sister,' said Larry. 'All the same, Fatty, I wish you could have a snoop round their caravans!'

'So do I,' said Fatty. 'But I don't see how I can. I mean, it stands among a lot of others, and I'd easily be seen prying round in the daytime – and at night they'd be in the caravan, and I wouldn't *dare* to go knocking at it!'

A voice broke into their conference. It was Eunice's! 'Frederick! Are you in your shed? Don't you know it's lunchtime, and if you want to go to the first meeting this afternoon, you oughtn't to be late.'

'Oh, blow Eunice!' said Fatty, in disgust. 'Is it as late as that? Gosh, yes it is! Well, we seem to be up against a blank wall. Think about it, will you, and telephone me if anyone sees a way out! ALL RIGHT, EUNICE, I'M COMING!'

The others slipped quickly out of the shed, avoided Eunice, and went out of the little gate that led into the back lane. Fatty stripped off his filthy things, cleaned his face and dressed himself. He arrived five minutes late for lunch and sat down, apologising.

'Sorry. Didn't notice the time!' he said. 'Yes, I'll have some ham, please, Mummy.'

He took up his knife and fork, and then discovered that he had forgotten to clean his nails. They were still full of dirt he had forced into them! He tried to hold his knife and fork with bent fingers, so that his nails did not show. His mother noticed at once.

'Frederick! What's the matter, dear? Have you hurt your hands?'

Everyone immediately looked at Fatty's curiously-bent fingers.

'Oh, it's nothing,' said Fatty. 'Just a touch of cramp, that's all.'

Eunice at once took hold of his right hand and straightened the fingers as if to get the cramp out. 'The best thing is to . . .' she began, as Fatty snatched his hand away. But his mother had already seen the filthy nails and looked coldly at Fatty.

'Please go and do your nails, Frederick,' she said, and Fatty fled, conscious of the shocked eyes of Mr Tolling, his mother and Eunice. Thank goodness his father had gone back to his work!

'We shall be late, we shall be late,' fussed Mr Tolling, when Fatty came back and lunch proceeded on its leisurely way. 'Frederick, are you sure you can be ready when Eunice is? Have you your ticket? We really must start soon. I do hope you will have a most enjoyable afternoon!'

Fatty was certain he wouldn't. He was sure that he would not find the escaped prisoner at the Coleopterist conference. No, he would much more likely be found in a caravan in Barker's Field. What a *nuisance* to have to go to such a dull meeting – and with Eunice, of all people!

14. A VERY INTERESTING AFTERNOON

It was only about seven minutes' walk to the Town Hall. Mr Tolling hurried along, with Eunice and Fatty just behind. Quite a number of other people were hurrying along to the Town Hall too! Fatty was surprised to think that there were so many beetle-lovers staying in Peterswood.

He was also surprised to see how many of the men wore moustaches and beards. 'Is it a sort of uniform with coleopterists to wear hair on their faces?' he enquired of Eunice.

'Don't be silly,' she said. 'Look, there's the wonderful Maria Janizena, the one who hatched out all those eighty-four beetles from Thibet.'

'Oh yes, the 168 twins,' said Fatty, remembering. He stared at the great Maria Janizena and shuddered. 'She looks very like a big beetle herself,' he said in a low voice to Eunice. 'And those things sticking up in her hat are rather like the horns my stag beetles had.'

He expected Eunice to be angry and scornful at such a disrespectful remark, but to his surprise she gave a sudden giggle. 'Don't,' she said. 'Father will hear.'

They went up the steps of the Town Hall just behind Mr Tolling. When he was almost at the top, Fatty had a shock. Mr Goon was there, standing beside a man who held a long list in his hand, apparently helping with the checking of the members.

Mr Goon must have got some idea that the man we want will come here, thought Fatty, at once. Now who told him that? The Chief Inspector? Or has he worked it out himself, as I did – that the man is interested in insects, and so will come to the conference – and may probably even be a member!'

Mr Goon was even more surprised to see Fatty than Fatty was to see him. He scowled, and then looked quickly down the list held by the man standing near him. Mr Tolling presented his ticket, and Eunice presented hers. Mr Goon then barred Fatty's way.

'Sorry,' he said. 'Only ticket holders admitted.'

'Oh – *I'm* vouching for him. He's my guest for this conference,' said Mr Tolling, much to Goon's annoyance. He let Fatty past, glaring at him. That boy! Always turning up where he wasn't wanted. Did *he* think too that that escaped prisoner might be somewhere about in this peculiar conference?

Fatty sat down with Eunice and Mr Tolling. He began to study the people around him. They all looked extremely earnest, almost as if they had come to church. The few women looked even more serious than the men. The wonderful Maria Janizena was up on the platform with the other big noises, the spiky things in her hat nodding to and fro as she spoke to the men on each side of her.

'Aren't there any beetles to see?' asked Fatty. 'Is it going to be talky-talk all the time?'

'There's a show of beetles in another room, I think,' whispered back Eunice. 'There usually is. Very, very precious too they are – lots of them from different collections! We'll go and see them afterwards. I'll show you some that my father caught. Very rare ones.'

Fatty came to the conclusion that beetle-lovers

were very much alike to look at – they were either bald and bearded, or bushy-haired and bearded. The few who had no moustache or beard stood out among the crowd, and it was only a minute's work to discover that not one had a curving scar above his upper lip.

Not that I really had a hope to see one, thought Fatty. Gosh, I wish I'd thought of disguising myself and painting a scar above my mouth, and coming here. Goon would have been too thrilled for words!

He ran down the list of names of members obligingly lent to him by Eunice. Some of them were foreign and very peculiar-sounding – no help to Fatty at all. He began to feel that it was an utter waste of time to come to the meeting. The only thing that would be any real help would be to pull at a few moustaches and see if they came off and were hiding any scar beneath! But that, unfortunately, was impossible.

The meeting was even duller than Fatty had feared it might be, though Mr Tolling appeared to enjoy it very much, listening intently to every word that was said by the speakers on the platform.

Fatty began to yawn, though he tried his hardest to stop. Mr Tolling gave him a stern look, but somehow that made Fatty yawn all the more.

He looked round to see if Mr Goon was still at his place by the door. Yes, he was – presumably to stop any gatecrashers. As Fatty looked at him, he yawned – a most prodigious yawn that set Fatty off again. He caught Fatty's eye and glared. Pest of a boy – copying his yawn like that! Goon spent a pleasant few minutes thinking of some of the things he would like to say to Fatty if only he had the chance.

At last, when Fatty was almost asleep, the meeting was over. 'Now we go to the other room to examine the specimens,' whispered Eunice. 'They're really interesting. I'll show you Father's.'

Goon was already in the outer room when the members filed in. Round the room were trestle-tables and on them were big cases, glass-fronted, in which there were specimens of many different kinds of bettles.

'Are there any *live* beetles?' Fatty asked Mr Tolling who, with gleaming eyes, was already examining a case of curious horned beetles.

'Oh yes, there should be,' said Mr Tolling. He spoke to someone beside him, a man whom Fatty had seen sitting on the platform. 'Good-afternoon, Sir Victor – may I congratulate you on your speech? And do you happen to know if there are any cases of live beetles – my young friend here wants to know.'

'Oh yes, yes,' said Sir Victor, whose beard reached almost down to the bottom of his waistcoat. 'But we had a sad accident yesterday, when we were arranging them – two cases were carelessly handled, fell, and broke. Mercifully, most mercifully, we were able to capture all the live beetles but one.'

'Aren't you showing those beetles then?' asked Mr Tolling, disappointed.

'Yes. It so happened that the old woman engaged to come as a cleaner this week has a daughter who runs what is, I believe, called a flea circus at some local Fair – and as these people have well-made display cages for their performing insects, we were able to borrow two of them. *Most* fortunate! Look, there they are over there – in some ways they are better than ours for display purposes!'

Fatty was interested to hear this, as he had seen the flea cages that very morning at the Fair. What was the name of the bad-tempered girl who owned them – Lucita? He looked along the row of display cages and recognised two that were like the one the old woman had shown him that morning. Live beetles were running about in them.

Behind the two cages was the old woman herself, duster in hand. So this was the 'new job' she had spoken about to Lucita – she had taken work as a cleaner while the conference was on. Fatty took a good look at her and wondered if *she* knew anyone with a scar that curved above his upper lip.

Fatty decided to speak to her. She would never recognise him as the boy she had seen in the flea circus tent that morning, for he now looked totally different.

He spoke to Mr Tolling as they leaned over the cases of scurrying beetles. 'I'm sure I saw cages like these at Peterswood Fair,' he said. The old woman heard him, as he meant her to.

'They'm borrowed from there,' she said in her cackling voice. 'They'm flea cages from the flea circus, young sir.'

Mr Goon loomed up majestically. 'Get on with your work, woman,' he said, shocked that a cleaner should talk to anyone at the conference. The old creature gave him a sharp look out of screwed-up eyes and moved away with her duster, flicking it here and there.

'Wonderful creatures, beetles, Mr Goon,' said Fatty, in the extra-polite tones that Mr Goon disliked and distrusted. 'Have you see the Seven-Spotted Helmeted Kicking Beetle from Ollaby-Oon in Grootenburgenstein?'

'Gah!' said Mr Goon, and gave Fatty one of his fiercest glares. He moved away ponderously. That boy! Him and his helmeted beetles – that was a dig at *him*, of course, because he wore a helmet!

Mr Tolling was extremely surprised to hear Fatty speak of a Seven-Spotted Helmeted Kicking Beetle from Ollaby-Oon in Grootenburgenstein, wherever *that* was.

'Er – that is a new kind of beetle to me,' he said. 'Are you sure you've got the name right, Frederick?'

'Well, it might be the *Five*-Spotted one I mean,' said Fatty. 'I'll just have a look round the cases and see if they've got the beetle I'm thinking of.'

As Fatty had invented the beetle that very minute, it was not likely that he would find it displayed anywhere, nor did he intend to look. An idea had suddenly come into his head. He moved off, leaving Mr Tolling to gaze earnestly into every case to see if by any chance the beetle Fatty had quoted was being shown.

The old woman was dusting vigorously just behind where Goon was now standing. It had occurred to Fatty that it might be rather interesting to go over to Goon and ask him a question that might also interest the old woman, Mrs Fangio.

'Oh – Mr Goon – I'd just like to ask you a question, if you don't mind,' said Fatty, politely.

Goon stared at him suspiciously. *Now* what was up?

'What's that?' he said.

'Well, I wondered if you had seen a man here with a thin scar curving above his upper lip,' said Fatty, in a voice loud enough to reach old Mrs Fangio, busy dusting behind the big policeman.

Mr Goon was startled – especially as he himself had been looking out all the afternoon for exactly what Fatty had just described. So Fatty was on the same job as he was – trying to spot that escaped prisoner! *Why* had the Chief Inspector told this toad of a boy anything about the case? He began to swell with rage, and his face turned a familiar purple.

But Fatty was not watching Goon. No, he was looking closely at the old woman standing just behind. Her back had been turned when he asked the question, and for a few seconds she kept it turned, standing suddenly very still. Then she swung round and looked at him – a puzzled, half-amazed look that turned in a twinkling to an extraordinarily malevolent glare that shocked him.

Then she turned round and began dusting again, moving away as she flicked her duster here and there.

Mr Goon was saying something to Fatty in an exasperated voice, but Fatty had no idea what it was. He had discovered what he wanted to know – that the old woman knew what he meant, just as her daughter Lucita had known – yes, both of them knew the man with the scar!

Did they also know where he was hiding? Was

he in Peterswood – perhaps in the caravan colony? Well, that was something that Fatty meant to find out!

15. TEA PARTIES

Fatty soon began to feel bored. He was longing to get back home and work out what he could do next. To his delight, he discovered that Eunice was bored too.

'I thought you adored beetles,' he said.

'Well, I don't,' said Eunice. 'Nor would you if you'd been to as many beetle shows as I have. But I have to back my father up, and go with him. Can't we go off and have some tea somewhere?'

Fatty began to think that Eunice wasn't so bad after all. 'But what will your father say?' he asked.

'Oh, I'll just tell him that you've kindly asked us both out to tea, and I don't want to disappoint you,' said Eunice.

'But I *haven't* asked your father,' said Fatty. '*Must* we? I really don't want to hear another word about beetles today or ever.'

'*He* won't come,' said Eunice. 'Nothing will

make him leave this conference and the beetles until he's *turned* out. You'll see.'

Eunice was quite right, and Fatty marched out with her, giving Mr Goon a condescending nod as he passed him.

'Hey,' said Mr Goon, whose mind was still puzzling about Fatty's curious question to him. 'Hey – a word with you, please, Frederick. About that man – You Know Who . . .'

'Another time, Mr Goon,' said Fatty, exasperatingly, and ran down the steps of the Town Hall.

'What man does the policeman mean?' asked Eunice, curiously. 'Why did you speak so shortly to him – he's nice. That's the one who helped me to fight that awful old tramp the other day. The one who was in your shed, smoking a pipe, and was so violent, you know.'

'Yes – *I* know,' said Fatty. 'I know that tramp very well indeed. As well as I know myself in fact. And he's *not* violent, nor does he smoke a pipe.'

'You don't know *any*thing about him!' cried Eunice. 'You weren't there – you only came along afterwards.'

'I was there all the time, if you'll pardon me contradicting you,' said Fatty.

'I wish you wouldn't talk in riddles,' said Eunice, pettishly. 'You're supposed to be intelligent, but honestly no one would think it sometimes. I consider it was really brave of me to tackle that tramp. You're only saying that he wasn't violent just to make out that I'm not brave after all.'

'Let's drop the subject,' said Fatty, feeling sure that he would tell Eunice the truth about the tramp if the quarrel went on any longer. 'Look, here's a tea shop. Will this one suit Your Majesty or not?'

'I'm not going to have tea with you if you talk like that,' said Eunice, beginning to be afraid that at last she had met someone who could exasperate her to tears.

'Right,' said Fatty, in his extra-polite voice. 'I'll go in here and have tea, and you can go into another tea shop and have tea. I'll come in and pay your bill when you've finished. Will *that* suit you?'

Eunice glared at him and gave in. She followed him into the little tea shop and sat down. 'I'll have buttered toast and some of those cream cakes,' she said.

'Very good idea,' said Fatty, and gave the order. The waitress brought an enormous pile of buttery toast and a dish of marvellous cakes.

'I can't possibly eat all this toast,' said Eunice.

'You don't have to,' said Fatty. 'Half is mine.'

'You're slimming,' said Eunice. 'You surely can't be so weak-minded as to eat half that buttered toast and half those cakes!'

'Gosh, *why* do I keep on forgetting I'm trying to be good?' groaned Fatty, looking longingly at the two full dishes. Eunice had trapped him properly! It *would* be weak-minded to eat his share, now that she had reminded him he was slimming – and yet he couldn't bear to sit and watch her gobble up the whole lot, as she most certainly would. Greedy pig!

Then, to his enormous delight, he saw Pip and Bets passing the shop. He shot out of his seat and hurried to the door. 'Pip – Bets – come on in and have some tea with me? Quick!'

In delighted surprise, Pip went into the tea shop, followed by Bets. 'Eunice is here too, but you don't need to bother about her,' said Fatty. 'Just tuck in well, both of you!'

So they did, much to Eunice's annoyance. 'Aren't *you* having any?' asked Bets, in surprise, seeing Fatty's empty plate.

'No. I'm being strong-minded,' he said, and grinned at Eunice's scowl. 'Eunice and I have been to the beetle show. Goon was there – he tried to keep me out.'

'Fatty, you didn't spot You Know Who, did you?' asked Bets, in a low voice. But Eunice's ears were quick, and she heard.

'Who's You Know Who?' she asked, with her mouth full of toast.

'I can't make out what you say when you've got your mouth full,' said Fatty, reprovingly. Eunice gave a snort and emptied her mouth. 'I *know* you've all got something on between you,' she began. 'Some secret you're not telling me. I daresay it's something silly, but it isn't good manners to keep talking secrets when I'm with you.'

'We don't,' said Pip, taking a cake.

'All right then – who's this You Know Who?' said Eunice.

'Sorry,' said Fatty. 'Can't tell you. Actually it's a police secret that we just happened to get to know about.'

'Oooh, what a fib!' said Eunice, disbelievingly. 'Police secret indeed! I don't believe it.'

'Fine!' said Fatty, irritatingly. '*Don't* believe it then. That suits *us* all right.'

Eunice lost her temper and went a bright red. 'You're mean! You're ill-mannered! And I warn you that I shall jolly well ferret out your silly secret, whatever it is – and I'll tell everyone about it!'

'Perhaps that's why we don't tell you,' said Fatty, politely. 'In case you do tell everyone about it. Anyway, thanks for warning us.'

Eunice got up from the table and stormed out, much to the amazement of the other people in the shop. Fatty grinned at Pip and Bets. 'She managed to eat a very good tea before she departed,' he said. 'Have some more cakes? I'm longing to have one. I didn't dare to while Eunice was there, in case she thought I was weak-minded. But, after all, getting fit doesn't mean absolutely *starving* myself!'

He ordered another plateful, and examined it closely.

'Which do you want, Bets?' he asked.

Bets laughed. 'I don't mind – but I know what *you* want, Fatty!' she said, and put an éclair and a cream bun on his plate. He grinned at her.

'You always read my thoughts, young Bets,' he said, and she smiled, delighted. Good old Fatty. How could that awful Eunice be so rude to him?

Fatty told Pip and Bets about his afternoon at the beetle conference, and the question he had asked Goon in front of Mrs Fangio, the old woman from the Fair. 'I just wanted to see if she jumped or seemed frightened, when I asked Mr Goon about the man with the scar,' he said.

'And did she?' said Pip.

'Yes. When she first heard me asking, she stood absolutely still,' said Fatty. 'Then she turned round, looking really amazed – and then gave me such a wicked look! Whew! If looks could have killed, I'd be lying there dead in front of her.'

'Don't say things like that, Fatty,' said Bets. 'Why *should* she have looked at you like that?'

Someone came and sat down at the next table. 'Don't say any more,' said Fatty. 'Let's go to

Larry's and all have a talk about it. Waitress, can I have the bill?'

It was quite a large bill, and for the hundredth time Pip and Bets marvelled at the amount of money Fatty always seemed to have. Just like a grown-up, Bets thought as he paid the bill and tipped the waitress.

They all went up to Larry's, and soon the five of them, and Buster whom they had collected on the way, sat down in Larry's summerhouse. Fatty told of his afternoon's doings again.

'That old woman called Mrs Fangio, Lucita's mother, got a job as cleaner at the Town Hall this week,' he said. 'And I suppose when there was a difficulty over the broken beetle cases, she suggested borrowing Lucita's performing flea cages – she would get a bit of money for that, of course. Perhaps that was what made Lucita so annoyed with her yesterday – she may have taken them without asking her.'

'Quite likely,' said Larry.

'Tell Larry and Daisy what happened when you asked Mr Goon about the man with the scar,' said Bets.

Fatty retold the incident. 'So, you see, it's quite obvious that not only Lucita knows about the man with the scar, but her mother does too. You know I can't help wondering if they are hiding him,' said Fatty.

'I'm pretty sure they are,' said Larry. 'Or at least they know where he *is* hiding. I wonder what relation he is to them. His photo is so like Josef – and like Lucita too – that he really must be related to them. And yet you say that Lucita said there were only she and her twin brother in her family, and her old mother. I'd ask the Chief Inspector about it, if I were you, Fatty.'

'I think I will,' said Fatty. 'And I think that, if I possibly can, I'll slip out tonight and go down to Barker's Field and see what I can pick up about the Fangios. I'll put on my tramp clothes – what a shock for Eunice if she sees me again!'

They talked a little more, and then Fatty departed with Buster. He debated whether to ring up the Chief Inspector at home, or from a call box. Eunice might be somewhere about at home. But there was someone already in the public call box so he had to wait till he got home. Then, after making sure that Eunice was not in sight, he telephoned Chief Inspector Jenks.

'Sir, it's Frederick Trotteville here,' he said. 'I've not got much further with that case, so far – but I want to know if you can tell me something, sir. It's about the man with a scar. I've spotted two people very like him to look at – twins – a brother and a sister, surname Fangio. But they say there aren't any others of their family, only themselves and their old mother. Could this other fellow be a cousin or some sort of relation, do you think?'

'Shouldn't think so,' came back the Chief's clear voice. 'He's apparently got no family, as you probably saw in those notes. His surname is Harris – or so he says. It's probably just a fluke that you saw any likeness.'

'Blow!' said Fatty, and put down the receiver. '*That* clue's gone west then!'

16. ADVENTURE FOR GOON
- AND EUNICE

No sooner had he put down the receiver than he heard a little scrambling noise from somewhere in the hall. Someone had been listening! Fatty hunted round, but whoever it was must have run up the stairs.

I bet that was Eunice! he thought. Bother her! I didn't *really* think she meant to spy on me. I shall have to be really careful when I go out disguised as an old tramp again tonight!

He gave Eunice a sharp look when he went into the dining-room for the evening meal at seven o'clock. She looked at him demurely – too demurely. He felt sure she had listened in to his telephone conversation. Still, what had she gained by it? Only that he was apparently looking for a man with a scar – who had a likeness to twins called Fangio. *That* wasn't going to help her much!

He suddenly thought of an idea and grinned as

he ate his soup. 'What's the joke, Frederick?' asked his mother. Fatty cast hurriedly about in his mind for some joke to tell her.

'Well, I was just remembering Mr Goon's face this afternoon when I asked him if he had seen the Seven-Spotted Helmeted Kicking Beetle from Ollaby-oon in Grootenburgenstein,' said Fatty, much to Mr Tolling's amazement. He put down his soup spoon and stared at Fatty, interested.

'The Seven-Spotted *Helmeted* Beetle,' he said. 'I must have missed that. I really must see it tomorrow. I will ask that policeman to show me where it is.'

'Yes, do,' said Fatty. 'He'll be interested to hear about it again.'

'*Frederick*!' said his mother warningly, sure that the helmeted beetle was a make-up of Fatty's, especially thought of for the helmeted Goon.

'Yes, Mother?' said Fatty, turning an innocent gaze on Mrs Trotteville. She shook her head at him and gave it up. But Mr Tolling didn't. He pursued the subject of helmeted beetles for some time, and Fatty learnt, to his great surprise, that there really *were* 'helmeted' beetles, and that apparently Mr

Tolling knew every one of them, which bored the whole table considerably.

'Shall we have another game of chess tonight?' asked Eunice, turning to Fatty as the meal ended with beetles still the subject of conversation.

'No, thanks,' said Fatty, briskly. 'I've got to do some cross-country running tonight. I haven't done any today, and it's a fine night. Another time, Eunice.'

'I'll come with you,' said Eunice. 'I could do with a bit of exercise too. It's lovely running this time of the evening. I often do at home.'

What a truly exasperating girl! Didn't she *know* when she was not wanted? All right, Fatty would give her the shock of her life!

'I'll go and change into a tracksuit and wait here for you,' said Eunice, quite determined not to let Fatty out of her sight. If he thought he was going to rush off to Larry or Pip, then she was going to come too. She didn't see why she should be left out of any excitement going on.

Fatty didn't say a word. He disappeared down to his shed and hurriedly dressed himself in his tramp clothes once more. He made up his face, stuck on the shaggy brows, and put in the prominent false teeth – and, finally, drew a horrible scar all down one cheek!

The man with a scar! he chuckled to himself. Look out, Eunice – here he comes!

He went out of the shed and locked the door. He stole up the garden and came to the house. He knew that his parents and Mr Tolling had left to have a game of bridge with some friends. Only Eunice would be in the sitting-room, waiting for him.

Buster, shut up in his bedroom, was whining dolefully, as he always did when Fatty was going out without him. Eunice heard him up there, and thought that Fatty must be with him. She sat patiently waiting in the sitting-room, keeping a sharp ear for stealthy footsteps, in case Fatty thought of going running without her.

She heard what she was listening for – stealthy footsteps! Where did they come from? Outside the window, surely! Eunice tiptoed to the window and peered out – and there, staring at her from a bush, was the tramp – the horrible old fellow that she had seen in Fatty's shed before! But this time he had a dreadful scar running down his face.

Eunice stared in horror! 'Help!' she cried. 'Here's that tramp again. Help! Frederick, where are you? That tramp's here again! Frederick!'

Jane, the maid, came running in at once. 'What is it?' she cried. But by that time, Fatty had gone from the bush. He knew that Jane's sharp eyes would recognise him through his disguise; she had seen him as an old tramp far too often!

Eunice pointed to the bush where she had seen Fatty. 'He was there – that tramp again,' she said. 'What shall we do? Everyone's out! Where's Frederick, isn't he in his bedroom?'

'I'll go and see,' said Jane. But the only occupant of Fatty's bedroom was Buster, who flew down the stairs at top speed as soon as Jane opened the door, wondering what Eunice's screams had been about.

'Frederick wasn't in his room,' reported Jane. 'He must have gone without you, Miss.'

'Oh dear. I think I'd better ring up the police,' said Eunice. 'Yes, I must. I think somebody ought to come up and have a look round. Why, the house might be burgled tonight!'

So Eunice rang up the police, and Mr Goon answered promptly. 'Police here. Who is it?'

'This is Miss Eunice Tolling, staying with Mr and Mrs Trotteville,' said Eunice. 'I want to report seeing a horrible old tramp here, like the one I saw on Sunday.'

Goon frowned. Now, what was this? He remembered Eunice perfectly, of course – but he also knew that that tramp on Sunday was *not* a tramp. And he, Goon, was NOT going on a wild tramp-chase again, not for anyone!

'Right, Miss. I'll take a few notes,' said Goon. 'Sorry I can't come up, but there's business here to detain me.'

'But you *must* come up!' cried Eunice. 'I tell you, it's the same man – and I got a closer look at him this time – he's got a horrible scar on his face.'

Goon got quite a shock. 'A *scar*?' he said. 'Are you sure?'

'Yes. Oh do come along here quickly,' begged Eunice. 'You might be able to catch him. Buster's in the garden too, looking for him, I expect.'

That piece of news did not please Mr Goon at all. He never liked Buster to be loose if he was anywhere near him. Still, a man with a *scar*! That really sounded something! Suppose he was the escaped prisoner? What a feather it would be in Goon's cap if he could catch him – *and* in that pest of a boy's own garden!

'Where's Frederick?' he asked.

'Out cross-country running,' answered Eunice.

Good! thought Goon. So *he's* out of the way. Well, I'll go up straight away.

He mounted his bicycle and pedalled up to the Trottevilles' house. He left his bicycle just inside the front gate and went quietly round to the garden door and through it. 'Miss!' he called cautiously, and gave Eunice and Jane such a fright that they both screamed loudly.

'Oh, it's you,' said Jane. 'What do you want to come creeping in on us like that for?'

'Well, I didn't want to give that fellow any warning,' said Goon. 'Now – where's this bush you saw him in, Miss? And – er – where's that dog?'

'He's still about, I think,' said Jane, which made poor Goon feel very nervous indeed.

'You both come with me and we'll work through the garden,' he said. 'And if that dog appears, you call him, Miss. He might think I'm the tramp and go for me.'

So they all three worked through the garden, poking into every bush. There was no sign of Buster, which delighted Goon very much.

After almost an hour's search, Goon gave it up. 'That tramp's gone,' he said. 'Wish I knew where. I'm looking for a fellow with a scar, and it'd be a feather in my cap if I could lay my hands on him. Whereabouts was this scar, Miss? Just above his upper lip, I suppose?'

'Oh no, all down one cheek,' said Eunice in surprise. 'Whatever made you think it was just above his mouth?'

Goon stared at her, bitterly disappointed and really angry. 'But – but I thought you meant – oh well, I suppose you couldn't know where the scar ought to be. Blow it, it's not the man I thought it was. It must have been – oh *no*! – yes, it *must* have been that toad of a boy disguised again! And you said he'd gone *running*! What do you mean by telling me such fairy tales!'

Eunice stared at the angry policeman in dismay. 'I don't know what you're talking about,' she said. 'And I will *not* be talked to like this. I shall go to bed.'

And away she went, holding her head high. How DARE that horrid policeman speak to her like that.

Jane laughed. 'There goes Miss High and Mighty!' she said. 'You look hot and bothered, Mr Goon, sir. You come along into my kitchen and I'll make you a cup of tea, and give you one of Cookie's shortbread biscuits. For all we know, Miss Eunice didn't see anyone at all – just a moving shadow!'

Mr Goon removed his helmet, wiped his hot head, and graciously accepted Jane's invitation. He sat in her kitchen enjoying himself, telling her tales of his valour, and of the numberless arrests he had made. He didn't hear quiet footsteps coming to the lighted kitchen window. He didn't see a scarred face peering in at him. He didn't even guess that Fatty had come back, still in his tramp clothes, and was even now getting out of them down in the shed.

Goon suddenly caught sight of the kitchen clock and was horrified to see the time. 'I must go. Where's my helmet?' he said. 'My word, how the time's gone. Goodnight to you, Miss, and thank you.'

He blundered out into the garden and went to find his bicycle. To his consternation, it was gone! 'I *know* I left it just here – and it's gone! It's been stolen!' he said. 'That fathead of a girl is the cause of this – bringing me away from all my work to hunt someone I thought was the man with the scar. Gah! Now I've got to walk home.'

And walk home he did, only to find the telephone ringing as soon as he got in. NOW who wanted him? If it was *another* tale about a tramp, he'd go mad!

But it was Fatty's smooth, confident voice. 'Is that you, Mr Goon? I have to report that there is a bicycle leaning by our kitchen door. I don't know whose it is, but possibly you have had one reported to you as stolen.'

'You – you pest!' shouted Goon into the telephone. 'You found my bike by your front gate, I know you did – and you took it away and hid it till I left – and now it's by your kitchen door, you say. Well, WHO put it there? That's what *I* want to know. WHO put it there?'

But there was no answer except a chuckle. The phone went dead, and Goon groaned. Now he had got to walk all the way back and fetch his bicycle! All right, Frederick Trotteville, you just wait – you'll get paid back one day!

17. FATTY HAS A SURPRISE

While Mr Goon and Eunice and Jane had been searching feverishly for the old tramp, Fatty had been having quite an interesting time. He had hurriedly left his garden by the little gate at the bottom, as soon as he heard Goon coming on his bicycle. Then he had made his way towards the river.

Barker's Field is the one near old Barker's farmhouse, he thought. If I meet anyone in this tramp get-up, I'll ask if they can tell me of any old barn I'd be allowed to sleep in. Gosh, what a scream Eunice let out when she saw my face peeping out of that bush! I hope Mr Goon and she had a wonderful time hunting all through the garden!

He put on a limp whenever he met anyone, and suddenly decided to cut himself a stick from the hedgerow. He could use it as a walking-stick – and it might come in useful if there were any loose dogs at the caravan camp.

He cut himself quite a stout hazel staff, and set off again. He came at last to the caravan field and stood looking at it. Which caravan was the Fangios'? There were about twenty caravans standing about, some modern, some old. Most of them had lights on inside.

No one seemed to be about, so Fatty grew quite bold. He peeped into a nearby caravan, standing on one of the wheels to reach the window. The curtains were pulled across but a crack had been left between them. Two people sat inside, one sewing, one reading. Man and wife, probably, quite decent-looking people.

He went to the next caravan – a very modern one. A dog barked as he came near, and Fatty decided he wouldn't go any further. He crossed the field and came to an old caravan that badly needed repainting. The night was now coming down quickly, and Fatty pulled out his torch. There was no light in this van. Perhaps it was empty?

It was. It smelt musty as he opened the door, and he shut it again quickly. Pooh! He went down the steps and looked round again. This sort of thing wasn't going to get him very far!

As he went to yet another caravan, someone came down the steps and spotted him in the darkness. 'Who's there?' called a man's voice.

'Only an old fellow who wants a doss-down somewhere,' said Fatty, in a high cracked voice. 'Can you tell me if there's a haystack anywhere, Mister?'

'Come in here and we'll give you a cup of tea,' said the voice. 'The farmer doesn't like tramps. He'll set his dog on you if you go on to his land. Let's have a look at you.'

Fatty limped up the caravan steps. It was an old caravan, but the inside was fairly clean, though not very comfortable. The man who had spoken to him was an oldish fellow with a kindly face. Inside was another old man.

'My brother,' said the first man. 'He's blind. We make pegs and baskets to sell, and we ain't got much money, but we can always spare a cup of tea. Can't we, Steve?'

'Ay,' said the blind man, and put out his hands to clear away a mess of cane and half-made baskets near him. 'Sit you down.'

Soon Fatty was sitting down drinking a very

strong cup of tea. 'I'm looking for some people called the Fangios,' he said. 'Do you know them? I was told they had a caravan here.'

'Oh ay,' said the first man. 'Their caravan is over yonder.'

'Two of them, there are,' said the blind man. 'Brother and sister.'

'No, three now,' said the brother. 'An old woman, their mother. Proper old tartar she is, and strong as a horse. Chops up all the wood, and carries buckets of water as good as any man! Her daughter, Lucita, she's a sulky young woman, she is, but the brother's all right.'

'Yes, that's Josef,' said the blind man. 'He takes my baskets to fairs for me, when they're round about here, or to the market, and sells them. He's a good lad. Are they relations of yours?'

'Not exactly,' said Fatty. 'They wouldn't know me now. I'm a lot different from the last time they saw me! Ah, this tea's good – black and strong, how I like it!'

'We've got a loaf and some marg if you want a bite,' said the blind man. 'Cut him a bit, Bill.'

'No, thanks,' said Fatty, hurriedly, touched by

the generosity of these poor old men. Bill turned up the wick of the lamp a little, and looked at Fatty, sizing him up.

'You can sleep here in our van if you so wish,' he said, after a moment.

'Well, thanks all the same, but I think I'll be getting on,' said Fatty. 'That tea was just what I wanted!'

'You got a bad scar there, above your mouth,' said Bill. 'Like a snake! How did you get that?'

Blow! thought Fatty. I forgot I'd painted on that wonderful scar! He laughed, and answered the old fellow. 'Oh, that's nothing. Can't go through life without a few scars – that's right, ain't it, Bill?'

A small noise came from outside the caravan, and the blind man lifted his head. 'That's that old cat,' he said. 'Let it in, Bill.'

Bill opened the door and a thin tabby cat came in, with bitten ears. 'Is this yours?' asked Fatty. 'It looks half-starved.'

'Nay, it's not ours,' said Bill, pouring a little milk into a saucer. 'It belongs to them Fangios, but seems to me they don't never feed the poor critter.'

Fatty watched the cat lap up the milk and an idea came into his head.

'I'll take it to the Fangios' caravan, if you'll show me which it is,' he said.

They let the cat finish the milk and then Fatty picked it up. It would be a marvellous way of having a look into the Fangios' caravan if he took back their cat!

The old couple bade him goodnight, pointing out the Fangios' caravan – a fairly big, quite modern one, and then shut their door. Carrying the mewing cat, Fatty went over towards the caravan.

As he came near, the door opened and a voice called out, 'Puss, Puss, Puss – come along in!'

Oh, good! thought Fatty. That sounds like Josef. As he came near, a figure ran down the caravan steps, still calling.

'I've got your cat!' called Fatty. 'I'm bringing it.' Someone came up to him, a dark shadow in the starlit night, and felt for the cat.

Fatty switched on his torch. It was old Mrs Fangio, not Josef. 'Now, Minnie, Minnie,' she said, and took the cat. 'Did Jo and Lucita turn you out then, the bad ones?'

'Minnie came over to Bill's caravan,' said Fatty. 'They gave her some milk.'

The old woman fondled the scrawny cat and Fatty waited in hopes of being asked into the caravan. He was longing to have a good look round it to see if there was anyone else there besides the Fangio twin, but no invitation came. Instead the old woman turned her back and went back to the caravan without another word. Fatty switched on his torch so that she could see to get up the steps. She certainly looked a dirty untidy old woman, and Fatty smiled to see the enormous old carpet slippers she was wearing, as she went up the steps, clutching the cat. She didn't even say goodnight to him, but slammed the door quickly.

He waited a little while in the darkness, and then he sidled towards the caravan. He meant to look in at one of the windows. If only there was a crack to see through, he might spot something interesting – maybe a fourth person – *with a scarred face!*

But the curtains were drawn tightly across. Not a chink had been left. Fatty was bitterly disappointed. He was standing on the big wheel, and was just about to get down when he heard voices – angry voices – coming from the caravan.

He listened, but the window was shut and he could not make out the words. Blow! And then suddenly he stiffened and held his breath.

There was a woman's voice – that would be Lucita's – or maybe old Mrs Fangio's – and there were two men's voices – *two!* One shouted something, and before he had finished, another man's voice began to shout back. There was a quarrel going on, and two of the quarrellers were men! Could one be the man with a scar? How Fatty longed to be able to peep in and see!

He suddenly had a shock. Someone came across the field, and walked right up to the Fangios' caravan. Whoever it was rapped at the door. Fatty simply didn't know what to do – there he was, perched on the high wheel, not daring to jump down in case the visitor saw him. He decided to stay where he was.

Someone opened the door. 'Who is it?' said Lucita's voice.

'It's Fred. Ask Josef if he's coming with us – we're going to have a game of darts.'

'Josef, Fred wants you,' called Lucita. She turned back to Fred. 'I'll come with you too,' she said. 'I'm sick of being cooped up in this caravan.'

And while Fatty was still perched precariously on the wheel, the three went off across the field together. Now, thought Fatty, only the old woman – and the other man, whoever he was – were in the van. HOW could Fatty have a peep and see? He got down quietly from the wheel, and was about to go round by the door to see if by any chance it had been left open, when someone came down the steps. Fatty crouched back into the shadows. Who was it? The old woman – or the second man?

He couldn't see. The figure went quickly away into the darkness and was lost. Fatty blundered after it for a few paces, but gave it up. No, he would go and peep into the caravan and see who was left there! If anyone saw him and came after him he would take to his heels and run. But he MUST see who was there!

He went quickly up the steps. The caravan door was shut, but he didn't think it could be locked because he had not heard a key being turned. He took the handle and began to turn it very slowly.

Then he pushed at the door and opened it inch by inch. There was not a sound from inside. Fatty was quite ready to leap down the steps and run off at top speed at the first sound!

He got the door half ajar, and still there was no sound. Then he flung it wide open, meaning to take a quick look round, spot who was there, and race off.

The door swung right back and Fatty looked swiftly into the untidy van. There were two sleeping-bunks, one above the other, and an old mattress rolled up below one – a folding table, two chairs, and an oil-stove. An oil-lamp hung from the roof, giving quite a good light.

But there was nobody there! Fatty stood on the top step, raking the van from corner to corner with startled eyes. There seemed nowhere for anyone to hide – well, then, where was the fourth person he had heard shouting?

Fatty was so astonished that he quite forgot that he could easily be seen by anyone outside the caravan, outlined clearly against the light from inside. And suddenly there came a yell.

'Hey, who's that at the Fangios' van? Hey you
– what you doing?'

18. FATTY TELLS HIS TALE

Fatty just had time to leap down the steps and run for his life before two men from the next caravan came at him. He tore over the grass towards the gate that led out of the field.

The men chased him, shouting. Fatty suddenly caught his foot in something and fell headlong. The men gained on him at once and, just as he got up, one of them shone a torch on him.

'Get him, quick!' he shouted – but before either of the men could grab him, something leapt out of the darkness, snarling and growling – something small and fierce.

It was Buster! He had trailed Fatty all the way from his house down to the field. Now he threw himself into the fray, snarling so fiercely, and giving such nasty little nips, that the two men drew back in fear.

Fatty raced off again, and Buster followed,

pausing every now and again to look back at the two angry men. They made no attempt to go after Fatty.

'He was going to rob the Fangios' van,' said one. 'We'd better report him to the police. Did you get a look at him? What a nasty bit of work!'

'Yes. I saw him clearly,' said the other man. 'He'd got a scar down his face – did you see it? I'd know him again all right if ever I saw him.'

Fatty didn't stop running till he was well away from Barker's Field. Then, panting, he sat down on a roadside seat, and made a fuss of the delighted Buster.

'You couldn't have come at a more convenient moment,' he said. 'I really was in a bad spot, Buster. Those men would have yanked me off to old Mr Goon, I bet they would! Whew! I nearly broke my leg when I fell down. I shall have a bruise the size of a saucer tomorrow. Well, come on, Buster, old thing. Thanks a lot for tracking me so well!'

Fatty went the rest of the way slowly, his leg paining him. He was quite glad of the hazel stick he had cut! His pretended limp had become a real one.

He talked quietly to Buster as he went along.

'You know, Buster, old fellow, this has been quite an exciting evening – but I'm blessed if I know what to make of things. I feel sure that the man with a scar is being hidden by the Fangios – but WHERE? I heard his voice in the caravan, I'm sure I did. *Could* I have been mistaken? No, I don't think so.'

'Wuff,' said Buster, sympathetically. 'Wuff, wuff.'

'I've a feeling that *all* the Fangios are in the plot,' said Fatty. 'And I've a feeling too that they're all angry about it for some reason. Don't they want to hide the fellow with a scar? If so, why are they doing so? For money? Perhaps he was in prison for stealing, and hid the money before he was caught. Perhaps now he's out, he's hoping to get it when the coast is clear – and won't tell the other three where it is? But where on earth is he *hiding*?'

Fatty got back to his shed at last, stripped off his disguise, cleaned his face, and went indoors to have a bath. He was thankful to see that Eunice had gone to bed. His parents and Mr Tolling were not yet home.

He rolled into bed at last, Buster beside him in his basket. Fatty let his hand hang down from the bed so that Buster could lick it goodnight.

'You're a good friend, Buster,' said Fatty, sleepily. 'Goodnight. I want to think things out but I'm too tired. My brain isn't working. I'll have to call a meeting tomorrow and let the others do some thinking!'

But the others were no better than Fatty at solving the tangle that this particular mystery had got into! Hearing that Eunice was going out with his mother that morning, Fatty promptly rang Larry and Pip and ordered a meeting at ten o'clock sharp down in his shed.

They all came punctually, anxious to know what had happened. Fatty had lemonade and biscuits ready, and they sat down prepared for a most interesting time. NOW what had Fatty been up to?

'Well,' began Fatty, 'you know that I planned to go down to Barker's Field and see if I could gather any information there, don't you? Actually, I did get quite a lot but, unfortunately, I can't make head or tail of it. So we'll *all* have to set our brains to work and find out what's happening.'

'Go on, then,' said Larry. 'We won't interrupt.'

Fatty began his tale, telling first of all how he had scared poor Eunice by appearing in his tramp clothes again, plus a scar down his face! When he related how she had telephoned Goon and made him cycle up to the house, they all roared.

Fatty went on with his tale. 'Well, I went down to the field. First of all, I went to a caravan where two nice old men lived, and they gave me a cup of tea and told me where the Fangios' caravan was. And would you believe it, while I was there, I had a real bit of luck because the Fangios' scrawny old cat came mewing up their steps for some milk!'

'Gosh, so you took the chance of taking it over to the Fangios' caravan, I suppose?' said Pip.

'Quite right,' said Fatty. 'I went over to it, carrying the cat. When I got near, I heard someone calling for the cat and I thought it was Josef, but it was old Mrs Fangio shouting, "Minnie, Minnie!" I gave her the cat and hoped she would ask me into the caravan, but she didn't. I switched on my torch to light the old woman up the steps of the caravan, but she never even said thank you. Gosh, she did look a sight with her dirty old shawl and carpet slippers on her feet, waddling up the steps! Anyway, bang went the caravan door, and that was that.'

'What happened next?' asked Bets, listening to every word, and thinking how well Fatty could tell a story!

'Well, I thought I'd stand on a wheel and peep into the caravan,' said Fatty, 'and just see if a fourth person was there, and if so whether he had a scar or not! So up I got, but the curtains were too closely pulled. I was just going to get down when a quarrel began in the van. I heard the old woman's voice – or it might have been Lucita's – and I also heard TWO men's voices!'

'Wow!' said Pip, his eyes shining. 'Did you really? Who was the other fellow then?'

'I don't know. Anyway, there was a fine old quarrel, with shouts and yells,' said Fatty. 'In the middle of it, someone came over to the caravan, and rapped on the door. I was scared stiff, but it was only somebody called Fred who wanted Josef to go and have a game of darts with him. The quarrel inside the van stopped, and Josef – and Lucita too – went off with Fred.'

'So the old woman and the second man were left in the caravan?' said Daisy.

'Yes. Well, I got down off the wheel after a bit – and just then someone came out of the caravan and went quietly down the steps!'

'Who was it?' asked everyone.

'I couldn't see – it was maddening!' said Fatty. 'I daren't switch on my torch, of course. Anyway, it had to be either old Mrs Fangio or the other man. So I made up my mind I'd open the caravan door and take a quick look in to see who was left alone there – the old woman or the man – and *perhaps* it would be the man with the scar!'

'Gosh!' said Larry. 'This is really exciting. Hurry up – what happened?'

'Well, I *did* open the door,' said Fatty, 'and I did look all round the van – and, believe it or not, there was nobody there! The van was empty. And I'm *certain* there was nowhere that a person could hide without my seeing them.'

There was an astonished silence. 'But Fatty,' said Larry, 'you *must* have been mistaken in some way. I mean, if old Mrs Fangio and the other man were in the van together, and only one went out, the other was still left. That's only common sense.'

'*I* know!' said Pip. 'You thought you only saw *one* person going out, after Josef and Lucita had left – but probably in the darkness there were *two* – going off very quietly in case someone saw them.'

Fatty hesitated. 'It does seem the only explanation,' he said. 'But I'm pretty certain that only three people left that caravan – and yet the fourth disappeared also! I can tell you, I was pretty puzzled.'

'What did you do next?' asked Bets.

'Well, someone saw me outlined against the light in the Fangios' van, thought I was a thief, and came after me. I took to my heels, of course, and raced off. Then I caught my foot in something and crashed to the ground – my word, I've got a bruise on my leg this morning. Look!'

Everyone exclaimed at the enormous black bruise that Fatty very proudly displayed. 'The men didn't catch you, did they?' asked Bets, anxiously.

'No. But it was a very near thing,' said Fatty. 'Old Buster turned up at that very moment – and he scared the men so thoroughly that I was able to get up and race off at top speed! You should have heard him snarling! Talk about a fierce dog – he sounded like an Alsatian, a Labrador, and a Scottie all rolled into one!'

'Good old Buster,' said Bets, patting him. 'What a good thing he turned up. I suppose he trailed you all the way there, Fatty.'

'Yes. Eunice must have let him out of my bedroom,' said Fatty. 'Good thing she did! I might have been languishing in a cell down at the police station by now! Well, what do you make of all that? Anyone got any ideas?'

Nobody said a word for a minute or two. They were turning Fatty's story over and over in their minds. It was certainly rather a curious one!

'I still think that *two* people must have left the van together, after Josef and Lucita had gone,' said Pip at last. 'And I think, too, that the second man in the van – the man whose voice you heard quarrelling with Josef – may very likely have been the man with the scar.'

'I think that too,' said Larry, and the others agreed. 'Right. What do we do next?' asked Fatty. Before anyone could answer, Buster began to bark loudly and then ran to the door.

'Someone's outside,' said Pip. 'I bet it's Eunice!'

It was – a very annoyed Eunice too. 'Why didn't you tell me there was a meeting down in your shed, Frederick?' she demanded. 'Why do you leave me out of things? Surely you could let me share in what you're doing, just for a few days? And WHY did you go off running without me last night? That awful old tramp came back – and Mr Goon came and was very rude to me.'

'Sorry, Eunice,' said Fatty. 'Well, do join us – have a spot of lemonade and a biscuit!'

The others glanced at one another. Had Eunice overheard anything of Fatty's story? Well, she wouldn't have been able to make much of it, if she had. They looked at Fatty, pouring out lemonade very politely.

What was he going to do next? This mystery seemed to be in a fine old tangle!

19. GOON IS A NUISANCE

Eunice then began to tell everyone all about her fright over the tramp the night before, and described the horrible, scarred face that the man had. They listened politely, longing to laugh, knowing that it had only been Fatty in disguise again. In the middle of the story, Jane came and knocked at the door.

'Frederick, it's the policeman, Mr Goon, to see you,' she said.

'Blow!' said Fatty, getting up. 'It's about that tramp, I suppose. Eunice, you'd better come with us. After all, *you* saw him. I didn't.'

'Don't you let Mr Goon be rude to me, Frederick, will you?' said Eunice.

'I will certainly see that he treats you with the utmost respect,' said Fatty, firmly. 'But just you stand up for yourself, Eunice – don't let him make out that that tramp is all a fairy tale of yours.'

'It's a great pity Jane didn't see him too,' she said. 'Look, there's Mr Goon.'

Goon was waiting on the path that led up to the house. He was not going to let Fatty slip away. Oh no – he had had important news that morning, that tied up with the old scarred tramp that that girl Eunice had said she'd seen last night. He had changed his ideas now about the tramp being Fatty, but he wanted to be quite sure about it. He had, in fact, wanted only a quiet word with Fatty, and he was annoyed when he saw Eunice and the others too.

'Er – can I have a word with you, Frederick?' he said. 'Alone?'

'What about?' said Fatty. 'If it's about the tramp last night, you must ask Eunice here – she saw him.'

'Yes, I certainly did see him,' said Eunice. 'And what is more, as I told you last night, Constable, Frederick had gone off on some cross-country running. *He* can't tell you anything about that tramp, because he wasn't here.'

'Yes, yes, I see,' said Goon. 'So you went off running, did you, Frederick, you didn't spend the evening at home?'

'Good gracious no, Mr Goon,' said Fatty, sounding surprised. 'I was miles away.'

'Ah, that was one thing I wanted to be sure of,' said Goon. 'You see – I half-thought *you* might have been that old tramp Eunice here said she saw.'

'*Well*!' said Eunice, in a rage. 'Do you suppose I'm such an idiot as not to be able to tell whether a tramp is a tramp, or whether he's Frederick Trotteville? I tell you, HE – WAS – A – TRAMP, Mr Goon. A horrible fellow. Very like the one I saw on Sunday, except that he had a scar.'

'Ah, that's what I wanted to know too,' said Goon, taking out his notebook. 'Now, did you notice very, very carefully exactly how big the scar was, and what position it was in?'

'Well, I didn't go out and get hold of the tramp's chin, and peer at the scar, or take a ruler to measure it, if that's what you mean!' said Eunice. 'I was in too great a fright to do anything but *notice* it.'

'Ah, so long as you noticed he was *scarred*!' said Goon. 'I had a report from somewhere else last night to say that there was a tramp trying to break in, with intent to steal – and *that* tramp had a scar on his face too! So you can see, Miss, why I'm glad that you spotted that *your* tramp had one too!'

'Don't call him *my* tramp!' said Eunice, annoyed. 'Well, fancy that fellow going on somewhere else to break in. It *must* be the same tramp. He certainly did have a scarred face.'

Fatty had become very interested. Was this tramp with the scar who had been reported for breaking in somewhere, none other than Fatty himself – reported by the two men who had seen him opening the door of the Fangios' caravan? Or was he quite another scarred man, from somewhere else – possibly the prisoner they were after?

'Mr Goon,' said Fatty, 'where was this fellow trying to break in last night?'

'Never you mind,' said Goon, irritatingly. 'But from what I've heard, he's certainly the fellow we're after. That scar proves it. He'd have been caught last night all right by the men who reported him, but for a dog that came out of nowhere and attacked them.'

Aha! thought Fatty. That was old Buster. So *I* was the 'tramp' those two men reported. Mr Goon *hasn't* got hold of the right man, thank goodness.

But he's hot on the trail, though he doesn't know it, because I'm pretty certain the real scarred man *is* being sheltered by the Fangios, down in that caravan camp. What a pity the two men reported me – now Mr Goon will be searching the camp himself and, being a policeman, he can do it much better than I can!

'Do you want to ask me any more questions?' said Eunice, tired of watching the policeman write voluminously in his notebook.

'No, thank you, Miss,' said Goon. 'You've put me on the right trail, I think. I'll just get my bike and be off. That reminds me – HOW did my bike take itself out of your front garden and put itself by your kitchen door last night, Frederick?'

'I'll work it out when I've got time,' said Fatty, with a perfectly straight face. 'Was it trying to come to look for you in the kitchen, do you think?'

'Gah!' said Goon in disgust. 'You'll cut yourself one day, you're so sharp!'

And away he went up the path, hoping sincerely that his bicycle hadn't disappeared again!

'What do you suppose Mr Goon is going to do now?' asked Pip.

'I *imagine* that he'll ask Chief Inspector Jenks for a search warrant and a couple of men – and go and search the caravan camp in Barker's Field,' said Fatty, gloomily. 'And as I think that that man with a scar *must* be there somewhere, Goon is likely to pull him in. And *I* put him on to the right place to search by being stupid enough to get caught by those two men last night!'

'What *is* all this?' said Eunice, puzzled.

'Oh gosh, I forgot you were here, Eunice,' said Fatty. 'Well, I suppose we'll *have* to tell you something of what is going on, or you'll keep on worrying us.'

'I certainly shall,' said Eunice. 'I must say I think you're pretty mean to keep things secret, especially when that old tramp I saw has something to do with it. I shall go and ask your mother what's happening, if you don't tell me.'

'Tell-tale,' murmured Pip, and got a furious look from Eunice. 'Frederick,' she said, 'tell me, please. I'll help you if I can. You seem to be doing some kind of detective work – and I'm good at that too.'

Fatty groaned. 'Is there anything you're *not* good at, Eunice?' he asked. 'Now listen – briefly, this is how things stand. There's an escaped prisoner, with a scarred face, somewhere in the district. He's actually been seen. We have been keeping a look out for him, but we haven't been lucky, so far. We were told to look for him in crowds, where perhaps he might not be noticed – the Fair, for instance – and even the beetle meetings, as one of his interests is insects.'

'Oh! I might have sat next to him!' said Eunice, quite scared. 'What's he like? I've gathered that he has a scar on his face, of course.'

'He's got sharp eyes,' said Pip. 'And a thin mouth . . .'

'And thick, dark hair,' said Larry. 'And he's medium height.'

'And his hands are very knobbly and bony,' said Daisy. 'And . . .'

'And we feel that possibly some people called the Fangios, who run the flea circus at the Fair, and also the shooting range, may be hiding him,' said Fatty. 'Because they go all peculiar when we mention men with scarred faces! Even that old cleaner woman at the beetle show, who is also a Fangio, got a shock when I mentioned a man with a scar.'

'I see,' said Eunice. 'Yes, I remember that old woman. Where does she live? At the Fair?'

'No, the Fangios have a caravan down in Barker's Field,' said Fatty. 'And what we're afraid of now is that Goon is on the same trail as we are – though not for the same reason – and may search that camp and get *our* man! What a feather in his helmet, if so.'

'I don't like that policeman,' said Eunice. 'I'm on your side. I'd like to help, Frederick. What are your plans?'

'Well,' said Fatty, 'let's go down to the shed again. I don't know that we've really got any plans yet.'

So Eunice went down to the shed with the others, quite determined to show them that she was as good a detective as any of them.

It proved difficult to think of a really good plan, but at last they decided that if Goon *did* get a search warrant for the camp, they simply must be there too. At least they must be in at the finish, even if Goon won the victory!

'What's the time?' said Fatty. 'Gosh, the morning's nearly gone! Listen, Mr Goon can't get a search warrant before this afternoon. One or other of us must haunt Barker's Field the whole time, from say two o'clock onwards, so that warning can be sent to the rest of us if Mr Goon arrives with other policemen.'

'Yes. That's a good idea,' said Pip. 'We can watch two at a time, so that there is always one to send off to warn the others. I'll watch with Bets. We can pretend to be picnicking, or something.'

'And I'll watch with Larry,' said Daisy.

'And I'll watch with you, Frederick,' said Eunice.

'You can't,' said Fatty. 'You've got to go to the beetle conference. And if you do, just keep an eye on that old cleaner woman, will you? – Mrs Fangio.'

'I *wish* I hadn't to go to this afternoon's meeting,' said Eunice. 'I'd much rather be with you. Who will you send to tell the others, Frederick, if anything happens while you are watching?'

'Buster,' said Fatty. 'I can tie a note to his collar and just say "Go to Larry" and he'll be off like a shot. And Larry could phone Pip.'

'Oh yes, I suppose you *could* do that,' said Eunice. 'Well, I'll try and take my turn with you

after tea, Frederick, the ____ ____'t be alone. Hey,
this is rather exciting, isn't it?'

'*I* don't think so,' said poor Fatty. 'It's bad ____ ____ough
to come to a full-stop, just when you've got some
interesting clues – but it's worse to have someone
like Mr Goon going over your head, and winning
by accident, so to speak!'

'Bets and I will be at the field at two o'clock,'
said Pip. 'Larry, you relieve us at four, and bring
your tea. Then Fatty can have his turn after tea
with Eunice.'

'Right. See you all later,' said Fatty, and the
meeting ended. Fatty watched them all leaving
the shed. The fun's over, he thought. Mr Goon's
really holding the reins now, although he doesn't
know it!

20. WATCHING AND WAITING

Eunice went off to the beetle meeting that afternoon with her father. Mr Tolling was quite disappointed that Fatty didn't want to come as well. But Fatty was firm.

'I really must do a few jobs for my mother,' he said. He felt that he could not listen to any more beetle talk. Mr Tolling had lectured them during the whole of lunchtime on the extraordinary habits of the family of Gulping Beetles of Ruahua in New Zealand. He only stopped when Fatty began to make the most peculiar swallowing noises, which alarmed his mother considerably.

'Frederick, are you choking?' she said anxiously, half getting up from her chair.

'No, Mummy, no, it's listening to all that about the gulping beetles,' said Fatty, faintly. 'I can't seem to stop gulping myself.'

Eunice gave a squeal of laughter, but Mr Tolling

could not see anything funny at all. Fatty caught his mother's stern eye and stopped gulping. He was very, very glad when at last Mr Tolling, complete with umbrella and gloves, and attended by Eunice, left for the Town Hall.

'I'll keep an eye on that woman!' hissed Eunice to Fatty as they left, causing her father to gaze at her in surprise. What woman? And what *was* Eunice looking so excited about? Really, she was getting as bad as that boy, Frederick!

Pip and Bets were down in Barker's Field just before two o'clock. They had decided to take their books on wild flowers, and to hunt for some. Then, when they had a bunch, they could perhaps sit down somewhere near the Fangios' caravan and keep a watch, in case Goon came.

Nobody bothered about them at all, and nothing happened of any interest. They just sat there, not far from the Fangios' caravan, pretending to look at their flower books. The caravan was shut, and nobody seemed to be there.

'I expect that girl, Lucita, has gone to the Fair to show off her performing fleas,' said Pip. 'And the young man – what was his name? – Josef – is looking after the shooting range.'

'And old Ma Fangio will be dusting away at the beetle conference,' said Bets. 'This would be quite a good time for Mr Goon to come and search their caravan. I wonder if there is anyone hiding in there this very minute?'

'They're very quiet, if so,' said Pip.

At four o'clock, Larry and Daisy came along to take their turn and Pip and Bets departed. Nothing happened while Larry and Daisy were there, either. They picnicked, chatted with a small child who came wandering up, and read their books. They kept an eye on the caravan, but nobody went in or out at all. Goon did not appear either. Altogether, it was really rather dull. They were glad when Fatty turned up with Eunice.

'Nothing to report,' said Larry. 'And Pip had no news either. How long will you sit here, Fatty? When do you think Mr Goon will come – if he does come?'

'I don't know. But I think if he hasn't come by seven, I'll ring up the Chief Inspector and see if Mr Goon *is* trying to get a search warrant,' said Fatty. 'It would be a help to know.'

'Right,' said Larry. 'Well, good luck. Give me a ring if you want me to come down after our supper, and keep watch.'

'Thanks,' said Fatty.

'Isn't this *fun*?' said Eunice, as she settled down in the grass near Fatty. But Fatty was in a gloomy mood and didn't respond at all. The Fangio caravan still remained shut, and was silent and apparently empty. Fatty began to wonder if his reasoning had been all wrong. Was he correct in thinking that the scarred man was being hidden by the Fangios?

After all, the only *real* clue we have is the fact that Lucita and Josef both look rather like the photo of the man with a scar, thought Fatty, and Lucita seemed surprised and angry when I mentioned a scarred man – and so did her mother. But that's absolutely the only reason why I think they may be hiding the fellow. It seems pretty thin reasoning really.

Eunice soon got bored with Fatty. 'I'll take a look round the camp,' she said, getting up. 'I'm bored sitting here.'

'No, don't wander about,' said Fatty. 'You'll only

draw attention to us. Sit down again. Tell me about the meeting this afternoon.'

'There's nothing to tell,' said Eunice, rather sulkily. 'I saw that cleaner woman. I watched her all the time to see if she did anything suspicious.'

'But how *could* she do anything suspicious? Don't be silly,' said Fatty.

'Well, she might have. You told me to keep an eye on her,' argued Eunice. 'So I did. She stared back at me – in fact we had quite a staring-match. I don't like her.'

'Well, look, here she comes!' said Fatty, suddenly. 'Don't stare though – she may recognise you. Eunice, I said *don't* stare!'

But Eunice did. Mrs Fangio was coming over the field, her shawl over her dirty grey hair, and her wrinkled face as brown as a berry. She saw Eunice, as she came near the caravan.

'Ho! So you're here, are you?' she said. 'What did you stare at me for all the afternoon? *I* saw you – rude little girl!'

'Don't talk to me like that,' said Eunice, in her high and mighty way.

'I'll talk to you how I like,' said Mrs Fangio,

who seemed to be in a very bad temper. 'And just get away from here, see? This is a caravan camp, and you've got no business here, no, nor that boy neither. You can clear out, both of you.'

'Well, we won't,' said Eunice. 'How dare you talk to me like that!'

'I'll show you!' said Mrs Fangio, and she came quickly up to where Eunice sat. Fatty leapt up, afraid that the angry old woman was going to attack Eunice.

'Now!' he said, 'there's no need for . . .' But he didn't finish what he was going to say, for the angry old woman pushed him so hard that he fell backwards, landing heavily on the squealing Eunice. Mrs Fangio gave a strange, hoarse laugh and went up the steps of the caravan, unlocking it with a key.

'Oh, Frederick, you squashed all the breath out of me!' cried Eunice. 'Get off! What are you doing?'

Fatty slid off the angry girl, feeling considerably astonished. Bad-tempered old woman! Fatty heard the sound of laughter, and saw two or three children nearby, pointing at him.

'Come on, Eunice. Let's get away from here,'

said Fatty, feeling most humiliated. The old woman had taken him quite by surprise. To think he had gone down flat like that! Fatty hoped that Eunice would hold her tongue about it.

'I'm going back home,' announced Eunice. 'I've had enough of this. Horrible old woman! She might set the son and daughter on us too, when they come back. This was a silly idea of yours, Frederick.'

'All right. We'll go back,' said Fatty, quite shaken. They walked by some small children, who sent a volley of squeals after them. Eunice was longing to tick them off but Fatty wouldn't let her.

'Now just you shut up for a bit,' he said. 'If you hadn't stared at that old woman when I told you not to, this wouldn't have happened.'

'You hurt me when you fell on me,' Eunice complained. 'Do you mean to say you fell down because that silly old woman pushed you? Well!'

'I just wasn't expecting it,' said Fatty. 'Now do be quiet, Eunice. I want to think.'

As soon as they got back, Fatty rang up the Chief Inspector. 'Frederick Trotteville here, sir. Er – I wonder if you'd tell me if Mr Goon has got in touch with you recently about the escaped prisoner case, sir? Several things have happened, and . . .'

'Yes, I know. And Goon wanted a warrant to search a caravan camp,' said the Inspector's voice. 'I said he could have one tomorrow. Have you unearthed any fresh news about the case, Frederick?'

'Well, no, sir,' said poor Fatty. 'I mean, I've got clues that just don't seem to lead anywhere. I can't help thinking that the only thing to do *is* to search the camp.'

'Right,' said the businesslike voice at the other end of the line. 'Sorry about it, Frederick, if you were hoping to solve the case. But you can't always be successful, you know. Good-bye.'

Poor Fatty. He felt very down in the dumps as he went in to the evening meal that night, and nobody could get a word out of him. Eunice offered to play chess with him afterwards.

'No, thanks,' said Fatty, feeling quite certain she would beat him tonight. 'I'm going up to bed soon.'

'Good *gracious*!' said Eunice, surprised. She gave a most annoying little giggle.

'Cheer up!' she said. 'You're *really* going to bed, I suppose, Frederick? You're not going to slip out again for anything exciting, are you?'

'As if I'd tell you!' said Fatty, and went upstairs with Buster, leaving Eunice wondering if he *did* mean to slip out again after all. Well – she would keep a watch and if he did, she would follow him.

Fatty did mean to slip out. He had forgotten all about getting fit that day and had eaten too much. He had decided that he would put on his running shorts and go down to the caravan camp for one last look round – just for luck.

It's my last chance, he thought. Mr Goon will be there tomorrow, with his search warrant, and if there is anything to be found, he'll find it! Blow – blow – BLOW!

21. FATTY IN TROUBLE

At about half past nine, Fatty slipped quietly down the stairs, in his singlet and running shorts. He thought that nobody had heard him, as he went out of the side door.

But the watchful Eunice had not only heard him, but had seen him too! She was in her room, with the door a little ajar and she saw him creeping by. She had put on a tracksuit, and wore her running shoes, ready for running too. Her heart beat fast. Fatty might be angry, but she was just going to show him that she could run too – and could outwit him as well!

She went out of the side door like a shadow and heard the click of the little side gate. She ran to it and out into the road. Yes, there was Frederick, running fast. Off went Eunice too!

She soon realised that he was off to the caravan camp, so it was easy to follow him, without getting too near. A little later, they were both in the big field, with the quiet caravans standing about here and there.

Some had lights on. Some hadn't. Fatty made his way to the Fangios' caravan, which was lit inside. Eunice followed like a shadow. Fatty disappeared under the van and Eunice stood in the shadow of a tree and waited. What was Fatty going to do?

Suddenly the caravan door opened and something shot out, landing near Eunice. She jumped as she felt something soft and warm sliding against her bare legs. It was a cat!

'Dirty little beast!' cried a voice from the caravan. 'Stay out there!' The door slammed. The cat mewed pitifully, frightened, and Eunice bent to stroke it. Then something else happened. The caravan door opened again, and someone came down the steps.

'Minnie, Minnie, Minnie!' said a voice. 'Poor Minnie! Where are you? Did they kick you and throw you out, the beasts? Minnie, Minnie!'

The cat left Eunice and went over to whoever it was nearby. Eunice stood as still as a mouse.

Had Fatty heard all this? She hoped he would be careful, hiding under the caravan. If that was the old woman, she wouldn't be at all pleased to find either Fatty or Eunice there!

Fatty was still under the caravan. He too had heard what had happened. He kept perfectly still, hardly breathing, for on no account must the Fangios know that he was there! He heard someone walking down the steps, and heard the calls of, 'Minnie, Minnie, Minnie!'

The old lady after her cat again, I suppose, he thought, and then in alarm he felt the cat against him! That would never do! If it mewed, the old woman would certainly grope under the van for it.

'Minnie, Minnie – oh, you've gone to hide under the van again,' said the voice. 'Here, puss, here!' And then to Fatty's awful horror, Mrs Fangio came crawling under the van too. He tried to creep backwards, away from her, but she heard him and a very hard hand caught hold of his arm.

'Who's this! Who's this!' she cried, and called loudly. 'Josef! Lucita! Come here!'

Before they could come, the old lady had dragged Fatty out from under the van. He could not bring himself to struggle too hard, for to fight with a woman was something Fatty could not do.

And then Josef was on top of him, and Lucita was there with a torch! The cat gave a frightened howl and disappeared.

'It's that boy – the boy who was here before!' hissed Mrs Fangio, evidently afraid of attracting attention from the nearby vans. 'Why does he spy on us? Josef, take him to that old caravan and lock him in. Gag him first. See, here is my shawl.'

The shawl was pulled tightly round poor Fatty's face, and somebody tied his arms behind him. Struggling hard, and kicking out, he was half-dragged, half-carried to the smelly old caravan he had peeped into the night before. He was thrown in, and the door was locked.

Fatty was extremely angry. To think that he had been caught as easily as that! But how fierce and strong that old woman was! What a horrid old woman! And yet how gentle she had been with the cat!

Fatty lay still in the smelly caravan, trying to get back his breath. Pooh! The smell nearly made him sick! He lay and thought rapidly. What was he to do? He couldn't shout because he was gagged. He couldn't try to open the door because his arms were tied behind his back. Perhaps he could kick at the door and get help? No, that would bring other caravan folk here, and he might be given a bad time – especially if the Fangios came along too!

And then, as he lay there, he heard an anxious voice outside. 'Frederick, are you all right?'

Gracious goodness, it was Eunice! Fatty could hardly believe his ears. EUNICE! She must have followed him all the way to the camp. Well, thank goodness she had. Perhaps she could get him out of this mess.

He drummed on the wooden floor with his heels to let her know that he was alive and kicking. He heard her rattling at the door, but it was locked, and there was no key.

Then he heard her climbing up to stand on the wheel to look through the small window. It was broken, but was far too small for her to climb through to help Fatty.

'Frederick, it's me, Eunice,' she said.

Fatty could not say anything because of the shawl tied tightly round his mouth, but he drummed hard with his feet again. Eunice shone her torch in at the window and gave a gasp when she saw poor Fatty lying there gagged and bound. 'Frederick – listen!' she said. 'I'm going to tell you what I think I'd better do. Drum two or three times with your feet if you agree, but only once if you don't.'

Fatty heard and drummed thankfully with his feet. Good old Eunice! Now, had she a sensible plan?

'I can't unlock the door and I can't get in at the window,' she said. 'I'm frightened of trying to get help from the caravan people in case the Fangios interfere and catch me as well. So, I'm going to go straight back to your home and get help. Is that all right?'

Fatty drummed vigorously with his feet. Yes, that was fine! Thank goodness she hadn't suggested going to Goon.

'I'll tell your father what has happened and leave it to him to say what's best to do next,' said Eunice. 'Well, I'm going now, Frederick, though I hate leaving you like this. I shall run all the way. It won't be long before you get help.'

Fatty drummed again. What a blessing Eunice

had followed him! He heard her jump down from the caravan and then he lay still and began to think about the whole mystery. Those Fangios – where *were* they hiding that man – that second man whose voice he had heard during the quarrel in the caravan? Could there be a false bottom to the van? He hadn't thought of that.

Well, if there is, Mr Goon will find it in the morning, he thought. To think that old Mr Goon will at last have solved a mystery before I have!

He wondered how far Eunice had got. If she ran, it wouldn't take her long to get home and raise the alarm. Probably his father would telephone Chief Inspector Jenks. Well, he wouldn't be very pleased about *that*!

Eunice had shot off through the field to the gate, being careful not to be seen. It was a very dark night, and a mist was coming up from the river. Eunice ran through the gate and away up the road, and then stopped at a corner. She gazed into the mist that was now hiding familiar landmarks.

Blow! This mist is going to make things difficult, thought Eunice. Well – I think I turn up here.

And she promptly took the wrong road! She ran on and on, looking for a corner that never came. She stopped at last, and looked round and about fearfully. Where in the world was she?

'*Don't* say I've lost my way!' she groaned. 'I'd better ask at some house or other. Blow this mist!'

But there were no houses to be seen! Eunice had taken the path to the river, and now there was nothing but fields. She was on the path beside the river – and as she stood there, she heard the water not far off.

She left the path and took a few paces to one side – and stopped with a gasp. Yes, there was the river!

'Well, now I'm *completely* lost!' said poor Eunice. 'I don't even know whether to go forward or backward – or turn off to my right. Certainly I can't turn off to the left or I'll be in the river! I wish this mist would clear!'

She tried walking to the right but gave up and came back to the path again. There was nothing but a field of long wet grass on the right. 'I'd better walk straight along the path,' decided Eunice. 'I'm bound to get somewhere then!'

So off she went, shining her torch in front of her. But she was now on the long, long river path to Marlow, and it seemed as if the way would go on stretching into the swirling mist for ever and ever. Eunice was almost in tears.

Just when I have to get help quickly! she thought, and went on and on. Then she realised that her torch was giving out. The beam it threw was getting faint. She was very frightened then. She might easily walk into the river if her torch no longer lit her way.

She gave a sudden exclamation. What's this? An old boathouse! If only I could get in there and wait till daylight! I simply daren't go on with my torch giving out.

It was easy to make her way into the dilapidated old boathouse. There was an old boat there, and Eunice scrambled into it thankfully. She made herself as comfortable as she could with sacks and a rotting tarpaulin.

Now I must just wait for daylight, she thought. There's nothing else to do! Oh, *why* did I lose my way when it was so very, very important that I should get help quickly?

She felt sure that she would not be able to sleep – but in five minutes' time, she was fast asleep and dreaming. When she awoke, the daylight was streaming in at the dirty window of the boathouse. Eunice could not for the life of her think where she was!

Then she remembered, and jumped up, stiff and cold. Oh dear, how could I have slept like that? What's the time? Gracious, it's half past seven! Poor, poor Fatty – what must he be thinking!

She made her way out of the boathouse and saw a path running from it across the field beyond. That's the path to take, she thought, thankfully, and away she went. Soon she was on the outskirts of Peterswood.

She ran up a road, recognising it as one she had been in before. A little way up a boy and a girl were swinging on a gate, waiting for the postman.

'Why, it's Pip!' said Eunice, thankfully. 'And Bets! I'd better tell them what's happened.'

Pip was most surprised to see a dirty, tired, most untidy Eunice padding up to his gate. 'You *are* out early!' he began, but she interrupted him.

'Pip, listen! Fatty's in trouble. He's lying in a

caravan in Barker's Field, gagged and bound. I went to fetch help last night and lost my way in the mist. I'm only just on my way to his house now.'

'Good *gracious*!' said Pip, startled. 'I'll go and telephone Larry and we'll go down to the field at once. You'd better go on to Fatty's house and give the news there. Whatever happened? Tell me quickly!'

Eunice told her story in a few words and then went off again, not feeling at all happy. Pip and Bets rushed off to telephone Larry. What a thing to happen to poor old Fatty!

22. THE MAN WITH A SCAR

Larry was most astonished at Pip's news and very concerned. 'I don't see that we can do anything else but go round to old Mr Goon and get him to come with us and set Fatty free,' he said, gloomily. 'It's maddening, because he'll gloat like anything.'

'Yes, and he's going to search the camp this morning for the man with a scar,' said Pip. 'He'll gloat even more when he finds him – in front of us too, probably! Well, get on your bike, Larry, and meet me at Mr Goon's as quickly as you can.'

In four minutes, both boys were at Goon's house, knocking at the door. The housekeeper, Mrs Boggs, opened it, surprised to see them so early.

'You can't see Mr Goon,' she said. 'He's gone down to the caravan camp with two other constables to do a bit of searching for something. That's all I know. If you want him, you'll have to go there.'

'Oh, thank you,' said Larry, disappointed. He was just turning away when an idea came to him. 'I think I'll telephone Chief Inspector Jenks, Pip,' he said. 'You know, Mr Goon's spiteful enough to leave Fatty in that caravan for ages, and if there's no key, we won't be able to let him out ourselves.'

The woman let them in to telephone, though she wasn't very pleased, and stood over them all the time. Larry could not get on to the Chief himself, who wasn't there, but left an urgent message for him. Then the boys went off to Barker's Field on their bicycles, to find Daisy and Bets awaiting them.

'Mr Goon's here, if you want to speak to him,' said Daisy, eagerly. 'Which is the caravan that Fatty is in, Larry?'

'I've no idea,' said Larry, looking round at the crowd of vans all over the field. 'Come on, Pip – we'll just go and tell Mr Goon about Fatty, and make him ask the Fangios for the key.'

The caravanners were all in a state of indignation and curiosity. Goon was at his most pompous, ordering people to stand back or to come forward, or to remain where they were. He and the two constables with him had already gone into two or three caravans and searched them thoroughly.

Larry went up to Goon. 'Mr Goon,' he said, 'we want your help, please. Fatty is locked up in one of these caravans here – we don't know which – and we want you to get it unlocked and set him free.'

Goon was astounded. What! That boy actually locked up in one of these vans? Why? Who locked him in? He was just about to ask Larry a few questions when he thought better of it. No. Let that pest of a boy stay locked up as long as possible – until he, Goon, had found the man with a scar, and *then* he'd let Fatty out so that he could watch his triumph. Aha! This would be one time Goon was on top and Fatty was nowhere!

'I can't interrupt my duties,' he told Larry, pompously. 'I'll see to that big friend of yours when I've finished the business I'm on. Now clear off!'

Larry was very angry. 'Come on, Pip,' he said. 'We'll go and find the van ourselves and see if we can't get Fatty out.'

They were joined by Daisy and Bets, and quickly made a round of the vans. As practically all the caravan people were out of their vans, standing about talking, and watching Goon and his men, it was easy to tell the two or three caravans in which Fatty might be locked up, for the doors of these were shut.

'This is the one,' cried Pip, standing on the wheel of one and looking in through a small broken window. 'I can see Fatty – he's lying on the floor, gagged, with his arms tied behind him. Fatty! Poor old Fatty! It won't be long now before we've set you free.'

The four children looked at the door. It was old and frail, and the boys felt sure they could break it down. 'Come on – all together!' said Larry.

Crash! The door fell from its hinges with hardly any trouble. Larry climbed over it and untied the shawl from Fatty's face, and undid the ropes that bound him. He sat up, looking extremely tired. He worked his arms about to get the stiffness out of them.

'What happened?' he said, and the boys told him how Eunice had lost her way in the mist, and how she had seen Pip when at last she made her way back early that morning. 'And that wretch of a Mr Goon's got his search warrant and is searching the caravans now,' ended Pip.

Fatty groaned. 'This is a miserable affair, isn't it?' he said. 'If that fellow with a scar is in the camp, Mr Goon is sure to find him – and *how* he'll boast over us!'

'Do you want to wait and see who it is?' asked Larry.

Just then Bets heard shouts of excitement coming from the other side of the field and looked out to see what was causing them. 'Hey!' she said. 'I do believe it's the Chief arriving – with two of his men.'

'Whatever for?' said Fatty, in disgust. 'Now he'll see Mr Goon on top and us nowhere! Whatever made *him* come?'

'Well – I phoned him,' said Larry, rather crestfallen.

'Well, you *are* an idiot,' said Fatty. 'He's the last person I want to see! I think I'll slip off without speaking to him. I feel pretty awful, and I'm filthy.'

'Oh, Fatty, don't look so miserable,' said Bets. 'Please don't. It's not like you!'

'Right. I won't!' said Fatty, and gave her a rather tired grin. 'Come on. Let's go.'

They all went down the caravan steps, Fatty finding himself curiously wobbly. 'Look – Mr Goon's just got to the Fangios' caravan,' said Daisy, thrilled. 'Oh, Fatty, do you think they'll find anyone hidden there – rolled up in a mattress or something?'

Josef, Lucita, and old Mrs Fangio had been ordered to come out of their caravan, while it was being searched. Josef went down the steps, looking angry, Lucita seemed scared, and old Mrs Fangio clutched the cat, and called out something rude in her cackling voice.

Just at that moment, Chief Inspector Jenks arrived at the caravan too. Goon was very surprised to see him, and wished suddenly that he had sent to rescue Fatty from the locked caravan.

'No results yet, Chief,' said Goon, saluting. 'Of course, the man with a scar that was reported to us from this camp yesterday may have gone.' Then, with a wave of his hand, he sent his two helpers to search the Fangios' caravan.

'What's all this about?' cackled old Mrs Fangio, indignantly. 'We ain't done nothing!'

Fatty was standing watching. He was frowning. He remembered that quarrel in the caravan – there *had* been two men there, he knew there had – and certainly Lucita and Mrs Fangio had been there too. And yet, when three people had left the caravan, it had been empty. The fourth person had apparently vanished into thin air! Would the two constables find his hiding-place? As he stared, the two men came down out of the caravan and shook their heads.

'Nothing there,' they said.

'Right,' said Goon, and turned to the Fangios. 'You can go back,' he said and the three went up the steps, grumbling among themselves.

It was just at that very moment that something exploded in Fatty's mind, and the whole mystery became as clear as crystal! The man with a scar? Yes, of *course* Fatty knew who it was! How could he have been so blind?

He gave a kind of yelp, and Goon and the Chief turned in surprise. 'Why, you're here, Frederick,' began the Chief. 'How did you . . .?'

He stopped, for Fatty was gripping his arm fiercely.

'Sir! I can show you the escaped prisoner – the man you want, the man with a scar!' he half-shouted.

'What's this?' said the Chief, astonished. 'What do you mean? Where is he?'

'I'll show you!' shouted Fatty, and he pushed Goon roughly aside and ran up the caravan steps. Josef and Lucita had gone inside, but the old woman was still at the top, holding the cat and watching the crowd below with a mocking look on her wrinkled, screwed-up face.

Fatty took hold of her arm, gripping it tightly. He snatched at the shawl round Mrs Fangio's head and ripped it off. Then he grabbed off the dirty white hair – and below it was thick brown hair!

'A wig!' shouted Fatty. 'And wipe her face and clean off its painted wrinkles – and you'll find the scar!' He suddenly lunged at the wrinkled face and rubbed the upper lip with the shawl before the old woman could dodge aside. He gave a shout of triumph. 'See – the scar is there. Here's your man, Chief, here's . . .'

But the astonished and furious man he held swung round his fist and knocked Fatty off the top of the caravan steps. Then he leapt straight into the watching crowd, sent them flying and raced off, holding up his skirts as he went. The old woman was a man, fierce and strong!

But one of the Chief's men overtook him easily and, holding him in a grip of iron, he and the other man frogmarched him to the long black car.

Everyone was so astounded at Fatty's sudden performance that there was quite a silence at first. Then what a hullabaloo! Bets was really frightened.

'Come on, little Bets,' said the Chief, picking her up and setting her on his shoulder. 'This is no place for you. Goon, you and your men disperse the crowd please. You can report to me later. Bring in the two Fangios there for questioning.'

Lucita began to wail. 'We didn't have nothing to do with it! He *made* us help him. He's our cousin and we owe him money, we didn't want to help him, did we, Josef?'

'He's a bad 'un!' shouted Josef. 'Always was. You let us alone, we ain't done nothing wrong!'

As Goon seemed to be struck helpless with surprise, the two men he had with him made the Fangios come down, and then took them off, howling and shouting. Everyone followed.

The four children followed too, with Bets on the Chief's shoulder. The first prisoner was now in the big black car, shouting something very loudly out of the window.

'What's he saying?' said the Chief, puzzled. 'Something about a *cat*?'

'Yes,' said Fatty. 'He's yelling, "Somebody look after that cat, somebody look after that cat!" Little does he know that it was the cat that gave his secret away!'

'I must have a little talk with you, Frederick,' said the Chief. 'Your performance was truly dramatic – but was it necessary to give it just then? Couldn't you have let me know the facts *quietly*?'

'No, sir, I couldn't' said Fatty. 'I only knew them myself at that very moment. They came on me like a flash! I'd like to tell you about it, sir. Can you come back home with us, and I'll make my report?'

'I think I'd better,' said the Chief. 'My word, you gave Goon the shock of his life when you ended the whole thing so dramatically. He almost fainted with surprise!'

Fatty looked back over his shoulder. Goon was staring after him, his mouth open, and his helmet decidedly crooked.

'I expect he's saying, "Gah!"' said Bets. 'He looks

like it. Poor old Mr Goon – he might so easily have solved the mystery first.'

'Look – there's Eunice – and Buster,' said Fatty, suddenly. 'Gosh – and my father and mother too! I hope Eunice didn't scare them too much when she got home and told them I was locked up in a van!'

'Frederick, what *is* the meaning of all this?' said Mr Trotteville, looking anxious and upset. 'Eunice came home with such a tale – oh, good morning, Chief, you here too! What in the wide world has been happening?'

'Well, sir, if you'd allow me to come back with you, I've a few questions to ask Frederick here,' said the Chief, politely. 'I'm really as much in the dark as you are.'

'Yes, yes – come back by all means,' said Mrs Trotteville. 'Frederick, have you had any breakfast?'

'No. Nobody has,' said Fatty cheerfully, patting a most excited Buster. 'Except the Chief. I expect he's had his, haven't you, Chief?'

'I certainly have,' said the Chief. 'Ah, I see you have a car – good. Will it take us all?'

'*We've* got our bikes,' said Larry. 'We'll bike up as quickly as we can. See you later!'

23. WELL DONE, FATTY!

Jane was most amazed to see so many arriving for breakfast. She and Cookie began to fry eggs and bacon at top speed and to make pieces of toast.

Eunice found a moment to have a word with Fatty. She looked very downcast. 'I lost my way last night,' she said. 'I'm awfully sorry, Frederick. I went for miles and miles in the mist!'

'Never mind!' said Fatty, grinning. 'Cheer up!'

'Well, now, Frederick, would you like to tell me what led up to your truly remarkable performance this morning?' asked the Chief, when breakfast was on the table. He sat down in a chair and took out his notebook. 'Right from the time when I first informed you of the man with a scar, and asked you to keep an eye open for him.'

'Well, sir – there were a whole lot of odd *clues*, but none of them seemed to fit together,' said Fatty. 'I mean, we spotted the likeness of the Fangios to the photo of the scarred man – but you told us he'd got no relations – and *they* said they'd only got their old mother . . .'

'Yes. Actually, he's a cousin,' said the Inspector, 'as no doubt you heard the twin Fangios calling out this morning. A cousin they're ashamed of and afraid of. That explains the likeness between them that you were clever enough to spot.'

'Yes. That was really the beginning of it all,' said Fatty. 'Well, quite a lot of things seemed to be clues after that. I mean, the insects, such as the fleas and the beetles. Mrs Fangio was mixed up with both, so I just thought that a love of insects was in the family, so to speak. Another clue was that they all behaved strangely when I asked them if they knew a man with a scar. That's what made me think of going down to the caravan camp where they lived, and having a look round.'

'Excellent idea,' said the Chief. 'Go on.'

'Well, there were other clues, sir – clues that I didn't really recognise,' said Fatty. 'Large carpet slippers, for instance. I saw Mrs Fangio wearing them, but didn't imagine that they were really her own – I mean, *his* own – I just thought the old woman had borrowed them from Josef. I didn't guess that they meant that a very large foot was inside them – the foot of a man, not an old woman! And then there was the quarrel in the caravan, when I heard *two* men's voices, and yet only one man was there! And I just didn't have the sense to fit the second voice on to somebody who *was* there – I couldn't understand why there were only three people when there *should* have been a fourth! Of course, the *second* man's voice belonged to old Mrs Fangio, who was using her – I mean, his – proper man's voice in the quarrel! She usually put on a sort of cackling old woman's voice!'

'All very complicated for you!' said the Chief. 'I can quite see how puzzling everything must have been. Anything else?'

'Yes – the cat,' said Fatty, ruefully. 'I forgot the scarred man was fond of cats. Actually, I thought it was perfectly natural for an old woman like Mrs Fangio to be fond of the cat, especially when the others were unkind to it. I was blind! I got all the clues and I never saw what they added up to!'

'She even had knobbly hands,' put in Bets, 'and we noticed them specially!'

'And I never thought of how easily a wrinkle could disguise a scar,' groaned Fatty. 'Of course, I see now that she – he, I mean – was very clever at disguising himself, and even kept his face all screwed up, so that the false wrinkles and real ones couldn't be distinguished.'

'He's known to be a master at disguise,' said the Chief, 'if that's any comfort to you!'

'Well, it is a bit,' said Fatty. 'But after all, *I'm* pretty good at disguising myself too, sir. I ought to have seen through his.'

'What made you *suddenly* see through Mrs Fangio?' asked Pip. 'I mean, one moment you were as upset as anything – and the next, you were yelling like mad, and tearing up the caravan steps!'

'I don't quite know,' said Fatty. 'It seemed as if all the muddle of clues in my mind, about fleas and beetles and carpet slippers and voices and quarrels and the cat and wrinkles and knobbly hands, fell into place – oh yes, *and* something else, sir! Of course! That's what *really* made it click!'

'What?' said everyone, eagerly.

'Well, old Mrs Fangio, as I thought she was, pushed me right over two nights ago,' said Fatty. 'I

smashing tea at the best cake shop in Peterswood
– and oh, by the way, what about that cat?'

'What cat?' said Eunice.

'The Fangios' cat!' cried Bets. 'Oh, of course!
They won't want it, poor thing. We'll fetch it, Fatty.'

'And it shall have the time of its life because it
helped us to solve the mystery of the missing man!'
finished Fatty. 'What do you say to that, Buster?'

'Wuff,' said Buster, and wagged his tail
vigorously. WUFF!'

thought it was just a lucky blow on her part. A
it was a *man's* blow, not a woman's. I rememb
thinking that at the time, without even guessing
was a blow from a man! And it was *that* that made
everything click into place. I thought, "It was a *man's*
fist that pushed me down," and then I knew I was
right, and suddenly the whole mystery was solved.
Well, Chief – I think that's about all. But gosh, I
thought Mr Goon was going to win this time! I just
got in by the skin of my teeth.'

'Well, my congratulations, Frederick,' said the
Inspector, standing up. 'And, as I think I have said
before, I am looking forward to having you on my
staff some time in the future – and if anyone gives
you a push then, it will be me, not Mrs Fangio!'

And away he went with the six children and
Buster to see him off.

'I want a bit more breakfast,' said Fatty,
returning to the dining-room.

'Oh, Frederick – you've forgotten your fitness
regime!' said Eunice. Fatty gave a determined snort.

'Today is to be a day of celebration, my dear
Eunice!' he said. 'Buns, lemonade, and ice cream
at eleven. A good lunch in the middle of the day. A

THE MYSTERY OF THE STRANGE MESSAGES

CONTENTS

1. MR. GOON iS ANGRY

Mr Goon, the village policeman, was in a very bad temper. He sat at his desk, and stared at three pieces of paper there, spread out before him. Beside them were three cheap envelopes.

On each sheet of paper, separate words were pasted in uneven lines. 'They're all words cut out of some newspaper,' said Mr Goon. 'So's the writer's handwriting wouldn't give him away, I suppose! And what nonsense they make – look at this one now – "TURN HIM OUT OF THE IVIES!" What does *that* mean, I'd like to know. And this one – "ASK SMITH WHAT HIS REAL NAME IS". Who's Smith?'

He stared at the last piece of paper. 'CALL YOURSELF A POLICEMAN? BETTER GO AND SEE SMITH.'

'Gah!' said Mr Goon. 'Better put them all into the wastepaper basket!' He took one of the envelopes and looked at it. It was a very cheap one, square in shape, and on each one was pasted two words only.

Mr goon

Each word was pasted separately, as if cut from a newspaper. Goon's surname had no capital letter, and he nodded his head at that.

'Must be a fellow with no education that put my name with a small letter,' he said. 'What's he mean – all this business about some place called "The Ivies", and a fellow called Smith? Must be mad! Rude too – "Call myself a policeman!" I'll tell him a few things when I see him.'

He gave a sudden shout. 'Mrs Hicks! Come here a minute, will you?'

Mrs Hicks, the woman who came to clean for Mr Goon, shouted back, 'Let me wipe me hands and I'll be there!'

Mr Goon frowned. Mrs Hicks treated him as if he were an ordinary man, not a policeman, whose frown ought to send her scuttling, and whose voice ought to bring her in at top speed.

After a minute or two she arrived, panting as if she had run for miles.

'Just in the middle of washing-up,' she began. 'And I think I'd better tell you, Mr Goon, you want a couple of new cups, and a . . .'

'I've no time to talk about crockery,' said Mr Goon, snappily. 'Now see here . . .'

'And me teacloth is just about in rags,' went on Mrs Hicks. 'How I'm supposed to wash up with . . .'

'MRS HICKS! I called you in on an official matter,' said the policeman, sternly.

'All right, all right,' said Mrs Hicks, in a huff. 'What's up? If you want my advice on that fellow who goes round stealing the vegetables off our allotments, well, I can give a good guess. I . . .'

'Be quiet, woman,' said Mr Goon fiercely, wishing he could clap her into a cell for an hour or two. 'I merely want to ask you a few questions.'

'What about? I've done nothing wrong,' said Mrs Hicks, a little alarmed at Goon's angry face.

'Look – see these three letters you brought in to me?' said Goon, pushing the envelopes over towards Mrs Hicks. 'Well, where exactly did you find them? You said one was in the coal shed, on the shovel.'

'That's right,' said Mrs Hicks, 'set right in the middle of the shovel it was. And all it said on the envelope was "Mr goon" and I brought it straight in to you today.'

'And where did you say the others were?' asked Mr Goon, in his most official manner.

'Well, one come in through the letter box some time,' said Mrs Hicks, 'and you weren't in, so I put it on your desk. And the second one was on the dustbin lid, sir – stuck there with a bit of sticky paper. Couldn't help but see it when I went to empty the dustpan. And what I say is, it's pretty strange to have notes all . . .'

'Yes, yes,' said Mr Goon. 'Have you seen anyone sneaking about round the back? Somebody must have climbed over the fence to put the notes in the coal shed and on the dustbin.'

'I haven't seen no one,' said Mrs Hicks, 'and what's more, if I had, I'd have taken my broom and given him a whack on the head. What's in the notes, sir – anything important?'

'No,' said Mr Goon. 'It's probably all just a silly joke – you don't know of any place here called "The Ivies", do you?'

'"The Ivies"?' said Mrs Hicks, considering. 'No, I don't. Sure you don't mean "The Poplars", sir? Now, a nice gentleman lives there, sir, I clean for him each Friday when I don't come to you, and he's ever so nice to me, he . . .'

'I said "The *Ivies*", not "The Poplars",' said Mr Goon. 'All right. You can go, Mrs Hicks. But keep an eye on the back garden, will you? I'd like to get a description of whoever it is leaving these notes about the place.'

'I will that, sir,' said Mrs Hicks. 'And what about me getting you a couple more cups, sir – one broke in my hand, and . . .'

'Oh, *get* the cups,' said Mr Goon. 'And I don't want to be disturbed for the next hour. I've important work to do!'

'So've I,' said Mrs Hicks. 'That kitchen stove of yours is just crying out for a good clean and . . .'

'Well, go and stop it crying,' snapped Mr Goon, and heaved a sigh of relief as Mrs Hicks disappeared in a huff.

He studied the three notes again, puzzling over the cut out, pasted on words. What newspaper had they been cut from? It would be a help to find out, but Goon could see no way of discovering that. Who had sent them – and why? There wasn't any place called 'The Ivies' in Peterswood.

He took up a local directory of roads and houses again, and went through it carefully. Then he picked up the telephone receiver.

When the phone was answered he asked for the postmaster. 'PC Goon here,' he said, importantly, and at once he was put through to the right department.

'Er – Postmaster,' said Goon, 'I want a little information, please. Is there a house – possibly a new one – called "The Ivies" here in Peterswood?'

'"The Ivies"?' said the Postmaster. 'Let me think – Ivies. No, there isn't, Mr Goon. There's "The Poplars", though, that might be . . .'

'It is *not* "The Poplars",' said Goon. 'I'm also looking for someone called Smith, who . . .'

'Smith? Oh, I can give you the addresses of at least fifteen Smiths in Peterswood,' said the Postmaster. 'Do you want them now?'

'No, I don't,' said Mr Goon, desperately, and put down the receiver with a bang. He gazed at the three notes again. No address on them. No name at the bottom. Where did they come from? Who had sent them? Did they mean anything – or was it a stupid joke?

A joke? Who would dare to play a joke like that on *him*, PC Goon, representative of the law for Peterswood? An uneasy feeling crept over Mr Goon, as a vision of a big boy with a broad grin on his face came into his mind.

'That boy! Frederick Trotteville!' he said, out loud. 'He's home for the holidays – and he won't have gone back to school yet. Gah! That toad of a boy! He'd think it was clever to send me notes like this – sending me off on a false trail – putting me on a wrong scent – deceiving me and making me look for houses called "The Ivies". GAH!'

He sat down to do some work, but at the back of his mind was the continual thought that it might be Fatty Trotteville playing a joke, and he found himself unusually slow with the making out of his reports. In the middle of his second report, Mrs Hicks came running in, breathless as usual.

'Mr Goon, sir – here's another of them notes!' she said, panting as if she had run a mile, and putting another of the familiar square envelopes down on Mr Goon's desk. He stared at it. Yes, his name was there as usual, pasted on the envelope. 'Mr goon'. No capital letter for his surname – so it was obviously from the same sender.

'Did you see anyone? Where did you find it?' demanded Mr Goon, slitting it open very carefully.

'Well, I went to hang out my dishcloth – and a real rag it is too,' said Mrs Hicks. 'And when I put my hand into the peg bag, there was this letter – on top of the pegs!'

'Was anyone about?' asked Mr Goon.

'No, the only person who's been this morning is the butcher boy with your chops,' said Mrs Hicks.

'BUTCHER boy!' said Goon, starting up, and making Mrs Hicks step backwards in fright. 'HO! Now we know where we are! Butcher boy! Did you see this boy?'

'No, sir. I was upstairs making your bed,' said Mrs Hicks, alarmed at Goon's purple face. 'I just called out to him to leave the meat on the table, and he did because I found it there, and he went off whistling, and . . .'

'All right. That's enough. I know all I want to know now,' said Goon. 'I'm going out, Mrs Hicks, so answer the telephone for me till I'm back. And you'll be glad to know that's the last of these notes you'll find. Butcher boy! *I'll* butcher boy him! I'll . . .'

'But Charlie Jones is a *good* lad!' said Mrs Hicks. 'He's the best boy the butcher ever had, he told me so. He . . .'

'I'm not thinking of Charlie Jones,' said Mr Goon, putting on his helmet, and adjusting the strap. 'Ho no – I'm thinking of someone else! And that someone else is going to get a nasty shock.'

Mrs Hicks was puzzled and curious, but not another word would Mr Goon say. He strode out of his office, fetched his bicycle, and rode off. In his pocket were the four notes he had received. He thought over the fourth one as he rode down the street. Ten words, cut out from newspapers again, and pasted on the sheet. 'YOU'LL BE

SORRY IF YOU DON'T GO AND SEE SMITH.'

It's that big boy, Frederick Trotteville, I'm certain it is, thought Goon, pedalling fast. Ha – he disguised himself as a butcher boy again, did he? Well, he's done that before, and he's made a great mistake doing it again! I can see through you, you toad of a boy! Wasting my time with idiotic notes! I've got you this time. You just wait!

He turned in at Fatty's gate, and rode up the drive to the house. At once, a small Scottie raced out of the bushes, barking gleefully at the policeman's ankles.

'You clear orf!' shouted Mr Goon. 'Bad as your master you are! Clear orf, I say!'

'Hello, Mr Goon!' said Fatty's voice. 'Come here, Buster. You can't treat your best friend like that! You seem in a hurry, Mr Goon.'

The policeman dismounted, his face red with pedalling so furiously. 'You keep that dog off me,' he said. 'I want a word with you, Frederick Trotteville. In fact, I want a long talk. Ha – you thought you were very clever, didn't you, sending all those notes?'

'I really don't know what you're talking about,' said Fatty, puzzled. 'But do come in. We'll have a nice cosy chat together!'

2. A NEW MYSTERY, PERHAPS?

Fatty took Mr Goon in at the side door and then into the sitting-room. 'Is your mother in – or your father?' asked Goon, thinking that it would be good for them to see their wonderful son properly ticked off by him.

'No, they're out,' said Fatty. 'But Larry and the others are here. I'm sure they would be interested to hear your little tale, whatever it is. We've been a bit dull these holidays, so far – no mystery to solve, Mr Goon. I suppose you haven't one that you want any help with?'

'You'd talk the hind leg off a donkey, you would,' said Mr Goon, glad to get a word in. 'So those friends of yours are here, are they? Yes, you bring them in. Do them good to hear what I've got to say!'

Fatty went to the door and gave such a loud shout that Mr Goon almost jumped out of his skin. It made Buster come out from under a chair and bark madly. Mr Goon glared at him.

'You keep away from me, you pest of a dog,' he said. 'Frederick, can't you send that animal out of the room?'

'No,' said Fatty. 'Buster, sit!'

There was the sound of feet coming down the stairs, and Larry, Daisy, Pip and Bets rushed in, eager to know why Fatty had yelled so loudly. They stopped short when they saw the stout policeman.

'Oh – hello, Mr Goon,' said Larry, surprised. 'What a pleasant surprise!'

'So you're all here, are you?' said Mr Goon, glaring round. 'Hatching mischief as usual, I suppose?'

'Well, not exactly,' said Pip. 'Fatty's mother is having a jumble sale, and we're turning out the attic for her to see what we can find. Have *you* got any jumble to spare, Mr Goon – a couple of old helmets that don't fit you, perhaps? – they'd sell like hot cakes.'

Bets gave a sudden giggle, and then retreated hurriedly behind Fatty as Goon looked sternly at her.

'Sit down, all of you,' commanded Mr Goon. 'I've come here about a serious matter. I thought I'd see what you've got to say about it before I report it to Headquarters.'

'This sounds very, very interesting,' said Fatty, sitting on the couch. 'Do sit down too, Mr Goon. Let's all be comfortable and listen to your bedtime story.'

'It won't do you any good to be cheeky, Frederick, I can tell you that,' said Mr Goon, seating himself majestically in the biggest armchair in the room. 'No, that it won't. First of all, why weren't you upstairs in the attic with the others?'

Fatty looked astonished. 'I brought some jumble downstairs to stack in the garage,' he said. 'Then I heard old Buster barking and came to see who the visitor was. Why?'

'Ho! Well, let me tell you that *I* know what you've been doing this morning!' said Goon. 'You've been putting on that butcher boy disguise of yours, haven't you? Oh yes, I know all about it! You got out your striped butcher boy apron, didn't you? – and you put on that red wig – and . . .'

'I'm sorry to say that I didn't,' said Fatty. 'I agree that it would have been much more exciting to parade round as a butcher boy, than to stagger downstairs with smelly old jumble – but I must be truthful, Mr Goon. You wouldn't like me to tell a lie, just to please you, would you? I'm afraid I *haven't* been a butcher boy this morning!'

'Ho! You haven't – so you *say*!' said Mr Goon, raising his voice. 'And I suppose you didn't leave a note in my peg bag when you came to my house? And you didn't leave one on my coal shovel and . . .'

Fatty was too astonished for words. So were the others. They looked at one another, wondering uneasily if Mr Goon had gone mad. Peg bags? Coal shovels? What next?

'And I suppose you thought it was *very* clever to stick a note on my dustbin lid?' went on Mr Goon, his voice growing louder still. He stared round at the silent children, who were all gazing at him, astounded.

'Where will you put the notes next?' he said sarcastically. 'Go on, tell me. Where? I'd like to know, then I could look there.'

'Well, let's see,' said Fatty, frowning hard. 'What about inside a watering can – if you've got one, have you, Mr Goon? Or in your shopping basket . . .'

'Or on his dressing-table,' said Larry, joining in. 'He wouldn't have to go and look for a note there. It would be right under his nose.'

Mr Goon had gone purple. He looked round threateningly, and Bets half-thought she would make a dash out of the door. She didn't like Mr Goon when he looked like that!

'That's not funny,' said Mr Goon, angrily. 'Not at all funny. It only makes me more certain than ever that you've planned those silly notes together.'

'Mr Goon, we haven't the least idea what you're talking about,' said Fatty, seeing that the policeman really had some serious complaint to do with notes sent to him. 'Suppose you tell us what you've come about – and we'll tell you quite honestly whether we know anything about it or not.'

'Well, I *know* you're mixed up in it, Frederick,' said Goon. 'It – it *smells* of you. Just the sort of thing you'd do, to make a bit of fun for the others. But sending anonymous notes isn't funny. It's wrong.'

'What are *anonymous* notes?' asked Bets. 'I don't quite know.'

'They're letters sent by someone who is afraid to put his name at the end,' explained Fatty. 'Usually anonymous notes have no address and no signature – and they're only sent by mean, cowardly people. Isn't that so, Mr Goon?'

'That is so,' said the policeman. 'And I tell you straight, Frederick, that you've described yourself good and proper, if you sent those notes!'

'Well, I didn't,' said Fatty, beginning to lose patience. 'For goodness' sake, Mr Goon, come to the point, and tell us what's happened. We're completely in the dark.'

'Oh no, you're not,' said Goon, and took the four notes from his pocket, each in their envelopes. He handed them to Fatty, who slid the notes out of their envelopes, one by one, and read them out loud.

'Here's the first note. All it says is "Ask Smith what his real name is". And here's the second.

"Turn him out of The Ivies." And this one says, "Call yourself a policeman? Better go and see Smith". And the last one says, "You'll be sorry if you don't go and see Smith". Well – what strange notes! Look, all of you – they're not even handwritten!'

He passed them round. 'Whoever wrote them cut the words out of newspapers – and then pasted them on the sheets of writing paper,' said Larry. 'That's a common trick with people who don't want their writing recognised.'

'This is really rather peculiar,' said Fatty, most interested. 'Who's Smith? And where is the house called "The Ivies"?'

'Don't know one,' said Daisy. 'But there's "The Poplars" – it's in our road.'

'Gah!' said Mr Goon, aggravated to hear 'The Poplars' suggested once more. Nobody took any notice of him.

'And there's "The Firs",' said Bets, 'and "The Chestnuts". But I can't think of any house called "The Ivies".'

'And this Mr Smith,' said Fatty, staring at one of the notes. 'Why should he have to be turned out of "The Ivies", wherever it is? And why should Mr Goon ask him what his *real* name is? It must be someone going under a false name for some purpose. Most peculiar.'

'It *really* sounds like a mystery!' said Pip, hopefully. 'We haven't had one this hols. This is exciting.'

'And the notes were put into a peg bag – and on a coal shovel – and stuck to the dustbin,' said Fatty, frowning. 'Isn't that what you said, Mr Goon? Where was the fourth one?'

'*You* know that as well as I do,' growled the policeman. 'It came through the letter box. My cleaning lady, Mrs Hicks, found them all. And when she told me that the butcher boy arrived this morning, at the same time as the last note – well, I guessed who was at the bottom of all this.'

'Well, as *I* wasn't that butcher boy, why don't you go and question the *real* butcher boy?' said Fatty. 'Or shall I? This is really interesting, Mr Goon. I think there's something behind all this!'

'So do I. *You* are, Frederick Trotteville!' said Mr

Goon. 'No – don't you keep telling me it wasn't you. I know you well enough by now. You'll come to a bad end, you will – telling me fibs like this!'

'I think we'll bring this meeting to an end,' said Fatty. 'I never tell lies, Mr Goon, never. You ought to know that by now. I've had my jokes, yes – and played a good many tricks. But I – do – NOT – tell lies! Here – take the letters, and get your bicycle.'

Mr Goon rose up majestically from his armchair. He took the letters from Fatty and then threw them violently on the floor.

'You can have them back!' he said. 'You sent them, and you can keep them. But mind you, if ONE MORE of those notes arrives at my police station, I'll go straight to Superintendent Jenks and report the whole lot.'

'I really do think you'd better do that anyhow,' said Fatty. 'There may be something *serious* behind all this, you know. You've got a bee in your bonnet about me – I don't know a thing about these anonymous letters. Now please go.'

'Why didn't you have the envelopes and the writing paper inside tested for fingerprints, Mr Goon?' said Pip, suddenly. 'Then you'd have known if Fatty's were there, or not. You could have taken his too, to prove it.'

'As it is, we've all handled the notes, and must have messed up any fingerprints that were there already,' said Fatty. 'Blow!'

'Fingerprints! Bah!' said Goon. 'You'd be clever enough to wear *gloves* if you sent anonymous notes, Frederick Trotteville. Well, I've said my say, and I'm going. But just you mind my words – ONE MORE NOTE, and you'll get into such trouble that you'll wish you'd never been born. And I should burn that butcher boy rig-out of yours, if I were you – if it hadn't been for you acting the butcher boy this morning, I'd never have guessed it was you leaving those notes.'

He went out of the room and banged the door so violently that Buster barked in astonishment, and ran to the door, scratching at it eagerly.

'Be quiet, Buster,' said Fatty, sitting down on the couch again. 'Hey, you others – what do you think about these notes? A bit mysterious, aren't they?'

Larry had picked them all up and put them on the table. The five looked at them.

'Do we do a little detective work?' said Larry, eagerly. 'Goon's given it up, obviously – shall we take it on?'

'Rather!' said Fatty. 'Our next mystery is now beginning!'

3. MR GOON iS WORRiED

Mr Goon cycled home, very angry indeed. Fatty
always seemed to get the best of him somehow
– and yet, the policeman felt that he, Goon, had
been in the right all the time. That boy had given
himself away properly by disguising himself as the
butcher boy again. He'd done it once too often this
time! Ah well – he could tell Mrs Hicks that he
had solved the business of those notes, and given
someone a good ticking-off!

He flung his bicycle against the fence, and went
into his house. He found Mrs Hicks scrubbing the
kitchen floor, a soapy mess all round her.

'Oh, there you are, sir,' she began. 'Look, I'll
have to have a new scrubbing brush, this here
one's got no bristles left, and I can't . . .'

'Mrs Hicks, about those notes,' interrupted Mr
Goon. 'There won't be any more, you'll be glad
to know. I've been to talk to the one who wrote

them – frightened him almost to death, I did – he admitted everything, but I've taken a kindly view of the whole matter, and let him off this time. So there won't be any more.'

'Oh, but you're wrong, sir,' said Mrs Hicks, rising up from her knees with difficulty, and standing before him with the dripping scrubbing brush still in her hand. 'You're quite wrong. I found another note, sir, as soon as you'd gone!'

'You couldn't have,' said Mr Goon, taken aback.

'Oh, but I did, sir,' said Mrs Hicks. 'And a funny place it was in too. I wouldn't have noticed it if the milkman hadn't pointed it out.'

'The milkman? Why, did *he* find it?' said Mr Goon, astonished. 'Where was it?'

'Well, sir, it was tucked into the empty milk bottle, stood outside the back door,' said Mrs Hicks, enjoying the policeman's surprise. 'The milkman picked up the bottle and, of course, he saw the note at once – it was sticking out of the bottle neck, sir.'

Mr Goon sat down heavily on a kitchen chair. 'When was the note put there?' he asked. 'Could it have been slipped in some time ago

– say when the butcher boy was here?'

'Oh no, sir. Why, I'd only put out the milk bottle a few minutes before the milkman came,' said Mrs Hicks. 'I washed it out – I always do wash my milk bottles out, I don't hand them dirty to the milkman, like *some* folks – and I put it out nice and clean. And about three minutes later, along came Joe – that's the milkman – and puts down your quart, sir, and picks up the empty bottle.'

'And was the note in it then?' asked Mr Goon, hardly able to believe it.

'Yes, sir. And the milkman, he says to me, "Hey, what's this note for? It's addressed to Mr Goon!" and he gave it to me, sir, and it's on your desk this very minute.'

'Exactly when did the milkman hand you the note?' asked poor Mr Goon.

'About twenty minutes ago, sir,' said Mrs Hicks. Goon groaned. Twenty minutes ago he had been with all five children – so it was plain that not one of them could have been stuffing a note into his empty milk bottle then. Certainly not Fatty.

'You look upset, sir,' said Mrs Hicks. 'Shall I make you a nice hot cup of tea? The kettle's boiling.'

'Yes. Yes, I think I could do with one,' said Goon, and walked off heavily to his little office. He sat down in his chair.

Now what was he to do? It couldn't have been Fatty after all. There was someone else snooping about, hiding notes here and there when no one was around. And good gracious – he had left all the notes with those five kids! What a thing to do! Mr Goon brooded for a few minutes and was glad to see Mrs Hicks coming in with an enormous cup of hot tea.

'I put in four lumps,' said Mrs Hicks. 'And there's another in the saucer. You've got a sweet tooth, haven't you? What about me getting a new scrubbing brush, now we're on the subject, and . . .'

'We're *not* on the subject,' said Mr Goon, shortly. 'Put the cup down, Mrs Hicks. I've something difficult to work out, so don't disturb me till my dinnertime.'

Mrs Hicks went out, offended, and shut the door loudly. Goon called her as she went down the passage.

'Hey, Mrs Hicks. Half a minute. I want to ask you a question.'

Mrs Hicks came back, still looking offended. 'And what might you be wanting to know?' she said.

'That butcher boy – what was he like?' asked Goon, still vainly hoping that he might have been Fatty in disguise. 'And did he really bring some meat – the meat you ordered?'

'Of course he did!' said Mrs Hicks. 'Two very nice lean chops, the kind you like. I told you before. And I told you I didn't *see* the butcher boy, I was upstairs. But it was him all right. I know his whistle. And I heard him calling over the fence to the next-door kid. It was Charlie Jones all right. What's all the mystery, sir?'

'Nothing, nothing, nothing!' said Mr Goon, feeling very downhearted. It couldn't have been Fatty after all; it *must* have been the real butcher boy. He might have guessed that when Mrs Hicks told him that his chops had come. Fatty wouldn't have known that chops were ordered. Oh, what an idiot he had been!

He caught sight of the note on his desk. Same

square, cheap envelope. Same pasted on bit of paper, with 'Mr goon' in cut-out letters. What was inside this time?

He slit the envelope open. He paused before he took out the note. He remembered what Larry had said about fingerprints. There *might* be some on the writing paper inside. Goon fetched his own gloves and put them on. They were thick leather ones, and he found it very difficult to get the thin sheet of paper out of the envelope, while wearing such bulky gloves.

At last it was out, and he unfolded it to read. He saw the usual cut-out words and letters, all pasted on a strip of paper, which itself was stuck on the sheet of writing paper.

'WHY DON'T YOU DO WHAT YOU ARE TOLD, EGG-HEAD?', he read, and grew crimson in the face. WHO was writing these rude notes? Just wait till he got his hands on him!

He forgot all about his cup of tea, and it grew cold. Poor Goon. He simply could *not* make up his mind what to do! Why, oh why, had he gone to see Fatty that morning, and left behind all the other notes?

I can't go and report things to the Super now, he thought. If I do, I'll have to tell him I went and told everything to that Trotteville boy – and he'll telephone him and tell *him* to take over. He's always in the middle of things, that boy – always doing me down. What am I to do?

Goon sat and worried for a long time. If only he could catch whoever it was delivering these notes! That would be the thing to do! He would soon solve everything then, once he got his hands on the fellow! Yes, that was certainly the thing to do. But how could he watch for him every minute of the day? It was impossible.

Then a sudden thought came to him, and he brightened. What about his nephew, Ern? What about asking him to stay with him for a while, and give him some pocket money to keep a watch for him? Ern was smart.

Leaving his cold tea, he went out to Mrs Hicks, who was sitting down enjoying her second cup of tea.

'I've got to go out,' he said. 'Be back by teatime. Keep a look out in case anyone else comes with a note.'

'But your chops, sir,' began Mrs Hicks. It was no good – Goon was off on his bicycle, riding at top speed to Ern's home. Mrs Hicks sighed and poured herself out a third cup of tea. Well, if he wasn't back by dinnertime, she would have those chops herself!

Meantime Fatty and the others had been busy discussing what seemed like a new, and rather sudden, mystery. They were in the middle of it when Mrs Trotteville came home from her shopping, hoping to find that all the jumble had been taken from the attic, and neatly stacked into the garage. She was not very pleased to find so little done.

'Well! You said you could get everything downstairs for me by the time I came back, so that I could look over it,' she said. 'Whatever have you been doing?'

Nobody said a word about Mr Goon's visit. Mrs Trotteville was always displeased if she thought that Fatty had been 'meddling in mysteries' again. She was tired of Mr Goon coming along with complaints of his doings.

'Sorry, Mummy! We'll finish everything this

afternoon,' said Fatty. 'Larry and the rest can easily come along again. Anyway, we've got quite a few things out in the garage already.'

'I should hope so!' said his mother. 'I've got to look over everything, mend what can be mended, and price each thing. And by the way, Frederick, I've the names and addresses of a few people in Peterswood who have said that they will be pleased to give some jumble for the sale, if you go and collect it on a barrow.'

'A *barrow*!' said Fatty. 'Do you mean I'm to borrow the gardener's old barrow and trundle it through the streets? No, thank you!'

'I've arranged with the builder to lend you *his* barrow,' said his mother. 'Well, I suppose it's a handcart, really, not a barrow. Larry can go with you to help you. It's for a good cause, so you can do your bit, surely?'

'You have an awful lot of good causes, Mummy,' said Fatty. 'Still, I'd rather have a mother with too many, than one with none at all! All right, I'll do some collecting round and about for you. Larry and Pip can both help me.'

'We'll come this afternoon and clear out the attic properly,' promised Larry. 'What time? Half past two?'

'Yes,' said Fatty. 'And I vote we all go out to tea at the best tea shop in the village. We'll be hungry after our hard work.'

'Well, I'll pay for a good tea,' said his mother, laughing.

That afternoon, the five, with Buster continually getting in their way at awkward moments, carried down an enormous amount of jumble from the big attic – and, just as they were in the very middle of it, a piercing whistle was heard coming up the attic stairs.

'Whoever's that?' said Fatty, startled. He looked down the steep little flight of stairs. 'Gosh! It's ERN! Ern, what on earth are you doing here?'

'Come on down,' said Ern. 'I got something to tell you. I'm staying with my uncle – he fetched me this morning.'

'Staying with Mr *Goon*!' said Fatty, disbelievingly. 'But you detest him! Half a mo – we'll all be down and hear what you've got to say. My word, Ern, this *is* a surprise! We'll be down in a tick.'

4. ERN'S NEW JOB

Everyone was amazed to hear that Ern had suddenly come to stay with Mr Goon. They hurried down the attic stairs at top speed. Ern was delighted to see them.

'Well,' said Fatty, clapping the boy on the back. 'Still the same old Ern!'

And, indeed, Ern looked exactly the same as he had always looked, though he had grown a little. He was still rather plump, and his cheeks were as brilliant red as ever. His eyes bulged a little, just like his uncle's. He grinned happily at everyone.

'Coo! You're all here. That's a bit of luck,' he said.

'Let's go down to my shed,' said Fatty. 'We can talk without being heard there. Do you think we've got enough stuff out of the attic to satisfy my mother? The garage will soon be so full that it won't take Dad's car!'

'Yes, we've done enough,' said Larry, who was feeling really tired after carrying so many heavy, awkward articles down the steep attic stairs. 'I want a rest.'

So off they all went, out of the side door, down the garden path, to Fatty's secluded little shed at the bottom of the garden, well-hidden among shrubs and trees.

The winter afternoon was now getting dark, and Fatty lit a lantern, and also an oil-stove, for the shed felt very chilly. Soon the glow spread over the six children and Buster, as they sat together, glad of a rest after so much hard work.

'I won't offer anyone anything to eat,' said Fatty, 'because we're all going out to tea, Ern – and my mother's paying, so we can have what we like. You can come with us.'

'Coo!' said Ern, delighted. 'Thanks a lot.'

'What's all this about your uncle asking you to stay with him so suddenly?' asked Fatty.

'Well, I was just eating my dinner with Mum and my twin brothers, Sid and Perce, when my uncle comes sailing up on his bicycle,' began Ern, thoroughly enjoying all the attention he was getting. 'And Mum says, "Look who's here!" And we looked, and it was Uncle Theophilus . . .'

'Oh! I'd forgotten that was Mr Goon's name,' said Bets, with a squeal of delight.

'Well, Sid and Perce, they bolted upstairs straightaway,' said Ern. 'They're scared stiff of Uncle because he's a policeman – and I was going too, when Uncle yelled at me and said, "You stay here, young Ern. I got a job for you to do. I want you to help the law".'

'Go on, Ern,' said Fatty, enjoying the way Ern imitated Goon.

'Well, Uncle was sort of pally and slapped me on the back, and said, "Well, how's the smart boy of the family," and that made me and Mum proper suspicious,' said Ern. 'And then he said he wanted me to come and stay with him, and do a bit of snooping round for him – and I was going to say no, that I wouldn't, straight off like that – when he said he'd pay me proper wages!'

'Did he now?' said Fatty.

'Loveaduck, I've never had much money in my life!' said Ern. 'But I was smart, I was. I said,

"Done, Uncle – if you throw in an ice cream a day as well!" And he said, "Right, if you come along with me now".'

'So you came?' said Bets. 'Did your mother mind?'

'Oooh no – she's glad to get rid of one or other of us for a few days,' said Ern. 'She just said, "What sort of a job is this?" And my uncle said, "Can't tell you, it's secret. But Ern here's smart, and he'll be able to do it all right." Coo, I never knew my uncle thought so much of me.'

'I hope he'll be kind to you,' said Daisy, remembering how unkind Goon had been to the boy on other occasions when he had stayed with him.

'Well, I've told him straight, I'll go back home if the job don't please me,' said Ern, boastfully. 'Job! Funny business it is, really. It's just to keep a look out for anyone snooping about the house, hiding notes anywhere, when Uncle's out and can't keep watch himself. And if I do see anyone and describe him good and proper, I'm to get paid a bonus.'

'So Goon has made up his mind I'm *not* the

guilty one!' said Fatty. 'Did he tell you anything else, Ern?'

'No,' said Ern. 'But he said I could skip along here this afternoon, and you'd tell me anything you wanted to – and I was to say he'd made a mistake. He says you can burn those notes he left, and don't you bother about them any more. He can manage all right.'

'He thinks we'll give up solving the mystery of the notes, I suppose,' said Pip. 'Well, we shan't, shall we, Fatty?'

'No,' said Fatty. 'There certainly is something decidedly strange about those notes. We won't burn them. We'll hang on to them. I vote we have a meeting down here tomorrow morning, and consider them carefully.'

'Can I have a look at them?' asked Ern, filled with curiosity.

'They're indoors,' said Fatty. 'Anyway, it's almost time we went out to have our tea. Got your bike, Ern?'

'You bet,' said Ern. 'It's a bit of good luck for me, isn't it? – getting so much money. I can buy you all ice creams in a day or two – pay you back a bit for the ones you've bought me so many times.'

He grinned round at the five children, and they smiled back pleased with his good-natured suggestion. That was so like Ern.

'How are Sid and Perce, your two brothers?' asked Pip. 'Does Sid still suck that awful toffee?'

'No. He's on to chewing-gum now,' said Ern, seriously. 'He got into trouble at school over that toffee – couldn't spit it out soon enough when the teacher got on to him about it. So now he buys chewing-gum. It's easier to manage, he says. Perce is all right too. You should have seen him and Sid scoot upstairs when Uncle arrived this morning. Atom bombs couldn't have got them up quicker!'

They all laughed. Fatty stood up. 'Well, let's go,' he said. 'Ern, if your uncle is at home tomorrow morning, you come and join our meeting. You may as well listen to our plans, seeing you're more or less in this affair too.'

'Oooh, I'd love to,' said Ern, overjoyed. 'I might bring my latest pome to read to you. It's not quite finished, but I'll try and think of the ending tonight.'

Everyone smiled. Ern and his poems! He did try so hard to write them, but nearly always got stuck in the middle. They all went out of Fatty's shed, and he locked it behind him carefully. No grown-up was allowed to see what treasures he had there! All his many disguises. His make-up. His false teeth and moustaches and whiskers. Mr Goon's eyes would have fallen out of his head if he had seen them.

They switched on their bicycle lamps and rode off to the tea shop, Buster in Fatty's bicycle basket. They left their bicycles outside the shop and went in, Buster keeping close to heel. 'A table for six, please,' said Fatty, politely.

Soon they were all sitting down enjoying a truly marvellous tea. Fatty's mother had handed out a generous reward for their hard work, and that bought a very fine tea indeed – but wasn't quite enough to pay for ice creams each as well, so Fatty delved into his own pocket as usual.

'I vote for scones and honey to begin with, macaroons to follow, and either éclairs or meringues after that, with ice creams to end with,' suggested Fatty.

'Loveaduck!' said Ern, overcome. 'I wish I hadn't eaten so much dinner. What about Buster?'

'Oh, Buster can have his usual tit-bits,' said Fatty, and gave the order to a most amused waitress.

'Are you sure that all this will be *enough*?' she said, smiling.

'Well, no, I'm not quite sure,' said Fatty. 'But that will do to start with!'

It was a hilarious meal, and Ern made them all laugh till they cried by telling them of Sid's mistake over his chewing-gum the day before.

'You see, Perce had got out his clay-modelling set,' began Ern, 'and he was flattening out some of the clay to work it up properly, like. And Mum called him, and off he went. Then Sid came in, and what does Sid think but that them flat pieces is some of his chewing-gum! So into his mouth they went. He didn't half complain about the taste – said he'd take it back to the shop – but he wouldn't spit it out, he said he couldn't waste it. And then Perce came back, and there was an awful row because Sid was chewing up his bits of clay!'

Everyone roared with laughter at Ern's peculiar story. 'Quite revolting,' said Fatty.

'Simply horrible. But very funny, the way you tell it, Ern. Don't, for pity's sake, repeat the story in front of my mother, will you?'

'I'd never *dare* to open my mouth to your mother,' said Ern, looking quite scared at the thought of telling a story about Sid and Perce to Mrs Trotteville. 'Coo – even my uncle's scared of your mother, Fatty. What's the time? I've got to get back to my job sharp at half past five, because Uncle's going out then.'

'Well, you'd better scoot off,' said Fatty, looking at his watch. 'When you're paid to do a job, young Ern, it's better to give a few minutes more to it, than a few minutes less. That's one of the differences between doing a job honestly, and doing it dishonestly! See?'

'Righto, Fatty,' said Ern, slipping out of his chair. 'I'll do anything you say. So long! See you tomorrow, if I can.'

'Good old Ern,' said Pip, watching the boy make his way to the door of the tea shop. 'I hope old Goon will treat him all right. And if he doesn't pay him as he promised, *we'll* have something to say about that!'

'Can anyone eat any more?' said Fatty. 'No? Sorry, Buster, but everyone says no, so it's no use wagging your tail like that! Well, I feel decidedly better now, if rather fuller. I'll have to try some cross-country racing again.'

'What! In this cold weather!' said Pip. 'It would make you so hungry, you'd eat twice as much as usual – so what would be the good?'

'I hoped you'd say that, Pip, old thing,' said Fatty, with a chuckle. 'Well, we'll get home. Tomorrow at half past ten, all of you. I've got a little job to do tonight, before I go to bed.'

'What's that?' asked the others.

'I'm going to use my fingerprinting powder, and see if I can find any unusual prints on the sheets of paper those messages were pasted on,' said Fatty.

And so, all by himself in his shed, Fatty tested the sheets for strange fingerprints, feeling very professional indeed. But it was no use – the sheets were such a mass of prints, that it would have been quite impossible to decipher a strange one!

'There are Mr Goon's prints – and all of ours,' groaned Fatty. 'I do hope Mr Goon doesn't mess up any new notes. He *ought* to test for prints as soon as he gets one. Well, I hope this *is* a mystery boiling up. It certainly has the smell of one!'

5. A MEETING –
AND THE FIRST CLUE

Next morning, Fatty was waiting for the others down in his shed. He had biscuits in a tin, and lemonade in a bottle. He also had the four notes set out in their envelopes.

Larry and Daisy were the first to arrive. 'Hello, Fatty! Solved the mystery yet?' said Daisy.

'I don't somehow think it's going to be very easy,' said Fatty. 'That box is for you to sit on, Daisy. I've put a cushion on it – and there's a cushion for Bets too.'

Pip and Bets arrived almost immediately, and then Ern came running down the path. Buster greeted him loudly, leaping round his ankles. He liked Ern.

'Hello, everybody,' said Ern, panting. 'Am I late? I thought I wouldn't be able to come, but Uncle said he'd be in all morning, so here I am. I'm on duty this afternoon.'

'Has he paid you anything yet?' asked Bets.

'No. He says he'll pay me each dinnertime,' said Ern. 'I asked him for a bit in advance, but he wouldn't give me any. If he had, I'd have bought some sweets and brought them along for us all, but I'll do that tomorrow.'

'Thanks, Ern,' said Fatty. 'Tell us – did you have any luck in seeing anyone snooping around, placing notes anywhere?'

'No. No luck at all,' said Ern. 'Uncle's quite disappointed there's no more notes. I watched him testing the one he got yesterday morning for fingerprints. All that powder and stuff! Beats me how it fetches up fingerprints!'

'Oh! Did Goon test for fingerprints too?' said Fatty, interested. 'Did he find any? The note he had wouldn't have any prints of ours on it – it would show up a strange print at once.'

'Well, it didn't show *any*thing,' said Ern. 'Not a thing. Uncle said the writer must have worn gloves. Didn't mean to be found out, did he?'

'No, he didn't,' said Fatty, looking thoughtful. 'It rather looks as if he was afraid that his fingerprints would be recognised . . .'

'And *that* would mean that he'd had them taken already for some reason,' said Larry, at once. 'So he might be a bad lot – might have been in prison.'

'Yes, that's true,' said Fatty. 'I wonder if the man who writes the notes is the one who's putting them all about Mr Goon's garden. No wonder Mr Goon wants to spot him, if so.'

'Coo,' said Ern, looking startled. 'Do you think he might be dangerous? Do you think he'd shoot me if he saw me spying for him?'

'Oh no, I shouldn't think so!' said Fatty. 'I don't think you *will* spot him, Ern. He'd be very careful indeed. I wish I knew what he meant by these notes, though. And why does he go to so much trouble cutting out letters and words from the newspapers, and putting them laboriously on strips of paper, and then sticking the strips on writing paper. Why couldn't he just disguise his writing? It's easy enough to do!'

'It might be easy for you, Fatty, but not for most people,' said Daisy.

'You say you saw and heard nothing at all to make you think anyone was around, and that no note was found this morning?' said Fatty to Ern. 'I wonder if that was because you were there? Who is in the house when Mr Goon is out?'

'Only Mrs Hicks, the woman who comes in to clean,' said Ern. 'She's not there all the time, anyway. And I don't believe she'd notice anyone around unless they rang the bell or banged on the knocker. Why, she never even noticed the boy next door when he hopped over the fence to get his ball.'

'The boy next door? Did *he* come over?' said Fatty, at once. 'It's possible someone might pay him to slip the notes here and there.'

'Well, I watched him like anything,' said Ern. 'I was peeping out of the bedroom window, see – and I saw two kids playing ball next door – and suddenly their ball came over the fence. And then the boy climbed over, got his ball, and went back, looking all round in case my uncle came rushing out. He didn't have any note – he just picked up his ball and ran for his life.'

'He doesn't *sound* suspicious,' said Fatty, and the others nodded in agreement. 'Still, you've got to suspect *any*one who comes, Ern.'

'Righto. I'll even give the next door cat the once-over if he comes,' said Ern, grinning.

'Now let's consider these notes carefully,' said Fatty, and spread them out in a row on the table. 'I'll read them all out again. Listen, everyone – you too, Ern – because you haven't heard them before.'

Fatty picked up the first one. 'Number one – "Ask Smith what his real name is". Number two – "Turn him out of The Ivies". Number three – "Call yourself a policeman? Better go and see Smith!" Number four – "You'll be sorry if you don't go and see Smith".'

'And I can tell you number five,' said Ern, eagerly. 'It was on Uncle's desk when he was doing the fingerprint test, and I saw it. It said, "Why don't you do what you're told, egg-head?"'

Everyone laughed. Ern grinned. 'Uncle didn't like that,' he said.

'Well,' said Fatty, 'what does anyone gather from these notes?'

'There's a house called "The Ivies" somewhere,' said Bets.

'And a man called Smith lives in it,' said Daisy.

'And it's not his real name, it's a false one,' said Larry.

'And if he's using a false name, there must be some reason for it,' added Pip, 'and possibly it means that at one time or another, he's been in trouble – and doesn't want people to know his real name now.'

'But why should the writer of these notes want him turned out of "The Ivies"?' said Fatty, frowning. 'And what reason would there *be* to turn him out? Well – until we find "The Ivies", it's impossible to do anything. To find a house called "The Ivies" must be our very first step.'

'I suppose we can't find the writer of the notes, can we?' suggested Daisy. 'It might be a help if we knew who *he* was!'

'How can we?' asked Larry. 'He doesn't give a thing away, not a thing – not his handwriting, not his fingerprints, nothing! He's so very careful that he's spent ages and ages snipping printed letters or words out of newspapers and pasting them on the sheet!'

'I wonder if we could find anything out about him from these little snippings,' said Fatty, gazing at them. 'Newspapers are printed on both sides. There might be a guide to us in something on the *other* side of the snippings. I rather think the man is using only *one* newspaper. The letters all seem to be the same type of printing.'

'But goodness me – we can't *un*paste the letters from the sheets,' said Bets.

'I could,' said Fatty. 'It would be a very tricky job, but I think I could. I've got some special stuff somewhere for that very purpose, but I've never yet used it. I'd forgotten about it. I might be able to do something tonight. It's worth trying, anyhow.'

'Yes. And, surely, we *ought* to be able to find the house called "The Ivies"?' said Daisy.

'I've looked in the street directory and examined the names there of every house in Peterswood, and I'm sure Mr Goon has too,' said Fatty, gloomily. 'There isn't a single one called "The Ivies", not a single one.'

'What about Marlow?' said Daisy. 'There might be a house called "The Ivies" there.'

'There might. And there might be one in Maidenhead and one in Taplow,' said Fatty. 'But it would take absolutely ages to look up all the houses in the directory.'

'What a pity the man took the name of Smith – the man who apparently lives at "The Ivies",' said Pip. 'There are so many Smiths.'

'Yes. I looked them up in the telephone directory to start with,' said Fatty. 'There are dozens there – and this man may not even be on the telephone. We can't go ringing up all the Smiths in the neighbourhood to find out if any of them have a false name!'

'No. Of course not,' said Pip.

'Well, I simply do not see how we can even make a start,' said Larry. 'Have you any ideas, Fatty?'

'None,' said Fatty. 'Ern – what about you?'

Ern looked startled. 'Well – if *you* haven't got any ideas, it isn't likely I would,' he said. 'You're the cleverest of us all, Fatty, you know you are.'

'Let's have a biscuit and some lemonade,' said Fatty. 'And Ern, what about that poem of yours? Did you bring it along?'

'Er – well, yes, I did,' said Ern blushing, and dived into deep recesses of his clothing. He brought out a little black notebook, and opened it.

'Read away,' said Fatty, handing round the biscuits. 'We're waiting, Ern.'

So Ern, looking very serious, read out his newest 'pome' as he called it.

The Old, Old House
by Ern Goon

There was a poor old house
That once was full of folk,
But now was sad and empty,
And to me it spoke.
It said, 'They all have left me,
The rooms are cold and bare,
The front door's locked and bolted . . .'

Ern stopped, and looked at the others. 'Well, go on, Ern – it's very good,' said Fatty, encouragingly.

'I'm stuck there,' said Ern, looking miserable. 'It took me six months to write those lines – and now I can't go on. I suppose you can't help me, Fatty? You're so good at making up poetry.'

Fatty laughed. 'Yes – I can tell you how your poem goes on, Ern. Here, let me read what you've written – and when I come to the end of it, I'll let my tongue go loose, and maybe we'll see what the end of the verse is. Here goes!'

And Fatty began to read Ern's poem out again. He didn't stop when he came to where Ern had finished. No – he went straight on, just as though he was reading more and more lines! No wonder Ern stared in the greatest astonishment!

> There was a poor old house
> That once was full of folk,
> But now was sad and empty,
> And to me it spoke.
> It said, 'They all have fled,
> My rooms are cold and bare,
> The front door's locked and bolted,
> And all the windows stare.
> No smoke comes from my chimneys,
> No rose grows up my wall,
> But only ivy shrouds me,
> In green and shining shawl!
> No postman brings me letters,
> No name is on my gate,
> I once was called The Ivies,
> But now I'm out of date.

The garden's poor and weedy.
The trees won't leaf again,
But though I fall to ruin,
The ivy – will – remain!'

There was a silence after this. Everyone stared at Fatty in astonishment and admiration. Ern hadn't a word to say. He sat open-mouthed. How DID Fatty do it? He, Ern, had slaved for six months over the first few lines – and then Fatty had stood up and recited the rest. Without even THINKING! And Ern sorrowfully confessed to himself that Fatty's lines were much better than his.

He found his tongue at last. 'Well, it's what I thought. You're a genius, Fatty, and I'm not. That's your pome, not mine.'

'No, Ern. It's yours. You *began* it, and I expect that's how it was meant to go,' said Fatty, smiling. 'I shouldn't have been able to think of the ending, if you hadn't thought of the beginning.'

'It beats me. It really does,' said Ern. 'Hey – fancy you putting in that bit about "The Ivies" too – and the ivy growing up the wall. Well, even if it had no name on the gate, like you said, anyone would know it was still "The Ivies", because of its "green and shining shawl!" – that's a lovely line, Fatty. You're a real poet, you are.'

But Fatty wasn't listening to Ern's last few words. He stood still, staring into space, and Bets felt quite alarmed. Was Fatty ill?

'What's the matter, Fatty?' she said.

'Well, don't you *see*?' said Fatty, coming to himself again. 'What I said in the verses – even if there's no name on the gate, even if the house hasn't *got* a name, it must still have got the *ivy* that gave it its old name. Why don't we go out and look for a house *covered with ivy*? We can easily cycle all round and about. We might find the very house we want!'

'Loveaduck!' said Ern, in awe. 'You're a one, Fatty. You really are. You make up a pome – and it gives us the first clue! I never knew anyone like you – honest I didn't!'

6. LOOKING FOR IVY!

The six children began to talk about Fatty's sudden brainwave. Of course! Any house once called 'The Ivies' must certainly be covered with ivy, or there would be no point in giving it such a name!

'But why wouldn't it *still* be called "The Ivies"?' asked Daisy.

'It's an old-fashioned sort of name,' said Larry. 'Maybe it's owned now by someone who just prefers a number for their house. The house opposite ours used to be called "Four Towers" but now it's simply "Number Seventeen" with the "seventeen" written out in full.'

'I think you're probably right, Larry,' said Fatty. 'Well, the thing to do is to go round looking for houses covered with ivy. I don't imagine that anyone would have the ivy pulled up, if they bought the house, because it clings to the wall so tightly, and sends its tiny rootlets into every nook and cranny. The ivy will still be there.'

'A green and shining shawl,' quoted Ern, who still hadn't recovered from Fatty's ending to his poem. 'Coo, Fatty, you're a wonder! To think of you standing up there, and . . .'

'Forget it, Ern,' said Fatty. 'You could do it too if you let your tongue just go loose. Practice is all you need. Now, let's go on with the discussion. We're all agreed then that the next thing to do is to search for an ivy-covered house with just a number, since we know there isn't a single house in Peterswood called "The Ivies".'

'It might have another *name*,' said Bets.

'Yes, you're right, Bets,' said Fatty. 'It might. The people who called it "The Ivies" might not be there now. They might have moved.'

'Still, we know that people called Smith live there – if what those peculiar notes say is true,' said Daisy.

'So, whenever we find a house covered with ivy, we have to try and find out if the people in it are called Smith,' said Larry, triumphantly. 'I really feel as if we're getting somewhere now.'

'I bet my uncle won't think up anything as clever as this,' said Ern, thoroughly enjoying himself.

'He didn't hear Fatty's verses,' said Pip. 'If we hadn't heard them either, we'd not have thought of that clue – looking for an ivy-covered house that wasn't *called* "The Ivies". Fatty, when can we go and look for this house?'

'No time like the present,' said Fatty. 'Got your bike, young Ern? Then you can come with us.'

'Suppose my uncle asks me what I've been up to this morning?' said Ern. 'Shall I tell him I haven't seen you?'

'Certainly *not*,' said Fatty, shocked. 'Any untruths of that sort from you, Ern, and you don't come to any more meetings. You ought to know by now what we think of people who don't tell the truth.'

'I'm sorry, Fatty,' said Ern, humbly. 'But I just didn't want to give anything away. My uncle's bound to ask me to tell him everything we said – and I don't want him to worm things out of me. I just thought it would make it easy, like, to say I hadn't seen you.'

'Never you take the easy way out if it means being dishonest or untruthful,' said Fatty. 'You've got a lot of things to learn, young Ern, and that's one of them.'

'I'll do anything you say, Fatty,' said Ern. 'Am I to tell Uncle what we've decided then?'

Fatty considered. 'Well – I can see it's difficult for you, Ern. If you refuse to say anything, your uncle may be horrible to you. You can tell him we're all going out to look for houses covered with ivy. Let him make what he likes of that.'

'But *he'll* go out and look for them too,' objected Ern.

'Well, there's no law against anyone looking for ivy-covered houses,' said Fatty, going out of the shed. 'Come on, everyone. Let's go. Brrrrr! It's cold out here. Buster, are you coming?'

Buster certainly *was* coming. He tore out after the others, barking, and Fatty locked the door carefully behind them.

Soon they were all on their bicycles, and they rode to the end of Fatty's lane. There they dismounted at Fatty's command.

'It would be a waste of time for us all to go together,' said Fatty. 'We'll go in pairs, and try to examine every road in Peterswood. Got your notebooks, everyone? As soon as you see an ivy-covered house, stop. Note if it has a name, or a number, and the street it's in. Don't bother about *new* houses anywhere – ivy takes years to grow. We must look out for an *old* house. Bets and I will go this way – you others decide which street *you'll* explore.'

Bets went off with Fatty, Ern cycled away with Pip, and Daisy and Larry rode off together. 'Meet at this corner in an hour's time!' yelled Fatty, as they parted.

Fatty and Bets rode slowly up the first road. 'You examine the houses on one side of the road, and I'll watch the ones on the other,' said Fatty.

They cycled along together, but to their disappointment not one house had any ivy at all growing up the walls. They turned down another road, and Bets suddenly gave an exclamation. 'Here's a house that's green from top to bottom, Fatty.'

'But not with ivy, Bets,' said Fatty. 'That's creeper – ordinary Virginia creeper. At least, that's what our gardener calls it. Bad luck!'

Down another road, riding very slowly this time, as there were big houses here, standing right back from the road, and difficult to see because of trees in the front gardens.

'Here's one covered with ivy!' said Fatty at last. 'Look, Bets!'

'Yes. But it's got a name on the gate,' said Bets. 'See – Barton House.'

'Well, we know we shan't find a house called "The Ivies",' said Fatty, 'because there's none in the directory. We'll have to put this down, Bets. Now wait while I get my notebook.'

He took it from his pocket and wrote quickly, Bets peeping over his shoulder. 'Barton Grange. Old house, with ivy almost up to roof. In Hollins Road.'

He shut his notebook. 'Good. That's one ivy-covered house, anyway. I wonder if anyone called Smith lives there. We'll have to find out.'

They only found one more ivy-covered house and that was quite a small one, in Jordans Road.

It had obviously once been a cottage belonging to the big house nearby, but had been sold and now had its own little garden, and a hedge round it.

'What's it called?' said Fatty. 'Oh, it hasn't a name – just a number. Number 29, Jordans Road. It looks well-kept – nice curtains at the windows, neat garden. I say, Bets – what about going to ask if people called Smith live here? You just never know your luck!'

'You go, Fatty,' said Bets, who was always shy of strange people.

'Right,' said Fatty, and leaned his bicycle against the trim little hedge. With Buster at his heels, he went in at the gate. I bet someone called Cholmondley or Montague-Paget lives here, he thought, just when I'm looking for a nice short, straightforward Smith!

He rang the brightly-polished bell. At once a dog began to bark inside the house, and Buster stiffened. Fatty picked him up immediately. He didn't want a dogfight on the doorstep!

Someone came up the passage to the front door, and it opened. At once a Pekinese flew out, dancing round excitedly, barking at the top of its voice. Buster wriggled in Fatty's arms, and began barking too.

'Come here, Ming!' said the little old woman at the door, and Ming obeyed, still barking. 'What is it you want?'

'Er – I'm looking for someone called Smith,' said Fatty, politely. 'I don't know if you can help me.'

'Smith? Well, that's *our* name,' said the old lady. 'Who are you? And which of us do you want – me or my husband?'

For once, Fatty was taken aback. He hadn't for one moment imagined that he would find a Smith in an ivy-covered house so quickly, and he hardly knew what to say! But Fatty was never at a loss for long.

'Er, I'd like to see Miss Annabella-Mary Smith,' he said. 'That's if she's here, of course.'

'Oh, you've got the *wrong* Smith,' said the old lady, briskly. 'There's no *Miss* Smith here, only a Mr and Mrs Smith – my husband and myself. Wait – my husband's here. He may know of another Smith somewhere near. John! Come here a minute, will you, dear?'

A nice old man appeared, with a wrinkled, kindly face, and twinkling eyes. Fatty liked him at once. His wife repeated what Fatty had said.

'Miss Annabella-Mary Smith?' he said. 'No, I don't know anyone of that name in this road anyway. We used to live in the big house next door, you know, and knew everyone in the district – but the place was too big for us and we moved into this little place – used to be our gardener's cottage, and very cosy it is too!'

'Was it ever called "The Ivies"?' asked Fatty, hopefully. Mr Smith shook his head.

'No. It was just called "The Cottage",' he said. 'Sorry I can't help you.'

'I'm very sorry to have bothered you,' said Fatty, pleased to have met such a nice old couple. He went back to Bets and told her what had happened.

'I felt rather mean, bothering such nice people,' he said, putting Buster down. 'Well – although their name is Smith and they live in an ivy-covered house, they can't be anything to do with the Smith in those notes. That little place used to be called "The Cottage" not "The Ivies".

Come along – on with the search, Bets. I wonder how the others are getting on!'

Bets and Fatty were astonished to discover that there were no more houses with ivy in the roads they rode along. 'Ivy must have gone out of fashion,' said Bets. 'There are plenty of houses with roses on the wall, and clematis and wisteria and creeper – but no ivy! Well, I must say ivy is a dark, rather ugly thing to cover a house with, when you can get so much prettier things to grow up the walls. What's the time, Fatty?'

'Time to meet the others,' said Fatty, looking at his watch. 'Come on, let's see how they've got on. Better than we have, I hope. Certainly we found an ivy-covered house, and people called Smith – but not the ones we want!'

They cycled off to the corner where they were to meet the others. Larry and Daisy were there already, waiting patiently. Ern and Pip arrived soon after, Ern grinning all over his face as usual.

'Any luck?' asked Fatty.

'We're not quite sure,' said Pip. 'Let's go to your shed, Fatty. We can't talk here. We'll all compare notes, and see if we've got anything useful!'

7. PIP AND ERN HAVE SOME NEWS

Soon all six, with Buster running round busily, were sitting once more in Fatty's shed. He produced some chocolate biscuits, and Buster sat up and begged at once.

'No, Buster. Think of your belly,' said Fatty, solemnly. Buster barked loudly.

'He says, "You jolly well think of *yours*, Fatty!"' said Bets, with a chuckle. 'I'll only have one, thank-you. It's getting near dinnertime, and we're having steak and kidney pudding – I don't want to not be hungry for that!'

'Well, any news?' asked Fatty, producing his notebook.

'You tell yours first,' said Pip.

'There's not much,' said Fatty. 'Bets and I found one big ivy-covered house called Barton Grange, in Hollins Road. Ivy almost up to the roof. We'll have to find out if it was ever called "The

Ivies". And we found a nice little cottage, with no name, in Jordans Road, Number 29 – AND the people who live there are called Smith.'

Everyone sat up in surprise. 'Goodness, you don't mean to say you've hit on the right house and people straightaway!' said Larry, astonished.

'No. Apparently the house once belonged to the gardener of the big place next to it, and was called "The *Cottage*" – not "The Ivies",' said Fatty. 'And the Smiths weren't the right Smiths either. Most disappointing! We'll have to rule it out, I'm afraid. Well, what about you, Larry and Daisy?'

'Absolutely nothing to report,' said Larry. 'We did see one old ivy-covered house – ivy right up to the roof, so it must have been quite an old house.'

'But its name was Fairlin Hall,' said Daisy. 'And it was empty. We rode in at the drive because we couldn't see the house properly from the front gates. We guessed it would be empty because there was a big board up outside that read, "To be Sold".'

'It looked a dreadful old place,' said Larry. 'Old-fashioned, with great pillars at the front door, and heavy balconies jutting out everywhere. I wonder if people ever sat out on those stone balconies in the old days.'

'It looked so lonely and dismal,' said Daisy. 'It really gave me the shivers. It reminded me of the line in that poem, Fatty – "All my windows stare". They did seem to stare at us, as if they were hoping we might be coming to live there, and put up curtains and light fires.'

'But we ruled it out because it was called Fairlin Hall, and was *empty*,' said Larry. 'No Smith there!'

'Quite right,' said Fatty. 'What about you and Ern, Pip?'

'We found *two* ivy-covered houses,' said Pip. 'And one really might be worthwhile looking into, Fatty. Ern and I agreed that it *might* be the one!'

'Ah, this is better news,' said Fatty. 'Out with it, Pip.'

'Well, Ern found the first one,' said Pip, seeing that Ern had taken out his notebook, and was looking hopefully at him, eager to enter into the debate.

'It was called "Dean Lodge", and was in Bolton Road,' said Ern, in a very businesslike voice, flicking over the pages of his notebook, as he had seen his uncle do. 'Ivy-covered to the roof – well, almost to the roof. And it wasn't empty, like the one Pip talked about. It had people in it.'

'Called Smith?' said Bets.

'No. Afraid not,' said Ern, looking hard at his notebook as if he needed to refer to a list of names. 'Me and Pip decided it might be a likely place, as the people who lived in it first *might* have called it "The Ivies". So we decided to ask if anyone called Smith lived there now.'

'And was there?' asked Fatty.

'No. The milkman came up just as we were looking at it, and I asked him,' said Ern. 'I said, "Anyone called Smith live here, mate?" And he said no, it was the Willoughby-Jenkins, or some such name, and they'd been there sixteen years and he'd brought them their milk every single morning of those sixteen years, except the two days he got married.'

Everyone laughed at Ern's way of telling his little tale. 'Now you, Pip,' he said, shutting his notebook.

'Well, the house I spotted was in Haylings Lane,' said Pip, referring to *his* notebook. 'Not a very big one, and not very old. Actually, it isn't really a house now, it's been made into half-shop, half-house, and over the front gate is a notice. It said, "Smith and Harris, Nursery-Men. Plants and shrubs for sale. Apply at house".'

'*Smith* and Harris!' said Fatty, interested at once. 'And you say the house is ivy-covered?'

'Well – not exactly *covered*,' said Pip. 'It had a kind of variegated ivy growing halfway up the whitewashed walls, the leaves were half-yellow and half-green – rather unusual, really. We thought perhaps as Smith and Harris grew shrubs and things, they probably planted one of their own ivies there, to cover the house. But the place wasn't called "The Ivies". It was just called "Haylings Nursery" – after the lane, I suppose. I told you it was in Haylings Lane.'

'Yes,' said Fatty, thoughtfully, 'I can't help thinking that your house is the most likely one, Pip. Ivy up the walls – owned by *Smith* and Harris – and it *might* have been called "The Ivies" before they took it over.'

'Well, what shall we do next?' said Ern, eagerly. 'Loveaduck – whatever would my uncle say if he knew all we'd been doing this morning!'

'Let's quickly run over the ivy-covered houses we've all discovered,' said Fatty, 'and make up our minds which are definitely no good, and which are worth enquiring into. I'll take Bets' and mine first.'

He ran over them quickly. 'Barton Grange, Hollins Road. Ivy-covered. Well, I suppose we'd better find out if people called Smith lived there, and if it was ever named "The Ivies". Then there was the house we found in Jordans Road, but we've ruled that out already, because it was never called "The Ivies". Then there's the house called Fairlin Hall, that Larry and Daisy found – but it's empty, so that's no good.'

'So that only leaves Haylings Nursery, owned by Smith and Harris,' said Pip. 'I vote we enquire into that! If that's no good, we'll find out a bit more about Barton Grange in Hollins Road, the one you and Bets found, Fatty.'

'I wonder if my mother knows who lives in Barton Grange,' said Fatty. 'She's lived in

Peterswood so long, she knows practically everybody. I'll ask her. Gosh, look at the time! And there's our dinner call! Hurry up, all of you, you'll get into a row!'

'Oh my goodness!' said Ern, in a panic. 'What will Uncle say if I'm late! And he's supposed to pay me my first wages at dinnertime. Good-bye, all!'

He raced off to get his bicycle, and Larry and the others rode away at top speed too.

'I'll phone you later!' Fatty shouted after them, and ran indoors to his own lunch. How the time flew when there was detective work to be done! He washed his hands, slicked back his hair, and went into the dining-room, to find his mother just about to sit down herself.

'So sorry I'm a bit late, Mummy,' said Fatty, sliding into his seat.

'It will be a nice surprise for me when you decide to be punctual, Frederick,' said his mother. 'What have you been doing this morning?'

'Oh, just messing about with the others,' said Fatty, truthfully. 'We did a bit of cycling. Mummy, can you tell me something? Who lives at Barton Grange – the big house in Hollins Road?'

'Barton Grange – let me think now,' said his mother. 'First the Fords lived there – then the old man died and his widow went to live with her daughter. Then the Jenkins came there – but they lost all their money and left. Then the Georges came – now what happened to them? I know they left very hurriedly indeed – there was some trouble . . .'

'And then did the Smiths come?' asked Fatty, hopefully.

'The Smiths? What Smiths?' said his mother, in surprise.

'Oh, I don't really know,' said Fatty. 'Anyway – who's there now? It wouldn't *be* people called Smith, would it?'

'No. Nothing *like* Smith,' said his mother, decidedly. 'Yes – I remember now – it's old Lady Hammerlit. I don't know her at all – she's bedridden, poor old thing. But why are you so interested in Barton Grange, Frederick?'

'Well, I was – but I'm not now,' said Fatty, disappointed to find that no Smiths lived there. 'Mummy, I suppose you don't know any place that was once called "The Ivies", do you?'

'Frederick, what *is* all this?' asked his mother, suspiciously. 'You're not getting mixed up in anything peculiar again, are you? I don't want that unpleasant Mr Goon here again, complaining about you.'

'Mummy, he's got *nothing* to complain about,' said Fatty, impatiently. 'And you haven't answered my question. Was there *ever* any house called "The Ivies" in Petswood – its name will have been changed by now. We've heard of one – but nobody seems to know of it now.'

'"The Ivies"?' said Mrs Trotteville. 'No, I don't think I've ever heard of it. I've lived in Petswood for nineteen years, and as far as I remember there never *has* been any place called "The Ivies". Why do you want to know?'

Fatty didn't like the way his mother was questioning him. He wasn't going to tell any fibs, and yet he couldn't give away the reason for his questions, or his mother would at once complain that he was 'getting mixed up in something peculiar again'.

He reached out for the salt – and upset his glass of water. 'Oh *Frederick*!' said his mother, vexed. 'You really are careless. Dab it with your napkin, quick.'

Fatty heaved a sigh of relief. The subject was certainly changed now! 'Sorry, Mummy,' he said. 'Hey, what was that story you used to tell about the man who sat next to you at a big dinner party one night – and told you what a big fish he had caught, and . . .'

'Oh yes,' said his mother, and laughed. 'He stretched out his arms to show me how big it was, and said, "You should have *seen* the fish –" and knocked a whole dish of fish out of the waiter's hand all over himself. He certainly saw a lot of fish then!'

Clever old Fatty! No more awkward questions were asked about "The Ivies" after that. His mother happily related a few more amusing stories, to which Fatty listened with great enjoyment. In the middle of them, the telephone rang.

'You answer it,' said his mother. 'It's probably your father to say he'll be late tonight.'

But it wasn't. It was Ern, and he sounded very upset indeed.

'That you, Fatty? I say, my uncle's in an awful

temper with me because I wouldn't tell him all we did this morning. He won't pay me my wages. And he says I'm not to go home, I've got to stay here. What shall I do? Shall I scoot off home? I don't want to, because it's so nice to be in the middle of a mystery with all of you.'

'I'll come up and see Mr Goon,' said Fatty, sorry for poor old Ern. 'You stay put. I'll be up in half an hour's time!'

8. FATTY PAYS A
CALL ON MR GOON

Fatty kept his promise to Ern. As soon as he had finished his lunch, he put Buster in his bedroom and told him to stay there.

'I'm going to see your enemy, old Mr Goon,' he told Buster, 'and much as you would like to go with me and snap at his ankles, I don't feel that it would be wise this afternoon, Buster. I've got to get poor old Ern his wages!'

Fatty fetched his bicycle and rode off, pondering as he went about what to tell Mr Goon. He decided to tell him everything that had happened that morning, even about Smith and Harris.

If the Smith of Smith and Harris *is* the man written of in those notes, and he's using a false name to cover up some misdeed or other, I suppose it would sooner or later be a job for Mr Goon to take over, Fatty thought. He'd have to find out what the fellow had done – and why he should be turned out of 'The Ivies' – if that's the place that is now called 'Haylings Nursery'. Anyway, I can't let poor old Ern get into trouble.

He arrived at Goon's house, and knocked vigorously at the door. Mrs Hicks arrived in her usual breathless manner.

'There now!' she said. 'I've just bin reading the tea leaves in my after-dinner cup of tea – and they *said* there would be a stranger coming to the house!'

'How remarkable,' said Fatty, politely. 'Tell Mr Goon that Frederick Trotteville wishes to see him, please.'

Mrs Hicks left him standing in the hall, and went into the policeman's office. He scowled at her. 'Bring that boy in,' he said, before she could speak. 'I saw him through the window. I've got something to SAY to him!'

Fatty walked in and nodded to Mr Goon. He knew that the policeman would not ask him to sit down, so he sat down at once, without being asked. He wasn't going to stand in front of Mr Goon like a schoolboy called in for a talking-to!

'Ah, Mr Goon,' he said, in an amiable voice. 'I felt I should like to see you for a few minutes. About Ern.'

'Ern! I'm *tired* of Ern!' said Mr Goon. 'Thinks he can come here and eat me out of house and home, go out when he wants to, solve mysteries, and cheek me into the bargain. *And* expects me to pay him for all that!'

'But didn't you promise to pay him?' asked Fatty, in a surprised voice. 'I must say that Ern has done very well, so far. Where is he?'

'Upstairs. Locked in his room,' said Mr Goon, in a surly voice. 'And I'd like to tell you this, Frederick Trotteville – I haven't time to waste on you. I've business to do this afternoon, see?'

'Right, Mr Goon,' said Fatty, standing up at once. 'I only came to tell you what Ern and the rest of us had been doing this morning. I thought you'd like to know.'

'But that's what I *asked* Ern! And all he said was that you'd gone hunting for houses covered with ivy!' said Mr Goon, almost exploding with wrath. 'Telling me tales like that! Making fun of me! I ticked him off properly for telling me untruths. Then he had the cheek to ask me for his money!'

Fatty looked sternly at Mr Goon. 'Ern was quite right, Mr Goon. He told you the absolute truth. We *did* go searching for ivy-covered houses – and if you were half as bright as that young nephew of yours, you'd guess at once *why* we decided to do such a thing.'

Mr Goon stared at Fatty in surprise. Ern had told him the truth, had he? But why go after ivy-covered houses? Then it all dawned on poor Mr Goon at once. Of course – they were looking for houses that *might* have been called 'The Ivies' at some time or another! Why hadn't *he* thought of that?

'Well, I'll go now,' said Fatty, politely. 'I wouldn't punish Ern, Mr Goon. He was telling you the truth. But obviously you don't want to hear any more about the matter, so I'll go.'

'No! No, sit down,' almost shouted Mr Goon. 'You tell me about these here ivy-covered houses.'

'I wouldn't dream of holding up your work,' said Fatty, and began to walk out of the room.

Mr Goon knew when he was beaten. 'Here!

You come back, Frederick,' he called. 'I've made a mistake, I see it all now. I'd like to hear anything you've got to say.'

'Fetch Ern down then,' said Fatty. 'He's in on this. He did some very good work this morning. You ought to be proud of Ern, not disbelieve him, and lock him up and refuse to pay him. The work he did this morning was worth a lot!'

Mr Goon began to wonder if he had made a great mistake about Ern. According to Fatty, Ern was much cleverer than he had thought him. Oh, Ern *could* be smart – he knew that – but to hear this boy, Frederick Trotteville, talking about him, you'd think Ern was really *brainy*.

'Well, I'll get Ern down,' he said, and got up heavily from his chair. He went upstairs and Fatty could hear him unlocking Ern's door. Ern shot out at once and came down the stairs two at a time, and ran into the office.

'I heard your voice, Fatty!' he said, gladly. 'Coo, you're a real brick to come. How did you make my uncle let me out?'

'Listen, Ern – I'm going to tell him quite shortly about this morning,' said Fatty, quickly, hearing

Mr Goon treading heavily down the stairs. 'But I want *you* to tell him about the house that you and Pip discovered – Haylings Nursery, run by Smith and Harris, see? I've decided that he'd better know about it.'

Ern just had time to nod before Mr Goon came into the room. He sat down and cleared his throat.

'Well,' he said, 'I hear that the tale you told me wasn't far off the mark, young Ern. If you'd told me a bit more, I'd have listened.'

'But you *wouldn't* listen, Uncle,' said Ern. 'You just roared at me when I asked for my money, and rushed me upstairs and . . .'

'Well, I'm sure your uncle is quite willing to pay you now,' said Fatty. 'I've told him you were a great help this morning. In fact I think he should pay you double. You and Pip were the most successful of us all.'

'Here! I'm not paying Ern double money,' said Mr Goon at once.

'In that case, I shall not say any more,' said Fatty, and stood up. 'You've been unfair to Ern, Mr Goon, and I should have thought you'd have liked to make it up to him a bit. My word, he did some good work this morning. He and Pip may have put us on to the track of Mr Smith.'

'What! The Smith mentioned in those notes?' said Goon astonished.

Fatty nodded. 'Maybe. We don't know for certain, of course. You'll be able to judge if you hear what Ern has to say. But as I consider the information is worth double pay, I won't give Ern permission to tell you unless you pay him – and pay him now, in front of me.'

Ern's rather bulging eyes bulged even more when he heard Fatty talking to his dreaded uncle in such a cool, determined voice. He gazed at Fatty in awe and admiration. What a friend to have!

Mr Goon's eyes bulged too – not with admiration, but with wrath and annoyance. He glared at Ern and Fatty. But again he knew he was beaten. That toad of a boy! He was somehow always just a little bit ahead of him. Mr Goon heaved a great sigh, and delved into his trouser pocket. Ern's eyes brightened as he heard the clink of coins.

Goon brought out the money. He put it on the table beside Ern. 'Here you are,' he said.

'But mind – if I think you don't deserve it, back it comes!'

'You keep it for me, Fatty,' said Ern, hurriedly passing it to Fatty. 'So's I don't spend it all at once, see?'

Fatty laughed and pocketed the money. He didn't trust Goon any more than Ern did. 'Well, now you can tell him what we did this morning, Ern,' he said. 'He knows that we went out hunting for ivy-covered houses – you told him that, and he didn't believe you. But he knows it's true now, and he knows *why* we went. I'll just say, Mr Goon, that we found a fair number of ivy-covered houses, not one of them called "The Ivies" of course, or it would be in the directory – but that we decided that the only one worth looking into was the one that Ern and Pip found together. Now you do the talking, Ern.'

Ern told his story well. He described Haylings Nursery, half-shop, half-house, well covered with variegated ivy, and told about the board outside, 'Smith and Harris'.

'And we were going to find out if the Mr

Smith was the one mentioned in the notes,' finished Ern.

'But I decided that perhaps that was *your* job, not ours, Mr Goon,' said Fatty. 'If it *is* the Mr Smith, then, according to the notes, it's a false name – and you can probably easily find out what his real name is, by making a few enquiries into his past.'

'H'm!' said Goon, most interested. 'Yes – yes, I can. And you've been wise to come to me about this, Frederick. This is a job for the police, as you said. *I'll* take this over now. You keep out of it. I think there's no doubt that the Smith in "Smith and Harris" is the man who is going under a false name – a criminal who's been in prison, probably. Well, if so, there will be a record of his fingerprints, and we'll soon find his name.'

'How will you get his fingerprints?' asked Fatty, with much interest.

'Oh, I have my own ways of doing that,' said Goon, putting on a very cunning expression, which Fatty didn't like at all.

'Well, it isn't by any means certain that this fellow Smith is anything to do with those notes, you know,' said Fatty, getting up. 'Better be a bit careful, in case he isn't, Mr Goon.'

'You don't need to give *me* any instructions,' said Goon, annoyed. 'I've been in the police force long enough to know my way about.'

Fatty said good-bye and went. Ern was told to go and keep his usual watch from his bedroom window, in case anyone turned up with another note. Goon finished some reports and then decided to go and interview Mr Smith of 'Smith and Harris'. Ha – good thing that big boy had had the sense to tell him about it. And fancy young Ern discovering the house! Goon brooded for a while over the money he had parted with.

Good mind to go and get it off him, he thought. No, I can't – he's given it to that big boy. Well, I'd better get down to Haylings Lane, and see this Mr Smith.

He went to get his bicycle, passing through the kitchen where Mrs Hicks was reading the tea leaves in her cup again. Mr Goon shouted.

'You and your tea leaves!' he said. 'Waste of time!'

He went out of the kitchen door and shut it

with a bang. Lazy, careless woman – always breaking things, always having cups of tea, always . . . Mr Goon's thoughts stopped suddenly as he saw something that gave him a real shock.

One of those anonymous notes! Yes, it must be. It lay on the kitchen window-sill – a cheap square envelope, and on it was 'Mr goon' just as before, with a small letter for his surname. He stared at it in amazement.

Well, *Ern* must have seen who put it there – and so must Mrs Hicks! No one could have come across the garden to the kitchen window-sill without being seen! He strode indoors with the letter.

'ERN!' he yelled. 'ERN! Come down here. And you, Mrs Hicks, you sit still. I've got a few questions to ask you both. Ho yes – I certainly have!'

9. ERN GETS INTO TROUBLE
- AND SO DOES MR. GOON!

Ern had heard his uncle's stentorian call, and leapt up, scared. *Now* what was the matter? Thank goodness he had handed that money to Fatty.

He tore down the stairs, two steps at a time. 'What is it, Uncle? What's the matter?'

Mrs Hicks was sitting in her chair, looking very startled, staring at Mr Goon.

'See here Ern,' said Mr Goon, in a voice of thunder. 'See here – another of those notes I told you about. Put on the window-sill outside the kitchen here! Mrs Hicks! How long have you been sitting here, facing the window?'

'About three minutes,' said Mrs Hicks, looking quite taken aback. 'I did my washing-up, and then sat down for my second cup of tea. Not more than three minutes ago.'

'Did you see anyone come into the garden?' demanded Goon.

'Not a soul,' answered Mrs Hicks. 'Well, bless us all, is that really another of them ominous letters, sir – or whatever you call them? And left on the window-sill too! What a nerve!'

'You *must* have seen someone put it there,' said Goon, exasperated.

'Well, it wasn't there ten minutes ago, that I do know,' said Mrs Hicks. 'Because I opened the window to throw out some bread to the birds, Mr Goon, and I'd have noticed at once if that letter was there. I'm not blind. And don't you glare at me like that, Mr Goon, you make me feel very uncomfortable!'

'Well, someone must have come over the fence, crossed the garden, and actually placed the note on the sill within the last ten minutes,' said Goon. 'Ernie *must* have seen them, even if you didn't. Ern, did you see anyone?'

'No, no one,' answered Ern, puzzled. 'No one at all.'

'Then you couldn't have been watching,' said Goon, losing his temper.

'I *was* watching. I was sitting at my window all the time,' said Ern, indignantly. 'I tell you, nobody came into the yard, NOBODY!'

'Then how did this note get here?' shouted Goon. 'There's Mrs Hicks here in the kitchen, and you upstairs at the window – and yet someone steals into the yard under your very eyes, leaves the note on the sill and goes away again.'

'Well, I dunno!' said Ern, bewildered. 'If *I* didn't see anyone, and Mrs Hicks didn't either, there couldn't have *been* anybody. Unless he was invisible!'

'Now don't you cheek me,' said Mr Goon. 'Invisible indeed! I don't suppose Mrs Hicks would see anything under her nose except tea leaves, and . . .'

'Don't you sauce *me*!' said Mrs Hicks, annoyed.

'And as for Ern, here, he must have been reading one of those comics of his!' said Goon. 'Ern – tell the truth. YOU WEREN'T WATCHING!'

'I was, Uncle, I was,' said poor Ern, retreating as his uncle came forward towards him. 'I do honest work. You paid me to watch, and I do watch when I'm up there. I tell you nobody came into that garden since you sent me upstairs.'

Goon shook his fist at him, but Ern ducked and

the policeman's fingers caught the edge of a table. He danced round in pain. Ern tore out of the house at top speed. He snatched up his bicycle and rode off on it. He wouldn't stay with his uncle one more hour! Disbelieving him like that! Mrs Hicks hadn't seen anyone. Well, if *she* hadn't, how could *he* have seen anybody!

Mr Goon tore open the square envelope, then saw Mrs Hicks staring open-mouthed, and stamped back into his office. The note was in message form again, made with cut-out letters as before. Goon read it. It was even more puzzling than the others.

'When you see Smith, say SECRETS to him. Then watch him show his heels.'

'Gah!' said Mr Goon, in disgust. 'What's it all mean? *Secrets*, now! What secrets? All right, I'll say "secrets" to this Mr Smith at Haylings Nursery when I see him! I'm getting tired of this. That boy Ern! Sitting upstairs like that and letting the fellow who writes these notes come and put one on the window-sill under his very nose – and I paid him double!'

He was just going out again to get his bicycle

when he stopped. Hadn't he better telephone that big boy and say another note had arrived – and tell him how badly Ern had behaved? Very dishonest of Ern it was, to take his money, and then not do his job. And most ungrateful too.

So Goon telephoned a rather surprised Fatty and told him about the new letter, and what it contained. Fatty noted it down at once. 'When you see Smith, say SECRETS to him. Then watch him show his heels.'

Goon went on to tell him about Ern, and how he had failed to spot anyone coming into the garden with the note. 'Reading his comics, that's what he was doing, instead of paying attention to his job, as he was paid to do,' grumbled Goon. 'Can't let Ern get away with behaviour like that, you know – taking money for what he doesn't do. You'd better let me have that money back.'

'Sorry, Mr Goon, but you paid Ern for what he'd *already* done, not for what he was *going* to do,' said Fatty. 'That money is Ern's. What are you going to do now? Go to see Smith and Harris?'

'Yes,' said Goon. 'But about that money? If

Ernie comes up to you, you tell him I want half of it back, see?'

Fatty put down the receiver, cutting off any more remarks from the angry Goon. He felt sorry that Ern had failed to see anyone coming into the garden with another note – in full daylight too. The messenger certainly had a nerve to do a thing like that!

He heard the sound of a bicycle bell outside in the drive and looked out of the window. It was Ern, panting with his exertions to reach Fatty's house at the first possible moment.

'Hello, Ern,' said Fatty. 'Your uncle's just been on the phone. I hear there's another anonymous note – put on the window-still under everyone's nose, apparently. How on earth was it that you didn't spot whoever brought it? Apparently it happened while you were supposed to be watching.'

'I *was* watching,' said Ern, indignantly. 'You told me to do my job honestly, and I did. I tell you, Fatty, as soon as Uncle sent me upstairs to watch, I sat at my window and glued my eyes on the yard. I did, really. I saw some bread dropping into the yard, and I guessed it was Mrs Hicks throwing some out to the birds. She says the note wasn't on the window-sill when she threw out the bread.'

'And after she threw it out, you still kept your eyes glued on the yard below?' asked Fatty, doubtfully. 'Didn't Mrs Hicks see anyone either?'

'No. No one. Well, if *she* had, I'd have seen him too, wouldn't I?' said Ern, half-angry. 'She was sitting opposite the window – she could almost have reached out and touched it! Well, if *she* didn't see anyone, how could *I*? I just don't understand it, Fatty. The note *must* have been there when Mrs Hicks threw out the bread – and she didn't see it – that's the only explanation.'

'I suppose it is,' said Fatty. 'There's something really strange about it though, I can't just put my finger on it. Well, I expect your uncle will cool down again, Ern. You can stay here for tea though, if you like. I don't think there's much point in your going back to do any more watching – there isn't likely to be another note today!'

'Oh thanks, Fatty. I'd like to stay here,' said Ern. 'Can I help you with anything?'

'Yes. I'm going to pack up some of the jumble to take to the village hall some time,' said Fatty. 'You can help me with that. I wonder how your uncle will get on with "Smith and Harris". It's *possible* that Smith may be the man mentioned in the notes. Well, we shall soon know.'

Mr Goon was not getting on very well in his afternoon's work. In fact, he was having rather a bad time. He had arrived at the nursery in a bad temper, owing to Ern's failure to spot the messenger who brought the last anonymous note. He rode in at the gate at top speed and almost knocked down a man coming up the path wheeling a barrow.

'Look where you're going!' shouted the man, as a flowerpot crashed to the ground. Goon dismounted, and spoke in his most official manner.

'I want to see Smith and Harris.'

'Well, you're speaking to half of them,' said the man, setting the barrow legs down on the path. 'I'm Harris. What do you want? I've got a licence for my dog, and one for my radio, and one for my van, and . . .'

'I haven't come about licences,' said Goon, with a feeling that the man was making fun of him. 'I want to see Mr Smith.'

'Oh, now – that's rather difficult,' said Mr Harris, rubbing his chin, and making a rasping noise as he did so. 'Yes, rather difficult.'

'Is he in the house?' said Mr Goon, impatiently. 'Or out in the nursery gardens?'

'No, no. You won't find him there,' said Mr Harris, who had taken a real dislike to the bumptious policeman. 'I couldn't rightly put my finger on him at the moment.'

'Well, I *must* see him,' said Goon. 'It's important. Don't put me off, please. Take me to him.'

'Oh, I haven't time to do that,' said Mr Harris. 'It's too far to take you when I'm busy, like. I've only one man working for me, and time's precious.'

Mr Goon began to feel exasperated. Where was this elusive Mr Smith? He decided to put a leading question.

'Is Mr Smith his real name?' he asked, bluntly. Mr Harris looked very startled indeed. He stared at Mr Goon and rasped his rough chin again.

'Far as I know it is,' he said. 'Known him

all my life, I have, and he always went by the name of Smith, since he was a tiddler. You being funny?'

'No,' said Mr Goon shortly, disappointed to hear that Smith's name was apparently correct. 'Er, can you tell me if this place was ever called "The Ivies"?'

'And why should it be?' demanded Mr Harris. 'It was Haylings Nursery when I bought it, and Haylings Nursery afore that, and probably Haylings Nursery afore you were born, Mr Nosey Policeman. What's this about "The Ivies"?'

'Well, you've got ivy growing up the wall,' said Mr Goon, beginning to feel very foolish, and wishing he had looked up how old the Haylings Nursery was. 'Now please – I want you to show me where Mr Smith is.'

'All right. Seeing as you insist,' said Mr Harris, and leaving his barrow on the path, he took Mr Goon indoors. He led him to a big round globe of the world, and swung it a little, so that South America came into view. Mr Harris then pointed to a town marked there.

'See that place Rio de Janeiro? Well, *that's*

where he is. Retired there twenty years ago, he did, and I carried on by myself – but I still keep the old name going – "Smith and Harris". You catch the next plane there, Mister, and ask him if his name's Smith. He won't mind telling you.'

And with that he burst into such a roar of laughter that Goon was almost deafened. Very angry at the joke played on him, the policeman departed, looking as dignified as he could. But right to the end of the lane he could hear Mr Harris's delighted guffaws.

Why hadn't he let that big boy interview Mr Harris? It would have done him good to have that silly joke played on *him*. Policemen should be treated with more respect! Mr Goon was very annoyed indeed.

10. FATTY COMES TO A FULL STOP

Mr Goon never told anyone all that had happened at Haylings Nursery. When Fatty phoned him that evening to ask if he had had any success, Mr Goon said very little.

'There is no Mr Smith there now,' he said. 'He left the firm twenty years ago. It was a waste of my time to go there. Is Ern with you, Frederick?'

'Yes. I'm just sending him back to you,' said Fatty. 'He's been a great help to me this afternoon – nice of you to send him up, Mr Goon. Thanks very much.'

Goon was astonished. Hadn't Ern told Fatty how angry he had been with Ern? Well, Ern could stay another night with him, and then he could go home. He wasn't much good as a watcher, and as for paying him another penny, he wasn't even going to *think* of it!

Ern arrived, wondering how Goon was going

to treat him. He sent him out to have his supper with Mrs Hicks in the kitchen. 'Got some work to do,' he said, and Ern fled thankfully to the warm kitchen.

He sat down by the fire, and watched Mrs Hicks making some pastry. 'Funny how neither of us saw that fellow, whoever he was, bringing that note this afternoon,' said Ern.

'Well, I wasn't really looking,' said Mrs Hicks. 'I was just sitting here with my teacup, reading the tea leaves, like I always do. *You* couldn't have been looking either, young man. You can tell fibs to your uncle, if you like, but you needn't tell them to me. You just wasn't looking!'

'Oooh, I *was*,' said Ern. 'I tell you I never took my eyes off that yard. Never once. When I'm paid to do a thing I do it, see? And I never saw anyone – all I saw were the birds flying down to peck at the bread you threw out.'

'Oh, you saw me doing that, did you?' said Mrs Hicks. 'Well, it's funny you didn't see who brought that note then, because he must have come along just after that – as I was telling your uncle.'

'He *couldn't* have come then,' said Ern. 'I tell you I was watching all the time, Mrs Hicks. *I'm* not making a mistake, I know I'm not.'

'Are you telling me that *I* am, then?' said Mrs Hicks, looking so fierce that Ern felt quite alarmed. 'You just be careful of that tongue of yours, young Ern, else not a mite of supper do you get.'

Ern subsided, feeling puzzled. Everyone was cross with him just now – but on the whole it was safer to sit with Mrs Hicks in the kitchen rather than with his uncle in the office. He wondered if Mrs Hicks would like to hear his 'pome'. It might put her into a better temper.

'I write portry, Mrs Hicks,' he said.

'Well, I shouldn't think that's very difficult, is it?' said Mrs Hicks. 'I'd write it meself if I had time.'

This was rather damping. Ern tried again. 'I'd like to know what you think of my last pome,' he said. 'Can I say it to you?'

'If you like,' said Mrs Hicks, still rolling the pastry vigorously. 'Silly stuff really. I used to do reciting at school meself.'

'But this is something I made up,' said Ern. 'At least, I made up some of it, and a friend of mine made up the other half.' And with that he stood up and recited his verses – and Fatty's – about the 'Poor Old House'. He didn't see Mr Goon at the kitchen door, standing amazed at Ern's recital. He almost jumped out of his skin when he heard his uncle's voice at the end.

'Have you taken to poetry writing again, Ern?' said Mr Goon. 'How many times have I told you it's a waste of time? Do you remember that rude poem you wrote about me once? Well, *I* haven't forgotten it, see? And what's all that about "The Ivies" in that poem? Don't you go putting secret information like that into your poems. You give me that notebook of yours and let me see what other poems you've got there.'

'No, Uncle. My notebook's private,' said Ern, remembering that he had put into it notes of the meetings he had had with Fatty and the others.

'Now, look here, young Ern,' said Goon, advancing on him, and Ern promptly fled out of the back door. He saw a black shadow moving before him, and yelled.

'Uncle! There's someone out here! Quick, Uncle!'

Mr Goon rushed out at once – and ran straight into Mrs Hicks' washing-line, which was hung with overalls, two sheets and a dark blanket. The line broke, and Mr Goon gave a yell as the blanket folded itself round him.

Poor Ern! He really had thought that the washing blowing in the darkness on the line was somebody in the yard. When he saw his uncle staggering into the kitchen with the washing dragging behind him on the broken line, he knew there was only one thing to do – and that was to rush up to his bedroom and lock himself in!

That meant going without his supper, but at least he still had his precious notebook and at least he was safe from his uncle's anger. Judging from the noise downstairs he was lucky to have escaped in time. Why, oh why had he ever said he would come and help his uncle? Never again, thought poor Ern. Never again!

Meanwhile, Fatty was feeling that he had come to a full stop where the mysterious notes were concerned. They hadn't found a house called 'The Ivies', or even one with ivy growing up it that *had* been called 'The Ivies'. Neither had they found the right Smith. Was there anything else to do?

Only one thing, thought Fatty. And that will be a terribly fiddling job. I'd better try and get the letters and words off, that are stuck on to the sheet of writing paper. I might find something printed on the other side to help me – I might even find out what newspaper they come from. If it was, say, a Bristol paper, the odds are that the writer of the notes comes from Bristol – or if it turns out to be a Manchester paper, maybe he comes from Manchester. Not that that will be much help.

So he went down to his shed that evening and set to work. It was indeed a horribly fiddling job. In the middle of it, his lamp flickered and went out.

'Blow!' said Fatty, and gathered up his things by the light of a candle and went indoors. He sat himself down in his bedroom to finish the job.

He found a few interesting things as he tried to get the pasted-on letters off the strips they were stuck on. The word 'goon' for instance, which was, in every case, apparently part of a whole word – it was not made of four separate letters. Fatty stared at it. 'goon'. It must be part of a whole word. But what word had 'goon' in it. He couldn't think of any.

As he went on with his work, a tap came at the door, and his mother came in. 'Frederick, have you taken my library book?' she asked. 'Good gracious, whatever are you doing? What a mess!'

'I'm just solving a – well, a kind of puzzle really,' said Fatty. His mother picked up the cut-out piece of paper he had just put down – the bit with 'goon' on.

'Goon,' she said. 'What a funny puzzle, Frederick. Is this part of "Rangoon" or something?'

'*Rang*oon!' said Fatty. 'I never thought of Rangoon. It's about the only word ending in "goon", isn't it, Mummy? Has Rangoon been in the papers much lately? Has anything happened there? Would the name be printed a lot in our papers?'

'Well no – I can't remember seeing anything about Rangoon,' said his mother. 'Oh Frederick, you *have* got my library book! Really, that's too bad of you.'

'Gosh, sorry, Mummy – I must have brought it up by mistake,' said Fatty. 'It's almost exactly like mine, look.'

'Would you like me to stay and help you to sort out this puzzle?' asked his mother. 'I like puzzles, as you know.'

'Oh no, Mummy, thank you, I wouldn't dream of bothering you,' said Fatty hastily, afraid of some awkward questions as to where he had got the 'puzzle' from. 'It's hopeless, really. I expect I'll have to give it up.'

And that is exactly what poor Fatty had to do, after struggling with it for at least two hours. There was nothing on the other side of the pasted-on letters that could help him to identify any newspapers – only odd letters that might have come from any part of any paper. It was very disappointing.

'*That* idea's no good then,' said Fatty, putting the bits and pieces back into the envelope. 'Waste of two hours! I'm at a dead-end. Can't find any clues at all – and even when there was a chance of actually *seeing* that fellow who delivers the notes, Ern doesn't see him. He must have had forty winks – he couldn't have failed to see him if he was really awake. Blow! Where do we go from here? I'll call a meeting tomorrow morning, and we'll see if anyone has any ideas.'

So next morning, at ten o'clock sharp, everyone was at Fatty's, including Ern. Ern was feeling a bit happier. His uncle had had a nice letter from Superintendent Jenks that morning, about some small case that Goon had apparently handled quite well – and the big policeman had beamed all through breakfast. He read the letter to Ern three times, very solemnly.

'Now if *I* had done what *you* did yesterday, and sat looking out of that window of yours, keeping watch, and hadn't even *seen* something going on under my very nose, I wouldn't be getting letters like this,' said Goon.

Ern didn't argue. He nodded his head and helped himself to more bread and butter and marmalade. He made up his mind to go up to Fatty's immediately after breakfast and tell him he was going home. He was sure that his uncle wouldn't pay him any more wages, and he wasn't going to stop with him for nothing!

So Ern was at the meeting too. When they were all in the shed, Fatty told them of his failure the night before. 'Mummy came up and offered to help me,' he said. 'But I was afraid she'd ask me awkward questions. She did say that she thought the word "goon" with the small letter instead of the capital one, might be part of *Ran*goon. And it *might*, though I can't think how it could help us! I gave up trying to find a clue by unpasting the letters in the messages. And now I don't really see what else we can do.'

'Well, there's only *one* thing left,' said Daisy, 'and that's that place that Larry and I found. What was it called now – Fairlin Hall. The place that was empty. I just wondered if it might be worthwhile finding out if it had *ever* been called "The Ivies".'

'But you said it was empty,' said Fatty. 'You saw a noticeboard up, saying that it was for sale.'

'Yes, I know,' said Daisy. 'But I went by it today – just out of curiosity, you know – and I saw something interesting.'

'What?' asked everyone at once.

'Well, I'm sure there was smoke coming out of a chimney at the back,' said Daisy. 'I couldn't be *quite* certain – the chimney might have belonged to a house I couldn't see. But it did *look* as if a chimney belonging to Fairlin Hall itself was smoking.'

'Well! This certainly needs investigating,' said Fatty, cheering up at once. 'There might be someone hiding there – Smith, perhaps! I vote we all cycle down straightaway and have a snoop round. What about it, everyone? Come on!'

And out they all rushed to get their bicycles, with Buster barking madly round them. Was this a clue to the mystery – or wasn't it? A smoking chimney! If only it *did* belong to Fairlin Hall!

11. THE CARETAKERS AT FAIRLIN HALL

The six cyclists, with Buster panting behind, rode through Peterswood at top speed. It was most unfortunate that they should meet Mr Goon round a corner. He was on his bicycle too, and Ern, being in the middle of the road, almost ran into him.

'Ern!' yelled Mr Goon, wobbling dangerously. 'I'll teach you to – here, where are you going, Ern? ERN!'

But Ern, and the others too, were away up the road, Ern looking scared. 'Hope he won't come after me,' he said. He looked round, and to his horror saw that Mr Goon had swung round and was pedalling furiously some way behind them.

'Can't let him see us going into Fairlin Hall,' panted Fatty. 'We'll go right past it, and up Cockers Hill. Mr Goon will soon be left behind then.'

So they swept past Fairlin Hall, each trying to

see whether smoke was coming from any chimney, turned the corner and made for the steep Cockers Hill. Up they went, more slowly now, hearing Mr Goon's shouts for Ern faintly behind them. Bets began to giggle.

'Oh dear! Mr Goon will be as red as a beetroot when he's halfway up this hill! It's rather a shame, Fatty.'

'He doesn't *need* to follow us up it,' panted Fatty. 'Look behind, Bets. Has he dismounted yet?'

Bets glanced behind. 'Yes, he has. He's standing still, mopping his head. Poor Mr Goon! We'll soon shake him off.'

They came to the top of Cockers Hill, sailed down it thankfully, and then made their way back to the road in which Fairlin Hall stood. There was no sign of Goon anywhere. They put their bicycles against the wall, and stood at the gate entrance, looking into the drive.

'See what I mean,' said Daisy, eagerly. 'Isn't that smoke from one of the chimneys right at the back of the house?'

'Yes. I think it is,' said Fatty. 'What an ugly old place! Look at those great pillars at the front door

– and those heavy stone balconies. It must have been empty for years.'

He went to look at the 'For Sale' board, and noted the estate agent's name on it. 'Paul and Ticking,' he said. 'It wouldn't be a bad idea to go and ask them for particulars of this place – we might find out if it had ever been called "The Ivies".'

'Yes. That's a good idea!' said Pip. 'Well, shall we snoop round the place and see if anyone's about? We must find out if that smoking chimney belongs to the house.'

'Yes,' said Fatty. 'I'll go with Bets. You stay here, you three, out of sight, with Buster. Bets and I will go round to the back of the house, calling Buster, as if we'd lost him, and if anyone *is* there, they'll probably come out to us. When we've stopped yelling for Buster, you can let him go, and he'll come to us.'

'Right,' said Larry, catching hold of the little Scottie by the collar. Fatty and Bets made their way down the overgrown drive, Fatty calling 'Buster, Buster, where are you?' at the top of his voice. Buster nearly went mad trying to follow, and was extremely angry with Larry for hanging on to his collar. He almost choked himself, trying to get away.

Fatty peeped into the windows he passed. The house was as dismal inside as it was outside. Great empty rooms, dirty and dreary, with filthy windows, and faded paint – Bets shivered and turned her face away.

They rounded a corner and came to the kitchen end. There was a line across a yard, with clothes blowing on it – aha, there was certainly someone here then! Fatty nudged Bets and glanced upwards. Bets did the same and saw a chimney above, smoking. Daisy had been right.

'Buster, Buster, where are you, you naughty dog!' shouted Fatty, and whistled piercingly.

An oldish woman came out of the kitchen door, thin and sad-looking, but with a kindly, rather sweet old face. 'Have you lost your dog?' she said.

'He's somewhere about,' said Fatty truthfully. 'I do hope I didn't disturb you. Isn't this place empty? I saw a "For Sale" notice outside.'

'That's right,' said the woman, pulling her shawl round her. 'We're caretakers. The house was left quite empty for years, but tramps kept breaking in – so the agents put in caretakers. We've been here for fifteen years now – and we hope the place *won't* be sold, because we don't want to be turned out!'

Buster suddenly came rushing round the corner, and barked madly when he saw Fatty. He was most indignant at being held so long by Larry who, of course, had let him go as soon as Fatty had stopped calling him.

'Ah, there's your dog,' said the old woman. 'He couldn't have been far away. I sometimes wish *we* had a dog. Three times since we've been here there's been burglars – though what they expect to find in an empty house, I *don't* know!'

A voice called her from indoors, and then someone coughed long and painfully. 'That's my poor husband,' said the old woman. 'He's ill. I suppose you aren't going back to the village, are you? I ought to go to the chemist and get him some more medicine, but I don't really like leaving him.'

'Of course we'll leave a message at the chemist for you – or better still, we'll pop down and get the medicine ourselves and bring it back!' said Fatty. 'We've got our bicycles.'

'Well, that would be really kind of you,' said the old lady. 'I'll just get the bottle,' and she hurried indoors.

'Wonder if their name is Smith,' said Fatty, in a low voice. 'Shouldn't think so. Obviously they're just caretakers who've been here for years. Ah, here she comes.'

'Here's the bottle,' said the old woman. 'And here's the money for the medicine. Ask for the same prescription as before, please.'

'Er – what name shall I say?' asked Fatty.

'Smith,' said the old lady. 'Mr John Smith. The chemist will know.'

'Right,' said Fatty, startled to hear that there *was* a Mr Smith in this ivy-covered place. He glanced at Bets, and saw that she was astonished too. 'Come on, Buster, old thing. We'll be back in about ten minutes, Mrs Smith.'

'You're kind, really kind,' she said, and gave them a smile that made her old face quite beautiful.

Fatty and Bets ran back up the drive with Buster at their heels. Fatty's thoughts were in a whirl. Was this another wrong Smith – or could it be – could it *possibly* be the right one?

'What an awfully long time you were,' said Larry. 'What happened?'

Fatty told the others briefly, as they wheeled their bicycles into the road. 'Two caretakers there – been in charge of the house for fifteen years. And the name is SMITH! What do you think of that?'

'Come on, we're going to the chemist,' said Bets.

'What on earth for?' demanded Pip.

'Tell you as we go,' said Fatty, which was really rather a dangerous thing to do, as the other four were so keen to hear Fatty's tale that they rode in a close bunch as near to him as possible, their pedals almost touching! However, they arrived at the chemist's safely, and Fatty went in with the bottle, planning to get a little more information about the Smiths if he could.

'For Mr Smith?' said the chemist, who knew Fatty. 'How's the old fellow? He's been ailing for the past year. He really ought to get out of that damp old place, and go and live by the sea – but they're as poor as church mice.'

'Mrs Smith seemed very nice,' said Fatty. 'I don't know her husband.'

'He's a strange fellow,' said the chemist, writing out a label. 'Sort of scared. Hardly ever goes out, and when his wife was ill and he had to come in to get medicine for her, he hardly opened his mouth. I guess they don't want that old place to be sold – they'd have to look for somewhere else to go to, and that's not easy these days, when you're old and poor.'

'Who used to own Fairlin Hall?' asked Fatty.

'I've no idea,' said the chemist. 'It's been empty for years – long before *I* came here. Falling to pieces, I should think. It's a dismal place. Well, there you are. Please give my kind regards to the old lady. She's a pet, and simply worships the old man.'

'Thanks,' said Fatty, and went out with Bets. 'We'll go straight back to Fairlin Hall,' he said to the others, who were waiting outside. 'I'll see if I can get any more information out of Mrs

Smith. Then we'll go the estate agent. We simply MUST find out if that house was ever called "The Ivies" – if it was, we're really on the track of the mystery!'

They all went back to Fairlin Hall, and Fatty and Bets once more went round to the back door, this time with Buster free, dancing round them. The kitchen door was shut, and they knocked.

'If that's the medicine, would you leave it on the doorstep?' called the old woman's voice. 'I'm just seeing to my husband. He's had a nasty coughing attack. Thank you very very much.'

Fatty put the bottle down on the step, rather disappointed at not being able to get any more information. He took a quick look round. The yard was very clean and tidy. Spotless, well-mended curtains hung at the windows – the only clean windows in the house! The doorstep was well-scrubbed. A washed milk bottle stood there, waiting for the milkman.

'Well, Mr Smith *may* be a man with a false name and a mysterious past of some sort,' said Fatty, as they went back to the others. 'But there's nothing wrong with the old lady. Even the chemist said she was a pet. I liked her, didn't you, Bets?'

'Yes, I did,' said Bets. 'Oh dear, I do hope nothing horrid will happen to Mr Smith, it would make his wife so unhappy. The man who wrote those notes didn't seem to like him at all, did he? I wonder what he meant by telling Mr Goon to say SECRETS to him.'

'Can't imagine,' said Fatty. 'Well now, off we go to the estate agent's. Hello – what's all the noise going on outside the front gates?'

Fatty soon found out! Mr Goon had come cycling by and had suddenly seen Larry, Daisy, Pip – and Ern! He also saw Fatty's bicycle and Bets', leaning against the wall, and felt very curious indeed. He had dismounted heavily from his own bicycle, after making sure that Buster was nowhere around, and demanded to know what they were all doing there.

'Just having a bit of a rest,' said Pip. 'Going up Cockers Hill at top speed was tiring, Mr Goon. I expect you found it so, too.'

'I don't want any cheek,' said Mr Goon, glaring at Pip. 'Where's that big boy gone? What's he here for? Ho – another ivy-covered house! Snooping round again, I suppose. Well, you won't find much there – it's empty, see? Ern, you come here.'

Just at that moment, Fatty and Bets and Buster came out of the gate, and Buster ran barking in delight towards his old enemy. Goon leapt on his bicycle at once, and rode off quickly, shouting to Ern.

'You come back with me, young Ern. I've got a job for you, delivering messages. You come at once, Ern.'

'Better go, Ern,' said Fatty. 'Who knows, he may give you some more wages at dinnertime, if you do some work for him this morning!'

'What a hope!' said Ern, in disgust. 'All right, Fatty. I'll go, if you say so. I'll be down at your place as soon as I can to hear your news. So long!'

And away he went after his uncle, looking so doleful that the others couldn't help laughing. 'Now to the estate agent's,' said Fatty, mounting his bicycle too. 'I feel we're getting somewhere now!'

12. MR GRIMBLE TALKS

The estate agent's office was in the middle of the High Street, and its window was set out with all kinds of very dull particulars of houses for sale.

'I hope you won't be too long, Fatty,' said Pip. 'It's a bit boring for the rest of us, waiting about while you and Bets do the work.'

'Sorry!' said Fatty. 'Yes, you're right – I've been making you wait about half the morning. Look, go into the café, and order what you like. It's gone eleven o'clock, I should think. I'll pay. I've still got heaps left from my Christmas money. Bets, you go too, and order me two macaroons and an ice cream.'

'Oh *Fatty*, didn't you have any breakfast!' said Bets. But Fatty had already disappeared into the estate agent's office. A young man was there, very busy at a big desk. In a corner, at a much smaller desk, sat a clerk, an older man, round-shouldered and shabby.

'Well, what can I do for *you*?' said the young man.

'Have you any particulars about Fairlin Hall?' asked Fatty, politely. The young man stared at him.

'That old place! You're not thinking of buying it, by any chance, are you?' he said, and laughed.

'Well, no,' said Fatty. 'I'm – er – interested in its history, to tell you the truth.'

'Well, I'm sorry, but I haven't time to give you a history lesson,' said the young man rudely. 'The place has been empty as long as I can remember – since before I was born. We're hoping to sell it as a school of some sort, but it's in such bad condition, nobody will buy. It's got no history as far as *I* know!'

The phone rang at that moment, and the young man picked up the receiver. 'Mr Paul here,' he said. 'Oh *yes*, Mrs Donning. Yes, yes, yes. Of course, of course. No trouble at all. Do give me all the particulars.'

It was quite plain to Fatty that he wasn't going

to get any help from the bumptious Mr Paul, who was evidently one of the partners in the business of Paul and Ticking. He turned and made for the door.

But as he passed the old clerk in the corner, he heard a few quiet words. 'I can tell you something about the house if you like.'

Fatty turned and saw that the old man was trying to make up for Mr Paul's rudeness. He went over to his desk.

'Do you know anything about the place?' he said, eagerly. 'You know it, don't you? – covered with ivy from top to bottom.'

'Oh yes. I sold it to its present owners twenty-one years ago,' said the clerk. 'It was a lovely place then. I and my wife used to know the old lady who lived there. Ah, Fairlin Hall was well-kept then – it had four gardeners, and you should have seen the rose garden! I was talking about it to old Grimble only the other day. He was head gardener there, and knew every corner of it.'

Fatty pricked up his ears at once. Surely an old gardener would know far more about Fairlin Hall than anyone else. He might be pleased to talk about the old place, too.

'Perhaps you could give me Mr Grimble's address,' he said. 'Does he still work?'

'Oh no, he's retired. Just potters about his own garden,' said the old clerk. 'I'll scribble down his address for you.'

'Er – was Fairlin Hall ever called anything else?' asked Fatty, hopefully.

'I believe it was – but I can't remember,' said the old man. 'But perhaps I can look it up for you.'

'Potter!' said Mr Paul, putting down the telephone receiver, 'it's very difficult for me to telephone, with you jabbering in the corner.'

'Sorry, Mr Paul,' said poor old Potter, and hastily pushed a piece of paper over to Fatty, who shot out of the office before the rude Mr Paul could admonish him too. Ugh! Fancy that old clerk having to put up with young Mr Paul's rudeness all the time! Fatty glanced down at the piece of paper he had been given.

'Donald Grimble,' he read. 'Primrose Cot, Burling Meadows. Gardener.'

He ran across the road to the café, where all

the others were now sitting round a table, eating macaroons. Buster greeted him loudly as usual, barking as if he hadn't seen Fatty for at least a month.

'You haven't been long, Fatty,' said Bets. 'I've only taken two bites of my macaroon. Have one – they're lovely and fresh. All gooey.'

'Did you find out anything?' asked Larry.

Fatty told them about the rude Mr Paul and the nice old man in the corner who seemed so scared of him. Then he showed them the piece of paper. 'Donald Grimble used to be head gardener at Fairlin Hall,' he said, 'and apparently knew every corner of the place. He's retired now – but I bet he can tell us plenty about it. If ONLY we could find out if it has ever been called "The Ivies"! I can't help thinking that old Mr Smith, whose medicine we got this morning, *must* be the Smith referred to in those anonymous notes.'

'We've got time to go and see Mr Grimble this morning,' said Bets. 'But what excuse can we make? He'll wonder why we're so interested in the old place. He might think we were making fun of him, or something.'

'I know! Let's buy a pot with some unusual plant in at the florist's,' said Daisy, 'and go and ask him to tell us what it is! Then we can get talking.'

'Daisy, that's a very bright idea,' said Fatty, approvingly, and Daisy went red with pleasure. 'That will mean we can all go, instead of most of you waiting about outside. I'll have another macaroon, please.'

'I suppose you're counting, Fatty?' said Pip, handing him the plate. 'You've had three already, and they're expensive, you know. Even *your* Christmas money won't last long if you empty plates of macaroons at this rate.'

'Have an ice cream, Pip,' said Fatty, 'and stop counting how many macaroons I eat. Bets, aren't *you* going to have an ice cream? You'd better feed yourself up, because I'm going to make *you* take the pot-plant in to old Mr Grimble!'

'Oh *no*!' said Bets. 'Why can't one of the others?'

'Because you have a very nice smile, Bets, enough to melt the crabbed old heart of even a fierce head gardener!' said Fatty.

Bets laughed. 'All right, I'll do it for you. Shall Daisy and I go and buy the plant now, while you others are finishing? We can't eat another thing.'

'Yes. Here's the money,' said Fatty, but Daisy pushed it away. 'Oddly enough, *I* have some Christmas money left too!' she said. 'Come on, Bets – let's leave these guzzlers, and go to the flower shop.'

They were back again with a small plant just as the three boys and Buster came out of the café, looking rather well-fed.

'Please, Mr Grimble,' said Bets, looking up at Fatty with a smile, 'could you tell me what this plant is?'

Fatty laughed. 'Fine, Bets! But be sure to get *us* into the picture somehow, so that we can come and listen – and so that I can ask questions!'

They went off to Burling Meadows on their bicycles. Primrose Cot was a small cottage standing by itself in a beautiful little garden. Not a weed showed in the smooth grass lawn. Nor was there a weed in any of the beds, either. The hedges were trim and neat. Early snowdrops showed their little white bonnets under a tree, and yellow aconites wore their pretty green frills just beside them.

'That must be old Mr Grimble sawing logs at the bottom of the garden,' said Fatty, seeing a sturdy old man there, a battered hat at the back of his head, and the dark blue apron of a head gardener over his corduroy trousers. 'Let's go into the field nearby and speak to him over the hedge.'

So they went down a side path into the field that skirted the bottom of Mr Grimble's garden. Bets called to him over the hedge. 'Please, are you Mr Grimble?'

'Yes, I am,' answered the old fellow, peering over at Bets. 'What do you want with me?'

'Oh please, could you tell me what this plant is?' asked Bets, with her sweetest smile, and handed up the pot. 'It's got such pretty leaves, and I do want to know its name. You know the names of every plant, don't you, Mr Grimble?'

Grimble beamed down at her. 'Well, I know a tidy few, dear. This here plant is a young Coleus – but you want to take it home and keep it in the warm. It don't like cold air.'

'Have you ever grown Coleuses?' asked Bets.

'Oh aye! Thousands,' said old Grimble. 'I used to work at that old place, Fairlin Hall – I were head gardener there for years – and I always kept one corner of the heated greenhouse for them Coleus. Pretty things they are, with their patterned leaves – all colours!'

'Oh, Fatty – he used to work at Fairlin Hall,' called Bets, anxious to bring the others into the conversation. 'Wasn't that the place we saw this morning – you know, where that old woman lives, whose husband we fetched medicine for.'

Fatty came up at once, pleased with Bets. The others followed, amused at her little performance.

'Good morning,' said Fatty, politely. 'Yes, we did go into the front drive and round to the back this morning. We didn't see much of the garden though.'

'Ah, it's a terrible place now,' said Grimble, sadly. 'I worked there, man and boy, for years, and was made head gardener. You should have seen my roses – 'twas a show-place, my rose garden. I never go down that road now – can't abear to see my old garden gone to ruin.'

'The house is absolutely *covered* with ivy now,' said Pip, putting in a word himself. 'Even the chimneys are green with it. Was it covered with ivy when you were there, Mr Grimble?'

'Oh yes, but not as thick as it is now,' said Grimble. 'My father planted that ivy, so he told me. It weren't called Fairlin Hall then, you know. It were called "The Ivies".'

This welcome bit of news came so suddenly that all the children had quite a shock. So they were right! Fairlin Hall *was* once 'The Ivies'! It *was* the house spoken of in those anonymous notes. But how strange that the writer didn't know that it had a different name now – it had been called Fairlin Hall for years and years!

'Why was the name changed?' asked Fatty.

Grimble looked at him and said nothing for some twenty seconds. Then he spoke in a curiously sad voice. '"The Ivies" got a bad name,' he said. 'Something happened there. My master and mistress, Colonel and Mrs Hasterley, couldn't abear their home to be pointed at – it were in all the papers, you see – and they sold up and went. And when new people bought the place they changed the name. Yes, it were once "The Ivies" – but that's a long time since.'

The children were silent for a minute or two, and the old gardener began his sawing again, looking sad and far away.

'What happened?' ventured Fatty, at last. 'Was it – was it something bad that your master did?'

'Nay, he were as good a man as ever lived,' said old Grimble. 'It were his son, Wilfrid, that brought shame on the old place, and on his parents too.' And to the children's horror, tears gathered in the old man's eyes, and dripped on to his saw!

'Let's go,' said Fatty, at once. 'Come on – let's go.'

13. MR. GOON IS PLEASED WITH HIMSELF

The five murmured a quiet goodbye to old Mr Grimble, who took no notice at all. He was evidently lost in far-off memories, which were still powerful enough to upset him. They all felt very sorry to have made the old fellow weep. Bets felt tears in her own eyes.

'We shouldn't have asked him questions, Fatty,' she said. 'I feel dreadful about it.'

'Well, we couldn't tell that he would take it like that,' said Fatty, feeling rather uncomfortable himself. 'My word, though – we were right. Fairlin Hall *was* "The Ivies". I wonder what dreadful thing Wilfrid Hasterley did to bring the house such shame and notoriety – enough to make its name known all over the country, and force his parents to sell it.'

'We'd better find out,' said Larry. 'How can we?'

'I almost think I'd better ask Superintendent

Jenks about it,' said Fatty. 'If he can tell us what the shocking happening was, it might make all this business of the anonymous notes a bit clearer. It's plain that the writer wants old Smith to be cleared out of Fairlin Hall – and it's also plain that he, the writer, must have been away for a good long time, if he doesn't know that the name has been changed for twenty years or more. It's a proper mystery, this!'

'You'd better telephone the Super when you get home, Fatty,' said Larry. 'Gosh, it's almost one o'clock! Daisy, come on – we'll be late for lunch!'

Fatty went home thinking hard. There were a great many questions in this mystery that had no answers. Who was the writer of the notes? How did he keep putting them where Mr Goon could find them, and yet never be seen himself? Why didn't he know that 'The Ivies' was now Fairlin Hall, and had been for years? Why did he want Smith sent out of Fairlin Hall – and why did Smith apparently have a false name?

'Too *many* mysteries this time,' said Fatty, cycling home fast. 'Well, the time has come to tackle the Super about it. I'll telephone immediately after my lunch.'

He went to the telephone at two o'clock, hoping that the Super might have finished his own lunch. Alas, he was away in the north of England. His deputy, who knew a little about Fatty's amateur detective work, was sympathetic, but not very helpful.

'You could go and see Mr Goon, the constable in your village,' he suggested. 'He might be able to help you. In fact, Frederick, I think that is the thing you *should* do. I believe we have had information from Mr Goon that some rather peculiar anonymous notes have been arriving at his house, and if you know anything that ties up with those, it's your duty to inform him. I'll tell the Super when he comes back – but I don't expect him for some days.'

This was extremely disappointing. Fatty put down the telephone with a groan. Blow! Now he'd *have* to go to Mr Goon! The Super would not be at all pleased with him if he held up his information just because he wasn't friendly with Goon. He sat down and considered the matter.

Well, it's no good. I'd better get it over, thought Fatty. I'll cycle down to Mr Goon's house now. How cock-a-hoop he'll be to think I'm passing on my information to him. Well, I jolly well won't tell him HOW I got it!

Fatty fetched his bicycle and went off to Goon's, feeling decidedly down in the dumps. He knew quite well that Goon would pretend to the Super that *he* had found out most of the information himself, and give no credit to Fatty and the others. He came to Goon's house and knocked at the door. Mrs Hicks opened it, breathless and panting, as if she had been running a mile.

'Mr Goon's not in,' she told him. 'But Ern is. Do you want to see him? He's up in his room, watching out of the window. We had another of them ominous notes this morning.'

Fatty was interested. He went up to Ern's room, and found the boy sitting close to his window, his eyes glued on the yard below. 'I heard your voice, Fatty,' he said, without turning round. 'I'm on the watch again. We've had another note this morning – pegged to the washing-line it was!'

'What, right in the middle of the yard!' said Fatty, astonished. 'I must say the writer's bold. Nobody saw him, I suppose?'

'No,' said Ern. 'But nobody was watching. Funny note it was. It didn't say "The Ivies" this time. It said Fairlin Hall. "Ask Smith at Fairlin Hall what his real name is", that's what it said.'

'Oho! So the writer has at last found out that "The Ivies" has changed its name,' said Fatty. 'I suppose this means that your uncle has gone racing round to Fairlin Hall, Ern?'

'Yes,' said Ern. 'He wasn't half-pleased about it, either – getting in on Mr Smith like that. He doesn't know that you saw old Mrs Smith this morning, and found out so much.'

'Poor old Mr Smith,' said Fatty. 'I wouldn't like to be in *his* shoes when old Mr Goon asks him questions. He'll be pretty beastly to the poor fellow. I think I'll stay here till he comes back, Ern. He may have some news. Gosh, to think we've all been working so hard to find out if Fairlin Hall was once "The Ivies" – and now Mr Goon's been lucky enough to have the information handed to him in one of those notes!'

A scream came suddenly from downstairs, and made Fatty and Ern jump. 'That's Mrs Hicks,' said Ern, and they both ran downstairs. Mrs Hicks was lying back in the kitchen armchair, fanning herself with the dishcloth.

'What's the matter?' cried Ern.

'Another note!' wailed Mrs Hicks. 'I went to my larder just now – and there was a note, pushed in through the larder window – on top of the fish, it was. It give me such a turn, seeing it there. You go and get it, Ern. I'm getting so as I don't want to touch the things. Horrible ominous notes!'

Fatty went to the larder before Ern. He looked in at the open door, and saw the square envelope lying on top of a plate of fish, just beside the open larder window. He took it and tore it open, though he knew he ought to wait for Mr Goon.

'Found out about Smith yet, you dunderhead?' said the note, in the familiar cut-out, pasted letters.

'When did you go to the larder last, Mrs Hicks?' demanded Fatty.

'About twenty minutes ago,' said Mrs Hicks. 'The note wasn't there then, I'll swear it wasn't. I got some fish for the cat off that dish, and put it back again on the shelf.'

'It *couldn't* have been put there in the last twenty minutes,' said Ern, at once. 'Haven't I been watching out of that window for the last half-hour? You know I have!'

'Ah, but your friend went up to see you,' said Mrs Hicks. 'The note must have come then, when you were talking to him and not keeping a watch.'

'I *was* watching,' said Ern, angrily. 'I never took my eyes off the yard. Did I, Fatty?'

'Well, *I* heard you talking all right,' said Mrs Hicks. 'And when people talk, they can't watch too. *You'll* catch it from that uncle of yours!'

'I don't know how the messenger has the nerve to walk across the yard and back like that,' said Fatty. 'He must know that Ern was watching – he could easily see him at the bedroom window. It must mean that the messenger hides himself somewhere very near, and watches his chance.'

'That's it, sir,' said Mrs Hicks. 'Artful as a bagful of monkeys he is. I've never seen him – though once or twice I've thought I heard him. It scares me proper, it does.'

'There's Uncle,' said Ern, looking suddenly anxious. 'Loveaduck, won't he be angry with me when he hears there's another note, left under our noses – me watching and all!'

Mr Goon came in, whistling softly. 'Pleased with himself!' said Ern, looking at Fatty. Goon walked into the kitchen, calling to Mrs Hicks.

'A cup of tea, please, Mrs Hicks. Hello – you here, Frederick? And why aren't you watching at your window Ern?'

'Er – well, Mrs Hicks found another note, Uncle,' said Ern, warily. 'And she screamed, and me and Fatty, we shot down to see what was the matter.'

'Well, there won't be any *more* notes,' said Goon. 'Not as soon as the writer of them hears that old Smith has gone from Fairlin Hall. I sent him packing!'

'But why, Mr Goon?' asked Fatty, troubled to think that poor old Mrs Smith should have had to leave with her sick husband.

'Come into the office,' said Goon, who was looking very pleased with himself. 'Do you good, Frederick, to hear how the police can get to work and settle things.' Fatty and Ern followed him, leaving Mrs Hicks alone in the kitchen, looking annoyed at being left out.

'Sit down,' ordered Goon, and Ern and Fatty obediently sat down. Goon leaned back and put his fingertips together, looking at the two boys in a most irritating way.

'Well, acting on information received, I went round to Fairlin Hall – you probably don't know, but it was once called "The Ivies",' began Goon. 'And there I found this fellow Smith, talked about in those notes. His wife was most obstructive – said he was ill, and I wasn't to disturb him – such nerve to tell *me* that,' frowned Goon. 'Well, I soon told her I wasn't standing any nonsense, and pushed her aside . . .'

'Not really *pushed*!' said Fatty, horrified to think of the gentle old lady being roughly handled by the big policeman.

'Well, shoved, if you want a better word,' grinned Goon. 'And there was Smith, in bed

– *pretending* to be ill, of course. Well, I made him get out – couldn't let him get away with a lot of humbug like that – and I said to him, "Now then! What are you masquerading round under a false name for? You tell me *that*!"'

There was a pause, presumably for Ern and Fatty to exclaim in admiration of Goon's behaviour with the Smiths. As neither of them said a word, he went on, not at all taken aback.

'Well, the old woman got hold of my arm, and began to sob – all put on, of course. She said their name wasn't Smith, it was Canley – and that rang a bell with me, that did! *Canley!* He was a bad lot, he was – he sold the secrets of a new war plane of ours to the enemy, and he went to jail for years. Ha – and when he came out, he had to report to the police every so often, but he didn't – he just took a false name and disappeared! Helped by that wife of his, of course. She waited for him all the time he was in jail.'

'So that was what the word "SECRETS" meant, in that note,' said Fatty, quite disgusted with Goon's hard-hearted narrative. 'Smith – or Canley

– would react to that word at once, be afraid – and pack up and go.'

'That's right,' said Goon. 'And that's just what I told him to do – pack up and go! Can't have a man like that in a responsible position as caretaker.'

'But he was ill,' said Fatty, 'and his wife is old. Poor things.'

'Ill! No, he was putting that on,' snorted Goon. 'He might deceive you, but he couldn't deceive *me*. I told him he's got to report to me here tomorrow morning, then we'll go into all this. Then I left. Now we know what all those notes meant!'

'We don't,' said Fatty, shaking his head. 'All we know is that someone had a spite against old Smith and wanted him out of Fairlin Hall. We don't know what the real reason was. There must be *some* reason!'

'You'll wear your brains out, you will,' said Goon. 'There's no mystery left, so don't pretend there is. Think yourself lucky that I've told you the end of it – riddling about with Ivies and Smiths and Secrets. It's all plain as the nose on your face. I've settled it!'

He turned to Ern. 'You can go home, Ern. There's no more watching to do. I don't know who sent those notes and I don't care. He put me on to a man the police want to keep their eyes on – and the Super will be pleased about *that*! I'll get another Letter of Commendation, you see if I don't!'

'Well, you wouldn't get one from *me*,' said Fatty, standing up. 'You'd no right to treat a poor old woman and an ill man so roughly. And let me tell you this – you think you've solved this mystery – but you haven't! You'll never wear *your* brains out, Mr Goon – you don't use them enough!'

14. FATTY iS A GREAT HELP

Fatty stalked out of Goon's office, paying no attention to his snorts of anger. 'Go and get your things, Ern,' he said. 'You needn't go home just yet. You can come with me. Whatever Mr Goon says, this mystery isn't settled. There's a lot more to it than hounding old Smith out of Fairlin Hall!'

'Coo, Fatty! Can I really come with you?' said Ern, overjoyed. He shot upstairs, and was soon down again with his small bag. He didn't even say good-bye to his uncle.

'We'll call a meeting at once,' said Fatty. 'I'll telephone . . . no . . . I don't think I will. There's something else more urgent. Ern, the Smiths may still be at Fairlin Hall, packing up to go – arranging for their bits and pieces of furniture to be moved. Let's go down there and see.'

'Right. Anything you say,' said Ern, giving Fatty a worshipping look. Loveaduck! Fatty was worth ten Mr Goons any day, the way he always knew what to do!

In a few minutes they had cycled to Fairlin Hall, and went round the back to the kitchen quarters. As Fatty had thought, the Smiths were still there. But they were not packing!

Mr Smith was lying on the floor, and the old lady was kneeling beside him, weeping, and wiping his forehead with a damp cloth. 'John!' she was saying. 'John, I'm here. I'm going to get the doctor, dearie. Open your eyes! I'm going to get the doctor.'

She didn't even hear the two boys open the door and come in. Fatty had looked through the window, and had seen what was happening. She jumped violently when he touched her gently on the arm.

'Mrs Smith,' he said. 'I'll get the doctor for you. Let Ern and I lift your husband back into bed. He seems very ill.'

'Oh, he is, he is,' wept the old lady, recognising Fatty as the boy who had gone to the chemist for her. 'He's just had a terrible shock too – I can't tell you what it was – and we've been told to go. But where *can* we go – and him as ill as that?'

'Now listen,' said Fatty, gently. 'Let us get your husband back into bed. We'll get the doctor – and probably an ambulance, because I'm sure your husband ought to be in hospital. That's the first thing to do.'

He and Ern managed to get the old man back into bed. He murmured something and half-opened his eyes, then began to cough in a terrible manner. His old wife wiped his face with the damp cloth, and comforted him. Ern's eyes filled with tears, and he looked desperately at Fatty.

'Don't worry, Ern,' said Fatty. 'We'll soon put this right. Stay here and do what you can to help Mrs Smith. I'm going to telephone the doctor. Who is your doctor, Mrs Smith?'

She told him, and Fatty nodded. 'He's mine too – so that's fine. I'll be back soon.'

Fatty ran to the nearest kiosk to telephone, and Dr Rainy listened in surprise to what he had to say.

'Well, well – the poor old fellow! I saw him yesterday and told Mrs Smith I'd send an ambulance to take him to hospital, but she wouldn't hear of it. I'll get one along at once and arrange for a bed for him in the Cottage Hospital here. See you later!'

Fatty raced back to Fairlin Hall. The old fellow looked a little better, now that he was in bed again. 'But where shall we go?' he kept saying to his wife, who was fondling his hands. 'Mary, where shall we go? Oh, what a lot of trouble I've brought on you. I've always been a trouble to you, always.'

'No, no, you haven't,' said the old woman. 'It's I that's been the trouble – having that dreadful illness all those years ago, and being such an expense. You'd never have sold those secrets to pay the doctors, never have gone to prison if it hadn't been for me!' She turned to Fatty, and touched his sleeve.

'You're kind,' she said. 'Don't judge my old man hardly, whatever he says to you. He's paid for what he did, paid over and over again. But I was so ill, you see, and we needed money to get me better – and it was because he loved me that he did wrong.'

'Don't worry about anything,' said Fatty, touched by the old woman's confidence in him. 'He'll soon get better in hospital. The ambulance will be here in a few minutes.'

'When he came out of prison we changed our name, you see,' said Mrs Smith, weeping again. 'People point their fingers when you've done something wrong. We tried to hide ourselves away, but always somebody found out who we were. And then kind old Mrs Hasterley let us come here to caretake the house.'

'Mrs Hasterley!' said Fatty, surprised. 'Is she still alive? She owned this place when it was "The Ivies", didn't she?'

'Yes. She's an old, old woman now,' said Mrs Smith. 'Older than I am. You've heard of Wilfrid Hasterley, her son, haven't you? – he planned the biggest diamond robbery ever heard of – and got away with it too – though nobody ever knew where he hid the diamonds. He went to prison for it, and died there – and broke his father's heart. His mother never got over it either, and she sold this house at once. My, my, every newspaper in the kingdom had a picture of this house in it then – "The Ivies", it was called . . .'

'It was changed to Fairlin Hall after that, wasn't it?' said Fatty, listening with great interest.

'Yes. But somehow it never got sold,' said Mrs Smith. 'It had a bad name, you see. Poor Mr Wilfrid. He had some wicked friends. He wasn't really the bad one, he was just weak and easy-going. The other two were the clever ones. One went to prison with Mr Wilfrid – and the other was never caught. He fled away abroad somewhere – to Burma, I did hear say. Prison's a dreadful place, young sir – see what it's done to my poor old husband.'

'I think I can hear the ambulance, Ern,' said Fatty, raising his head. 'Go and see, will you? Ask them to come as far down the drive as they can.'

The old fellow opened his eyes. 'Mary,' he said, hoarsely. 'Mary. What will you do? Where will you go?'

'I don't know, John, I don't know,' said his old wife. 'I'll be all right. I'll come and see you in hospital.'

Ern came in at the door. 'There's two men and a stretcher,' he said, importantly. 'And an awfully nice nurse. The doctor couldn't come after all, but the nurse knows all about it.'

A rosy-cheeked nurse looked in at the door and took everything in at a glance. 'Is that my patient?' she said in a cheery voice to Mrs Smith. 'Don't you worry, dear – we'll look after him for you. Here, Potts – bring the stretcher right inside.'

Everything was done very swiftly indeed. It took less than a minute to get Mr Smith into the ambulance. He couldn't say good-bye, because he had another fit of coughing, but his old wife held his hand to the very last moment. Then the ambulance door was shut and the big van trundled up the drive and out of the gate.

'I can't pack and go tonight,' said Mrs Smith, looking dazed. 'I feel exhausted. And I've got nowhere to go.'

'Stay here tonight then,' said Fatty. 'I'll arrange something for you tomorrow. My mother will know what to do. But you're too upset and tired to bother about anything. The only thing is, I don't like to think of you staying here all alone at night, Mrs Smith.'

'I'll stay here with her,' said Ern, suddenly. The

whole affair had touched him as nothing else in his life had done. Ern longed to do something to help, he didn't care what it was – but he had got to do something, as he put it to himself. And to stay and look after the sad old woman was the only thing he could think of.

'You're a good-hearted fellow, Ern,' said Fatty, touched. 'Thanks very much. I was going to offer you a bed up at my house, as your uncle had sent you off – but if you'll stay here, I'm sure Mrs Smith would be glad.'

'Oh, I would,' said Mrs Smith, and actually gave Ern a little smile. 'There's a sofa in the next room he can have. What's your name, now – Ern? That's a kind thought of yours, my boy. I'll cook you a nice little supper, you see if I don't.'

'Well, I'll go home now, and see my mother, and get her to fix up something for you, Mrs Smith,' said Fatty.

'I can work, you know,' said the old lady, eagerly. 'I kept this little place spotless. I can sew, too. I'll earn my keep, don't you be afraid of that.'

'I'm not,' said Fatty, marvelling at the brave old lady. 'Now I know Ern will look after you well. Ern, what about making a pot of tea for Mrs Smith?'

'I'll do that,' said Ern. He went beaming to the door with Fatty. Then he pulled at his arm, and spoke in a low voice. 'Fatty, what shall I talk to her about? To keep her from worrying, you know?'

'Well, Ern – have you got your notebook with you?' said Fatty. 'What about reading her some of your poetry? I'm sure she'd like that. She'd be very surprised to think you could write poetry.'

'Loveaduck! I never thought of that,' said Ern, delighted. 'It might keep her amused, mightn't it? So long, Fatty. See you tomorrow.'

'So long, Ern – and thanks for all your help,' said Fatty, making Ern beam all over his red-cheeked face. He gazed proudly after Fatty as he disappeared into the darkness of the January afternoon. Ern was absolutely certain there was no one in the whole world to equal Fatty!

Fatty surprised his mother very much when he got home, just in time for tea. He looked so serious that she was quite concerned.

'Mummy, can you spare a few minutes for me

to tell you something?' said Fatty. 'I simply must have your help.'

'Oh, Frederick dear – you haven't got into any trouble, have you?' said his mother at once.

'Not more than usual,' said Fatty, with a grin that reassured his mother at once. 'Listen, Mummy – it's rather a long story.' And he plunged into the tale of the anonymous notes, the search for ivy-covered houses, Mr Grimble's tale, the Smiths, and Goon's treatment of them. His mother listened in amazed silence. What in the world would Frederick get mixed up in next?

Finally Fatty came to his main point. 'Mummy, as old Mr Smith has gone to hospital, and Mrs Smith's alone and has nowhere to go, could one of your good causes help her?' he said. 'She can do housework, and she can sew.'

'Why, she can come *here*!' said his mother at once. 'She can help me to make the new curtains. I'd love to have the poor old thing – and Cook's so kind she will make her really welcome in the kitchen. We're not far from the hospital too, so she can visit her husband easily, every day. She can come here, Fatty.'

Fatty got up and kissed his mother. 'I *knew* you'd think of something, Mummy,' he said. 'You always do. I'm glad I have a mother like you!'

'Well, Frederick – what a nice thing to say!' said Mrs Trotteville, pleased. 'I only wish the old lady had come here tonight. I don't like to think of her there in that big empty house, all alone.'

'Oh, Ern's staying there to look after her,' said Fatty. 'He's going to read old Mrs Smith his poetry. Ern will have a very pleasant night, Mummy!'

But he was wrong! Ern didn't have a pleasant night at all. Quite the opposite. Ern had a very disturbed night indeed!

15. FATTY HAS A PLAN

'Fatty, you won't forget that you promised to fetch jumble for me from one or two of my friends, will you, for the sale next week?' said Mrs Trotteville next day at breakfast. 'I told you I'd borrowed a cart for you to fetch it, didn't I?'

'Oh yes – I *had* forgotten,' said Fatty. 'But I'll do it, of course. You just give me the addresses and I'll see if I've time to go today. I'm just off down to Fairlin Hall now to get old Mrs Smith up here. I should think she could leave her bits and pieces of furniture down there, couldn't she, Mummy? Just till she knows when her husband's coming out of hospital, and where they're going?'

'I don't see why not,' said Mrs Trotteville. 'If old Mrs Hasterley gave her the job of caretaking, that policeman has no right to turn her furniture out. If he does, tell me. I'll go and see him about it.'

'Gosh, I'd like to be at the interview,' said Fatty, longingly. 'Are you afraid of *any*one, Mummy?'

'Don't be silly, Frederick,' said Mrs Trotteville. 'I'm certainly not afraid of Mr Goon. Get a taxi for old Mrs Smith, and bring her up here in it with her bags. Leave all the other stuff behind and lock the door. I could perhaps write to old Mrs Hasterley, and tell her what's happened.'

'Right,' said Fatty, and got up. 'I'll just phone for a taxi now – and tell the man to arrive at Fairlin Hall in an hour's time. That will give me time to scoot down and make sure she's ready.'

'I've told Cook about her,' said his mother. 'And she's going to put up a bed in her room for her. Now DON'T forget about my jumble, Frederick. I've given you the addresses.'

'Yes. I've got them in my pocket,' said Fatty. He went out of the room and telephoned for the taxi and then fetched his bicycle. He debated whether or not to telephone Larry and the others, to tell them the latest news, but decided he hadn't time.

He was soon cycling down to Fairlin Hall. It was a frosty morning and rather slippery, so he was careful as he rode round the corners. He hoped Goon was out on *his* bicycle too – slipping about all over the place! thought Fatty. Serve him right if he fell on that big nose of his. Scaring those poor Smiths out of their lives!

He rang his bicycle bell as he went down the drive, with Buster panting after him. He was most surprised to find the kitchen door locked when he tried to open it. Surely Ern and Mrs Smith were up! He banged loudly on it.

Ern's face peeped cautiously from behind the window curtain, making Fatty feel still more astonished! 'Come on, Ern – open the door!' he shouted. Almost at once he heard the key turned and the door opened. Ern stood there, looking pleased.

'Coo, Fatty – I'm glad you've come!' he said. 'We've had such a night!'

'Whatever do you mean?' asked Fatty, surprised. 'What happened?'

'Well – footsteps round the place. And someone trying to open the kitchen door. And noises, and people on the balcony, and goodness knows what,' said Ern. 'I was really scared. So was old Mrs Smith. Good thing I stayed to look after her.'

Fatty walked into the warm little kitchen. 'Good morning, Mrs Smith,' he said, 'I'm sorry you had a disturbed night.'

'It was those burglars again,' she said. 'My old man and me, we've often heard them trying to get in. Once they did get in, too, over one of the balconies – but there's nothing to steal in this empty old place. All they took was a mirror off one of the walls in the dining-room! I was glad of Ern here, last night, I can tell you. Real brave he was.'

'They did all they could to get in,' said Ern. 'Mrs Smith says the house is pretty well burglar-proof now – except the kitchen part, but as she and Mr Smith were living in these few rooms, the burglars avoided them. Not last night, though! Look, they broke this window – but they couldn't undo the catch!'

'Good thing you were here, Ern, or they might have bashed the door in, and wrecked the place,' said Fatty. 'Perhaps it was tramps looking for shelter. It was a cold, bitter night.'

'They went when I shouted,' said Ern, proudly. 'And I pretended there was a dog here, didn't I,

Mrs Smith? You should have heard me yapping. Like this!' And Ern broke into such realistic yaps that Buster looked at him startled, and then began to bark himself.

'That was a jolly good idea, Ern, to pretend there was a dog here,' said Fatty, and Ern beamed. 'Well, Mrs Smith, do you think you could get your bits and pieces together? My mother says she would be very glad if you could come and help her with her new curtains – you said you could sew, didn't you? We've put up a bed for you already.'

'I never knew there were such kind folk in the world,' said Mrs Smith. 'Never. I've packed already. I can't do anything about my furniture. It'll have to stay here till I can send someone for it. I don't think Mrs Hasterley will mind. I'd be glad to help your mother – if she's anything like you, it'll be a pleasure to work for her. I'll be able to see my old man, won't I, though?'

'Oh yes – the Cottage Hospital is quite near,' said Fatty. 'You'll be able to go every day. My mother will ring up the hospital when you arrive, and get the nurse to tell you how Mr Smith is.'

'Such kindness!' said the old lady, overcome.

'And this boy Ern here – he was such a comfort last night. And the poetry he read me! Well, I reckon he's a genius, I do really.'

Ern blushed. He knew he was no genius, but it was very very pleasant to be thought one! He helped Mrs Smith out with her things, ready for the taxi. 'You go with Mrs Smith in the taxi, Ern,' said Fatty. 'I've got my bicycle and Buster. Go down to my shed and wait for me, when you get there. You'll find some biscuits in the tin.'

'Oooh, thanks Fatty,' said Ern. He had been afraid that he would be sent home. Perhaps he would have yet one more day with Fatty?

The taxi came, and Ern put all Mrs Smith's things into it. He helped her in and then climbed in himself. He felt rather important. 'First time I've been in a taxi!' he said. 'Loveaduck, I'm getting grand!'

'I'll lock the back door and take the key,' said Fatty. 'I'd better return it to the estate agent and I'll warn them that burglars came again.'

He went back into the kitchen. It still had the Smith's things there – rather poor bits of furniture, a carpet, worn and old, the curtains.

They could really go on a cart, thought Fatty, and suddenly remembered that he had promised his mother to fetch her jumble.

He locked the door and walked to where he had left his bicycle. Then he and Buster went to the front gate. A man was standing there, hands in pocket. Buster barked at him and he kicked out.

Fatty felt rather suspicious. Why should the man be hanging about outside an empty house? Was he one of the men who had tried to break in the night before? Had he watched Mrs Smith and Ern leaving in a taxi? Fatty rode off to the estate agent's, wondering.

He walked into the office and was relieved to find that the young and conceited Mr Paul was not there. Only the older man was present, sitting in his corner. He recognised Fatty at once and smiled.

'I've brought you the back door key of Fairlin Hall,' said Fatty. 'There were caretakers there, as you probably know, and they've left. Their furniture is still there, though.'

'Well, that's nice of you,' said the old clerk. 'But you'd better keep the key in case the Smiths want to fetch their things. Were they given notice, or something? We haven't heard anything from Mrs Hasterley.'

'Er – Mr Smith fell ill and has gone to hospital,' said Fatty, thinking that was the best thing to say. 'And by the way, burglars tried to break in there again last night.'

The old clerk tut-tutted, and shook his head. 'Bound to get tramps and rogues trying to get in, when a house has stood empty for years,' he said. 'We've tried to make it burglar proof – but what it wants is people living in it, filling the house! By the way, it's a funny thing – but some people came in to enquire about it this morning. Two men. Said they might like to buy it for a boys' prep school.'

'Did you give them keys?' asked Fatty, at once.

'Yes. And I told them that a couple of old folk were there, caretaking,' said the man. 'I didn't know they'd gone.'

Mr Paul arrived at that moment and Fatty at once went, in case the old fellow should be admonished for wasting his time talking to him again! Fatty was very thoughtful as he rode home.

People enquiring about Fairlin Hall – so soon after the Smiths had gone? Could it be someone who had tried to force a way in last night? – and now, knowing that the house had no caretakers, had got the keys so that they would have the house to themselves? But what was the point of that?

I rather think I'd better keep some kind of watch on Fairlin Hall, thought Fatty, and at once his mind flew to a possible disguise. How could he watch the house without anyone guessing?

'Of course!' he said, aloud, making the panting Buster look up at him in surprise. 'Of course! I'll be a rag-and-bone man! I'll get that cart, and go and collect jumble! And I'll park my cart outside Fairlin Hall, and keep my eye on anyone going in and out!'

He cycled even more quickly and went down the drive to his own house at top speed, almost running down the baker. He went straight to his shed, and found Ern there, patiently waiting.

'Ern, I'm going to disguise myself,' said Fatty. 'Look, you go up to the house and telephone the others. Tell them to come here at once, if they can. I'll talk to them while I'm disguising myself.'

'Right,' said Ern, thrilled, and sped off to telephone. He wasn't very sure about it, but Mrs Trotteville, amused by Ern's serious face, got the numbers for him, and he delivered his message faithfully, saying every word so distinctly that it sounded as if he were reciting!

Meantime, Fatty was swiftly disguising himself. Dirty old rag-and-bone man, he thought. Those old corduroy trousers. That torn shirt. No tie. Scarf round my neck – that filthy white one will do. Awful old boots, now where did I put them? A cap – and that awful overcoat I found left behind a hedge one day!'

He got out his make-up box, and in ten minutes had transformed himself from a boy in his teens, to a wrinkled, dirty, slouching fellow, with protruding teeth, shaggy eyebrows and a ragged moustache.

Ern watched in unbounded admiration. 'Loveaduck!' he kept saying. 'Loveaduck, Fatty! How do you do it? You are a one, you are! My word, my uncle will chase you out of Peterswood, if he sees you!'

Fatty laughed. 'Here come the others,' he said,

as Buster barked. 'Let them in!' And in they all trooped – to stop in astonishment at the sight of the dirty old rag-and-bone man.

'FATTY!' squealed Bets. 'It's you! Fatty, you look *awful*! What are you going to do? Quick, tell us! What's up? Has something happened?'

16. RAG-A'-BONES!
RAG-A'-BONES!

Everyone crowded round the dirty old rag-and-bone man, thrilled. How did Fatty do it? Except for his twinkling eyes and too-clean hands, nobody would know he was anything but what he looked!

'Your hands – and your nails, Fatty,' said Bets. 'Don't forget those.'

'Go and fill this plant pot with some wettish earth, Bets,' said Fatty, retying his filthy neck-scarf. 'I think our gardener's out there, and if he sees me, he'll chase me off the premises.'

Bets rushed out with the pot and a trowel and filled it with damp earth. Fatty put his hands into it and made them really dirty. The dirt got into his nails too.

'You look simply terrible,' said Larry. 'And you smell a bit, Fatty. Must be that horrible overcoat.'

'Yes. It does smell,' said Fatty, sniffing at a

sleeve. 'Still, it's all in a good cause, as Mummy would say. Listen, and I'll tell you quickly what's happened this morning and yesterday.'

He swiftly outlined all the events, and Ern nodded in approval. That was the way to tell things – no 'ers' or 'ums', or stammerings – but everything set out absolutely clearly. Lovely to listen to! Everyone sat enthralled as Fatty related his tale at top speed.

'There's a few things I *can't* understand,' finished Fatty, 'and one is why the writer of those "ominous" notes, as Mrs Hicks calls them, is so set on getting old Smith out – I suppose he's got some kind of spite against him – and the other is how on earth do those notes get put all over the place at old Mr Goon's without anyone seeing them?'

'Right under my nose again yesterday!' said Ern. 'I was watching like anything, never took my eyes off the back yard, never once, not even when Fatty came into my room and spoke to me. And Mrs Hicks was down in the kitchen too, in full view of the window – and yet, there was the note, sitting on top of the plate of fish in the larder! And *neither* of us saw anyone come into the yard, or creep over to the larder window and pop the note on the fish! Beats me! Must have got an invisible cloak or something!'

'Do you know what *I* think?' said Daisy, suddenly. '*I* think it's Mrs Hicks who's putting the notes there! Putting them there herself! We once had a gardener who complained that someone was slipping into the garden and taking the strawberries, and there wasn't – Daddy caught *him* taking them himself! I bet it was *Mrs Hicks* with those notes, pretending it was someone else all the time!'

There was a silence after this speech of Daisy's. Fatty stared at her – and then smacked his hand in delight on the chest beside him, making Buster jump in fright.

'*Daisy*! What an idiot I've been! Of course – that's the only possible explanation! Mrs Hicks is being paid by someone to hide those notes at Mr Goon's – someone who doesn't want to be seen for some reason. I wonder who's paying her. Where does she live, Ern?'

'With her sister and little niece,' said Ern. 'To think she got me into all that trouble with my uncle! How *could* I see anyone delivering notes when all the time she must have had them hidden in her apron pocket? Just wait till I see that Mrs Hicks again.'

'No. Don't you say a word to her if you do see her,' warned Fatty. 'Let her think she isn't suspected at all. There won't be any more notes, of course, because old Mr Smith has been got rid of.'

'Maybe that's the end of the whole thing then,' said Pip.

'I don't think so,' said Fatty. 'No, I *certainly* don't think so, though Mr Goon does, of course. There's something more behind those notes than just spite against an old man. Well, I must go. Ern, you go and see how Mrs Smith is getting on, and ask my mother if you can do any jobs. She'll like that.'

'Can we come with you, Fatty?' asked Bets, longingly. 'Could we walk a little way behind you – just to watch you being a rag-and-bone man? You do look exactly like one – in fact, you look so awful that I'm sure Mummy would send you off at once if you came to *our* house!'

'I haven't overdone it, have I?' said Fatty, anxiously, and looked at himself in the glass. 'Do these false teeth that I've put on over my own stick out too much?'

'Oh no. They're fine,' said Larry. 'And I love the way your shaggy eyebrows go up and down. I do hope you meet Mr Goon.'

'Well, I don't,' said Fatty. 'If I do, I shall put on a foreign accent – or stammer or something, so that Mr Goon can't get any sense out of me. Well, so long. I'm going to get the cart now.'

He looked out of the shed window to make sure that the gardener was nowhere near, and then went rapidly to the garage. The cart was there, together with a good deal of jumble taken from the attics. Fatty piled some on, and then set off to Fairlin Hall. Perhaps he could catch sight of those men who had got the keys.

He sang out the usual rag-and-bone ditty. 'Rag-a'-bones! Rag-a'-bo-o-o-ones! Bring out your rag-a'-bo-o-o-nes!'

He hoped that nobody would, because he hadn't much money in his pocket, and didn't really want to pay anyone for jumble! He came safely to Fairlin Hall, and set down the cart. He took an old pipe out of his pocket and began to fiddle with it, keeping a watch on the house, trying to make out if anyone was there.

He couldn't see anyone, and decided to wheel his cart right into the drive. Perhaps he would be able to spot the two men who had gone to the estate agents for the keys, if he went down the drive. He decided not to shout his rag-a'-bone cry, but to go very quietly.

Ah – the men must be in the house – there was a small car at the front door. Fatty noted the number swiftly, and the make and colour. 'Brown Riley, AJK 6660.' Then he went on cautiously, wheeling his cart, making his way to the back door.

He stood in a corner, pretending to arrange the things on the cart, but keeping his ears open for any sound that might tell him where the men were, and what they were doing. He couldn't hear or see a sign of them.

He decided to go to the back door and knock, pretending that he had come to see the Smiths. But as he passed the window of the kitchen, he caught sight of a movement inside, and stopped. He peered through the window.

Two men were inside, one opening the cupboard doors, the other taking up the carpet, rolling it to one side. Fatty felt angry. What did they think they were doing? Robbing the poor old Smiths of the few things they had left behind?

Fatty went to the door and banged on it violently. There was an exclamation from inside and one of the men went to the window and peered out. He said something to the other man, and then opened the window. Apparently he hadn't a key to open the kitchen door.

The window swung wide open, and a thin-faced elderly man looked out, and shouted at Fatty.

'What are you doing here? Clear out!'

Fatty put on a real Cockney voice. ''Ere, mate, I've come to see me frens, the Smiffs,' he said. 'What you a-doin' of, messin' abart in their rooms? You ain't up to no good. I'll git the police in, see if I don't.'

'The Smiths have gone,' said the man, curtly. 'We're probably going to buy the house; we've got the keys to look over the place. Clear out, now, your friends have gone.'

'Well, what you a-doin' of then, wiv their things?' shouted Fatty. 'What you rollin' up that bit of carpet for? What you . . .'

'Now, now, now, what's all this?' said a familiar voice, and to Fatty's surprise and annoyance Mr Goon marched up to the window. 'That your cart in the drive, fellow? Take it out then. And who's this in the house?'

'Constable, remove this man,' said one of the men indoors. 'He says he's a friend of someone called Smith, but it's my belief he knew they were gone, and came to steal their bits of furniture. We've got the keys to look over the house, and suddenly saw this fellow at the back door.'

'Ho! So that's it, is it?' said Goon, roughly, and turned on Fatty. 'You clear orf, my man, or I'll march you off to the police station. What's your name?'

Fatty pretended to be scared. 'F-f-f-f-f,' he stammered, while Goon still glared at him. 'F-f-f-f-f . . .'

'Well, go on – get it out,' commanded Goon, taking out his notebook. 'Name *and* address.'

'F-f-f-f-fred,' said Fatty, 'T-t-t-t-t . . .'

'Fred,' said Goon, writing it down. 'Fred what?'

'T-t-t-t-t-t,' stammered Fatty, looking absolutely agonised. 'T-t-t.'

'All right, all right,' said Goon, shutting his notebook. 'I've got more important things to do than to stand here and listen to you. You go and get your tongue seen to – and take that cart out of this drive. If I set eyes on you again today, I'll run you in.'

'R-r-right,' said Fatty, and shot out of the drive with his cart, grinning. He stood at the front gate, wondering what to do. He had seen those two men, and noted what they looked like – he had got particulars of their car – he had watched them examining the Smiths' kitchen and the things in it, goodness knew what for . . . and he had had a successful few minutes with Goon. What next?

He moved on down the road, shouting 'Rag-a'-bones' at intervals – and then he saw someone he knew, hurrying along on the pavement.

It's Mrs Hicks, he thought, and his interest quickened. I suppose she's got the morning off. Where's she going in such a hurry?

He decided to follow her. If she had really been the one to hide those notes, then someone must have given them to her, and presumably she was being paid for hiding them at Mr Goon's. Goon, of course, was the only person who had the power to turn the Smiths out, so that was why the notes had been sent to him. It would be very, very interesting to find out who the sender was. It might throw quite a lot of light on the mystery.

Fatty trundled his cart after Mrs Hicks. Round the corner she went and round the corner went Fatty. Down a little hill and round another corner. And ah – Mrs Hicks turned in at a gateway and vanished.

Fatty trundled his cart along the gutter, and came to a stop outside the gate. He pretended to fiddle with his pipe again, examining the house as he did so. It was a fairly big one, well-kept, and looked comfortable. From between the curtains, he could see what looked like a gleaming brass ornament.

The name on the house was 'KUNTAN'. Who lived there? Was it someone who had given those notes to Mrs Hicks? He decided to go to the back door and ask for anything old and done for. Even if he had to give up all his money for junk, it would be worth it, if he could find the sender of those anonymous notes.

He went cautiously down the side entrance, and came to the back door. Beside it were piled wooden crates, with foreign words printed across them – empty crates, evidently unpacked, and then thrown out for firewood. One was already half-chopped up.

Fatty looked at them – and then one word made him stare in excitement. Just one word, stamped across each crate in big black letters – the name of the place the crate had come from.

'RANGOON'

17. A VERY LUCKY FIND

Fatty stared at the name on the crate, remembering how hard he had tried to think of a word with 'goon' as part of it, when he had tried to fathom why Mr Goon's name should have been spelt each time with a small letter g. 'Mr goon', not 'Mr Goon' had been on each of the envelopes containing those anonymous notes.

When I asked Mummy if she knew of any word with the four letters 'goon' in it, she suggested 'Rangoon', thought Fatty, remembering. And here's a crate with 'Rangoon' stamped across it. Can it be just chance – just a coincidence? Or is it a real clue – a clue pointing to the man who sent those letters to Mr Goon?'

He stared at the crate again. A man lives here who has friends in Rangoon, that's certain – friends who send him crates of something. Well, he might have Rangoon *newspapers* sent to him too – he might have cut out words and letters from them and taken 'goon' from the title of the newspaper – *Rangoon Times*, it might be, or something like that. Gosh, I think I'm on to something here!

He was still staring at the crate, when the back door suddenly opened and made him jump. He turned in fright, and saw Mrs Hicks there, being ushered out by a small, foreign-looking man.

Burmese! thought Fatty, at once, recognising the man's Burmese eyes, the brown complexion and black hair. And Rangoon is in Burma! Is this the fellow who sent those notes?

Mrs Hicks caught sight of him at once and frowned. 'Rag-a'-bones, rubbish, jumble, anythink bought!' said Fatty at once. 'Good price paid!'

'Do you want to get rid of any rubbish?' asked Mrs Hicks, turning to the Burmese man. 'This fellow will take it for you. Your yard looks pretty cluttered up. I can deal with him for you, if you like. What about those crates? – he'd buy them for firewood – I see you've already got plenty chopped up.'

'Yes, Meesees Icks,' said the Burmese man, and

nodded. 'You do beesinees wiz zis man. Much much rubbish here!'

And with that he shut the door. Mrs Hicks beamed. What a bit of luck! Now she could sell these crates and keep the money herself!

'You can have the crates,' she said. 'And I'll have a peep in the shed and see if there's any rubbish there.'

She disappeared into a small shed, and Fatty followed her. It was stacked with old junk, just as his mother's attic had been – but Burmese junk! A big brass tray, green with neglect, stood on its side in one corner. A broken gong was near it, and a pair of small Burmese idols in brass. Other curiously-shaped ornaments were thrown here and there.

'You could have some of these if you liked,' said Mrs Hicks. 'Cheap too – you could sell them for a good bit to a dealer. Take what you like.'

'Nobody wants junk like that,' said Fatty, knowing that he must bargain. 'Funny stuff, this – where's it come from? Does it belong to that gentleman there?' and he nodded his head towards the house.

'Yes,' said Mrs Hicks. 'Burmese, he is, but he married an English wife. I do sewing for her, but she's too stuck-up for me. Her husband's all right, though, and so are his two friends. Free with their money, and that's what I like.'

'What are the friends like?' asked Fatty, poking about among the junk. 'Burmese too?'

'No! English,' said Mrs Hicks. 'One's been in Burma for years, but the other's a close one – don't know where he's from, I'm sure. Never opens his mouth! Well, what about this stuff? Give me a good price and you can take what you like.'

'I can't sell trays and gongs,' said Fatty, giving the tray a kick with his foot. 'Now those crates out there – I could take some of those. And newspapers – old newspapers if you've got any. I can sell those to fishmongers and butchers. But this brass stuff – no, I wouldn't get a penny for it!'

'Go on!' said Mrs Hicks, disbelievingly.

'Well, I'll give you something for this ornament,' said Fatty, picking up a hideous little brass figure, 'for four of those crates – and any old newspapers you've got.'

'What – newspapers, and hardly anything for that there lovely brass ornament!' said Mrs Hicks. 'You're crazy!'

'No, I'm not. I know what I can sell and what I can't,' said Fatty, fingering the ornament with his dirty hands. He looked at Mrs Hicks from under his shaggy false eyebrows, and smiled, showing his awful protruding teeth.

'Go on, Missus. You let me buy what I can sell – four of those crates, and as many old newspapers as you've got – and one ornament.'

'All right,' said Mrs Hicks. 'You put four of those crates on to your barrow, while I fetch the newspapers. There's plenty stacked in the kitchen cupboard!'

Fatty grinned at her, showing his revolting false teeth again, and took the little ornament and the crates to his cart. He waited there for Mrs Hicks. Out she came with a vast number of newspapers, which she dumped in the cart.

'There you are,' she said. 'But you're a robber, that's what you are,' said Mrs Hicks. She took the money and put it into her pocket. Just as she did so, a car drew up at the house, and two men got out, the very two that Fatty had seen at Fairlin Hall! Fatty noted the car at once – aha – Brown Riley, AJK 6660. So those two men were staying here – they must be the two friends that Mrs Hicks spoke of – one who had come from Burma, and the other whom she said 'never opened his mouth'. Fatty took a good look at them.

Things were beginning to fit together nicely! Rangoon. Mrs Hicks and the notes. The two men who were staying here – was it one of them who had paid her to put the notes round and about Mr Goon's house and yard? And now they had been to Fairlin Hall!

They wanted to get the Smiths out because *they* want to take it – or to find something there, thought Fatty, with a surge of excitement. And what do they want to find there? Could it be – could it *possibly* be – the diamonds that were never found after the robbery? Whew! Everything's boiling up at once! My word!

He wheeled his cart away slowly, gazing at the men as they walked up to the front door of the house. He was longing to get out his notebook, and write down their descriptions!

He set off down the road with his cart, feeling quite in a daze. He suddenly caught sight of the name of a house on the other side of the road.

Gosh! That's one of the houses that Mummy asked me to collect jumble from, he thought. Well, as I'm so near, I'd better collect it. Let's see, it was Mrs Henry's, wasn't it?

Still in rather a daze, trying to sort out everything in his mind, Fatty pushed his cart up the drive of the house. He went to the front door, quite forgetting that he was disguised as a dirty old rag-and-bone man. He rang the bell.

Mrs Henry came to the door and stared. 'The back door is round there,' she said, pointing. 'But we've nothing for you today. Nothing at all.'

'Er – well, my mother said you'd have some old clothes, Mrs Henry,' said Fatty, politely. 'For her jumble sale you know.'

'Your *mother*,' said Mrs Henry, staring in amazement at this awful, dirty old fellow, with his shaggy grey eyebrows and filthy overcoat. '*I* don't know your mother. Who is she?'

'She's Mrs Trotteville,' said Fatty, and was most astonished when the door was banged in his face.

Then he suddenly realised that he was in disguise, and rushed off down the drive with his cart. Good gracious! How *could* he have forgotten he was a rag-and-bone man – whatever must Mrs Henry have thought?

Why did I mention Mummy's name? thought Fatty, with a groan. She's bound to ring her up – and Mummy won't be at all pleased. Well, I'll get home quickly. I'm longing to have a look through these newspapers and see if there are any from Rangoon. Mother didn't know how clever she was when she mentioned *Rangoon* to me!

He was soon back at his house and pushed the cart into the garage. He took one of the crates, with RANGOON stamped on it, and also the little brass ornament, and all the newspapers, down to his shed, keeping a sharp look out for the gardener as he went.

The others had all gone. Not even Ern was there. I bet they're having macaroons at the café again, thought Fatty, feeling suddenly hungry. Now to have a look through these newspapers!

He took them up one by one, and laid them down again, disappointed. The *Daily Telegraph*

– heaps of those. The *Daily Mail, Daily Express, Evening Standard* – wait now – what's this?

He had come to a magazine, printed on cheap paper. He looked at the title. '*The Rangoon Weekly*'. He scrutinised the type carefully – was it the same type as the letters and words in those notes? It really did look like it!

I'll get that anonymous note I have, in a minute, thought Fatty. I'll just look through a few more papers. Ah, here's another of those magazines – another *Rangoon Weekly*, but still in its wrapper. And here's another – but wait a minute, wait a minute! This one's all cut up! My word, *what* a bit of luck! I do believe this is one of the papers that the sender of those notes cut the letters from, that he stuck on to the notepaper! IT IS!

Fatty stared at the magazine he was holding. Bits had been cut from it. The 'goon' had been cut from the words *Rangoon Weekly*! Yes, not only on this page, but on the next one too! Only the 'Ran' was left in the word 'Rangoon' – the 'goon' had been neatly snipped away!

Fatty found that his hands were trembling. The jigsaw of the mystery was fitting together now.

Fatty had quite a lot of the pieces. Not many were missing! He went swiftly through the rest of the papers he had bought.

He found two more of the *Rangoon Weekly* magazines with letters and words snipped from them. He gazed at them in rapture. What a *wonderful* piece of luck!

He stood up and put the three snipped magazines into an envelope, opened a drawer and put them carefully inside. Then he locked the drawer.

'Very valuable evidence!' said Fatty. 'But evidence of *what*, I don't quite know. Funny mystery this – all made up of bits and pieces – but I'll make a proper picture of them soon, and then we'll see what it shows! Whew! I wish the others were here. Oh my goodness, there's Mummy calling! AND she's coming down to the shed. Whatever will she say when she sees an old rag-and-bone man here!'

18. FATTY REPORTS HIS DOINGS

Fatty hadn't time even to take out his horrible false teeth, before his mother opened the shed door.

She looked inside. 'Frederick, are you here?'

Fatty stood with his back to her, in the darkest corner of the shed. 'Yes, Mummy. Did you want me?'

'Frederick, Mrs Henry has just telephoned me,' began his mother. 'Do turn round, dear, I'm speaking to you . . .'

'Er – I'm in disguise, Mummy,' said Fatty, embarrassed.

'Turn *round*,' said his mother, and Fatty reluctantly faced her. She gave a horrified scream.

'FREDERICK! Come here! Into the light. How *can* you dress like that? Disguise indeed! Oh Frederick – *don't* tell me that you were the horrible rag-and-bone man that Mrs Henry just rang me up about? Surely, surely, you didn't really go there and say that your mother had sent you – that *I* had sent you.'

'Well, Mummy – it was a bit of a mistake,' began Fatty, his dirty face as red as a beetroot. 'I forgot I was in disguise, you see, and . . .'

'Don't talk such rubbish,' said his mother, really angry. 'How could you *possibly* forget you were in that horrible, revolting get-up? I'm absolutely ashamed of you, Frederick. To go to Mrs Henry's like that! Please don't bother about collecting any more jumble for me. If you're just going to make it a joke, and deceive my friends like that, and . . .'

'But, Mummy – I tell you I *forgot* for just a minute or two,' said poor Fatty. 'I'm most terribly sorry. I'll go and apologise to Mrs Henry. You see, I'd just discovered a few amazing things, and I was a bit dazed, thinking them out, but when *you* hear what's been happening, you'll be just as astonished, and you'll . . .'

'Stop all this rigmarole,' said Mrs Trotteville, angrier than Fatty had ever seen her. 'I don't wonder that Mr Goon gets annoyed with you if you wander about like that. Has *he* seen you in that get-up too? He has? Well, I suppose he'll soon be along here then, complaining as usual. I only hope your father doesn't hear about this.'

And away she went up the garden path, her skirt whisking angrily over the edges of the border. Fatty stared after her, quite shocked. *Now* he was in a fix! His mother would continue to be very upset with him – and yet he couldn't very well explain to her what had been happening. Life was going to be very uncomfortable indeed.

Fatty groaned heavily, and began to remove his make-up and various pieces of disguise. Out came the awful teeth, and off came the shaggy grey eyebrows. He stripped off the smelly overcoat and hung it up, and bit by bit became himself again.

He looked at himself in the glass. Yes, his face was clean now. Should he take the cart out and go and collect the jumble his mother had asked him to? Should he go and apologise first of all to Mrs Henry and get *her* jumble?

No, Fatty thought *not*. Let it all blow over for a day. He would sit down now and write out a report of the morning's happenings. Nothing like writing everything down, to get it straight in his mind!

Fatty found his pen, and took out his notebook. He wrote rapidly.

About half past twelve he heard the sound of voices. It was the others coming to see if he were back again. Fatty shut his notebook and went to the shed door.

'Oh, you're back, Fatty!' said Bets, pleased. 'Any luck this morning?'

'Plenty,' said Fatty, grinning. 'Some good and some bad.'

'Oh – what was the bad?' asked Daisy, anxiously.

'Well, in a fit of absent-mindedness, I went to Mrs Henry's front door to collect her jumble while I was in my rag-and-bone man get-up,' said Fatty. 'And, also absent-mindedly, I told her that my mother had sent me to her!'

There was laughter at this and horrified exclamations. 'You surely didn't say that your mother was *Mrs Trotteville*, did you?' said Pip. 'Well, *Fatty* – I never thought you could be such a prize idiot! She'll telephone your mother, and you'll get into an awful row.'

'She did, and I have,' said Fatty, soberly. 'My mother is not on speaking terms with me now.'

'Loveaduck!' said Ern. 'The things you do, Fatty. What was the *good* luck?'

'Well, I've just written a sort of report on what happened,' said Fatty. 'To get things straight in my mind, really. I'll read it to you.'

He opened his notebook and read from it. 'Dressed up as rag-and-bone man. Went to watch Fairlin Hall. Saw car there, Brown Riley, AJK 6660. Guessed it had brought the two men who had got the keys of the place from the agent's. Went to back door and saw men in kitchen, peering into cupboards, taking up carpets, etc. They saw me, and told me to clear out. Then Mr Goon arrived . . .'

'Oh *no*!' said Bets. 'Oh dear!'

'Mr Goon arrived and the men told him to send me off. He asked my name, and . . .'

'Oh, you didn't give it!' cried Daisy.

'No. I said it was F-f-f-f-f,' said Fatty, stammering. 'T-t-t-t-t . . . well, he just couldn't be bothered with stutterers, he said, so that was all right!'

The others laughed. Fatty turned to his notebook, and went on. 'I then left Fairlin Hall and went out, shouting like a rag-and-bone man. Saw Mrs Hicks coming along in a hurry and decided to follow her. I thought she might be going to the sender of the notes, to be paid. So I followed and she went into a house called Kuntan. I went to the back door, thinking I'd ask if they'd any rubbish.'

'Oh Fatty – how exciting!' said Bets. 'Is this the good luck part?'

Fatty nodded, and went on reading. 'Outside the door were crates with RANGOON stamped across them, evidently sent from Burma. Then the back door opened and out came Mrs Hicks, and behind her was a Burmese man – and he said she could sell me any junk she liked out of the shed. She told me she did sewing for the Burmese fellow's wife, and she also said there were two other men staying there – one from Burma, an Englishman, and another man, very quiet, that she knew nothing about.'

'Two men! Were they the two you saw at Fairlin Hall, Fatty?' asked Larry.

Fatty nodded, and went on reading. 'Mrs Hicks sold me a brass ornament, four of the Rangoon-stamped crates, and a great bundle of newspapers. I brought them here and examined them. Among them were some magazines, printed on cheap paper, called the *Rangoon Weekly*. Three of these were cut about – letters and words had been snipped from them, especially from the word "Rangoon", which, in several cases, had had the four letters "goon" cut from it.'

'Fatty!' shouted Pip. 'That's where the "goon" came from on those envelopes! Gosh, fancy you getting the very papers they were cut from!'

'Sheer luck,' said Fatty. 'Well, there you are – we know a lot now, don't we! The only thing we *don't* know for certain is – why did those men want to turn old Smith out of Fairlin Hall? Anyone any ideas?'

'Yes. What about that diamond robbery? The diamonds were never found!' said Pip, in excitement. 'Fatty, they must be hidden in Fairlin Hall somewhere! Wilfrid Hasterley must have hidden them there himself, and then gone to prison hoping that when he came out, he could get them again, and be rich!'

'Yes, and those two men you saw this morning

must have been the ones who planned the robbery with him!' cried Daisy. 'We know they didn't both go to prison . . . one went and hid himself abroad . . .'

'In Burma!' said Pip.

'And the other one, the one who was in prison with Wilfrid, must have some time been told by him that the diamonds were hidden at Fairlin Hall,' said Larry. 'Gosh, what a thing to happen! Fatty, what do *you* think about it all?'

'I agree with you absolutely,' said Fatty. 'And I'm sure that's why those fellows sent those notes about Smith to Mr Goon, having first found out that he had a shady past. The thing is, having been away so long, they didn't know that the name of "The Ivies" had been changed to Fairlin Hall!'

'It all begins to fit, doesn't it?' said Larry. 'Gosh, to think how we rushed round looking for ivy-covered houses! If only we'd known it was Fairlin Hall from the beginning, we could have got going much more quickly!'

'Fatty,' said Bets, earnestly. 'What about those hidden diamonds? Oughtn't you to tell

Superintendent Jenks all this?'

'He's away up north,' said Fatty. 'I telephoned – only to be told to report everything to Mr Goon! Mr Goon, who thinks that he's settled the whole affair – why, we're still right in the very middle of it! I wish I *could* tell the Super.'

'Can't you wait till he comes back, before you do anything else?' said Bets.

'What! And let those two men find the hidden diamonds!' said Ern, entering into the discussion for the first time. 'Coo, Fatty – let's you and me go and hunt for them! I bet those men will be there as often as they can, searching everywhere.'

'I rather think the diamonds must be in the kitchen quarters,' said Fatty. 'Otherwise, why try so hard to turn out the poor old Smiths?'

'I suppose the Smiths wouldn't know anything about the diamonds, would they?' said Pip. 'No, of course they wouldn't. But would they know of any secret place, Fatty, do you think? You know – a trap-door leading downwards – a secret cavity in a cupboard? Mrs Smith kept the place really clean, you said, and she probably knows every corner of it.'

'That's quite an idea, Pip,' said Fatty, considering it. 'She's here, you know, helping my mother with the new curtains. I could easily have a word with her. She might let something drop that would help us. Yes, that's quite an idea. But we've got to be quick if we're going to do any hunting ourselves, because now that the Smiths are out of the way, those two men will lose no time in getting the diamonds if they can.'

'When do you think of going then, Fatty?' asked Larry, feeling excited. 'This afternoon?'

'I don't see why not,' said Fatty. 'I've got the back door key. Yes, let's. But we'll have to keep a good look out for the men. Gosh, it's time for lunch! I must go because I don't want my mother to be any more annoyed with me than she already is. Look, will you all be at the corner with your bikes, at three o'clock?'

'You bet!' said Pip, thrilled. 'What about Ern?'

'Fatty's cook has asked me to the kitchen for dinner,' said Ern, proudly. 'Mrs Smith said some nice things about me, that's why. I'll be there at three too, with Fatty.'

'So long!' said Fatty, shooing them all out, and locking his shed hurriedly. 'Look here, Ern, as you'll be chatting with Mrs Smith over your dinner, you try to get a few hints about possible hiding-places, see?'

'Coo, yes, Fatty!' said Ern, delighted. 'I'll do my very, very best. Loveaduck – this isn't half a lark, is it!'

19. A DISAPPOINTING AFTERNOON

Fatty and Ern were at the corner before the others, waiting there with their bicycles. Buster was safely shut up in Fatty's bedroom.

'Well, did you enjoy your dinner, Ern?' asked Fatty.

'Oooh yes,' said Ern happily. 'Made quite a fuss of me they did. Especially Mrs Smith. She told your cook and Jane all about my portry.'

'You don't mean to say you read them any?' said Fatty, amused. Ern went red.

'Well, they kept on and on about it,' he said. 'So I read them one or two pomes. They liked the one about "The Ivies", Fatty – but I told them you wrote half of it. I wasn't going to let them think I'd written those *good* lines. Coo, Fatty, I don't know how you let your tongue go loose, like you say, and spout out portry by the yard, rhymes and all.'

'You do it like this, Ern, as I've told you before,' said Fatty, and rested his bicycle against the fence. He stood up and opened his mouth. Ern waited breathlessly. Fatty began to declaim at top speed.

> *Oh every time*
> *You want a rhyme,*
> *Then let your tongue go loose,*
> *Don't hold it tight,*
> *Or try to bite,*
> *That won't be any use!*
> *Just let it go*
> *And words will flow*
> *From off your eager tongue,*
> *And rhymes and all*
> *Will lightly fall*
> *To make a little song!*

'There you are, Ern, that's how you do it,' said Fatty, with a chuckle. 'You try it when you're alone. Just think of the first line, that's all – then let your tongue go loose.'

'I don't think I've got your sort of tongue,' sighed Ern, half-inclined to try it there and then.

'Coo, Fatty, it's funny, you know – you don't really care about writing portry, and I do, but I can't. And *I'd* give anything to write it, and you wouldn't, but you can.'

'You're muddling me, Ern,' said Fatty. 'Ah, here are the others. Good.'

Soon all six of them were cycling to Fairlin Hall. They sent Ern in to make sure the coast was clear. He came back very quickly.

'OK!' he said. 'No car at the front door. Nobody about at all, as far as I can see.'

'Come on then,' said Fatty. 'We'll hide our bikes in some thick bushes round the back, so that they can't be seen. We'll take it in turns to keep a watch out. Pip, you keep first watch.'

'Right,' said Pip, at once, though he was longing to go in with the others. 'If you hear me whistling "Over the Seas to Skye", you'll know there's something up.'

They put their bicycles behind a thickly-growing bush and went to the kitchen door. Fatty unlocked it, and looked round. 'I think we'll keep to the kitchen quarters,' he said. 'Let's see – there's the kitchen – a small scullery – and a room the Smiths had for a bedroom. Oh, and there's a tiny bathroom here as well, leading off the bedroom.'

'Where exactly do we look?' asked Bets. 'I've been trying to think where I'd hide diamonds away in these rooms, if I had to – and except for silly places like at the back of a drawer, or on the very top of a cupboard, I can't think of any.'

'Well, the hiding-place is sure to be pretty good,' said Fatty. 'A prepared one, perhaps – you know, a hole knocked in the wall behind a cupboard, and then the cupboard put back again.'

'Oh,' said Bets. 'Well, I'm pretty sure I shouldn't find *that*.'

The five began to hunt carefully. Every mat, every scrap of carpet was turned back. Every bit of furniture was moved. Then Bets went to a chest of drawers.

'No good looking in the drawers of that chest, Bets, old thing,' said Fatty. 'The furniture belongs to the Smiths, you know. Hello, what's this?'

Everyone turned at once. Fatty was down on his knees, trying to peer into a hole that was at the bottom of one corner of the kitchen wall. 'It seems to go back a little way,' he said. 'Gosh, I can see something there! Bets, can you get your tiny hand in and feel?'

Bets knelt down and tried to put her hand in at the hole. 'I can feel something!' she said excitedly. She stretched her fingers to the utmost and tried to get hold of whatever it was, with the very ends of her fingers. There was a sudden SNAP! and Bets screamed.

'Oh! My finger! Something caught it!'

'It's a mousetrap, isn't it!' said Pip, with a squeal of laughter. 'I know that SNAP! Mummy put a trap in my bedroom last night, and it went SNAP and caught a mouse.'

'Oh Bets, did it trap your fingers?' said Fatty, in concern, as Bets stood up, squeezing the fingers of her right hand.

'No. Not quite. The trap part just missed them,' said Bets. 'Oh, Fatty – and I thought I was reaching out for a bag of diamonds! and it was only just a mousetrap that the Smiths must have put into the hole!'

Fatty took his torch from his pocket and bent down to make sure, his cheek against the ground, as he flashed the light of his torch into the hole. 'You're right, Bets,' he said. 'It's a trap. What a disappointment. Still, a bag of diamonds wouldn't be pushed into a mouse-hole, of course! The hiding-place will be very much cleverer than that! Call Pip in, Ern, and take his place.'

Pip came in, rubbing his hands. 'It's cold out there,' he said, stamping his feet. 'Shouldn't be surprised if it's going to snow. Found anything?'

'Not a thing,' said Bets. 'Except a mousetrap.'

The hunt was a complete failure. Fatty gave up after a whole hour's search. It was getting dark, and he was the only one with a torch.

'No go,' said Fatty. 'I think probably only professional police searchers could find the diamonds. They may even be embedded in one of the walls – a hole could have been made, the plaster put back, and painted over. Short of pulling the walls to pieces, and taking up the floor, I don't see that we can do anything else! I vote we go and have tea somewhere.'

'You can come and have it at our house,' said Pip. 'Mummy's gone out, and she said if we cleared away ourselves and washed up, she would leave a smashing tea on the table. And if we break anything, we've got to replace it.'

'Jolly nice of your mother,' said Larry. 'Shall we go to Pip's, Fatty?'

'Yes. Splendid idea,' said Fatty. 'I'd have liked you all to come to my house for tea, but Mummy is very very distant to me at the moment. I really might be some third cousin she hasn't seen for years, and doesn't want to know. Poor Mummy – she'll never get over my going to Mrs Henry's disguised as a smelly rag-and-bone man. That overcoat did smell, you know.'

'It sure did,' said Pip. 'You smell of it a bit still, Fatty. Ern, you can come to tea, too, of course.'

Ern beamed. He had been afraid that he might not be asked. What would Sid and Perce say when he told them how he'd been here, there and everywhere? He was very happy indeed as he cycled up to Pip's with the others – but quite horrified when he suddenly met his uncle round a corner! Goon saw him at once and leapt off his bicycle. He caught hold of Ern's handlebars and Ern wobbled and fell off.

'What you doing here in Peterswood, Ern?' he

demanded. 'Didn't I tell you to go home? What you been doing all this time?'

'I asked him to stay with me,' said Fatty, in what Goon called his 'high and mighty voice'. 'Don't you want to know what happened to those poor old Smiths, Mr Goon – the ones you tried to turn out of their caretaking job?'

'All I know is they've gone, and good riddance to them,' said Goon. 'Smith was a traitor – didn't ought to be in any responsible job. The man that wrote those notes to warn me, was quite right.'

'Well, Mrs Smith is staying up at our house, helping my mother,' said Fatty. 'And Mr Smith is in the Cottage Hospital, very ill, but Mrs Smith can see him every day, you'll be pleased to know. At least I hope you *will* be pleased to know. You were very unkind to her, Mr Goon.'

'Don't you talk to me like that, you – you pest of a boy!' said Goon, furious at being ticked off by Fatty in front of Ern, whose eyes were nearly falling out of his head. 'And let me tell you this – Fairlin Hall's bin bought, see – and anyone going there will be TRESPASSING, and will be PROSECUTED. Those are the new owner's orders.

Two gentlemen have bought it – very nice too, they are, and very friendly. So you be careful, Frederick Trotteville.'

'Thank you for the news, Mr Goon,' said Fatty. 'I was rather expecting it. But why should you think I'd want to go there?'

'Oh, I wouldn't put it past you to go and move out all the Smiths' furniture,' said Goon. 'Always interfering in everything! Ern, you come with me.'

'I've been asked out to tea, Uncle,' said Ern, edging away. He leapt suddenly on his bicycle and rode away at top speed.

'Gah!' said Goon, in disgust. 'You've made Ern as bad as you are. Just wait till I get my hands on him!'

Goon rode away angrily. That Frederick Trotteville! Was he up to anything? Goon couldn't help feeling that there was still something going on that he didn't know about. Gah!

The others laughed and rode off again. They arrived at Pip's to find Ern waiting for them behind a bush. Soon they were sitting round a loaded tea table. Fatty wished he had gone to fetch Buster, because Mrs Hilton, Pip's mother, had left a plate of dog biscuits for him, smeared with potted meat, a meal that old Buster simply loved!

'Will the Smiths be able to get their furniture out before those men move in?' asked Ern. 'Mrs Smith was very worried about it at dinnertime. And she said that lots of things ought to be done before anyone else uses that kitchen. She said the kitchen range was extremely dangerous. And she said the sink smelt something awful. I did try to find out if there were any possible hiding-places, Fatty – but the only things she said were about the kitchen range, and the sink, and the coal-cellar, and the cold pipe in the bathroom, and the mouse-hole in the wall.'

'What did she say about the coal-cellar?' asked Fatty. 'We never examined that, now I come to think of it.'

'She said the steps down were so rickety she was afraid of breaking her leg,' said Ern. 'And she said the cold pipe in the bathroom ran so slowly that their baths were always too hot. It had a leak too, she said, and the sink . . .'

'Smelt something awful,' said Fatty. 'Hm. Nothing very helpful there – though I think we *ought* to have looked in the coal-cellar. I've a good mind to go there tonight, as a matter-of-fact. It'll be my only chance if those men are going to move in. Yes, I think I *ought* to have a squint at that coal-cellar.'

'I'll come with you, Fatty,' said Ern, eagerly. 'Do say I can.'

'No,' said Fatty. 'I shall go alone, if I do go, but I'm not certain yet. If only Superintendent Jenks was back, I'd go and see him, and ask for a couple of men to search those kitchen quarters. No, no more jam tarts, thank you, Pip! Ern, you'll go pop if you have any more. Try Buster's dog biscuits smeared with potted meat!'

'Well, they don't look half bad,' said Ern, and made everyone laugh. 'I've a good mind to try one!'

There wasn't much left on the table when they had all finished. 'Let's play cards now, Fatty,' said Pip. But Fatty shook his head.

'No. I want to go to the flower shop before it shuts,' he said.

'Why? To buy another Coleus plant?' said Bets, with a laugh.

'No – to buy a very expensive bunch of red roses for someone I've mortally offended,' said Fatty, solemnly. 'My mother! I simply cannot bear to go home and be treated like a bad smell – and Mummy really is very very annoyed with me. I feel rather bad about it, actually, she's such a dear. See you tomorrow! Mind you don't break anything when you wash up!'

20. FATTY INVESTIGATES

Ern had been told that he could sleep the night in Fatty's shed, if he didn't want to go home. He decided that he certainly would – and Ern had a very strong reason for his decision.

If Fatty was going down to Fairlin Hall that night, then he, Ern, was going too. Not *with* Fatty, because he might be sent back. He was just going to follow him, and make sure nothing happened to him.

Just suppose those men have moved in, thought Ern, anxiously. Fatty would be no match for them. I won't let him see me – but I'll keep watch, in case those men are there and hear him.

So, as he cycled back to Fatty's after Pip's tea party, Ern made his plans. He would leave his bicycle in a bush down the drive, at Fatty's house, so that as soon as Fatty went off, he could follow him. And if Fatty walked, well, Ern would walk

211

too. He felt in his pocket to see if his torch was there. Yes, it was.

Fatty was down in his shed when Ern arrived, looking through his notes. 'Hello, Ern!' he said. 'Did you break anything when you all washed up?'

'Not a thing,' said Ern. 'You ought to have stayed, Fatty. We played cards, and little Bets won the lot. Did you get some flowers for your mother?'

'I did,' said Fatty. 'And Mummy was very pleased. So that's settled. I'm not a nasty smell any more.'

'Are you really going down to Fairlin Hall tonight, Fatty?' asked Ern.

'I am – and you are *not* coming, so don't ask me again,' said Fatty. 'I shall creep down the stairs when the household is in bed. Ern, if you're sleeping down in this shed, I think you'd better have Buster, if you don't mind. He might bark the place down if I go without him.'

'Oooh, I will. I'd like to,' said Ern, who was very fond of the lively little Scottie. 'He'll be company.'

'Well, I must go in and make myself respectable,' said Fatty. 'They're expecting you to supper in the kitchen, Ern. You'd better write a bit more poetry to recite to them.'

'Oooh, I couldn't write it in such a hurry,' said Ern. 'It takes me weeks to write two lines, Fatty.'

'Rubbish,' said Fatty. 'Remember what I told you. Just let your tongue go loose, and it comes – it comes! Think of a good line to begin with, Ern – then let your tongue wag away as it likes.'

Fatty left him, and Ern opened his notebook. He looked at his 'portry'. If only he could think of it easily, like Fatty! It would be so very, very nice to stand up in the kitchen tonight and recite a new 'pome'.

'Well, I'll have another try,' said Ern, valiantly, and stood up. He worked his tongue about a little to get it 'loose' and then delivered himself of one line.

'There was a pore old mouse . . .'

He waggled his tongue desperately, hoping the next line would come spouting forth, just as it did when Fatty made up verses. 'There was a pore old mouse . . . mouse. There was a pore old mouse . . .'

'Snogood,' said Ern, flopping down again.

'Fatty's tongue must be different from mine. I wonder what's for supper tonight.'

At ten o'clock, Fatty said goodnight to his mother and father and went up to bed. He waited for half an hour and then he heard his parents come up, and the lights click off. He quickly put on his overcoat and slipped downstairs again, with a very quiet Buster at his heels. Buster's tail was wagging hard. A walk! At this time of night too!

It was snowing a little as Fatty walked down to his shed. He knocked quietly. Ern opened the door at once.

'Goodness – aren't you going to get undressed, Ern?' said Fatty, in surprise. 'I left you an old pair of pyjamas, didn't I?'

'I'm not sleepy yet,' said Ern, truthfully. 'Hello, Buster. Come on in. Well, good luck, Fatty.'

'Thanks. I'll be off,' said Fatty, and went down the path, the snowflakes shining white in the light of his torch. Ern waited a few seconds and then slipped out himself, pulling on his overcoat. Buster began to bark frantically as Ern shut the door. He leapt up and down at it, flinging himself against it. He was furious at being deserted by both Fatty *and* Ern.

Blow! thought Ern. I hope he won't wake everyone. Still, the shed's pretty far away from the house!

He hurried along down the garden path, into the drive and out of the front gate. He could just see Fatty passing under a street-lamp some way off. He followed quickly, his feet making no noise on the snow-covered path.

Fatty had no idea that Ern was following him. He went along quickly, feeling the key of the kitchen door of Fairlin Hall in his pocket. His mind went over what Ern had related to him. Kitchen range. Smelly sink. Leaking pipe. Coal-cellar. Yes – he'd certainly better examine that coal-cellar. It might make a splendid hiding-place.

Behind him plodded Ern. Fatty came to the drive of Fairlin Hall and turned down it cautiously, looking for lights in the house. Ern turned in after him, keeping Fatty in sight as best he could, a dark shadow in the distance.

Fatty could see no lights anywhere, but of course the electricity would not be connected yet. If the two men came, they would have to use torches. The Smiths had had an oil lamp in their kitchen, because no gas or electricity was on.

Those men will have to come pretty soon, certainly within the next week, I suppose, thought Fatty. I don't expect they *really* mean to buy it – all they want is to find the hoard of diamonds they stole so many years ago, and take them. Anyway, they've got the keys, so they can get in at any time.

He let himself in quietly at the kitchen door, and left it open, in case he had to run out quickly. He slipped through the scullery and kitchen, and went to the door that led from the kitchen to the hall. He opened it and stood there listening. He could hear nothing at all.

Slipping off his shoes, he padded into the dark hall and went to the bottom of the stairs. There was no light to be seen anywhere, and the whole house was heavy with silence. Almost as if it were listening, too! thought Fatty. Well, as there's absolutely no one about, I'll just examine that coal-cellar. I suppose it's outside, because I don't remember seeing a cellar indoors.

He put on his shoes again and slipped through the kitchen and out into the little yard. He didn't see Ern standing like a statue in the shadow of some bushes not far off; but Ern saw the light from Fatty's torch, and knew that he was going to examine the coal-cellar.

The Fairlin Hall coal-cellar was a truly enormous one. A large, heavy grating covered the entrance hole, and Fatty lifted it off, and peered down. A steep wooden ladder led downwards to what looked more like an underground room than a coal-hole. The ladder was rickety, as Mrs Smith had related to Ern, and Fatty didn't really fancy going down it.

He flashed his torch down the ladder, and came to the conclusion that if any diamonds had been hidden in the cellar they would have been discovered, for there was very, very little coal left – only a sprinkling over the stone floor.

Fatty went back to the house, and flashed his torch over the kitchen range. Was there any hiding-place at the back? No, not possibly. He went round the rooms methodically, trying to think of somewhere he hadn't examined that afternoon.

He suddenly heard a small sound, and stood still, listening. There it was again. What was it?

Was it someone opening the front door and shutting it? Fatty's heart began to thump a little. If it were the two men, they would probably come into the kitchen quarters to search. He switched off his torch and stood in the tiny bathroom listening intently.

Suddenly he felt a soft touch on the top of his head, and he stiffened in fright. It felt like a moth settling on his hair – but no moths were about in January.

There it was again – just a soft touch on his hair. Fatty put up his hand and felt the spot – and it was damp! He heaved a sigh of relief. Just a little drip of water from somewhere – probably from the leaking water pipe that Mrs Smith had told Ern about!

He stood there in the dark, listening for any further sound, but none came. He must have been mistaken. He took a step forward and switched on his torch again, looking up at the water pipe to see where the drip had come from.

It's from that loose joint, thought Fatty, seeing

a place where two pipes had been joined together. Gosh, it made me jump.

He reached up his hand and touched the joint. It was rather loose, so no wonder the water leaked out. A sudden idea flashed into Fatty's mind – an idea that made him catch his breath. Could it be – no, it *couldn't* be what he was thinking!

His hand shook a little as he held the torch up to the joint of the pipes. Why should there be a join there, held together by an iron band round the pipe? Could the pipe have been deliberately cut – could something have been slid into it – then the cut ends fixed together by the joint, hiding whatever had been forced into the pipe?

Fatty stood below the narrow little pipe, hearing the small noise that the tiny drip made every now and again. Mrs Smith had said that the flow in the cold water pipe was very poor – very slow – so slow that they couldn't make their hot baths cool! Was that because the pipe had been stuffed with something that impeded the flow of the water – stuffed with *diamonds*, perhaps!

Fatty flashed his torch on the joint again. It didn't look as neat a job as the other joints he could see. A surge of excitement made his heart begin to beat fast.

I believe I've got it! thought Fatty to himself. I really believe I have! My word – if Wilfrid Hasterley really did push all his diamonds into a water pipe and then sealed it up, he was a wizard at hiding things! I bet he put a few big ones in first, hoping they would jam together, and not be taken down to the outlet. Whew!

He had heard no more noises, and felt certain he was mistaken in thinking anyone had come into the house. He would surely have heard something more by now! He debated whether he should find the main water-cock and turn off the water. Then he might be able to hack off the pipe-joint, force the two ends of the little pipe apart, and peer into them.

But where *was* the water-cock? He hadn't the faintest idea. No good messing about, thought Fatty. I'll get back home – and tomorrow I simply MUST get in touch with the Superintendent, even if I have to telephone to the back of beyond!

He crept silently out of the little bathroom, shining his torch in front of him – and then he had the shock of his life! Someone pounced on him from a corner and gripped him so tightly that he couldn't even struggle!

Then a torch was shone into his face, and a voice exclaimed, 'Oh, so it's that big boy, is it? Why are you here again? What are you looking for? Go on, tell us, or we'll make you!'

Fatty saw two men – yes, the two he had been on guard against, and listening for! So he *had* heard something! What an idiot he had been not to go and investigate.

He began to shout at the top of his voice. 'Let me go! Let me go! Help! Let me go!'

'There's nobody to hear you!' said one of the men. 'Shout all you like! Go on – shout!'

21. ERN HAS A REALLY EXCITING TIME!

But there *was* somebody to hear Fatty, of course. Ern was still outside, shivering in the shelter of the bush he was hiding in. He almost jumped out of his skin when he heard Fatty's shouts.

They've got him – somebody in the house has caught him! thought Ern, shaking at the knees. What shall I do? I daren't go in – I'll be caught too if I do. Oh Fatty, what can I do to help?

He stole from the shelter of his bush and crept nearer to the kitchen door. He could hear a struggle going on as Fatty tried to kick the men on the shins.

'You let me go! Oh! You brute! Let go!'

Ern listened in anguish. He longed to go to Fatty's help, but what *would* be the sense of two of them being caught? Oh, poor Fatty! Ern strained his ears to hear what the men were saying.

'Lock him in this cupboard,' panted one of

them. 'My word, he's strong. Knock him over the head.'

'No. Be careful. I don't want a spell in prison again,' said the second man. 'Shove him in!'

Ern heard a crash as Fatty was pushed violently into the big cupboard, where the Smiths' brooms and brushes and pans still stood. Then there was a short silence. Not another sound from Fatty!

'Lock the door on him,' said a voice. 'He's knocked out for a bit, at any rate. My word, he gave me a kick that almost took off my knee-cap! Now come on – we've *got* to find those stones! We know they're here somewhere!'

Ern, his heart thumping so loudly that he felt the men must hear it, stood watching their torches flashing here and there, as they made their search for the hidden diamond haul. There was no sound to be heard from Fatty, not even a groan. Ern began to feel very anxious.

I must get help! he thought. I really must. But how? He stood and thought hard.

I'll go and stand at the front gate and stop the first person coming by, he decided at last, and he crept through the falling snow up to the gate. He waited, shivering, for a few minutes and then, to his delight, saw someone coming. It was a small man, hurrying along. Ern ran to him.

'Please will you help! Two men have got hold of a friend of mine in that empty house there. They've hurt him and locked him in a cupboard. Please come and help him.'

The little man looked quite scared. 'That's a matter for the police!' he said.

'Oh *no*!' said Ern, thinking of his uncle at once. 'No, I don't want the police here.'

'Well, all I can do is to telephone them for you,' said the man, and hurried off. 'It's the police you need!'

Ern was in despair. The last person he wanted to see was his uncle, the very *last*! He hurried back to the house, his feet making no noise over the snow. He peeped through the kitchen window. No sign or sound of poor old Fatty – but the men were obviously still there, for Ern could see the flash of their torches from the little bedroom.

He debated whether he dared to go in and unlock the cupboard door. No, he daren't. He couldn't possibly get Fatty out without making a noise. Ern's heart sank down into his shoes. I'm no good when there's trouble about, he thought, sorrowfully. No good at all. Fatty would know what to do at once. I wish I had better brains.

And then he jumped violently as something brushed against his leg, and then planted a wet lick on his hand. 'Oooh! What's that! Oh, it's *you*, Buster! Sh! How in the world did you get out?'

Buster wagged his tail. He knew quite well how he had got out! He had leapt up on to the chest of drawers in Fatty's shed, and had found the window open a little. He had squeezed himself through the opening and jumped to the ground. Then he had nosed his way after Ern's tracks and Fatty's, sniffing them easily all along the roads to Fairlin Hall.

But now Buster sensed trouble, and that was why he hadn't barked when he saw Ern! He put his paws up on the boy's knees and whined a very small whine, as if to say, 'Where's Fatty? Please tell me what's up?'

Then Buster heard the men inside the house and his ears pricked up at once. He ran to the door. He smelt Fatty's tracks, he smelt Fatty himself! Where was his master? What had happened to him? He ran to the cupboard and pawed at it. He knew Fatty was in there!

The men heard him and ran out of the bedroom. They flashed their torches on the little Scottie – and at the same moment he leapt at them. One man felt a nip on his ankle – then the other felt a glancing bite on his hand. He hit out at the excited dog, who bounded all round them like a mad thing, barking, and nipping them whenever he could.

One man ran out of the kitchen into the hall, and the other followed. Buster went too, and Ern heard him chasing them all the way up the stairs. Ern was almost weeping in relief. He raced to the locked cupboard and turned the key.

'Fatty! Quick! Come out!' he said.

Fatty was lying back on a collection of pails, pans and brushes. He stared up at Ern, still half-dazed.

'Ern!' he said in a weak voice. 'What's up?'

'Oh Fatty – you've an awful bruise on your head,' said Ern, in distress. 'Quick, I want to get you out of here. Can you stand? Let me help you.'

Fatty stood up with difficulty. Evidently the blow on his head had quite dazed him. Ern helped him anxiously out into the air.

'Let me sit down,' said Fatty. 'This cold air is making me feel better. I don't feel quite so dazed. Gosh, what happened? I'm just remembering! Ern, what on earth are *you* doing here? And is that Buster I can hear barking?'

'Fatty, don't bother about anything now,' said Ern, as the boy sat down heavily beside a bush. 'Old Buster is chasing the men who knocked you out. Stay here a minute and I'll just go and see what's happened to him.'

Ern went back cautiously to the kitchen. But before he could even look inside, he saw a lamp coming waveringly round the corner of the house, and stared at it in amazement. Who was this coming now? Then a loud and angry voice hailed him.

'ERN! What you doing here? Some fellow phoned me and said there was a boy here who wanted help – Ern, if it was *you* playing a joke like that on me, I'll – I'll . . .'

It was Goon! He leapt off his bicycle and strode

towards the terrified Ern, who promptly fled into the kitchen. Goon padded after him, quite convinced that Ern had got him out here in the snowy night just for fun.

And then Buster appeared at top speed! He had heard Goon's voice, and had come to investigate. He leapt at the policeman in delight and nipped his trousers at the ankle.

'What – that dog's here too! Is that big boy here as well?' thundered Goon. 'What's going on? I never heard of such doings in my life. Oh get off, you horrible little dog! Clear orf, I say! Ern, get him off. WILL you get away, dog?'

But Buster was having the time of his life. No Fatty to call him off, nobody to stop him from harrying his old enemy all he liked. It was too good to be true! He chased Mr Goon all round the kitchen, and then into the broom cupboard, where the angry policeman subsided among the same pails and brooms that Fatty had fallen on.

And then Ern suddenly saw the two men peeping round the door, and he crouched in a corner in terror, praying that they would not see him. One flashed his torch into the cupboard and saw the policeman there, with Buster on top of him.

'Look there – the police!' he cried in alarm, and slammed the cupboard door at once. He turned the key, locking the door. 'Well, thank goodness we've got rid of the dog, and locked up the policeman,' he said, in a shaky voice. 'I can't understand all this. Where's that boy gone that we knocked out?'

'He's lying under the bobby, I expect,' said the second man. 'He was quite knocked out. The policeman must have fallen on top of him, trying to get away from that vicious little dog. Phew! What a night! Do we search any more – or what?'

'No. We get back to Kuntan,' said the second man. 'My ankles are bitten all over! I must put some iodine on them!'

'Well, he can keep the policeman and the boy company till morning,' said his companion. Then he turned sharply. 'Hello – who's this?' he said, and he flashed his torch on to the corner where Ern was crouching.

And then Ern behaved magnificently. He reached up a hand and swept a whole row of kettles and pans off the shelf just above him. They clattered to the floor with an awful din, and startled the two men out of their wits. Then Ern leapt up into the air, hands above his head, and moaned in a horrible, hollow voice, 'I'm coming! I'm coming!'

The two men took to their heels and raced out of the kitchen door. This was absolutely the last straw – what with boys and policemen and dogs roaming about – and now this awful creature, whatever it was, clattering pans everywhere! The men were really terrified.

Ern looked out of the door after them, hardly able to believe that his sudden mad idea had acted so well. Then he heard a loud shriek, and wondered what had happened. Then came a crash, and angry voices.

What's up now? wondered Ern, uneasily. As the voices came no nearer, he tiptoed out of the kitchen door and went cautiously towards them.

'Coo – lovaduck! They've fallen down the coal-cellar!' he said. 'Fatty must have forgotten to put the grating back over it – and down they've gone! They must be hurt or they'd try getting up the ladder. Quick, Ern, my lad, you can do something here!'

And Ern flew to where the big heavy grating lay on the snow-covered ground. He dragged and pulled, pulled and dragged, panting hard. At last he got it half across the cellar-opening, and the men, who had been quite silent, hoping that perhaps their hiding-place would not be discovered, suddenly realised what was happening.

One gave a yell and began to climb the ladder, but the rickety rungs broke under his weight and he fell back into the cellar again. Ern at last pulled the grating right across. Then he flashed his torch down at the two angry, frightened men.

'You can stay there till you're fetched!' he said, and looked about for something else heavy enough to drag over the grating, to keep it down. He found the dustbin, and dragged it there, and then filled it with stones from a nearby rockery. He was very hot and tired when he had finished. The men yelled and threatened him with all kinds of terrible things – but Ern was feeling on top of the world, and took no notice.

Loveaduck, there's the men down the coal-cellar

– and uncle in the cupboard with Buster on top of him – I've done a good night's work, thought Ern, hurrying back to where he had left Fatty. If only poor old Fatty is feeling better!

Fatty was decidedly better. He was standing up wondering whether to go and join the row he could hear going on not far off. He didn't know that it was Ern well and truly imprisoning the men in the coal-cellar!

'Hello, Fatty,' said Ern's voice. 'You better? Come on, I'll take you home. You lean on me. No, don't ask any questions now – you'll be all right tomorrow. I'll answer them then.'

And so the still-dazed Fatty, frowning with an enormous headache, went slowly home, leaning on Ern's shoulder. His head was in a muddle. All he wanted was to lie down and rest in bed. Good old Ern, he'd explain everything to him tomorrow! Fatty simply couldn't be bothered to worry about anything just then!

22. A MOST SURPRISING FINISH

Ern slept the night in Fatty's room, so that if the boy wanted anything in the night he could get it for him. He curled himself up in a chair, dressed as he was, meaning to keep awake and think over the exciting happenings of the night. Coo, think of Uncle in that cupboard with Buster barking in his ear. A very very pleasant thought for Ern!

He fell asleep – and as for Fatty, once his headache had eased, he too slept like a log. He sat up in bed at half past seven next morning as lively as a cricket, and was most amazed to see Ern asleep in his armchair. His mind groped back to the evening before. What had happened?

I can remember as far as being attacked by those men – and being thrown into the cupboard – but all the rest is hazy, thought Fatty, and gently felt the bump on his head. I suppose they knocked me out. How did I get here?

'Ern! Wake up, Ern!'

Ern awoke with a jump and uncurled himself. He went to Fatty's bed. 'Coo, Fatty – you've got an awful bruise on your head,' he said. 'How do you feel?'

'Fine,' said Fatty, getting out of bed. 'Ern, how did I get back here? What on earth happened last night? How did *you* come into it? You weren't even there!'

'Oh yes I was, Fatty,' said Ern. 'You just listen. Get back into bed and I'll tell you the best story you ever heard in your life.'

'Well, make it short,' said Fatty. 'I've simply *got* to phone the Superintendent now!'

'Yes, you have. But there's no hurry,' said Ern, grinning. 'I've got everyone nicely in the bag for you.'

'What do you mean, young Ern?' demanded Fatty. 'Don't sit there grinning – tell me everything.'

'Well, my uncle's locked up in the cupboard where *you* were,' said Ern, 'and Buster's with him, and the two men are imprisoned in the coal-cellar. I scared them and they ran out and didn't see the opening – and fell down it. Good thing you didn't put the grating back, Fatty. I pulled it across the hole and, my word, it was heavy, and I stood the dustbin on top as well and filled it with big stones from the rockery.'

Fatty was too astonished to say a word. He stared at Ern as if he couldn't believe his ears. 'Is this true?' he said at last. 'How was it you were there?'

'I followed you,' said Ern. 'I was afraid something might happen to you. I left Buster in the shed, but he must have got out somehow. He chased those men all over the place.'

'Ern – thank you,' said Fatty. 'Thank you more than I can say. I made a mess of things – and you didn't. You – you did magnificently. My word, Ern, what a time you had!'

'Coo, I did!' said Ern. 'I dragged you out of that cupboard, Fatty, and put you outside in the drive – you did look awful. I was that upset and scared. Then suddenly I wasn't scared any more, and, well – I suppose I sort of went mad, and swept all the pans off the shelf, clitter-clatter, and booed at those men at the top of my voice, and chased them!' Ern began to laugh as he remembered. 'Honest, I didn't know I could do it.'

'You'll have to write a poem about it, Ern,' said Fatty, getting out of bed again. 'Well, I can see there's a lot of loose ends to tie up this morning! My word – fancy old Mr Goon having to spend the night in a cupboard with Buster – I bet he didn't enjoy that.'

Fatty was soon very busy indeed. He felt perfectly all right now, though the bruise on his head was sore. He telephoned immediately to the Superintendent's office and, oh, what a relief, he was there! Fatty was put through to him at once.

'This is an early call, Frederick,' said the Superintendent's crisp voice. 'What's up?'

'Plenty,' said Fatty. 'Superintendent, will you turn up details of a big diamond robbery over twenty years ago, when a Wilfrid Hasterley of "The Ivies", Peterswood, and two friends, got away with an enormous haul of diamonds.'

'I don't need to turn it up,' said the Superintendent. 'I was a young man then, and happened to be one of the men put on the job. Wilfrid got a jail sentence and died in prison.

One man fled abroad, and we never heard of him again. The other man went to jail, and came out a few months ago. We meant to watch him, hoping he'd know where Wilfrid had hidden the diamonds, but he was too wily and went to ground. What about it? It's a very old case now.'

'I know. But two of the men came back to Peterswood – to "The Ivies", which is now called Fairlin Hall,' said Fatty. 'And . . .'

'Frederick! You don't mean this!' said the Superintendent's voice, sounding amazed. 'Where are they?'

'Well, at the moment they're imprisoned in a coal-cellar at Fairlin Hall,' said Fatty, chuckling. 'And you'll be surprised to know that that was the work of young Ern, Superintendent – Mr Goon's nephew, you know.'

'Good heavens!' said the Superintendent, sounding more astonished than ever. 'What about Goon? Is he in on this too?'

'Well, he was at the beginning,' said Fatty. 'But he didn't last till the end, I fear. He gave up halfway. At the moment, I regret to say, he's locked up in a broom cupboard at Fairlin Hall, with Buster. He's been there all night.'

There was a dead silence, then the Superintendent spoke again. 'This isn't a joke, is it, Frederick?' he said.

'Oh no. It's all absolutely true,' said Fatty, earnestly. 'Can you come over? We could go down to Fairlin Hall and you can examine the various people there who are imprisoned in one way or another!'

'Right. I'll be along in twenty minutes,' said the Superintendent, briskly. 'With a few men. Meet me there, Frederick. Good heavens, this all sounds *quite* impossible!'

Fatty put down the telephone and turned to Ern, who was listening nearby. 'Ring up the others for me, Ern,' he said. 'Tell them to meet us at Fairlin Hall quickly – even if they're in the middle of breakfast. This is going to be exciting. I'm going to get some biscuits for poor old Buster – he'll be starving!'

In fifteen minutes time, Larry, Daisy, Pip, Bets and Ern were all in the drive of Fairlin Hall, in a state of the greatest excitement. Fatty was at the gate waiting for the Superintendent and his men. Ah, here they came in two black police cars. The Superintendent jumped out and said a few words to the man with him. Then he strode toward Fatty.

'Now let's get down to business,' he said, clapping Fatty on the back. 'Lead on!'

'We'd better rescue poor Mr Goon first,' said Fatty. 'And Buster too. I'm afraid Mr Goon will be in a fearful temper, sir.'

'That won't matter,' said the Superintendent hard-heartedly, 'Hello, Bets! You here! And all the others too! Well, I'm blessed!'

They all went to the kitchen door and Fatty pushed it open. A loud barking was coming from the locked cupboard. Fatty went over and unlocked it. Out leapt Buster, mad with joy at seeing Fatty again, and being free once more.

'Steady, Buster, steady,' said Fatty. There came a noise from the cupboard and Mr Goon walked out, looking as if he was about to burst with rage! He advanced on Fatty.

'*You're* at the bottom of this!' he roared. 'Toad of a boy! And you, Ern, what do you mean by getting me here in the middle of the night, and . . . oh . . . er . . . good morning, Superintendent. Didn't see you, I'm afraid. I've got a complaint to lay against this Frederick Trotteville. Always interfering with the law, he is, sir. After I'd settled a case, he goes on with it, poking his nose in, and . . .'

'That's enough, Goon, for the moment,' said the Superintendent. 'Where are these other men, did you say, Frederick?'

Goon looked astounded. Other men? What did the Superintendent mean? He followed Fatty and the others out into the yard. A voice came from the coal-cellar.

'Let us out! One of us has a broken ankle. We give up!'

Goon stared in surprise at the dustbin full of big stones, as one of the policemen heaved it off the grating. He stared even more when the grating was taken off too, and a constable shouted down into the cellar.

'Come on up – you're wanted for questioning. We know you're the fellows in that Diamond Case years ago.'

The men had to be dragged up, because the ladder had broken in half. Goon was overcome with astonishment. What *was* all this?

'We can explain everything,' said one of the men. 'You've got nothing on us. We only came back here to visit the old place – to see old Mrs Hasterley.'

'People don't live in empty houses,' said the Superintendent curtly. 'Frederick, we'll all go somewhere and talk over this, I think.'

'There's nothing to talk about,' interrupted Goon. 'It's just a case I cleared up myself. These fellows sent notes to me, telling me about a caretaker here – man run in for being a traitor – and . . .'

'Sir, could we go into Fairlin Hall for a few minutes?' said Fatty. 'There's still a little matter to be cleared up there, if you don't mind. We could go into the kitchen.'

'Very well,' said the Superintendent, and he and Goon, and all the children filed in. The Superintendent sat down in the old armchair.

'You know all about that long-ago diamond affair, sir,' began Fatty. 'Well, as soon as those two fellows you caught just now got together, when one of them came out of prison, they decided to come back here and find the diamond haul, which Wilfrid Hasterley had hidden safely away. They found caretakers in the kitchen quarters, so they couldn't search. They then discovered that Mr Smith, the caretaker, had a shady past – had sold some secret papers to a foreign government . . .'

'And I turned them out of here!' said Goon. 'Quite right, too. Couldn't have a fellow . . .'

'Quiet, Goon,' said the Superintendent. 'Go on, Frederick.'

'Well, as Mr Goon said, he turned them out – and so left the place clear for the two thieves to search,' said Fatty, 'which is exactly what they wanted! Well, *we* were on the trail, as well – we knew about the messages to Mr Goon, you see – and we guessed the two fellows were after the hidden diamonds. So we came to search too!'

'Gah!' said Goon, in disgust.

'Well, we didn't find them. But last night I came back here again, and the men were here too – and, to cut a long story short, sir, Ern here imprisoned the two men in the coal-cellar, got me out of a cupboard where I'd been locked, and . . .'

'But how did *Goon* get locked in?' said the Superintendent, looking suspiciously at Ern.

'Oooh, *I* didn't lock my uncle in,' said Ern, hastily. 'I wouldn't do such a thing. The *men* locked him in, sir.'

'And did those fellows give you any hint as to where the diamonds were?' asked the Superintendent, looking at Fatty expectantly.

'No, sir,' said Fatty. Everyone groaned – what a pity! No diamonds after all!

'Well, that's rather an anti-climax,' said the Superintendent, looking disappointed. '*Sure* you don't know where they are, Frederick?'

'Well – yes, sir, I think I *do* know where they are – though I haven't *seen* them!' said Fatty.

WHAT a sensation that made! Everyone gaped at Fatty, and the Superintendent stood up at once.

'You *know* where they're hidden!' he said. 'You actually *know*?'

'Well, I can make a jolly good guess,' said Fatty. 'If I were a plumber, I could find out at once.'

'A *plumber*? What do you mean?' said the

Superintendent. 'Come on, Frederick – no more mystery, please!'

'Well, sir – come into the bathroom,' said Fatty, and everyone squeezed into the tiny bathroom, even Goon. Fatty tapped the cold-water pipe, that still sent out a tiny drip at the loose joint.

'I think the diamonds are all jammed into this pipe, sir,' he said. 'It was Mrs Smith who first mentioned the pipe to me – she said the flow of water was very poor indeed. Then, when I examined it, I saw that the joint was loose – it's been badly done, sir, if you look – not a professional job at all. And I just put two and two together, sir, and thought, "Well, this is about the only place where nobody's looked! They must be here!"'

'Can't be!' said the Superintendent, staring at the pipe. 'What an idea! But what a hiding-place! What do *you* think, Goon?'

'Diamonds in a water pipe?' said Goon, scornfully, delighted at being asked his advice. 'Never heard of such a thing in my life. You have that pipe cut, sir – we'll flood the bathroom, but that's about all we'll do!'

The Superintendent went to the door and called out to one of his men. 'Get that hacksaw of yours, Sergeant!'

'Right, sir!' And in half a minute in came the Sergeant with an efficient-looking little saw.

'I want that pipe cut,' said the Superintendent, nodding his head at the little water pipe. 'The water's turned off, so there's only what's in the pipes. Cut below that loose joint, where the water's dripping a little.'

Everyone watched while the Sergeant did a little sawing – then water spurted out – and with it came two small sparkling things that fell to the ground, and lay there, glittering. Fatty pounced on them at once, and dropped them into the Superintendent's hand.

'Whew! Yes, they're diamonds all right,' he said. 'The pipe must be crammed with them! No wonder the water wouldn't flow through properly. Cut another place, Sergeant.'

The man obeyed – and there was no doubt of it, the pipe was full of diamonds – some big, some small, none of them any the worse for having lain in water for so many years.

'Sergeant, take a couple of men and empty the pipe,' ordered the Superintendent, looking extremely pleased. 'Frederick, you deserve a medal for this! Good work, my boy – as good as any you've ever done. Don't you think so, Goon?'

Goon didn't think so. Goon was busy blowing his nose loudly. Goon didn't want to answer *any* questions about Fatty at all. He was tired to death of Fatty and Ern, and all he wanted to do was to go home and have a nice hot cup of tea.

'I'll have to come and take a report about all this from you, Frederick, some time or other,' said the Superintendent, his hand on Fatty's shoulder. 'But now I must go and question those two men. My warm congratulations – and if I were you, I'd go and put something on that frightful bruise. One of the men did that, I suppose?'

'Yes. But I don't mind!' said Fatty. 'I gave as good as I got. Gosh, it *was* a night and a half, sir – and Ern here did as much as I did. More!'

'My congratulations to you too, Ern,' said the Superintendent. 'I shouldn't be surprised if you didn't have a little something coming to you as a reward for your good work.'

Ern blushed all over his face in surprise and delight. How he longed to be like Fatty, and let his 'tongue go loose'. What a 'pome' he would recite to the Superintendent! But all he could say was, 'I'm going to be a policeman some day, sir – and I'll be a Sergeant in no time at all – you see if I don't!'

'Gah!' said Goon, before he could stop himself, and marched off angrily. That Ern! And to think he'd paid him for helping him. What a waste!

'Let's all go back and have breakfast at my house,' said Fatty. 'I'm starving. Mummy will have a fit when she sees my bruise! Gosh, I do hope it doesn't go down before I'm back at school – I'll be the envy of everyone when I tell them how I got it. Well, Ern – how did you enjoy *this* mystery?'

'Loveaduck!' said Ern, beaming. 'It was smashing, Fatty. Thanks a lot for letting me in on it. Never enjoyed myself so much in my life. And don't forget – I've still got that money that my uncle gave me. I'll buy you all ice creams this morning, and that goes for Buster too!'

'Good old Ern,' said Fatty, and clapped him on the shoulder. And the others all said the same, making the boy blush as red as a beetroot. 'Good old Ern.'

EGMONT PRESS: ETHICAL PUBLISHING

Egmont Press is about turning writers into successful authors and children into passionate readers – producing books that enrich and entertain. As a responsible children's publisher, we go even further, considering the world in which our consumers are growing up.

Safety First
Naturally, all of our books meet legal safety requirements. But we go further than this; every book with play value is tested to the highest standards – if it fails, it's back to the drawing-board.

Made Fairly
We are working to ensure that the workers involved in our supply chain – the people that make our books – are treated with fairness and respect.

Responsible Forestry
We are committed to ensuring all our papers come from environmentally and socially responsible forest sources.

For more information, please visit our website at www.egmont.co.uk/ethical

---

Egmont is passionate about helping to preserve the world's remaining ancient forests. We only use paper from legal and sustainable forest sources, so we know where every single tree comes from that goes into every paper that makes up every book.

MIX
Paper
FSC® C018306

This book is made from paper certified by the Forestry Stewardship Council (FSC®), an organisation dedicated to promoting responsible management of forest resources. For more information on the FSC, please visit www.fsc.org. To learn more about Egmont's sustainable paper policy, please visit www.egmont.co.uk/ethical.